MINERVA WAS O[...]
ated rather tha[...]
dismaying of al[...]

Marriage was, of course, the only solution to the problem of such a daughter. As much as Lord Haran loved Minerva, and he really did dote on her, if she was not to have a most unhappy life, then she must be tamed. The institution of marriage would bring her to heel as her father had failed to do.

Behind the closed doors of the drawing room, the young man's sigh was nervous. He cracked his throat for the third time and Minerva, seated before him in an elephant-hide chair, smiled sympathetically.

He was the Viscount Ronald Templeton, the only son of a family of English aristocrats steeped in the bluest of blood. Nervous as he was, the fellow had a certain poise of the sort inbred since Agincourt. "Will you consider my proposal, Minerva?"

"That we marry?" She frowned. "I will consider it, Ronald. But not, I fear," Minerva added, "favorably."

"You do not look favorably on me," he summed up stiffly.

"Oh, Ronald. Don't pout. Why not simply regard it as a business venture which has not worked out?"

"I do not regard marriage as a business venture," the viscount protested.

"Of course you do." Minerva smiled. "And so does Papa. Particularly as regards the daughters of the House of Diamond. A Diamond son is born to wealth and power; a Diamond daughter is bred to breed for merger and influence."

Ronald Templeton was quite overwhelmed by her frankness. "Still, by your own description, tradition and family limit your options. Why not marry me, then?"

It was a point well taken. For an instant, Minerva was tempted to answer his question. But the answer was a secret she shared with no one. . . .

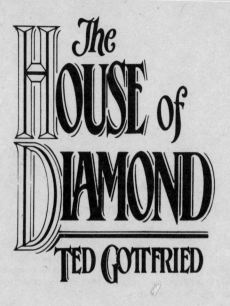

The HOUSE of DIAMOND

TED GOTTFRIED

LYNX BOOKS

New York

THE HOUSE OF DIAMOND

ISBN: 1-55802-026-8

First Printing/November 1988

The author of this work is a member of the National Writers Union.

This book is published by Lynx Books, a division of Lynx Communications, Inc., 41 Madison Avenue, New York, New York, 10010.
The name "Lynx" together with the logotype consisting of a stylized
head of a lynx is a trademark of Lynx Communications, Inc.

Printed in the United States of America

0 9 8 7 6 5 4 3 2 1

For my son, Daniel Gottfried
—my friend Dan—
Peace and Love

The author would like to express his gratitude for their help in the writing of this book to his wife Harriet Gottfried, his editor Chris Kinser, and his lifelong friend, Jewish culinary expert Mrs. Anne Kobrin.

The HOUSE of DIAMOND

PROLOGUE

MYTH HAS IT that when the founder of the Diamond financial dynasty, Zelik Diamant, lay on his deathbed, he was asked how a persecuted, despised, and ghetto-ized German-Jewish peddler such as he had managed to create the most prestigious and powerful interna-tional banking house in the world. What was his se-cret?

The full-bearded and venerable patriarch summoned his last bit of strength and pushed himself up on his elbows. "Buy low," he wheezed. He fell back to his pillow. "Sell high."

They were his last words. The next sound that passed his parched and wizened lips was a death rat-tle.

Of course, the story is apocryphal. There is no truth to it at all. It is merely the stuff of legend. The prin-ciple it expresses, however, is right on the mark. It is exactly how Zelik Diamant built his fortune. And it is the axiom by which his heirs operated from that day forward.

The House of Diamond would always buy low. They would always sell high.

But not too high.

BOOK ONE

1. FRANKFURT

MONEY-GRUBBING JEW banker!

The uniformed doorman of the Frankfurterhof silently cursed the Baron Immanuel von Diamant as he watched him cross the polished mahogany lobby on a Saturday morning in January of the year 1906. The fifty-four-year-old head of the Diamond family was a silent partner in the Steinburger chain, which had opened the dazzling new hotel a few years before. This made him, after a fashion, the Frakfurterhof doorman's employer. But that wasn't the reason for the doorman's reaction. He just hated Jews—particularly rich Jews.

Baron Immanuel von Diamant was, indeed, rich. He was quite the wealthiest of Frankfurt-born Jews, wealthier even than the Rothschilds, who had likewise originated there. But, like the Rothschilds, the baron no longer lived in Frankfurt; he only visited there frequently. During his periodic trips from Vienna to Frankfurt, the Frankfurterhof was Baron von Diamant's

home-away-from-home. The entire two top floors—the
Royal Suite and three other lavish suites—were set aside
for his part-time residency. The doorman was not unaware of such profligacy. Indeed, when off duty at the
local *brauhaus*, he often repeated to his cronies an an-
ecdote related to it.

When the baron was in Vienna, or elsewhere, the
doorman would point out bitterly, his elegant quarters
stood empty. They were not available for leasing by
other guests. Twice, though, they had been occupied
by others. On one occasion Baron von Diamant had
made them available as a courtesy to another "Jew
pig," a visiting member of the Warburg family. Another
time, diplomatically, he had instructed that his apartments be put at the disposal of Kaiser Wilhelm II and
a rather large hunting party accompanying him.

The German kaiser had accepted the loan of Baron
von Diamant's quarters in the Frankfurterhof because
his hunting lodge in the low mountains to the east of
Frankfurt was not available. The roof of the lodge had
been caved in by a tree felled during a summer thun-
derstorm, and repairs were still under way. "And so,"
the kaiser had joked, "I must sleep in the bed of the
Jew. However," he had added with that humor so
treasured by his inner circle, which viewed it as the
other, softer, side of his authoritarian paternalism,
"contrary to what we might expect, I did not wake up
with fleas, or with a hooked nose." The laughter at the
kaiser's bon mot was so convivial as to verge perilously
on being democratic.

" 'I did not wake up with fleas, or with a hooked
nose'!" Chortling, the doorman would quote the kaiser
to his cronies over many a stein of good, dark German
beer. "Our kaiser is not fooled by sly yids currying favor!"

Now the doorman's smile slashed through the gray

morning to greet the Baron Immanuel von Diamant as he exited the hotel. "A cab, Herr Baron?" he inquired ingratiatingly, moving to hail one of the horse-drawn coaches waiting at the hack stand up the cobblestoned street.

"No, thank you. I will walk."

"*Sehr gut*, Herr Baron." The doorman tugged his forelock.

The gesture was not lost on the baron. The head of the House of Diamond read people shrewdly. The doorman's tugging of his forelock may have been meant as a gesture of subservience, but to the baron it clearly conveyed Jew hatred along with its servility and arrogance.

Servility and arrogance were both familiar qualities to the man whose iron hand ruled the House of Diamond. He viewed them as two sides of the same German coin. The lowliest of Austrians might salute—a long finger casually flicking a cowlick—but the tugging of forelocks in Austria-Hungary had ceased with feudalism. Only in Russia, where the tsar saw to it that the peasants remained real peasants, and in Germany, where the concept of discipline was as eagerly granted from the bottom as it was demanded from the top, was respect still signaled by the forelock being tugged.

Deliberately, the baron did not acknowledge the gesture. He started up the dismal, wintry street, his stride brisk. The doorman's eyes, the hate once more unveiled, followed him. Filthy Jew!

But there was little in Baron Immanuel von Diamant's appearance as he picked his way through the rivulets of slush between the cobblestones of the narrow streets on this Saturday, the Hebrew Sabbath, that would have identified him as Jewish. His clothes were the fashionable garb of a Viennese aristocrat. He wore a winter overcoat of heavy merlton cloth with a beaver collar. It was cut straight and long and was unbuttoned high to the white silk scarf at his throat. It concealed the baron's dark gray, single-breasted, high-button suit with its narrow lapels and contrasting pearl-gray vest, as well as his pale blue shirt with its detachable stiff white collar and cuffs. A low-crowned, wide-brimmed derby hat sat with authority on his square-hewn head. He carried a silver-knobbed, right-angled walking stick, a gift from the aging Emperor Franz Josef of Austria-Hungary who was both the baron's patron and his dependent.

Beneath the derby, the baron's hair, steel gray and cropped short, was his one feature that was more German than Viennese. It led the aging Austrian emperor to sometimes refer fondly to Baron Immanuel as "my Jewish Prussian."

The baron's thin nose had the pinched look of an Austrian nobleman sniffing the heady air reserved to his caste. His eyes were gray-green and gave away nothing. His jaw was as stubborn as the posture of his six-foot athletic figure was relaxed; and his strong, pronounced cheekbones were softened by an unexpected dimple unhidden by his neatly trimmed side-whiskers. The ladies at the Viennese court thought him quite handsome in his mature fashion, and the newcomers among them were always surprised to learn that the attractive widower was a Jew. "But he doesn't look . . ." was a refrain that all too frequently wafted past Baron von Diamant's ears.

In any case, the baron thought to himself now as he moved briskly against the bleakness of winter-gray scenery, the pinpricks of Vienna are as nothing compared to the heavy-handedness of Hessian anti-Semitism. Such malevolence had permeated his boyhood. And even now, many years later, he could not walk from his hotel to that area that had once been the ghetto and his boyhood home without remembering, and without a sharp awareness that this was Frankfurt, this was Germany.

The doorman's forelock-tugging, his scarcely concealed hatred of Jews, stayed with the baron as he strode purposefully through the crooked byways toward the River Main where once had stood the toll gate to Frankfurt's ghetto. *Judengasse*, the ghetto, was long gone, and yet . . .

The doorman's attitude was increasingly typical, the baron thought bitterly, of the kaiser's Frankfurt subjects. Officially, following the unification of the German States into one nation, Jews had received citizenship in 1864; and in Frankfurt, by 1870, all the legal restrictions regarding Jews had been relaxed. In 1893, however, of the sixteen avowedly anti-Semitic candidates elected to the Reichstag, half were from Hesse, the State of which Frankfurt was the principal city. Ten years later, in 1903, Hesse elected eleven anti-Semites. Three more had been put in office in the most recent by-elections.

In such a climate, Baron Immanuel von Diamant had to consider the possibility of the clock being turned back for Jews. In the days of his grandfather, Zelik Diamant, and to a large extent during his father's lifetime, the Jews of Frankfurt-am-Main had been ruled by anti-Semitism. Back then, Jews had been forbidden by statute even to have surnames. The name Diamant in all its familial variations—von Diamant, Diamante, Diamond—had come about through usage, as "Zelik the diamond dealer" evolved into "Zelik Diamant," *Diamant* being the German word for the gem just as *diamond* was the English one and *diamante*, the Italian. It had taken courage back then to be Jewish. And the way things were going in Europe, courage might be required again.

Baron Immanuel von Diamant had such courage. He would stand with his people always. That was why he, a respectful if not always pious Jew, carried no money today, shunned all business, and walked to his destination as the Jewish Law decreed, rather than riding in comfort in a coach as befit his illustrious status.

His destination was a tall, narrow house in what had once been the Frankfurt ghetto. It was a modest enough edifice, but well cared for and possessed of a certain air of distinction in contrast to the run-down buildings pressing in on either side of it. At one and the same time it both stood out and was typical of the style of dwelling once forced on the Jews by the laws governing them.

Baron Immanuel von Diamant's mother insisted on remaining in the tall narrow, Gothic-style house in which all the Diamants had once been forced by law to live. She clung to this environment and to the old ways as if to life itself. Which was why, on this drab Sabbath, he was proceeding by foot to the now mostly Christian slum where the ghetto had once stood.

Every third Saturday, as well as on the Jewish High Holy Days, Baron Immanuel visited his mother. Rebekah Diamant was eighty-two years old, the wife of a baron, the mother of a baron, but she still refused to use the "von" in front of her name, and with the same stubbornness, refused to leave the house in the slums. "My home is my home; once they could make me stay; but now they can't make me leave; my home is my home." As well try to budge Gibraltar with a wooden pry.

Now, reaching the house with its four street-level archway entrances—once three had been used for various business enterprises, and only the fourth gave access to the Diamant living quarters; now those three were sealed off, serving only an exterior esthetic purpose—the Baron Immanuel paused just inside the doorframe before raising and letting fall the heavy brass door-knocker. He turned to the tiny box affixed to the right side of the doorway. This was the mezuzah. It contained a small portion of Deuteronomy in twenty-two lines handwritten on parchment. Softly, the baron spoke a traditional prayer. He then kissed his hand and pressed it against the mezuzah.

He knocked and was admitted by a round-faced matronly German woman with flaxen hair. "Hello, Bertha," he greeted her. "How are you?"

"Keeping quite well, Herr Baron." She curtsied and took his overcoat, derby, and walking stick. "Madam is in the parlor," she informed him.

The parlor was situated on the second floor, in the front of the house. Mounting the steep and narrow staircase, the baron smelled the mouth-watering aromas of the *cholent* cooking over a low flame in the oven of the kitchen below. Since his mother always insisted on preparing it herself, right down to the detail of setting the flame at just the proper temperature, in keeping with religious law it would have been cooking since before sundown on the previous evening. By the time Bertha, who was not Jewish and therefore eligible to labor on the Sabbath, took the cholent from the oven and served the dish of meat, potatoes, and dried beans, the aromas would have permeated the house all the way up to its fifth-floor gabled attic.

His mother had positioned herself to catch the late-morning sun in the parlor. Her narrow armchair, straight backed and hard by choice, was centered in a shaft of sunlight, making the finely lined skin of her face look particularly translucent and ethereal. Her small green eyes, however, were sharp as a sparrow's as she glanced up at her son's approach.

"Ha!" she greeted him. Her small, thin frame was

electric with energy, even in repose. "And what about the tsar?" It was her habit to start in mid-conversation, trusting that all her relatives had enough acumen to catch up.

"Hello, Mother." Baron Immanuel bent and kissed her cheek, which was cool and smoother to his lips than it appeared. "The Tsar of Russia is a fool and a tyrant and an anti-Semite. Worst of all, he lives in fear. That, of course, is very dangerous for Russian Jews."

"Do not pontificate, Immanuel. Please."

"You asked me, Mother." The hurt was slight, and he was patient.

"And do not be obtuse. You know I mean the tsar's *Protocols*."

She referred to an infamous anti-Semitic tract, *The Protocols of the Elders of Zion*, written by Sergei Nilus, a monk, at the behest of Tsar Nicholas II. The tsar, throughout most of his reign, had countered periodic peasant rebellions by instigating his subjects to pogroms against the Jews. When it became more difficult to channel their discontent that way, he had Nilus forge a document—*The Protocols of the Elders of Zion*—proving how a conspiracy made up of Jewish bankers and Jewish anarchists was planning to conquer the world. During the three years since 1903 when the *Protocols* first appeared, its message had gained wide acceptance not only in Russia, but throughout much of the rest of Europe as well. Everywhere anti-Semitism was on the rise.

"The *Protocols* continue to spread from east to west," Baron Immanuel answered his mother's question.

"Germany?" His mother's sparrow eyes narrowed.

"Yes. Only yesterday I saw them displayed in the bookstalls a few blocks from the Frankfurterhof."

"Eighty-two is a good age to be Jewish in a country

of anti-Semites," she decided. "One can always outwit them by dying."

"Not all Germans are anti-Semites, Mother. Not all Hessians. Not all Frankfurt Christians."

"Ahh, my son is so wise. So wise. But you are right. There are good Germans. And the good Germans will obey the law. Only tell me, my wise son, my eldest son, my son the baron, what will the law be?"

"So far—"

"Not so far. After that. Here in Hesse, from Frankfurt, we elect anti-Semites. Does the kaiser frown? Smile? Care? Or does he nod approval to Herzl's ghost and Zionism with one side of his face and wink at our Hessian Anti-Semites with the other?"

Such an old lady, his mother, to be thrusting her spear to the heart of the question! "The kaiser has signed a secret military agreement with the tsar," he told her with a sigh.

"So, then, I have my answer. The windows to be shuttered, the silver to be hidden, strong Jewish guards to be hired to guard my virtue." A lifetime of ghetto living made his mother bitter, sarcastic, and not impractical.

"What I just told you is very confidential, Mama."

"So I won't tell Bertha." More sarcasm. "After all, if she can't tell *milchikeh* dishes from *flaishikeh*"—plates used for dairy from plates used for meat in a kosher household—"how should she be trusted with state secrets?" Rebekah Diamant looked at her son then without irony. "You know this for a fact? That they have joined forces, the tsar and the kaiser?"

"Yes."

"How? I thought your closeness with Emperor Franz Josef excluded you from the kaiser's counsels."

"It does." Immanuel smiled thinly. "But it doesn't exclude my money. I hold notes for loans to one of Kaiser

Wilhelm's high-ranking and most trusted advisors. This secret," he added drily, "is interest on the loans."

"You look like your *zayde*." Rebekah went off on a tangent. "Like your grandfather, Zelik. But you don't behave like him, my son. Your zayde was never devious. You are devious."

"These are different times." Immanuel shrugged. "Survival dictates a certain deviousness."

"Survival, or prosperity?" Rebekah wondered.

"Would you have me be poor and less devious, Mama?"

" 'Measure profit. Never gouge.' " Rebekah quoted one of Zelik Diamant's strictures for conducting the House of Diamond's business. " 'Good will is future gain. Squeezing the *pfennig* is long-term loss.' "

"I try to live by that, Mama." The baron smiled wryly. "Not that the anti-Semites think so. They'd rather believe 'Buy low; sell high,' and every Jew a Shylock. I really do try to limit our House to fair profits. But competition in business is doubly difficult for us, and therefore doubly fierce. It's not always easy to know just what is fair."

"Our Lord Jehovah knows." The piety spoken, Rebekah smiled. Her smile was almost flirtatious. "So now tell me, my son. What devious action do you plan to take to counteract the threat of an alliance between the Russian father and our German kaiser?"

In answering, Immanuel did not have to explain to his mother the special relationship between the House of Diamond and the Austro-Hungarian Empire, nor his own favored position at the court of the emperor. She knew that, like his father before him, Baron Immanuel had seen to it that the House of Diamond continued to guarantee government bonds and make loans to the Austro-Hungarian Empire that kept it from bankruptcy and enabled it to compete in post–Industrial Revolution world trade through the building of long-line railroads and steamships for the transport of goods. She knew that Baron Immanuel was the emperor's confidante and most trusted advisor, and that her son made personal loans to him as well.

"Emperor Franz Josef has authorized me to feel out certain powerful people in France, England, and Italy regarding an entente to balance off the secret Russo-German agreement. After all, squeezed between Russia and Germany geographically as Austria-Hungary is, such an alliance is a direct threat to their trade and, therefore, to the House of Diamond investments," he told her.

"That does not sound so very devious," his mother pronounced. "Merely pragmatic."

"I am also personally underwriting a scheme aimed at convincing Tsar Nicholas that the anarchist plots that have been directed against his regime for the last fifteen years are being secretly financed by the kaiser."

"Now that," Rebekah said, adjusting the filagreed lace of her high-necked collar, "is devious." She paused and regarded Immanuel fondly. "Deliciously devious," she added. With those words, she rose and motioned to him to come closer so that she might take his arm. "The cholent is done," she told him. "Let us go down to dinner."

Over dinner, Rebekah inquired as to the health of the seventy-six-year-old Emperor Franz Josef. "How is the Emperor, His Majesty, the Exalted?" she inquired, invoking the designation used by Jews when referring to the ruler of Austria-Hungary.

"Remarkably well, considering his years and the pressures on him," Immanuel replied, savoring a forkful of *tsimmes*, the sweet carrot compote served with the cholent.

"The poor man. He has been through so much." It

was true. The Emperor Franz Josef lived always with
the Hapsburg curse, which had seen his brother Maximilian, the Emperor of Mexico, executed by the rebels
of Juarez, his son Rudolf a suicide in the lovers' death
pact of Mayerling, and his wife, the Empress Elizabeth
of Bavaria, assassinated by an anarchist while vacation-
ing in Geneva, Switzerland. "I wish him solace."

Franz Josef had solace, but Immanuel did not mention this to his mother, whose morality was inclined to
be old-fashioned. The emperor's ongoing relationship
with the actress Katharina Schratt, more than forty
years his junior, had been spicing up the court gossip
in Vienna since shortly after the death of the empress.

"The emperor's health is our good fortune," Rebekah
remarked.

From the inception of his reign fifty-eight years before, Emperor Franz Josef had championed the Jews
against Austrian and Hungarian anti-Semites. To Jews
like Rebekah Diamant, his rule represented a golden
age for Austria-Hungary. Even in Frankfurt, which was
German, the synagogue was filled to overflowing for
the services held on the emperor's birthday. Indeed, the
folklore passed on to Jewish children insisted that the
prophet Elijah had personally blessed the emperor and
promised him long life.

"Yes," Baron Immanuel agreed with his mother. "The
emperor's health is indeed our good fortune."

Bertha was clearing away the dishes from the mid-
day meal now. Baron Immanuel got to his feet and
helped his mother from her chair. They went back up
to the parlor. They would have their tea and warm
strudel from a cart there.

"Your young man has been to see me," Rebekah remarked, blowing on her tea-with-milk to cool it.

"Josef Rothko?" The baron smiled. "And could you
help him?" Young Josef Rothko was a Viennese gene-

alogist Baron Immanuel had recently hired to trace the history of the Diamant family. He was a bright and clever young man with a winning personality and quite knowledgeable in his field. The baron had sent him to Frankfurt with a letter to Rebekah asking her to cooperate with him regarding family relationships and lore in any way she could. Josef was also, he remembered now as he saw a familiar glint in his mother's eye, rather handsome in a craggy-faced, soft-eyed way.

"Is he married?" Rebekah wanted to know. There were always Diamant grand-nieces and cousins for whom husbands must be found.

"I don't believe so." And then, deliberately, the baron dimmed the light in his mother's eye. "I don't know if he's Jewish," he remarked.

"You don't know?" Rebekah was disapproving. "You couldn't ask?"

"It never came up, Mama."

"But how can he trace our family history if he's not Jewish?"

"He's a genealogist, Mama. It's his trade. His own religion has nothing to do with it."

"So you say, my son, the baron." Obviously Rebekah didn't approve. Then she had another thought. "You don't know if he's Jewish," she said. "But you don't know that he's not Jewish either. Isn't that so?"

"Yes, Mama. That's so."

"So he could be Jewish."

"He could be," the baron granted.

"You'll find out, Immanuel." It was not a request.

"Yes, Mama." He sighed. "I'll find out." The baron stood. "It's time for me to go, Mama. I have a business engagement. And since I have to walk back to the Frankfurterhof . . ."

"Have you been to the *shul* yet?" his mother inquired as she rang the little bell that would signal Bertha to bring the baron's overcoat, hat, and walking stick to the front door.

"No."

"Will you go to shul now?"

"Yes."

"And say a prayer for Zayde and one for your father?"

"Yes, Mama. Of course."

"You're a good boy, Immanuel." Humor once again lit her sparrow eyes. "Devious," she added, "but a good boy."

"I'm a man, Mama." He bent to kiss her good-bye.

"Of course. A man. And so, my son the man, you will see to it that the House of Diamond stops the tsar and that bully blowhard the kaiser from starting a war. Will you not?"

"You have my word, Mama. No war. Not in the immediate future, anyway. We and the Rothschilds are agreed. And that will give all the banking houses of Europe pause."

"Good." She raised her face and when he bent a second time, she kissed his cheek. "Don't forget Zayde and Papa during *kaddish*," she reminded him.

"I won't." The Baron Immanuel von Diamant left.

An hour later, he took off his prayer shawl at the synagogue and bid good-bye to the other men with whom he had been praying. He exited and began walking back toward the Frankfurterhof at a somewhat less brisk pace than before. It was still light out, however, still *Shabbas*, and so he had no choice but to walk.

As the baron reached the edge of what had been the ghetto, a coach pulled up alongside him. A familiar face peered out the window and greeted him. The baron returned the greeting with some surprise. "I didn't know that you were still in Frankfurt, Josef," he exclaimed.

"Well, I am, sir," Josef Rothko, the young genealogist, told him. "May I offer you a ride?" He half opened the door of the coach.

"Thank you, no." The baron looked at the light still in the sky. It was still too early. "I must walk back to my hotel."

"No, sir." Firmly, Josef Rothko contradicted him. "You must ride." From under his coat he produced a pistol with a long barrel and pointed it in the baron's face. "Please get in, and quickly."

Astonished, the baron got in the coach. Immediately, the driver cracked the whip over the horses, and the coach started off at top speed toward the outskirts of Frankfurt.

The head of the House of Diamond had been abducted.

2. VIENNA

IT WAS WELL before dawn when the Emperor Franz Josef was awakened. The old monarch's eyes opened blue and angry, forecasting the fierce resentment of the frown turning down his thin-lipped mouth. His instructions decreed that his sleep was never to be disturbed lightly, particularly when he shared his bed with Katharina. Nothing less than a declaration of war was sufficient cause.

The gravity of the face peering down at him from above the oil lamp stayed the emperor's anger. He patted Katharina, stirring from sleep to wakefulness beside him, and slid from the bed into the robe and slippers provided by the two nervous servants flanking the majordomo of the royal house. He followed the candle into the anteroom.

"What has happened?" The emperor was a slender man, not tall, but even in old age his posture was commanding, ramrod stiff in defiance of the rheumatism that beset him. He sat down on a Louis XIV sofa with curved gold-leaf legs, a remnant of a long-ago time when the Hapsburgs and the French Bourbons had sought détente through the exchange of such gifts as exquisite furniture and works of art—and royal princesses such as the unfortunate future queen, Marie Antoinette of France. He shivered visibly as he was informed of the abduction of the Baron von Diamant in Frankfurt.

"Have they killed him?" Under his bald pate, Franz Josef's thin face with its overwhelming mustaches revealed nothing of what he was feeling. He regarded Immanuel von Diamant, as he had the baron's father before him, as a friend as well as a trusted advisor and confidant. But a Hapsburg could not display concern, or any other emotion.

"We do not know, Majesty."

"Has there been word from the abductors? Ransom demands, perhaps?"

"Not as yet, Sire. But perhaps it is too soon."

"Perhaps." The emperor fell silent, thinking. Another cold shiver twitched his body. Damn Hofburg Palace! Its drafts had been a disgrace since the time of the Empress Maria Theresa. No wonder the Hapsburgs were regarded as haughty by their fellow European monarchs. Their uptilted noses and arrogant sniffing were the result of too many Viennese winters spent in this dank and drafty old castle. True Hapsburgs were constantly beset by sniffles. Yet the Hofburg was a symbol of Hapsburg monarchy, and as absolute as he insisted his power was, Franz Josef had never dared to assuage his tormented sinuses by ordering it to be razed. Symbols were all-important in keeping his subjects docile.

Now he blew his nose, and spoke again. "There are many considerations," he said carefully. "We must move hastily, but not too hastily. You may leave me now. But wait just outside the door," he told the majordomo, "so that my orders may be carried out quickly when I issue them."

The servants turned up the gaslight in the anteroom and then followed the majordomo out. As soon as the door closed behind them, the other door leading from the royal boudoir opened and Katharina Schratt, the emperor's mistress, emerged to join him. *"Liebchen?"* she asked.

As he told her what had happened, Katharina's eyes widened, accentuating their roundness, and confirming the soft contours of her face. Even with the ravages that sleep had visited upon her makeup, Katharina's expression was a permanent moue, a bow-shaped mouth balanced by twin red-apple cheeks. It was a visage suited to her physique. Tall and flaxen haired, Katharina boasted an hourglass figure, wide in the hips, narrow of waist, and with an overflowing bosom. An actress, she exemplified the ideal beauty of her time: abundant, fleshy, womanly. And if the expression on her face was a trifle vacuous, that, too, was in keeping with the universal male preference for a wink and a wallow between the sexes with no pretension to any communication of ideas.

Nevertheless, whereas Katharina looked the part, her relationship with the emperor actually ran counter to this prevailing masculine philosophy. She was his confidante, and behind her too-pretty features, she not only comprehended what he told her but formulated responses that sometimes startled Franz Josef with their incisiveness. "You are an actress playing a part!" he would accuse her. "The part is Dumb Dora, but really you are Athena, Goddess of Wisdom."

"Please, Sire, I am nothing of the sort. I am only your most humble and adoring subject."

"An old man's darling."

"The emperor's most fortunate subject," she would insist.

"And if I were not the emperor? If I were just some ordinary old man without distinction? Would you adore me then? Would you share my sheets if they were not royal silk?"

"But you are the emperor." Katharina was practical. "And of course that is why I adore you If you were like other men—and I do not just mean age—then I would not love you as I do."

"Even if I were young and broad of back and firm of limb? Young, with rippling golden muscles and flashing white teeth all my own?"

"Why, that would be very tempting." Katharina would laugh. "But nothing compared to being the woman loved by His Supreme Majesty, the Emperor Franz Josef of the Austro-Hungarian Empire."

"Birth does have its advantages." The Emperor would also laugh, but he would respond drily. In the back of his mind, always, was the one question he would not ask: Are you satisfied, Katharina? Forty years difference between us. He was seventy-six years old and sex was infrequent, if not impossible. Still, for him, it was by far not the most important part of their relationship. Like that ancient King of the Hebrews, Solomon, the warmth of a young body in his bed was all-important. Yes, all-important and life extending.

Nor was the warmth merely physical. Their talk, their rapport, warmed his soul as nothing else did. Following the murder of his wife, Elizabeth, his empress whom he had loved truly, if not always faithfully, since her fifteenth birthday when he had married her, the actress Katharina Schratt had rescued him from the depths of genuine despair. He trusted Katharina, loved her after his royal fashion, and basked in the young woman's adoration for him. But was she satisfied?

"My poor Highness." Katharina reacted now with words to the abduction. "You were so fond of the baron. And you trusted him."

"I did. I trusted Immanuel. I trust you. That is two people I can trust, and that is all." The emperor sighed. "It changes things."

"I know." She took his veined hand and held it, a gesture of sympathy. "How is it," she wondered, "that the kidnappers contacted you, rather than some dignitary of the House of Diamond?"

"The Baron von Diamant is my banker. My government depends on him as do I personally. It is quite reasonable that these abductors would notify me, the patron who so relies on him, rather than one of the other Diamonds who might be his rival and perhaps not quite so eager to secure his quick release."

"I see."

"It does change things," the emperor repeated. "Not just for me. For Austria. The economy of the nation, its prosperity, are quite dependent on the House of Diamond."

"But the House of Diamond is still there. It is only the Baron Immanuel—"

"Without the Baron Immanuel," the emperor cut her off, "the balance of power will change in the House of Diamond. And that will change the balance of power for all Europe. The Baron Immanuel was a friend to Austria. The other members of the House have other allegiances."

"I see."

"It is a very delicate time. The throne of the tsar rests on shifting sands, and the flirtation of the kaiser with him must be regarded as a serious threat to us. There is no stability in France. The sun never sets on the English Empire, and such constant and insistent daylight precludes sleep for all the other governments of Europe that must expand—that is to say, colonize—or perish of the inability to sustain our economies at home. Even the upstart Americans have run the Spaniards out of their hemisphere and are straining for delusions of imperialist grandeur by taking over the building of the Panama Canal from the French. With all this, the House of Diamond has involvement. But it was only the Baron Immanuel who held the interest of Austria-Hungary close to his heart."

"My poor Highness. Come back to bed."

"I cannot. The House of Diamond must be notified of the abduction. I must decide who, specifically, should be entrusted with the news."

"I understand." Katharina sat down beside him on the Louis XIV sofa and pulled his head down until it was cushioned on her ample breast. "But surely Lord Haran Diamond in London is the one to notify. He is Baron Immanuel's brother, the next-oldest member of the family, the obvious successor as head of the House of Diamond."

"That's true," the emperor granted, nuzzling into her soft flesh. "But it is also the problem. And, setting my personal feelings aside, I cannot overlook the possibility that there may be an opportunity in these circumstances to affect that succession, perhaps even to change it."

"You don't like Lord Haran?"

"Actually, I don't. He is both the most obtuse and the most arrogant Englishman I have ever met. If he were a German, he would be the kaiser."

"But he is a Jew!"

"Ironic, isn't it?" The emperor's dry, thin-lipped mouth tickled her bosom as he smiled. "Lord Haran is both a Jew and yet the very embodiment of the British Empire. He is the epitome of their power and pomposity. Even so," he added, "it is not my personal feeling that is important. What is important is that if Lord Haran gains control of the House of Diamond, he will use its influence overwhelmingly for England, and that will both work against Austria-Hungary and upset the balance of power in all Europe."

"Well, who else is there to take over the House besides Lord Haran?" Katharina wondered.

"There are the other heads of the major branches. There is the baron's cousin Carlo Diamante in Rome. Because of the Venetian trade, his branch of the family was once the most powerful. He has always been amenable to Baron Immanuel's exploitation of Italian natural resources and seaports for Austria's advantage. But he is a weak man, and if I were to throw my influence behind him, I would surely find myself sooner or later riding a lame horse."

"Who else?"

"There are two other cousins, Marcus and Noah Diamond, father and son, who are doing remarkably well with the new House of Diamond branch in New York City in North America. The Baron Immanuel has confided in me that he is impressed with them, although he has some reservations regarding their enthusiasm for investment in New World projects. He thought they may to some extent have been seduced by pioneer optimism, and so lean toward overexpansion. Still, he has seen fit to back them on the Panama Canal and to put House of Diamond resources behind the United States project to build it despite the French failure."

"The Baron Immanuel has a son," Katharina remembered.

"Yes." The emperor sighed, his warm breath making a whooshing echo in the deep valley between her generous breasts. "Philippe."

"Philippe?" She was surprised. "Surely that is a French name."

"He is the head of the Paris branch of the House of Diamond."

"But if he is the Baron von Diamant's son, isn't he Austrian?"

"Oh, yes. He was raised in Vienna and only left Austria as a young man to complete his education at Heidelberg. Philippe even has the faint trace of a dueling scar to attest to his lack of Frenchness."

"Then why—"

"Six years ago, when Philippe was twenty-five, upon the death of a great-uncle, he was sent to Paris to manage the branch until Baron Immanuel could consult with Lord Haran regarding which family member should next be in control in Paris. Despite the fact that even Philippe's father thought him a lightweight young scamp more interested in beautiful women than in the business of a great financial house, the boy took hold. He did so well that even Lord Haran was forced to agree that he should take over the Paris branch permanently. Shortly after that decision was reached, Philippe dropped the honorary Austrian 'von' from his surname and Gallicized his given name."

"But why?"

"It is their policy." The emperor shrugged. "The original founder laid down the precept that assimilation was necessary to good business. Thus our Baron Immanuel, although born a German, is an Austrian through and through. Lord Haran Diamond is the quintessential upper-class Englishman, snobbery and all. Carlo Dia-

mante in Italy thrives on pasta, and Philippe is a gour-
met, a roué, and a Francophile."

"But if the Diamants are so eager to assimilate, then
why do they cling to being Jewish?"

"Integrity." The emperor was quite serious. "It may
be good business to blend in with the prevailing culture, but it is bad for the Jew's eternal soul to foresake
the religion of his forebears. Believe me, I have discussed this with the baron—and with his father before
him—on more than one occasion. Their faith comes
first always. The family next. Then one's fellow Jews.
And only after those considerations is business foremost. Do you wonder at my admiration for these Hebrews?"

"Well, no. But still, they sound quite clannish, these
Jews, these Diamants."

"Oh, they are. But loyal to a fault. Loyal to one another, and loyal to those to whom they have pledged
fealty."

"I see." Katharina thought for a long moment. "Well,
then," she said finally, "to whom will you send word of
the Baron's abduction?"

"To the one least likely to do harm to Austria-
Hungary." With a sigh the emperor lifted his head from
the soft pillow of her bosom. He stood up and went to
the door and summoned the majordomo.

"A telegram," he told him. "Send it immediately. To
Philippe Diamant of the House of Diamond in Paris."
The emperor glanced at a large grandfather clock
standing in the hallway. It was still early morning there
in Vienna and in Paris. "You had best send it to his
home," he decided. "My dear Philippe," he dictated. "I
regret to inform you . . ."

3 . PARIS

PHILIPPE DIAMANT WAS not at home when the emperor's telegram was delivered before dawn to a sleepy servant at his fashionable town house on the Rue Saint-Antoine in Paris. Realizing its importance—it had come from the emperor in Vienna, after all—the servant took it to his master's personal secretary. The secretary had to be awakened, and he considered carefully before taking the responsibility of opening the envelope.

Finally, he decided to read the message, and doing so turned quite pale. He read it a second time. There was no mistake. Philippe's father had been kidnapped.

The secretary stared out the window, composing his thoughts. A wintry dawn was just breaking over the Eiffel Tower. "Monsieur Diamant did not sleep at home," he guessed.

"But he did, sir." The servant corrected the secretary. "The master rose early, dressed, and went out."

"How long ago?"

"Perhaps an hour, sir. No more."

"And he left no word where he might be reached?"

"The master said nothing, sir," the servant assured the secretary.

Merde!

It was not the first time. As conscientious as Philippe was about his stewardship of the Paris House of Diamond, he was nonetheless given to sudden and prolonged absences. He would give some instructions as to the conduct of business and then he would simply vanish. When he conveyed the orders, nothing in his manner would indicate whether or not he was going to be there to see that they were carried out. It kept the staff on its toes, the secretary supposed.

Often he would later reveal that his absence was related to some business coup he had brought off for the House of Diamond. It would be plain then that advance notice of his movements might have tipped off his rivals to his intentions. Always, when analyzed, there was a good reason behind his disappearances.

Still, this was different. No matter the business strategy involved, Philippe's father had been abducted, and he must be informed. Where could he have gone so early in the morning?

The answer should not have surprised anyone who knew Philippe. He was greeting the dawn in the clearing of a woods not far from the Palace of Versailles, about to participate in a traditional ritual that although outlawed was still dear to the hearts of many aristocratic Frenchmen—and to the vanity of some of their ladies.

One of these ladies, a young and beautiful countess, sat in a closed carriage behind some winter-bare chestnut trees fringing the clearing. The curtains of the carriage were drawn, but she was holding one aside with lace-gloved fingers to observe the scene. Under her cloak her pert bosom heaved with anxiety and her heart beat wildly. Her prayers were fervent, but treacherous.

Two of the men in the clearing had reached the end of their proscribed pacing and were about to turn and raise their arms in the classic dueling pose. Each held a loaded and cocked revolver in his right hand. When the referee dropped the white handkerchief from his outstretched hand, they would be free to fire. They would have two shots each—one from each barrel of the old-fashioned, powder-and-shot–loaded dueling pistols they wielded.

One of the men was the Count Evremont, husband of the beautiful young woman in the carriage. The other was Philippe Diamant. The countess's prayers were for Philippe.

They were, perhaps, not necessary. Philippe was known to be the most accomplished duelist in Paris, with the possible exception of the recently elected French Premier Georges Clemenceau himself. The faded crescent of the dueling scar on Philippe's left cheek attested to his expertise with the saber, but it was as a crack pistol shot that he was more renowned in Paris. He had fought many duels since coming to France, usually—as was the case now—with outraged husbands. He had lost none.

Philippe's irresistibility to certain ladies of society— usually the victims of marriages of convenience, the joining of aristocratic houses, or of wealth with breeding—was not difficult to understand. His conquests tended to be much younger than their husbands, bored, and eager to satisfy needs that their husbands could not. All this frequently came to a head upon first meeting with Philippe, whose handsome features were enhanced by a dashing air of wit and intelligence.

He was blond, and yet there was a decided swashbuckling swarthiness to his complexion. His wit was whiplike, sharp and incisive, but never lingering on any one target for long. He had an avant-garde sense of fashion and the slender but muscular figure to show it off—particularly evening wear—to best advantage. And, the promise smoldering in his green eyes always fulfilled, he was as uninhibited as a Montmartre gigolo between the sheets. So satisfying a lover was he that each new conquest was an advertisement for the next.

Now the handkerchief of the referee was dropped.

The Count Evremont, the latest husband to be cuck-olded by Philippe, raised his pistol. He aimed. His hand was shaking badly as he fired, and the shot went wild. Immediately, he fired his second and final round. The bullet grazed Philippe's shoulder, leaving a small rent in his pleated mauve shirt.

Philippe's gun was aimed at his adversary's heart. His hand was steady. Deliberately, he raised it, pointed the barrel at the gray and wintry early-morning sky, and fired his two shots in rapid succession. He bowed to the adversary he had spared. He turned on his heel and departed the clearing.

As he passed the coach, Philippe paused. He stroked his blond mustache with a long finger. "My dear Count-ess," he said, "perhaps it would be best if you did not drop by for an absinthe tomorrow evening."

From the coach there came a heartfelt answer, word-less, a sigh of regret.

4 . LONDON

BEHIND THE CLOSED doors of the drawing room, the young man's sigh was nervous. He cracked his knuck-les. He cleared his throat for the third time. Minerva Diamond, daughter of Lord Haran Diamond, smiled sympathetically.

Minerva, not quite twenty years old, was both the eldest and most troublesome of Lord Haran's six chil-dren. She was a rather plain young woman with mouse-brown hair and an unfortunate shambling gait. Her voice was deep and throaty despite the efforts of a suc-cession of governesses to impress on her that she must go up at least one octave to make it even minimally ladylike. She was nearsighted and because of this her gaze was so direct as to be disconcerting. Sometimes she wore spectacles, but she had an unfortunate habit of peering out at people from above them, which most found even more unnerving. It was true that when her deep brown eyes blazed with anger while expressing a firm conviction, her face took on an intensity that was almost beautiful. But since the holding of such firm convictions—and Lord Haran thought them truly outrageous ideas—was not ladylike or becoming, he discounted the notion of its being appealing.

Some women, her father was given to reflect, overcome their physical deficiencies by cultivating a certain charm, even a sensuality. Minerva was, he believed, devoid of both. She was not demure as might have befit her boyish figure, rather hoydenish, given to abrupt and unwomanly gestures, and remarks every bit as piercing as they were humorous. With neither great beauty nor womanly compliance to recommend her, Minerva was also outspoken rather than retiring, opinionated rather than modest, and—to her father the most dismaying of all her traits—quite self-confident.

Marriage was, of course, the only solution to the problem of such a daughter. As much as Lord Haran loved Minerva, and he really did dote on her, she could not stay a maiden forever. And if she was not to have a most unhappy life, then she must be tamed to womanhood. Spinsters were, after all, by definition the most unhappy of creatures. Yes, marriage, Lord Haran was satisfied, would do the trick. The institution would bring her to heel as her father had failed to do.

It was toward this end that he had allowed the sliding polished-wood doors to the Diamonds' drawing room to be closed, affording the two young people inside a certain expedient privacy. As if to balance the privacy of closed doors, the heavy Victorian window drapes had been drawn open to admit what stray shafts of afternoon sunlight might penetrate the London winter fog. In a pale pool of such light, a pool of tenuous existence, Minerva Diamond sat in an elephant-hide armchair and sympathized with the nervous young man before her.

Nervous as he was, the fellow had a certain poise of the sort inbred since Agincourt. His loose, fashionable flannel coat and trousers seemed as natural to his leisurely style as a second skin. Indeed, his nervousness was not a matter of character, rather of circumstance. He was, perhaps, not altogether thrilled with the task he had set himself.

He was the Viscount Ronald Templeton, the only son of a family of English aristocrats steeped in the bluest of blood. For eight generations, he could trace his family back without fear of finding a Celt, a plebeian, or a heretic. The lineage of the Templetons was pure British upper class and unimpeachably Church of England. If the young viscount betrayed an unaccustomed nervousness now, it was doubtless because circumstance had placed him on the brink of breaking with that tradition.

"I would like to speak to your father." The Viscount Templeton stepped over the brink.

"How nice." Minerva chose to be perversely obtuse. "He does so enjoy conversation with you."

The viscount reddened slightly, not sure if he was being twitted, or misunderstood. "I would like to speak with him about speaking to you, if you take my meaning," he explained.

"I'm not sure I do. You *are* speaking to me," Minerva pointed out.

An expression of dismay flitted across the viscount's features. He was fully aware that Minerva was not beautiful—he was prepared to ignore that fact just as he disregarded her Jewishness—but it had not occurred to him that she might be slow witted as well. "Let me clarify my intent." He spelled it out. "I am asking for your permission to speak to your father so that I may ask his permission to speak with you and ask you for your consent to our betrothal and eventual marriage."

"That does seem awfully roundabout, Ronald. Why don't you just ask me straight out? Now. Here."

"Custom and respect dictate otherwise. I have no wish to offend Lord Haran."

"Of course you don't." Minerva was well aware of the substantial liens the House of Diamond held against the Templeton estates in Surrey. Her father had been quite understanding and generous in extending loans to Ronald's father. As rich in lands as they were in heritage and influence at court, the noble Templeton family was habitually short of ready cash. Indeed, for three generations their state of genteel debt had been regarded as noblesse oblige. In this harsher modern time, however, only the goodwill of Lord Diamond stood between the Templetons and the auction block. "Still," Minerva continued, "we both know that Father is in his study waiting for you to trot back there so that he can agree to what he has already decided to agree to in order for you to trot back here and pop the question. I don't think he would be offended if we foreshorten the ritual. He might even appreciate the saving of wear and tear on the carpets between the parlor and his study."

Ronald frowned. Composure was his birthright, but it was only skin-deep. Was this unwonted forthrightness, he wondered, some trait peculiar to Jewish women of which he had hitherto been unaware? "Very well, then." He adapted to the situation. "Will you consider my proposal, Minerva?"

"That we become betrothed?"

"Yes.

"And subsequently marry."

He frowned. "Yes."

"I will consider it, Ronald. But not, I fear," Minerva added, "favorably."

This time there could be no mistaking the rush of blood to the young Viscount Templeton's cheeks. "You do not look favorably on me," he summed up stiffly.

"Oh, Ronald. Don't pout. It's really not so great a rejection, is it? I mean you are not in love with me any more than I am with you. Why not simply regard it as a business venture that has not worked out?"

"I do not regard marriage as a business venture," the viscount protested.

"Of course you do. And so does Father. Particularly as regards the daughters of the Diamond family. We are all of us trading markers for the House of Diamond."

"That is a dismaying characterization of arranged marriages," Ronald pointed out. "Many of them, after all, work out quite well."

"And many don't."

"Nor do many love matches."

"*Touché*, Ronald." She regarded him with surprise. "I apologize to you. Indeed, you are more perceptive than I have given you credit for being."

"And you, Minerva," he blurted out, "are more cynical than I would have guessed."

"We daughters of the House of Diamond have good reason to be cynical. We're traditional bargaining chips. For three generations our fathers have arranged marriages that have been either with distant Diamond cousins eligible to be brought into the firm, with business colleagues offering opportunities for advantageous merger, or with aristocrats such as yourself from a variety of countries in which the firm has interests.

"The sons of the House of Diamond," Minerva continued, "must marry either other Diamonds, or at the very least daughters of other prominent Jewish families. They're forbidden to marry outside the religion, for then they might themselves beget sons alienated from Judaism and family. But, with an eye toward increasing family influence in the royal houses of Europe, the daughters are frequently married off to gentile aristocrats. One of my aunts is a grand duchess of Rumania, while another has borne sons for the Bourbon line. And my cousin Tamar is a Venetian countess. We Diamond women tie the family to the great royal houses of Christian Europe, as well as to the mightiest banking houses both Jewish and gentile. Cynical? Of course I'm cynical. I have reason to be. A Diamond son is bred to wealth and power; a Diamond daughter is bred to breed for merger and influence."

"You should be careful how you talk, Minerva. Another person not of your faith might find his anti-Semitism much reinforced by such admissions."

"Really?" Minerva's laugh was a trifle harsh. "But why? Neither the Diamonds nor the Jews originated the practice of marrying off daughters for purposes of establishing alliances. The royal houses of Europe have been doing it for centuries, and right up to the present. The future Queen Victoria was long ago married off to a German prince. Her daughter Alice, by arranged marriage, wed Prince Frederick William of Prussia and became mother to the present Kaiser of Germany. Princess Alice's daughter Alexandra was betrothed to the present Tsar of Russia, and Queen Victoria's son, King Edward, in addition to being cousin to the kaiser and the tsarina, is also related to the royal houses of Greece, Rumania, Sweden, Denmark, Norway, and Belgium. All this the result of arranged marriages." Minerva sat back in triumph and then leaned forward again. "And oh, yes, since the Emperor Franz Josef of Austria-Hungary had a brother, Maximilian I of Mexico, whose queen was the Princess Carlotta of Belgium, it is probable that King Edward and the Austro-Hungarian Emperor are related through marriage to Belgian royalty as well. Shall I continue, or have I made my point?" Minerva inquired without pausing for breath.

"You have made your point." The Viscount Templeton was quite overwhelmed. "I concede that marriage for advantage is not a monopoly of either the House of Diamond or Hebrews generally. Indeed, you might have mentioned that it is quite common among the noble houses of England, as well as with the royal houses of Europe." He took a deep breath. "Still, by your own description, tradition and family limit your options. Why not marry me, then?"

It was a point well taken. For an instant, Minerva was tempted to answer his question. But the answer was a secret she shared with no one, not even, yet, with the person involved—the man with whom Minerva had fallen head-over-heels, the description being quite accurate, in love.

The man she loved was poor. He was foreign. Not even to Minerva's myopic and smitten gaze did he appear remotely handsome. And yet she loved him.

She had searched her mind for reasons while her heart silently jeered at the quest for logic where love is concerned. All that she possessed were feelings—and except for the love itself, only half-formed feelings—and they could not stand examination by the logic of Minerva's own usually sensible nature, let alone by any impartial standard. Instinctively, she recoiled from any further logical reasoning.

There was something openly vulnerable about the man she loved. It reminded Minerva of her own vulnerability, which she had long ago learned to disguise.

Of course, the stray puppy she had brought home when
she was ten years old had conveyed that same vulnerability.

Minerva had smiled to herself. It wasn't the same.
The man she loved was no puppy; he was a man. She
could sense the hidden strength beneath the diffidence
he cultivated. She might occasionally manipulate this
man, but she would never control him. He was no
puppy. There was a stubbornness much like her own
in his silence, his mutterings. Yes, he would be a difficult man, passive to a fault on the surface, a rock at his
core.

This was a reason to love a man? That he appeared
a milksop and was really a mule? Her father's daughter,
Minerva rejected that. It was no reason. She had no
reason that could stand up to even her own scrutiny.
No reason. She was in love. And she was quite prepared to scratch out the eyes of anyone who questioned the worthiness of the object of her love.

"Why not marry me, Minerva?" The Viscount
Templeton repeated his query.

"I am sorry, Ronald. I really do like you awfully,"
she told him. "But there will be other merchants'
daughters eager to receive your proposal. I am not the
only answer to your money difficulties."

Minerva was right. There were other merchants who
would be more than glad to link their names to that of
Templeton via their marriageable daughters. And Mi-
nerva Diamond was certainly a most difficult woman.
"I really must be going." He eased toward the door.
"Please do say good-bye to your father for me. Tell him
I remembered another appointment and that I apolo-
gize for hurrying off."

"I'll see to it, Ronald. Good-bye."

And then he was gone.

Minerva proceeded to her father's study. Lord Haran

looked up eagerly at her knock. But his face fell when he saw it was his daughter and not the Viscount Templeton. "I thought that Ronald would surely—?" The upper-class British cadences that Lord Haran had cultivated so carefully to cover traces of his Frankfurt birth trailed off.

"He had a previous appointment. He asked me to apologize to you for not stopping to say good-bye, but he was late."

Lord Haran crossed over to his ponderously Victorian desk of polished mahogany. He removed a silver, monogrammed snuffbox from the upper right-hand drawer. Turning away from his daughter, he took a pinch of snuff from the box and inhaled it deeply. Just as he turned back, however, a sneeze turned his face as ruddy as that of a country squire and his habitual monocle popped from the eye squinched to hold it.

Minerva suppressed a smile. Her father was the most compulsively British person she had ever met, far more so really than King Edward himself, who—and this, too, was a mark of her father's well-planned climb up the British social ladder—sometimes took dinner with them. Really, with his cheeks red and his eyes watering as he screwed his monocle back in place, he was the very image of John Bull.

"I thought surely that Ronald would want to speak to me regarding his intentions toward you." Monocle in place, color fading, Lord Haran had recovered.

"You always think that, Father. No matter who the young man is."

"I usually have good reason. I am a shrewd judge of English character and intentions. I would not hold the position I do in the English business world and in English society were this not so."

"Oh, Father, I don't doubt that. But when it comes

to reading the intentions of potential suitors . . . Well, you've been wrong before, and more than once."

"Have I?" The monocle focused like one of those newfangled electric searchlights blinding passersby in Piccadilly. It was true that this was not the first time such an occurrence had taken place, but he was beginning to suspect that the mistake was not his. "Or have you somehow—?"

"I, Father? Of course not," Minerva blithely lied. "You just have to accept that when it came right down to it, Viscount Templeton wasn't that attracted to me. Let's face it, Father, I am not a great beauty."

"You do have other qualities, by Jove."

"I do. But they are not readily appreciated by men less astute and loving than you, dear Father." Yet there is someone who might, just might, appreciate those qualities, Minerva thought. She was careful not to speak that thought aloud.

"Well, we shall just have to try again."

"I'm sure you will, Father." Ignoring his reference to a joint effort on their part, she placed the stress on the word *you*.

Lord Haran sighed. "I must return to my offices," he told his daughter. "They will think I'm not coming back from lunch."

"Have a nice day, Father."

"Good afternoon, Minerva."

The message from Paris was waiting on Lord Haran's desk when he sat down behind it. He opened and read it quickly. Then he read it a second time, more slowly, squinting with concern through his monocle.

This was terrible news. His brother abducted! Devastating. Lord Haran sat frozen with genuine concern for several moments. The conflicting emotions he had felt toward his older brother since childhood—admiration coupled with jealousy, inferiority with competitiveness, bitterness with respect—welled up to the surface of his consciousness. But his love was greater than his resentments, and he bowed his head and offered a quick and fervent prayer that his brother was still alive and that a way might be found to secure his release from whoever was holding him.

Responsibility forced Lord Haran to put his concern to one side. With Immanuel absent, he was now the one in charge of the House of Diamond. He must act quickly and prudently to protect the interests of the family.

Rome would have to be notified, and so would New York—but not immediately. As of now, he must act on the assumption that the news was contained. Frankfurt and Vienna knew, of course, and he would have to rely on Immanuel's people there to take prudent measures to protect Diamond interests, but to go no further until they received instructions from London. His nephew, Philippe, in Paris knew, and that was perhaps unfortunate—there was a warning in the Austro-Hungarian Emperor's notifying Philippe first, rather than him—but Philippe was in no immediate position to mount a serious challenge to Haran's authority. In any case, Philippe had an equal stake in preventing premature disclosure of the kidnapping.

The House of Diamond stock would plunge with the revelation. An abrupt and unanticipated change of management would precipitate a crisis in confidence among small and large investors. Their faith had been placed in Baron Immanuel von Diamant. He, Lord Haran Diamond, was less well known to them, untested, questionable. They would unload their holdings. With the ripple effect, world exchanges would go bearish on Diamond.

Such a reaction was inevitable. Advance knowledge

of the kidnapping was worth millions of dollars. That knowledge had to be both contained and acted upon. Time was of the essence.

Fleetingly, Lord Haran remembered the ethos of Zelik Diamant: "Measure profit. Never gouge. Goodwill is future gain. Squeezing the pfennig is long-term loss." In his position, his brother, Immanuel, would have taken pains to act within those guidelines. Lord Haran frowned so that his monocle cut into his flesh painfully. Survival! That came first.

Lord Haran made plans to implement the sale of House of Diamond stock at current rates, or even slightly below. It must be a subtle unloading, a movement of large blocks of stock in different exchanges: Tokyo, Hong Kong, Rio, Cairo, New York, and lastly London, Paris, Rome, and Vienna. As much as possible, it should be simultaneous so that the price would not slide, but plunge abruptly. When that plunge took place, they would stop selling. When the price of House of Diamond stock hit bottom—a delicate judgment—they would buy back in the same way they had sold, all at once. The stock would be devalued, but it would be in family hands—one of Zelik Diamant's immutable rules. Family control must always be maintained—and once the crisis subsided it would climb again.

The gain would be great. Too great? Gouging, rather than merely profiting? There was no time to weigh and measure the advantages of goodwill by Zelik's old-fashioned scale. There was only time, Lord Haran decided, to act.

In the short term, they would have to retrench. Any large investments the House of Diamond had been planning would have to be delayed. Every available cent of capital would be needed to take advantage of the buyback after the plunge.

Clearing both nostrils with twin pinches of snuff, Lord

THE HOUSE OF DIAMOND ♦ 41

Haran considered the effects. He made some rapid decisions. The last fifty miles of the trunk line connecting Vienna with Budapest would have to be delayed and the financing for the track laying diverted to capital funds. The House of Diamond would have to withdraw from the bidding for the Giotto frescoes in Florence. The Vatican curator would be delighted, as would Sotheby's. And, of course, there would be no money to underwrite the United States government bond issue to complete the construction of the Panama Canal.

By Jove! Lord Haran repositioned his monocle thoughtfully. It was terrible about Immanuel, really dreadful, but it was an ill wind that didn't blow a wisp of good toward Britain. Lord Haran had long opposed the building of the canal. He had been appalled when his brother had decreed funding for it. Might as well turn over half the world to non-British trade! Indeed, the Panama Canal was nothing less than a Sword of Damocles dangling over British merchant shipping. Lord Haran saw the situation quite clearly. Panama would be to the upstart Yanks what Suez had been to England. The world would be cleaved in two with cowboys colonizing and exploiting their half even as Britain civilized the Orient and Africa. Damned nonsense! North America was itself a colony, or had been, anyway. What business had they, half-savage still themselves, to think they might develop the jungles of Central and South America?

And to build a canal controlling shipping between the two great oceans of that hemisphere! Unthinkable! The trade routes would belong to the barbarians! The Panama Canal must not be built.

And Lord Haran had the power to see that it wouldn't be!

5 . NEW YORK

NOAH DIAMOND COULDN'T take his eyes off Olivia Hamilton, eldest daughter of the Virginia fox-hunting Hamiltons. The two young people were alone together in the small apartment of Olivia's aunt, who was away on a tour of the Greek Isles. The flat was in the ultra-respectable Fifth Avenue Hotel, a six-story white marble fortress that occupied one square block between Twenty-third and Twenty-fourth streets overlooking the sculptured gardens of Madison Square.

Noah, in love with this southern belle, had begun to feel that the affair was hopeless. His father did so decidedly. "You're naive, Noah," Marcus Diamond, the head of the New York House of Diamond, admonished his son. Long a widower himself, and with a keen eye for the ladies, Marcus was not oblivious of the willowy blonde's appeal to his twenty-three-year-old son. Olivia Hamilton was a challenge, a beauty, a prize well worth pursuing. But not for marriage. That road could only lead to misery. Yet when Marcus looked into his son's dark eyes, he saw an infatuation made up of more than physical desire. "Families like the Hamiltons," he told Noah bluntly, "don't let their daughters marry Jews. You're naive, my boy," he had repeated.

Noah did not welcome the advice. "And you're biased," he had snapped back at his father. "You want me to marry one of those German dumplings from up the avenue." He was referring to Fifth Avenue, which above Madison Square was lined with the fashionable brownstone town houses of the German-Jewish banking community.

"And why not?" Marcus had been both practical and sanguine. "You're a Diamond, my boy, a prize catch."

"Then take the hook yourself, Father." Noah's tone had been respectful, but chiding. "You're as much a bachelor as I am." Marcus's wife, Noah's mother, had died giving birth to her only child, Noah.

"But set in my ways, my boy. And I've already propagated. My duty to the House of Diamond is fulfilled. Yours, however, is not. And if you marry outside the faith, no matter how blue your bride's blood, you will break the family covenant."

"That's medieval. And I'm not going to marry some red-cheeked daughter of the Googs just to satisfy some barbaric family tradition." The Guggenheims—"the Googs," as they were known among the exclusive German-Jewish families of upper Fifth—along with the Loebs, the Seligmans, the Lehmans, the Baches, and the Strausses, were constantly trotting out marriageable daughters, nieces, and cousins for Noah's consideration. Noah was expected to marry one of them, but he wasn't interested in one of them. He was in love with Olivia Hamilton. What she felt, however, he wasn't at all certain.

Noah had just told Olivia in confidence about the abduction of the Baron Immanuel von Diamant in Frankfurt and she had responded by launching into a discussion of Sigmund Freud.

Noah was perplexed, to say the least. "What does Freud have to do with it?"

"He comes from Vienna, too," Olivia explained patiently.

" 'Too'?"

"Isn't that where your uncle who was kidnapped lives? At finishing school last term," Olivia continued her explanation, "one of the girls had just come back from Vienna. Her father is a doctor, and she said that the entire Viennese medical community was up in arms over this upstart Doctor Freud and his outrageous theories about women and sex. My friend's father was curious, and so he got hold of a copy of Freud's book that had caused all the uproar. It's called *Three Contributions to the Theory of Sex*. Later, after they came back home, my friend sneaked her father's copy out of his library and brought it to the academy, and we girls huddled under the covers after lights out and read it. It was quite—umm—provocative." Olivia combed slender fingers through her golden ringlets.

"Provocative, how?"

"In that Jewish way. You know. Describing how women feel about sex. Their yearnings and how they sublimate them. Things no Christian man could ever ferret out. Dignity would stop them cold."

"And Jews don't have dignity?" Noah was miffed.

"Not like my stodgy people, thank God. Why do you scowl, Noah? That smoldering Jewishness one senses reading Freud is what attracted me to you. It's why I agreed to meet you here tonight."

"I see." Actually, Noah believed her. Olivia probably wouldn't have agreed to meet a young man she considered her social equal under these circumstances—alone, with night falling, in a New York hotel apartment. With some young Harvard Brahmin from the right family with the right religion, she would have been risking her reputation. But with himself? Well, after all, whom could he tell? He didn't really know any of the people Olivia knew. He didn't travel in those circles. Olivia obviously felt more liberated with him. Evidently, there were some advantages to being Jewish not readily apparent to the Ivy League crowd.

"Not that my family would approve my being here alone with you like this," Olivia added frankly. "They wouldn't approve my seeing you at all. They don't like

Jews." Her tone indicated to Noah that, like each of their previous meetings, this one was in secret defiance of her people, and therefore titillating.

Even when flaunting her defiance, Noah reflected, Olivia was an imperious Hamilton of Virginia. Her family had settled in America in the late seventeenth century, established a plantation, imported African slaves to work it, and flourished. Her ancestors, high-ranking officers all, had stood with Washington at Valley Forge and fought beside Lee at First and Second Manassas and Gettysburg as well. They were not, however, according to Olivia, even remotely related to Alexander Hamilton, who had been, after all, born on the wrong side of the blanket, and was said to have had mulatto blood.

After the Civil War, the Hamiltons had had the good sense to marry wealthy Boston Brahmins, and so preserved their plantation way of life with barely a ripple of discomfort. The turn of the century found the Hamiltons thriving, fat with tradition, and puffed up with pride at a bloodline only mildly sullied by an influx through marriage of New England money.

"But I don't share my family's prejudices," Olivia assured him, a sweet smile on her face. Was it real? He honestly didn't know.

"I like your being Jewish. And I love the way you look so Jewish." Olivia, tilting her head to one side, looked completely ingenuous.

Did he really look Jewish? Noah wondered, and what did that mean? His hair and eyes were dark, his skin pale. And no matter how he brushed it, his hair snapped back to curliness. His nose arched proudly—more Greek-coinish than Hebrew, really, but Olivia would not make the distinction.

He pushed the subject from his mind. Olivia was sitting with her blond head cocked prettily to one side, waiting for him to respond. Noah understood that it made her feel bold to discuss his ethnic status and his religion, but it made him feel vaguely exploited. Deliberately now, he shelved the topic and picked up on what Olivia had been telling him before about Sigmund Freud.

"And is this Viennese doctor really so all-knowing about women's secret desires?" Noah wondered out loud. "Are your own secret desires really as he describes them?"

"La!" Suddenly the Virginia belle, Olivia rapidly fanned her flushed cheeks with a purely imaginary fan. "You do make me blush, sir. And I a woman alone in these rooms, and at your mercy."

It was pure playacting, of course, but Noah nonetheless felt a strong response to Olivia's flirting. He did want to marry her; his father had read him right, but had also underestimated his desire: Olivia's attraction for him was also quite sensual. The way she held her slender, long-legged body affected Noah strongly. He wanted to crush her cherry lips with his kisses, to overcome the arrogance of those cheekbones and bring tears of passionate joy to those cool gray-green eyes. Whatever pedestal he might have put her on, when Olivia played the coquette, it was passion he felt toward her, not schoolboy adoration.

Olivia recognized this, and had never been completely shy of it. With Noah, she carried the art of flirtation to an extreme; it became a kind of sensual foreplay that she would never have dared to have tried on the men of her own circle. "Of course," she teased, "Freud would say that I deliberately put myself in this position—alone with you in these rooms, at your mercy—because of my own desires."

"Is Freud right?" Noah asked eagerly. "Is that true?"

"There is some truth to it," Olivia replied softly, her eyelashes fluttering against her cheeks.

Noah moved to sit beside her on the settee. When he circled her shoulder with his arm, she turned to him, lips raised, inviting his kiss.

Noah's lips claimed hers and as their kisses became more urgent, their bodies strained against each other with more desire than decorum permitted.

Reluctantly, they finally drew apart. Looking deeply into each other's eyes, each read a message of desire in the depths. After a moment, it was Olivia who spoke.

"What will it mean to you—to the House of Diamond," she inquired breathlessly, "this kidnapping of your uncle?"

"Cousin," Noah reminded her as he fought back his feelings and put his arm around Olivia's shoulder again. She was dressed for the evening, her handkerchief-linen bodice with its elaborate embroidery supported by the narrowest of shoulder straps cut low and heart shaped to reveal deep cleavage. Her skin was a tawny gold, of a darker shade than his. She was very beautiful. "Don't you want to talk about Freud and libidos anymore?" he asked with only a hint of sarcasm.

"I think it would be prudent to shelve that topic for the moment." She was, however, still breathless. "Besides, I'm really interested. What effect will the abduction have?"

"That will depend on what happens between the baron's brother, Lord Haran Diamond in England, and his son, Philippe Diamant in Paris."

"Lord Haran is the one who's trying to stop your father from playing a major role in the financing of the Panama Canal," Olivia remembered.

"That's right. And now—with the baron out of the picture—Lord Haran is holding back the money." Noah nuzzled her neck. It was quite the most graceful and swanlike neck he had ever encountered. Olivia arched her neck receptively when his lips burned a kiss at the base of it.

"What will you do?" Olivia squirmed, further encouraging his intimacies.

"The canal won't wait." Noah's hand now encircled her small waist. "Father has already sent Lord Haran a wire pointing out that the word of the House of Diamond is at stake. It's a tenet of faith with the family that our pledge must be backed up. If not—"

"If not . . . ?" Olivia glanced down modestly at his hand, but instead of insisting on its removal, moved herself ever so slightly more closely into his embrace.

"One of two things." Noah's lips were at her ear now, his voice low, his breath tickling. "Either Morgan and Harriman, possibly Rockefeller, will underwrite the canal and reap the profits, or Father will pull out of the House of Diamond and use his own personal fortune to back up his pledge."

"Does he have the personal resources to do that?" Olivia wondered, impressed. She knew Noah Diamond was wealthy, but she had never considered that he might be in the same league as her own family.

"Not quite. He could borrow the balance from the Loebs or the Kuhns, but of course he doesn't want to do that. It would tie up all his money, and mine as well. And there has never been a break in the solidarity of the House of Diamond. We are a family institution, after all. Father is extremely reluctant to rupture that tradition."

Olivia held up her mouth to be kissed again. "And this Philippe Diamant in Paris can influence the situation?" Olivia moaned softly when the kiss was over.

"Perhaps. He was originally sent to Paris by his father the Baron at the time that France was forced to stop construction of the canal and sell it to the United

States. The Paris branch was very much involved in
the financing of that ill-fated French canal effort. The
scandal of that project brought down the Bank of
France, and the name of Diamond was badly tarnished
in France. It fell to Philippe to restore it. He did that so
successfully that he was put in charge of the Paris
branch."

"And will Philippe challenge the authority of his uncle in London?"

As much as he had no desire to discuss business matters, he sensed that Olivia would cut short their evening if he did not comply with this semblance of
conversation. Thus he continued, "Not directly. Still,
there's no doubt where Philippe stands. In his view,
control by Lord Haran reduces the House of Diamond
to an arm of the British government. Philippe knows,
as my father and I do, that for Lord Haran, what is
good for Great Britain is good for the House, and what
is good for the House must per se be good for England.
If he's pushed far enough, Philippe may well act to op-
pose his uncle's stewardship."

"And what would push him?"

"Lord Haran has curtailed all House of Diamond investment in anticipation of the market reaction to the
abduction. This stops us in New York as regards the
Panama Canal. It may also pull the rug out from under
Philippe in his efforts to buy the Cullinan Diamond. The
price it fetches will be astronomical. Only the wealthiest can compete. But whoever succeeds in purchasing
the Cullinan will either boast the world's most precious
jewel intact, or reap a tremendous profit by having it
expertly carved into smaller gems to be released slowly
over a period of time to an eager market."

"This Philippe Diamant," Olivia reflected, snuggling
into Noah's arms, "does indeed sound fascinating. Will

he succeed in acquiring the Cullinan Diamond, do you think?"

Noah's lips sought hers again with butterfly kisses as his hand moved up her side till his fingertips reached the gentle swell of her bosom. "Philippe is up against some formidable competition. Hearst, for one." Already the forty-three-year-old newspaper publisher and avaricious collector William Randolph Hearst had dispatched his agents to bid on the gem. "Also, a Russian grand duke representing the Tsarina Alexandra and both the Rothschilds and the Warburgs will be involved in the auction. And two prominent British financiers, as well." Lord Revelstoke of the House of Barings and Sir Everard Hambro had combined forces to bring the jewel back to London on the dubious, although patriotic, grounds that winning the Boer War gave England first claim to the South African diamond." The conversation was at last curtailed as Olivia's body yielded to his; Noah's breath caught in his throat, though he knew from previous experiences with this fair southern belle that it was only a matter of time before his desire was cut short. Expert in the arts of coquetry, Olivia Hamilton was not about to surrender her virtue to either Noah's, or her own, passion.

6. ROME

CARLO DIAMANTE WAS a simple man, the simplest, perhaps, of any of the branch heads of the House of Diamond. He enjoyed food and drink, sleep and sex, and took none of these pleasures for granted. Repetition never dulled their appeal for him. Each specially prepared dish, each new vintage, even each nap he took, and especially each time he made love was a fresh experience to be savored to the fullest. At forty-two years of age, Carlo Diamante was the quintessential Italian. A cousin twice removed of the Baron Immanuel von Diamant, his was the third generation of his branch of the family to reside in Italy. His great-grandfather, a brother of Zelik Diamant, had built the House of Diamond in Venice when Venice was still the crossroads of trade between Europe and the Near East. His grandfather had shifted to Naples, where, along with Kalmann Rothschild, he had helped finance the Kingdom of Naples, the Kingdom of Tuscany, and many other independent Italian states. With the unification of Italy, his father had opted for Firenze; and when the ascendancy of Rome was confirmed, Carlo Diamante had shifted his headquarters there from Florence.

Carlo was happy in Rome. "That's your trouble," the Baron Immanuel had told him on more than one occasion. "You're a happy man. Content. And so you lack drive. You're simply not hungry enough."

"It's true." Carlo had laughed his deep, baritone laugh. "I live well. I have a wonderful wife and six wonderful children."

"And a wonderful mistress," the baron had added drily.

"Of course." Again the laugh rumbled. Carlo thumped his barrel chest. "And you may be sure that Noella is a great asset to the Rome House of Diamond."

The baron had been able to do nothing but shake his head and laugh. It was true. Signora Noella Corri, who had for five years been Carlo Diamante's mistress, was the wife of the Italian Minister of Trade. The secrets she whispered in her lover's ear between caresses enabled the rather simple minded Carlo Diamante to hold his own with the more ambitious and perspicacious heads of the other House of Diamond branches. Even so, possessed of what Rebekah Diamant had once told her son Immanuel was *"a goyishe kopf,"* Carlo had no real head for business. He was too busy living his life to focus with any intensity on the day-to-day fluctuation of markets. Immanuel, who was very fond of his cousin Carlo, made allowances for his shortcomings. The allowances were based not only on his own fondness for his cousin, but also on the fact that Carlo was a third-generation Italian and he was operating in Italy where he understood the people and they understood him. This was an advantage that helped outweigh his shortcomings. Rome was not Frankfurt, or London, or New York. There was no one with Carlo's Italian temperament to replace him; consequently, on more than one occasion, the baron had turned a blind eye to Carlo's more inept business dealings.

"I'll miss the baron." Carlo sighed now to his mistress as he shifted his weight from her to lay his head on the pillow that should have been reserved for her spouse. "We understood each other."

"He covered up your mistakes, you mean." Signora Corri valued Carlo for many things, for thighs like the trunks of trees, for a head thick with black, curly hair and arms banded with muscles, for unending energy and honest sweat that bathed her with passion, but she did not mistake him for that which he was not. Her husband—a spindly, balding man with dry skin and a cold eye—had a brilliant grasp of the world's economy. Carlo was not like her husband; he could not be trusted to add up a laundry list. Still she kissed Carlo, a generous mouth melting over his like marzipan. "Have you heard from London?" she asked. Carlo had told her that Lord Haran was taking control and confided his fears regarding that frosty and demanding Britisher.

"Sì." Carlo shifted his position so that his head rested

on Noella's breast. "I have received my orders." His tone was both ironic and unhappy. "I am to withdraw the House of Diamond from the bidding for the Giotto frescoes in Firenze."

"He is making you bow to the Vatican?" Noella shifted disapprovingly. "Next he will be instructing you to sell off the collection of Renaissance art."

"You think that you are only jesting." Carlo turned over and exposed his left buttock. He wiggled it, not as an enticement, but as a signal that there was an itch he wished scratched. As Noella complied with long nails, he continued speaking. "Well, it is no joke. He is converting many of our investments to cash assets. Treasures the baron would never have parted with are being sold off. Sell-sell-sell is the order that's gone out to all the branches."

"Then at some point he will turn around and buy-buy-buy." Noella continued scratching thoughtfully. She was a shrewd, intelligent woman and had learned many things from her husband.

"Perhaps. But meanwhile he won't hesitate to sell the Renaissance collection, or the family silver, or the children if they will fetch a price."

"How are the children?" Noella inquired, giving Carlo's well-scratched buttock a final pat before covering it.

"Flourishing." Carlo's smile was broad, white teeth flashing. "The boys are bandits, the girls coquettes." He had three of each and adored them all. Indeed, he was a doting father, outgoing and generous, and all six returned his adoration.

"And Leah?" she inquired about his wife.

"A stuffed head." Carlo sighed. He also loved his wife—a truth that was a thing apart from his lust for Noella. "It's that damned winter wind off the Tiber. The snow blows right through our coach when she goes for the *mikveh*," he complained, referring to the Jewish ritual bath of purification. "Her eyes constantly water and she can't stop sneezing."

"I will tell you a remedy for her. Slice a raw onion very thin and lay the slices flat on a plate. Spread bees' honey on each slice. Cover it with another plate and set it outside in the winter night from dusk to dawn. Then bring it in and allow an hour to two hours for melting. This will form a syrup. Have Leah swallow a teaspoon of this syrup four times daily, and within three days her condition will noticeably improve. I guarantee it."

"Well, I will certainly have Leah try it. Thank you. It's very kind of you."

"Self-preservation. If you catch her cold, you will give it to me." But it wasn't the whole truth. Noella had never actually met Leah, but she had seen her with Carlo and he had never hesitated to discuss her. She felt as if she knew her. And while she didn't understand why it should be so, Noella's concern for his wife's health and well-being was genuine.

"And you will then give Leah's malady to the minister, which could have a deleterious effect on the entire Italian economy." Carlo laughed and slapped Noella's hip fondly.

"Not to mention the fact that it would keep him home in his bed." Noella laughed back and hugged Carlo. "And what would you do then?" she wondered.

"Insist that he move over." Carlo was calculating rapidly. His passion was renewing itself. Leah was expecting him home for dinner with the children in less than an hour. Still, if they wasted no more time . . .

"No, you wouldn't. If my husband knew about us, with your baron already abducted, that would be the end of your business career. You can be sure that he would see to it that there would be no more information from me."

"You're right. I would never survive that." Carlo was honest with her as he was with himself. "Now, turn over." He smiled as Noella quickly complied.

Less than an hour later, right on schedule, Carlo Diamante alit from his coach in front of his villa on the banks of the Tiber. The snow was falling softly, haloing the gaslight from the streetlamps. Carlo was hungry and looking forward to the chatter of children around the groaning board of his dinner table. But first, he decided, he would stop in the kitchen and give instructions to prepare the remedy that Noella had recommended for Leah.

As Carlo started to circle the high Italianate wrought-iron fence enclosing his property in order to enter through the servants' passage, a man blocked his path. He was a tall man, poised and well dressed, more slender than Carlo, and younger by perhaps fifteen years as well. "Excuse me, signore." He bowed. "I am Paolo Banducci. I wonder if I might have a word with you."

Carlo was annoyed, hungry, and beginning to feel the cold, but it was not in his character to be discourteous. "Of course." He knew the gentleman's name, having heard it in the exchanges. Paolo Banducci was an up-and-coming player, but as far as he could recall he had not met the young man before. "What can I do for you?"

"I would like to join with the House of Diamond in bidding for the Firenze frescoes."

"The Giottos?" Carlo's annoyance gave way to amusement. "Signor Banducci, surely you have been involved with the exchanges long enough to know that the House of Diamond does not sell shares in its bids and purchases."

"Of course. I wasn't asking you to sell me a share of

your offer. I rather thought you might want to include me in as a matter of prudent business."

Carlo stared at him through the softly falling snow. He may not have been the shrewdest of businessmen, but he recognized that there had to be something behind the young man's impudence. "And why would the House of Diamond want to do that?" Carlo inquired in a reasonable tone.

"For the same reason that you'll want to make arrangements for me to buy into your Renaissance art collection."

Carlo laughed pleasantly. "Ahh, my friend, but why not try the Vatican? Their collection is larger than ours." It was true, but it was also true that it was only slightly larger, and that no other collection in the world approached the House of Diamond Italian art holdings in either scope or value.

"Because"—Paolo Banducci returned Carlo's pleasant smile, and the expression made him look even younger—"the Pope is not sleeping with the wife of the Minister of Trade."

Carlo stared at him steadily. "Are you trying to blackmail me?" he said finally.

"Absolutely."

"And if I tell you to go to hell?"

"A note to your wife. A note to the minister. Dates. Places. Names of witnesses. Various other proofs." Paolo Banducci's tone was not that of a man who was bluffing.

"I see. And you want—?"

"A share in the House of Diamond bidding for the Giotto frescoes."

"On margin, I presume." Carlo was no longer smiling.

"Of course."

"But you see, I cannot accommodate you. The House

of Diamond will not be bidding on the Giottos." It was the truth. Lord Haran's instructions forbade it.

"The Minister of Trade will be desolate to learn that."

"I swear it!" The temperature was almost to zero, but Carlo was sweating.

"If it is so, then I will be truly sorry. But my course is unalterable. My next stop must be the home of Signore and Signora Corri."

Carlo thought for a moment. "All right," he said finally. He had no other option but to lie. "What I just said was not true. You can have a share of the House of Diamond bids on the Giottos on margin. Just how much of a share do you want?"

"Forty percent."

Carlo stared at him. "That much?"

"The Minister of Trade is said to have connections with the Black Hand. He would surely not hesitate to call on them in a matter involving his family honor."

"Very well, then." Carlo took a handkerchief from his pocket and patted the icy sweat from his forehead. "Forty percent. Call on me in my office." Carlo stepped around Paolo Banducci. "Buona sera, signore." He continued on his way to the kitchen entrance.

"On Thursday next." Paolo Banducci nailed it down. "Buona sera, Signor Diamante." He watched Carlo disappear into the snowfall. Then Paolo Banducci took out his pocket watch and opened it. Good. He still had time to catch the overnight train to Venice.

7. VENICE

THE DI FALCO palazzo commanded a view of the Grand Canal from the Rialto to the Bridge of Sighs, as well as of the smaller canals spiderwebbing through the islands and mud flats that made up the city of Venice. At approximately the same time that the overnight train for Venice bearing Paolo Banducci was leaving the Rome station, the Contessa Tamar di Falco, her husband, and her six-year-old son were standing atop the palace's rooftop loggia and staring inland from the Adriatic Sea at a sight on one of the mini-canals. They were peering through the snow—still falling here as it was in Rome—at a gondola being painstakingly poled through the ice-coated waterway.

Shivering, the gondolier was gamely belting out a Puccini aria as he strained to push his heavily laden craft through the frozen canal. There were six people, all male, huddled in greatcoats in the gondola. Their faces were pinched against the cold, their features no longer distinguishable to the Count and Countess di Falco observing them from the loggia of their palazzo. But when the boat had passed directly in front of the palace before, the little boy, Donald, had seen the passengers close up and run to fetch his mother.

"They look different!" Donald had exclaimed. "I never saw anybody who looks like them before. Who are they, Mother?"

The contessa could not answer his questions, but her husband, the Conte Guido di Falco, who joined them shortly afterwards, was able to shed some light on the mystery. "They are Japanese," he said. "And they are obviously determined that the winter cold won't stop them from taking in the traditional sights of Venice from a gondola."

"Tourists?" The twin scimitar brows above the contessa's remarkable violet eyes arched upward to indicate her amused amazement. "In January?"

"Well, actually, they are businessmen. I'm sure it's their first time in Venice, and probably it's the first time they've been out of their own country. It's natural that they should want to see the sights. You have to admire their persistence, considering the weather."

"I don't understand what Japanese businessmen are doing in Venice at all," the Contessa Tamar told her husband.

"The Russo-Japanese War, my dear. The Japanese won it," he reminded her.

"Oh, yes," Tamar remembered. "They signed that treaty last September, didn't they? Some place in the Americas, wasn't it?"

"In the city of Portsmouth in the state of New Hampshire in the United States." The conte smiled. "The world grows smaller."

"It certainly does." Tamar's dulcet tones indicated her disapproval. "I've always thought Russia was more Asian than European. Still, the Muscovites are a mighty power. I don't understand how those little Oriental people with the almond-shaped eyes could win a war with them."

"On land and sea," the conte explained drily. "At the Battle of Mukden some two hundred thousand Russian soldiers were slaughtered by Japanese infantry. And the Japanese Navy destroyed the Russian fleet at Port Arthur."

"An obscure Asian nation trounces Imperial Russia, and the victor and the vanquished choose to sign a peace treaty in one of the former British colonies in the

Western Hemisphere," Tamar summed up. "I don't understand it at all."

"Your English upbringing is showing itself, my dear," the conte chided his young wife. "It's more than a hundred years since the United States could be considered British colonies."

Tamar, who cared as little for the British as she did for any nation and who was used to deliberately ignoring her husband, dismissed his words. "Well, war or no war, treaty or no treaty, I still don't understand what any of it has to do with Venice. Why have these Japanese businessmen chosen to come here?"

"They were invited," Conte Guido di Falco's next two words claimed his wife's full attention, "by patriots."

The contessa brushed the snow from her smooth brow with her fur muff. "And you played a role in this invitation?" she inquired carefully. If her tone and her attitude had been light and uncaring before, they were no longer so. Tamar cared a great deal more about her husband's business dealings than she did about the patriotism of faraway nations.

"Yes. Winning the war has established Japan as a major player on the world stage. The Americans, and to a lesser extent the British and the French, may have established themselves as Japan's major trading partners, but they have not claimed Japanese allegiance when it comes to investment. There is surplus capital in Japan. Having won Korea and certain Manchurian ports from the Russians, they are looking to balance off their imports by developing an export trade. In other words, the Japanese want access to European markets, and they have the money to pay for it. It is in the interests of Italy, and of Venice as the major seaport on the Adriatic specifically, to provide that access."

"But the Italian ports, including Venice, are controlled by the Austro-Hungarians."

Conte Guido di Falco regarded his wife thoughtfully. She was a great beauty, and this had certainly been one of the main reasons he had contrived to marry her. The fact that she had been a daughter of the House of Diamond was certainly another reason. Her intelligence, and the incisive grasp of events she was displaying now, had been a delightful bonus. He congratulated himself on having married all these qualities. And yet these were not what continued to make Tamar irresistible to him. What made his wife the contessa irresistible was her ruthlessness.

"The Austro-Hungarians, sì." He answered Tamar with bitterness in his voice. "Franz Josef exploits Italy like some African colony. He owns Venice, and Venetian shipping fills the coffers of his treasury."

"Because the House of Diamond provided the money for him to modernize Venice and the other Italian seaports," Tamar reminded her husband with more than a touch of malice.

"Sì."

"*You* are joined to the House by marriage," she reminded him. "You have not suffered by Austrian development of the ports."

"I am an Italian patriot first and foremost. Your uncles know that."

"And now that Uncle Immanuel is no longer in control," Tamar astutely summed up, "you invite the Japanese to Venice and make plans to move against the Austro-Hungarian emperor who was his patron."

"Do not jump to conclusions, Tamar. Our talks with the Japanese are only exploratory."

"Of course, my dear. Exploratory." The contessa's smile was dazzling. "And in any case, I am only a woman and unequipped to fathom the intricacies of such matters."

"Naturally." The conte's laugh acknowledged that her demurrer was nonsense.

"I can't see them anymore." Little Donald had lost the gondola to the falling snow. "And I'm cold. Can't we go inside now, please?"

"Of course, my darling." The contessa took her small son by the hand and led him to the staircase leading down from the rooftop loggia into the interior of the palazzo. The three of them paused for a moment before descending, taking a last look at the elaborately shaped chimneys jutting into the distinctive Venetian skyline through the snow. With their domes and elaborate minarets, the rooftops of Venice made the city seem more Turkish than European.

The contessa's mind, however, was not on the scenery in front of her. Already she was reviewing what her husband had just told her. And her review quite accurately reflected that ruthlessness of character that Conte Guido di Falco found so irresistible.

Contessa di Falco had been born Tamar van der Diamant in Amsterdam, Holland, some twenty-eight years prior to that January evening in 1906. Her father had been Jacob van der Diamant, the younger brother of Baron Immanuel and Lord Haran. Her mother, Sophie, had been a Diamant second cousin from an obscure Brussels branch of the family. Jacob and Sophie had settled in Holland because that was where the Amsterdam Diamond Exchange was.

The Amsterdam Diamond Exchange had long been the largest and most important jewelry market in the world. As far back as the Inquisition, Diamant ancestors had fled to—and then from—Amsterdam. Jews, and therefore heretics, their struggle for survival had turned them to diamond smuggling during their short tenure there. Thus they had financed their migration to Frankfurt, and thus—at a much later date—they had come by their name.

Two hundred years after the Inquisition, Zelik Diamant, the founder of the House of Diamond, had expanded his banking business by setting up one of his sons in the diamond trade in Amsterdam. The son had never married, and after his death it had fallen to Zelik's youngest grandson, Tamar's father, Jacob, to take over the Dutch enterprise. Following in his predecessor's footsteps, Jacob had added the "van der" to the Diamant name as a means of blending into the Amsterdam business community.

When Tamar was five years old, her mother and father had taken her by train to visit Sophie's relatives in Brussels. The train they were on was blown up—some said by Flemish separatists, others by anarchists—and forty-two people died in the explosion. Both Jacob and Sophie van der Diamant were among those killed. Tamar, however, had been riding on the rear observation platform with her nursemaid and survived the blast unharmed.

The images of the tragedy were imprinted indelibly on Tamar's mind, however. Twisted steel, acrid smoke, the ripped flesh of the victims, the blood-soaked ground between the railroad ties, the moans of the injured and the dying, the anguished screams of those identifying their dead loved ones from mutilated and charred remains—such was the background to her parents' sudden death. It was this horror, this desolation, that remained with Tamar throughout the trauma of starting a new and very different life.

Over the objections of her mother's family in Brussels, Zelik and the Baron Immanuel decided that Tamar should be sent to London, where she would be brought up in the household of Lord Haran. Newly married and without any children of their own, the Diamonds considered their home to be the best place for the child. Here, at Haran's behest, the child's name was Anglicized to Diamond. Tamar's adored Dutch nursemaid was discharged, and a proper Scottish nanny was engaged to care for her.

The Scottish nanny's employment didn't last long. Lord Haran decided that the precocious and combative young Tamar would best be molded into a proper upper-class British young lady by being sent away to an exclusive girls' boarding school. It was only the first of a succession of such establishments that Tamar attended through her formative years. Because she was away so much, she really had very little contact with the family into which she had been adopted. The first of Lord Haran's children, Minerva, was eight years younger than Tamar and, though plain, much beloved by her parents. Tamar felt concern on the part of her relatives after her parents' death, but not love. Over the years, when she came home to Lord Haran's mansion for the holidays, which were always marked by the Jewish traditions to which Lord Haran insisted his household adhere, Tamar was witness to the affection and warmth of his growing family, but she never felt a part of it. Tamar's later relationships with the six children of Lord Haran were polite, but never close.

After her parents' death, Tamar never thought of herself as part of a family, and certainly not as a member of the English Diamond family. She missed her mother and father. The ache did not diminish; it only deepened. Defensively, she would not allow herself to feel sorry for herself. Instead, she became an emotional skeptic.

She respected the British uncle who had taken her in, but she developed no great affection for him. And as she progressed from childhood through adolescence, her skeptical outlook hardened into cynicism and the emotional shell that had formed when she was orphaned hardened with it.

Tamar's cynicism was to take on a bias against men, which would remain with her throughout her life. As perceptive as she was extraordinarily beautiful, Tamar was not far into her teens when she recognized not only that the House of Diamond had a pecking order based on gender, but also what that meant. The family was strictly patrilineal—wealth, control, power were traditionally passed from father to son, or from uncle to nephew, or even from male cousin to male cousin. Daughters and other female Diamonds did not inherit. There were no exceptions.

Diamond daughters might be married off to distant cousins to strengthen the bloodline or betrothed to the sons of other successful Jewish merchant families to cement business ties. Or they might be wed to one or another of the aristocratic gentile families with an eye toward spreading Diamond influence throughout the European power structure. Wherever they wed, they would bring substantial dowries, but control of this wealth would pass to their husbands. Tamar soon perceived that, born into one of the wealthiest families in the world, Diamond women would never themselves have a claim on any of their family's riches.

When as a young woman she came to understand this fully, Tamar was both shocked and infuriated. Naturally she related it to herself. Standing in front of her mirror, she saw herself for what she was: a prize bauble with no rights and no property she could call her own who would be offered in marriage wherever the greatest advantage to the House of Diamond might lie.

Hers was not an exaggeration born of egotism. Tamar was, indeed, a prize. She had blossomed into a great beauty, tall and regal, with luminous violet eyes, lips that were red and full, and a chin that was firm and habitually tilted at a haughty angle. The mantle of hair framing her visage was her crowning glory, curly and thick, blue-black and lustrous. Her figure was slender, with full breasts, but slim hipped and graceful and poised.

The period of her young maidenhood was the beginning of the Edwardian Era. Tamar's appearance exemplified the lovely maidens portrayed in the literature of the day, always innocent and virtuous, always subliminally toothsome in the eyes of the rogues who despoiled them. Early on, Tamar recognized that look on the faces of men. Convention said they treasured beauty like hers and were committed to protecting its purity. But Tamar understood that the reality was that lust filled the gazes of the men who looked on her and that it was secretly filleting her body from out of its clothes.

Tamar identified the Italian Conte Guido di Falco as such a man the very first time she met him. He was ten years older than she, quite handsome, suave and composed, the eldest son of a noble Venetian banking family that, while still important in Italian financial circles, had declined from the position of great power it had once held. To the House of Diamond he represented an opportunity to strengthen a family influence in Italy that had stagnated under the stewardship of Carlo Diamante in Rome.

Conte di Falco made little effort to hide the fact that he desired Tamar. Nor was he discouraged by her cool response to him. In a world of arranged marriages, he took it for granted that whatever Tamar's feelings might be toward him now, the honeymoon bed would condition her to a more receptive and loving attitude.

Nothing infuriated Tamar more than his confidence that his love and its techniques would melt her. She was helpless to alter her fate. The House of Diamond had decreed it, and that was that. But they could not stop her from seeing to it that Conte Guido di Falco married something less than that upon which he and the Diamonds had predicated their bargaining. Years later, her cousin Minerva was to adopt one method of discouraging unwanted suitors. Tamar, who had far less control over her uncle's wishes, adopted another method—not meant to discourage but certainly to defy—altogether.

Tamar contrived to have herself invited to the country manor of a former schoolmate for the weekend at the very time that the conte and Lord Haran were finalizing the conditions of the betrothal. The occasion was a ball to which were invited some two dozen unmarried young women and a like number of officers from a regiment of Scottish Grenadiers billeted at a barracks in the countryside. Among these officers was a handsome young man with curly ash-blond hair, a powerful physique, and apple cheeks given to easy blushes. Lieutenant Donald MacPherson was much valued by his fellow officers for his prowess as a regimental rugby player. He was also quite dazzled by Tamar Diamond, particularly when the already renowned young beauty selected him from among his fellow officers to escort her on a stroll in the gardens so that she might recapture the breath spent dancing. "You have a trustworthy look," she told him, and when she took his arm, he found his elbow pressed into flesh softer than any he had ever imagined.

"By a trustworthy look," she continued, just as if they hadn't been strolling for ten minutes or more in silence, "I mean that you would keep your own counsel, particularly if it involved the reputation of an innocent woman."

"Of course," he assured her, blushing. "I'm an officer of the Scottish Grenadiers."

"And a gentleman."

"And a gentleman," Lieutenant MacPherson confirmed.

"That moon is so romantic." She had turned her face up to his.

Lieutenant MacPherson did what any officer and gentleman who belonged to the Scottish Grenadiers would have done. He kissed Tamar. And she, with a certain amount of calculation, but with fire as well, kissed him back.

Leaving the gardens for a copse of woods, they embraced again, and perched on a grassy knoll, kissed still more deeply. And although Lieutenant MacPherson had no recollection of fumbling with buttons, he found his mouth moving over the tall and slender beauty's naked bosom. There on the grass he tossed her skirts to the starry sky and with her full and enthusiastic consent relieved Tamar of her virginity.

When it was over, Lieutenant MacPherson was gratified, but also chagrined. "It was my fault," he announced, officer and gentleman of the Scottish Grenadiers that he was. "I will speak with Lord Haran regarding marriage immediately, of course."

"That won't be necessary. He has, you see, already made other arrangements concerning my marrying."

"But—" Lieutenant MacPherson's cheeks were once again flaming red.

"What is your given name?" Tamar asked him.

"Donald."

And so Tamar named her baby Donald when it was born six months after her marriage to Conte Guido di Falco.

The conte did not question Tamar's choice of names. Whatever Guido thought, or felt, he kept his own counsel. Her husband was never anything but courteous and considerate of her outside the bedroom; he was never anything but passionate and demanding in their marriage bed. And he treated Donald always, without exception, as his own son.

Tamar did not regret what she had done. On the contrary, she regarded it as justified. If the House of Diamond was going to trade its women like stock certificates, then surely if anyone had been cheated, the blame must lie with those who were party to the negotiations from which her sex had excluded her. Let them trade in women, but not in virgins! Tamar had simply fulfilled her obligation to that vow.

She carried it further, as well. From the first day of her marriage, Tamar considered that her husband had bought her body, but not her fealty. She was determined not to fall in love with him or to be satisfied by his lovemaking. She really knew of no woman of her acquaintance in love with her own husband, so Tamar did not worry about that too much. But even more, she was determined not to grant him an exclusive right to her body.

Her first lover was a disappointment. Tamar was forced to admit to herself that she enjoyed her husband more. She had ended the affair quickly and waited a year before embarking on another one.

That, too, had been a disappointment. The reputation of Venice for romance, it seemed, was more secure in her husband's hands than in those of either Italian lover to whom she had granted her favors. Tamar waited a long time before embarking on a third affair, and then she chose carefully.

Some three months before that January night on the rooftop she had once again become involved with a man not her husband. This affair was infinitely more satisfying than the other two had been. And it had an advantage that the others did not. But it had one major drawback, too. Tamar's new lover made his home in Rome and only came to Venice sporadically.

Still, their separation gave her something to look forward to through the long winter nights. Her heart beat faster in anticipation of time spent with him. It was beating faster now, as she descended the stairs from the rooftop loggia with her husband and son.

Already Tamar was filing away the information her husband had imparted regarding Japanese investment in Italian port facilities. The coupling of business with love, power with desire, was the advantage this lover held above any other. Through him, she could gain all that she sought. Tomorrow she would see her lover, and she would certainly discuss what her husband had told her with him. He would be interested, even fascinated by it, but only after they made love. Ahh, tomorrow . . .

Tomorrow the Contessa Tamar di Falco would lie in the arms of Paolo Banducci.

8. FRANKFURT

WITH THE PASSING of weeks, terror and fear and even concern had given way to boredom. Time convinced the Baron Immanuel von Diamant that he was not to be tortured by his captors, but by ennui.

Not that he had been able to keep track of time. He thought it must now be February, but had only the haziest idea in terms of days and weeks of just how long had elapsed since the young genealogist Josef Rothko had shoved a pistol in his face. The period since then had been divided only by a coach ride that had moved him from one place of imprisonment to another.

His first prison, quite dungeonlike, really, had been the cellar of a farmhouse somewhere on the outskirts of Frankfurt. He had been guarded by two men and a woman. There may have been others, but these were the only ones he ever saw, and then only at dawn, noon, and dusk, when they brought him his meals and replaced his chamber pot. After the first day, he did not see Josef Rothko again until the evening some time later when he was moved to his second place of incarceration.

That night the sandy-haired young man, his craggy face as scrubbed clean and innocent-looking as ever despite his role in his employer's plight, had entered the basement cell carrying a candle in one hand and some garments over his other arm. "A change of clothing," Josef Rothko informed the baron. "I thought you'd be ready for one about now."

"Indeed." The baron welcomed any conversation. His other jailers were taciturn and came and went quickly with few words. "I am ripe for a change. No pun intended," he added drily.

"Not only your clothes will be changed. We're also moving you to a new location."

"Oh? Where?" The baron's gray-green eyes were carefully guileless.

Josef Rothko's boyish smile reminded the baron that it would have been absurd to expect any answer to that question.

"These fit well." Under the coarse wool blanket they had provided him, the baron had removed his trousers and drawers and put on clean underwear. The dimple flashed amid his overgrown side-whiskers. He was a man used to the caress of fresh linen and soft silk on his skin, and there was pleasure now in the feel of laundered drawers.

"They should. They're yours."

The baron looked at him questioningly.

"I stole them from your house in Vienna." Rothko's crinkly brown eyes were just as warm and friendly as before the abduction. "It wasn't very difficult. I came to know the layout quite well while I was working there with you on your family history."

"Little did I guess that you were a kidnapper rather than a genealogist." The baron stood, his six-foot height placing his square chin at the same level as Josef Rothko's soft eyes.

"I really am a genealogist. Actually, I'm a pretty good one."

The baron ignored the boast. "Are you a member of some organized group," he questioned, "or only a freelance brigand with your own band of merry men?"

"Ah, well." Josef Rothko again smiled his boyish smile.

"I only wondered if I was in the hands of gangsters, or business rivals, or some political organization." The baron smoothed his short-cropped iron-hued hair with the flat of his hand.

"You'll be told all in good time, Herr Baron." Joseph strode to the door of the cell and rapped for the guard to unlock it.

"Have you contacted my people? Am I being held for ransom?"

"All of your questions will be answered in good time," Josef Rothko repeated. When the door swung open, he motioned for Baron Immanuel to precede him through it. "Just now we are going on a short journey."

They put him in a coach, and then Josef Rothko, apologizing, blindfolded him. The baron, however, stayed alert. He recognized the change in the feel of the wheels under his haunches when they began rolling over cobblestones rather than the dirt road of the countryside. From the slight distance they had traveled, he judged that they had brought him back to Frankfurt. Shortly thereafter, his nostrils picked up the familiar and unmistakable odor of stale sewage. It was an ancient stench, and one this section of the city would never quite lose, even if it had been many years since the passing of the ghetto. The baron guessed that they must be on what had once been Jew Street, the ghetto's main thoroughfare.

Long before the baron's time, Germany's greatest writer, Goethe, had described the Judengasse. With the ghetto sprawling out on both sides of it, Jew Street, he wrote, ran "between the city wall and a trench." The trench referred to by Goethe was the open sewer into which flowed the garbage and excretion of the ghetto. It had been an ongoing disgrace, a health hazard the Jews were prohibited by law from altering. And now, as the baron's nostrils confirmed, its evil smell lingered on to memorialize the inhuman conditions that had once prevailed there.

When the baron was a boy, at sunset each night, and on the Christian Holy Days, the Frankfurt Hessian militia had sealed off the Judengasse with heavy chains. The toll gate to Jew Street was barred and guarded. After sundown, the ghetto became a jail of darkness.

By edict, five hundred families had been crowded into the ghetto back then—no more, no less. The Jews were permitted only twelve marriages a year by Frankfurt city decree. Nevertheless, the population grew with the birth rate.

It was against the law for Jews to own land either outside the Judengasse or within its confines. All the ghetto housing had therefore been Christian owned, and living space was at a premium. In the beginning, to the delight of the landlords, Jews had bid against each other for quarters, driving the rentals up.

But the elders of the Frankfurt ghetto, led by the rabbis, had put a stop to that. They assigned housing on the basis of tenure and need, and they maintained lists to make sure that space was allotted fairly. Some families had been forced to live five or six to a house, but the overcrowding was regulated and sometimes rotated to minimize suffering. And because the elders forbid competition for living space, an early form of rent control was enforced, and the landlords were prevented from exploiting the housing situation.

Since the ghetto was forbidden by law to expand its boundaries horizontally, it naturally grew vertically. All houses were built tall and narrow to accommodate as many people as possible while using up as little as possible of the precious land base. The drawback to this was that light and air were cut off, and the ghetto was turned into an even drearier environment.

The Jews of Frankfurt had been forbidden to engage in agriculture in any way. The ban included the selling of fresh fruit and vegetables, effectively excluding such foodstuffs from ghetto larders. Many of the childhood diseases common to the ghetto—scurvy, rickets, tuberculosis—could be traced to this ban.

Jews could not engage in handicrafts: Weaving, bricklaying, even plumbing, as well as many other forms of livelihood, were forbidden to them. Even now, the craft guilds excluded Jews as one means of limiting the competition. They had not been allowed to deal in silks—most silks were imported, and traveling Christian merchants had had that trade tied up since the Crusades—although they were permitted to sell woolens and to engage in a certain amount of tailoring. With looms forbidden them, the invention of the sewing machine by a French tailor, Barthelemy Thimmonier, in

1830 had been a major boom to ghetto Jews throughout Europe. And, of course, they were permitted neither to deal in nor to own guns, or any other weapons.

They could not, therefore, defend themselves against
the more violent forms of anti-Semitism. There were
no orchestrated pogroms in Frankfurt, as there would
be later in Russia and Poland, and no immolations as
there had been earlier in Spain and Portugal during the
Inquisition. But all the same, the Hessian troops billeted
locally had gone on periodic sprees in which the good-
natured beating of individual Jewish men by four or
five soldiers at a time and the casual torching of Jewish
shops and the raping here and there of a particularly
toothsome Jewish maiden were commonplace occur-
rences.

Back then the Jews of Frankfurt lived in fear. The
Baron Immanuel von Diamant had himself grown up
with it. That would change early in his lifetime, there
would be reforms, but when he was a boy the threats
and indignation of anti-Semitism were a part of his daily
life.

In addition to being forbidden to own land, Jews were
not permitted to rent living quarters any place in
Frankfurt except the Judengasse. Jewish merchant-
travelers were not even permitted to lease rooms at
any of the Frankfurt hotels. Still, minor exceptions did
evolve.

Back then, before the rule of Germany was central-
ized, the Prince of Hesse-Kassel, ruler of the principality of Hesse, of which Frankfurt was the major city, had
been inconvenienced by a delay in receiving a loan
from the banking house that was propping up his regime. The son of the Diamant family bringing the gold
from Amsterdam had been prevented from entering
Frankfurt because the laws forbade Jews from moving
about the city, or being admitted to the ghetto, after

sundown. Irked, the prince had issued an edict suspending the ban on renting city hotel rooms outside the ghetto in the case of certain favored Jews.

Specifically, it exempted the Diamants and the Rothschilds—his personal bankers. The Baron Gershon von Diamant, Immanuel's father, had taken regular advantage of the privilege. He planned his Viennese and other business trips so that he would return to Frankfurt on Friday, stay overnight at a small hotel in the city, and reenter the ghetto early on Saturday morning when the chains were taken down.

Now, blindfolded in the coach, as his nostrils flared at the centuries-old stench of the ghetto, the baron recalled what it had been like as a boy when he returned from such business trips with his father on the Sabbath.

"*Guten Tag* to my best Saturday customer," the taker of the toll the Jews had to pay to enter or leave the ghetto would sneeringly greet his father. The gatekeeper knew the Baron Gershon von Diamant well, had been admitting him for years of Saturdays through this gate. Indeed, he made the same remark every time. It was meant as a joke, but while Immanuel's father recognized the intent, he never acknowledged it with even the barest of smiles.

The joke had been that Baron Gershon von Diamant was the toll taker's *only* Saturday customer. The toll taker's job was a sinecure secured by nepotism, a featherbed by definition since Jews were forbidden by their religion to carry money on the Shabbas and so there was virtually no taking of Saturday tolls to enter or leave the ghetto. The Baron Gershon von Diamant and his son Immanuel were rare—if regular—exceptions.

Recognizing the mean-spiritedness behind it, Baron Immanuel's father had not admitted the joke. The toll taker's beady eyes twinkled with a dual message. As a good Christian, he knew that Scripture assigned Sunday as the Lord's Day. By celebrating on Saturday, the Jews flaunted that they were indeed Satan's creatures. But even so, how hypocritical that this make-believe gentleman, this Jew with his haughty airs, should break faith with his own pagan scripture.

Once, the boy Immanuel had heard the toll taker make a remark to some cronies regarding his father after they had passed. *"Des Königs* kike," the toll taker had snarled, unable to resist an alliteration that promoted the unpopular then-Prince of Hesse-Kassel to king.

That long-ago silent accusation of the gatekeeper notwithstanding, however, neither Baron Gershon von Diamant, nor his son Immanuel after him, had ever broken the Holy Law. Neither had ever carried money on Shabbas. Not once had his father passed the coins to the toll taker. Instead, Immanuel's father had utilized a Shabbas goy. Usually the term "Shabbas goy" referred to a Christian hired to open the synagogue, start the furnace, and light the candles for the Friday-night services. Such chores were regarded as labor, and from Friday sundown to Saturday sundown, the Talmud decreed that Jews were forbidden to work, just as they were forbidden to handle money. The Baron Gershon's Shabbas goy had been a servant at the small Frankfurt hotel where, thanks to the special dispensation, Immanuel and his father stayed on Friday nights. On Saturdays he accompanied them to the entrance to the ghetto for the express purpose of handing money to the gatekeeper.

This menial had always followed the traditional three paces behind them all the way from the hotel, although the Baron Immanuel's father had tried to keep him from doing so. When they reached the gate, he would shamble forward and pay the toll to the Judengasse toll taker. Then he would bow low and leave.

Behind the blindfold, the scene was still vivid in the baron's memory. The shambling Shabbas goy, the smiling hatred of the toll taker, his father's eyes hooded to conceal the pride flashing in their depths, himself taking it all in and hiding his emotions as he had been taught to do for as long as he could remember—the tableau would be a part of him always. He was the Baron Immanuel von Diamant, banker and confidant of the Emperor of Austria-Hungary, head of the international House of Diamond, important enough even to be kidnapped. But underneath it all he would always be that quiet boy standing beside his father while the Shabbas goy paid the gatekeeper the toll that would admit them to Jew Street.

Now the coach pulled off Jew Street to one of the side alleys and came to a stop. Josef Rothko helped the baron to get out and guided him to the street-level entrance of a dwelling. Still blindfolded, inside the house he was led up three flights of stairs. When they entered a room, the baron cracked his head on a slanted ceiling. He realized they must be in an attic at the top of the building, under a steeply slanted roof. This was typical of ghetto houses, which, because they were crowded so closely together, were especially vulnerable to the accumulation of rainfall and snow. His perception was confirmed when his blindfold was removed, and his eyes refocused in the murk of the gaslight.

"I will be leaving you now," Josef Rothko told him. He held out his hand.

The baron looked at the extended hand and raised one thin gray eyebrow. Josef Rothko shrugged and put his hand back in his pocket. A moment later he was gone.

During the weeks that followed, the baron had occasion to regret the frostiness of their parting. At least

with the young genealogist there had been some conversation. With his captors in the attic there was virtually none.

They were the same three who had guarded him in
the farmhouse. By listening to them talking to each
other, the baron was able after a while to put a name
to each of them. The older man, stocky with a heavy,
stolid face and a pronounced Polish accent, was Jerzy.
The younger, slender and dark with an olive complexion and large, limpid Arabian eyes, was Ammal. And
the woman, who was perhaps forty years old, was
called Gabrielle. Her manner was authoritative, and the
two men seemed to take their lead from her in Josef
Rothko's absence.

Despite the woman's name, the baron did not think
she was French. Her face, with its pronounced cheekbones and angular sweep and determined jawline,
looked more Slavic. There was no fat on her body, but
her build was slightly stocky, and her movements were
athletic. Usually uncommunicative, Gabrielle had once
or twice demonstrated that she could also be direct.

On one such occasion, she had deigned to speak to
the baron. He had initiated the exchange. "Are you
French?" he had asked, having only just learned her
name.

"I am stateless."

"I beg your pardon?"

"I'm a Jew like you."

While the baron was formulating his response, she
turned on her heel abruptly and was gone. The baron
was surprised. Gabrielle was nothing like those malleable and pious Jewish daughters of the ghetto he had
known as a boy. Neither did she resemble the female
members of the rich Jewish merchant families, those
modernized turn-of-the-century Rothschild, Warburg,
and Schiff women he found indistinguishable from

spoiled Viennese aristocratic court coquettes. Indeed, where women were concerned, Gabrielle with her shotgun over her shoulder and her cartridge belt strapped across her chest was something quite unique in the baron's experience.

On another level, the baron was relieved to have his woman jailer identify herself as Jewish. Since he had been abducted, he had been afraid that he might have fallen into the hands of organized anti-Semites. With the spread of *The Protocols of Zion*, there had been a proliferation of small, local anti-Semitic cults—many of them quasi-military—dedicated to visiting violence upon Jews to a lesser or greater degree. In particular they targeted prominent Jews like himself.

If Gabrielle was Jewish, then at least he knew he wasn't at the mercy of anti-Semitic bloodlust. But who, then, was holding him? None of his three jailers would enlighten him when he raised that question. It was only when Josef Rothko returned after a protracted absence that the baron finally got an answer.

"We are anarchists," Josef Rothko informed him.

"Anarchists." It was not good news. To be in the hands of anarchists was no safer than being at the mercy of anti-Semites. Baron Immanuel von Diamant was an international banker, and anarchists did not hesitate to kill men of wealth and power.

Indeed, hatred of capitalists was at the very root of anarchist theory. The founder of the movement, Pierre Proudhon, had posed the question some sixty years earlier: *"Qu'est-ce que c'est la propriété?"* What is property? And answered succinctly with three English words: "Property is theft."

In their drive to abolish property along with government, the anarchists had earned a reputation for ruthlessness. Over the last twelve years—from 1894 to 1906—anarchists had been involved in literally hundreds of violent crimes—bomb throwings, bank robberies, kidnappings, etc.—resulting in countless deaths and maimings, and the destruction of millions of dollars in property. During that period anarchists had assassinated nine heads of state—President Carnot of France, Premier Canovas of Spain, Empress Elizabeth of Austria, Italy's King Humberg, the Queen of Korea, Premier Stambulov of Bulgaria, the Shah of Persia, the King and Queen of Serbia, and President William McKinley of the United States. Most recently an anarchist had assassinated the Russian Minister of the Interior Vyacheslav von Plehve. There had also been failed attempts on the lives of many other members of the ruling class, including royalty and tycoons, aristocrats and high-ranking military officers. The anarchists acknowledged no national boundaries, and neither did the crimes committed in the name of anarchism.

"And what will you anarchists do with me?" Baron von Diamant asked Josef Rothko.

"That will depend on your family and your friends."

"There is a ransom being asked, then?"

"After a fashion."

"The House of Diamond will pay . . . up to a point."

"And what point would that be?" Josef Rothko wondered.

"Any amount within reason. My family is fond of me. They won't quibble when it comes to ransoming me. But they're not fools. Even where affections are involved there are limits in matters like this." The baron regarded him with a calm that he did not altogether feel. "Just how much are you asking?" he inquired.

"We aren't asking for money." Josef Rothko smiled slightly. "We are anarchists. We don't believe in money."

"I see. And what do you believe in? Aside from violence, that is?"

"We don't all believe in violence. Actually only a small percentage of anarchists do."

"That would be the small percentage with the dynamite, the guns, and the knives." The baron could not hide his sarcasm. "The small percentage who throw bombs, assassinate leaders, and cut off the ears of the rich men they have kidnapped. By the way," he asked, not without genuine fear, "is my ear to be cut off?"

"No. I assume that's only done to establish that those making the demands are serious about what they will do to their prisoner if the demands aren't met. In your case, our assumption is that we are being taken seriously and that we have established to the satisfaction of your family and friends that you are in our custody. And let me reassure you on one point, Herr Baron. Regardless of your eventual fate, you are not in the hands of people who are gratuitously bloodthirsty or cruel."

"Ahh. How fortunate for me. I have fallen into the hands of the humanist wing of the Anarchist Party."

"There is no Anarchist Party," Josef Rothko assured him. "We do not believe in organization, or hierarchies of any sort. Acts are taken by individual anarchists on their own initiative, or by small groups who have arrived at a consensus. The so-called 'international anarchist conspiracy' is a myth of your capitalist press."

"I see. Murder and mayhem by insane individuals rather than by an insane collective." In his present position, irony was the only luxury left to the baron.

"Some anarchists are insane." Unexpectedly, the young man agreed. "Their lives have made them so. If there is a division among anarchists, it is between intellectuals like myself who subscribe to the theories of Proudhon and Bakunin, but who have not themselves suffered with the masses, and the downtrodden—those who starve and are worked like animals in the factories and fields of rich men, those who die of the diseases endemic to their working and living conditions, the have-nots whose children perish in infancy and whose own life expectancy is less than half that of their masters. Some of them are driven mad by hunger and need, and they do commit desperate and deadly acts directed at their exploiters. Oppression is violent by definition, and violence begets violence."

"I am a Jew," the baron reminded him. "You do not have to tell me about the nature of hardship, or about violence."

"Your being a Jew is irrelevant. It's your being a wealthy banker that is pertinent to us."

"And in regard to me—there being no organization, no central committee, as it were—who will prevail? The intellectuals, or the killers?"

"Consensus will prevail. That, Herr Baron, is what has been happening during the time since we took you into custody. There has been discussion of all points of view. I will tell you the truth. There are those who favored cutting off your head and sending it in a hatbox to the London stock exchange as a warning to other international bankers. But they have been persuaded to modify their position."

"Then I am to keep not only my ears, but my head as well. That is a relief."

"For the immediate present."

"Somehow that modification does not make me feel more secure." The baron thought a moment. "You said before that you weren't asking for a monetary ransom," he said finally. "What are you demanding for my safe return, then?"

"People. Human beings."

"I beg your pardon?"

"We anarchists have our heroes." Josef Rothko's face took on a certain youthful shining quality, the glow of the true believer. "The oppressors deal with them harshly, and so they are mostly dead martyrs. A few, however, are still alive. They are in many jails, in many countries. We have drawn up a list. We are prepared to exchange you for them."

"How many countries?"

"Five."

"And why should these countries release anarchist prisoners to secure the release of one Jew?"

"Because the House of Diamond has power—either direct, or indirect—in each country and in each situation. We have chosen carefully. In every case your people have the leverage to exert pressure on the governments involved. If our heroes go free, then you will be released. If not . . ."

"If not?"

Josef Rothko looked momentarily unhappy. "If theorists saved your head initially by gaining agreement to a more humane consensus, Herr Baron, then you must understand that pragmatists, our men of action if you will, obtained quite another consensus as to your fate if our demands aren't met. You see, in a way, it is the fault of your men of power yourselves. You have stated too often that you will not make deals with anarchists. Some of our comrades believe you—that you will pay no ransoms, meet no demands—and this has pushed them into quite a hard-line position. And so if there are no results within the next ninety days, then—"

"I will be killed," the baron realized.

"Yes. You will be decapitated and your head sent to the London stock exchange in a hatbox."

"In a hatbox." Baron Immanuel von Diamant swallowed hard. Ninety days to live . . . three months . . . In a hatbox!

BOOK TWO

1.PARIS

DRAMA IS AN effective tool of seduction. Philippe Diamant had long known that. He had used this knowledge more than once to make a conquest. Melodrama, however, was something else. Melodrama was drama carried to the ultimate, and Philippe had an instinctive gentlemanly dislike for extremes. He never would have considered it or the actions he was prepared to embark upon if the life of his father, the Baron Immanuel, had not hung in the balance. He would never have considered his present plan of seduction if it were not a last resort. But with the necessity for immediate results and considering the nature of the woman involved, the times called for immediate and drastic action.

"The times, monsieur, they are difficult for thespians in Paris." Across the splintery wooden table of the working-class bistro in Montparnasse, the actor regarded Philippe with a mournful face. "The public, it hangs on the fate of France midway through the third act, and so what do they want of theater? I tell you, monsieur, Shakespeare was wrong. The play is not the thing. Real life is."

Philippe nodded, not really listening to the words so much as the quality of speech. The man's face was perfect for Philippe's plans—a cauliflower ear, a nose like an overmashed potato, sausage lips, crumpled eyes like baked beans, cheek and jaw as craggy as splintered chicken bones—a veritable mélange of picked-over features. The body, too, was barrel built and hulking, a bear complete with tufts of feral hair showing through the shirt he wore. The man was a perfect thug from top to toe. But his speech was all wrong. It was too mannerly, too stagey, the choice of words too literate, the diction too clear, the inflection too rhythmic.

"And then there is the typecasting." The actor poured freely from the bottle of red wine Philippe had ordered for them. "I am, monsieur, a trained actor. I can do Molière, Racine, even that wet handkerchief Dumas *fils*. But the directors! Alas, they have no imagination. They look at me, and always they see the highwayman, the peasant rogue, the traitorous villain."

Of course, that was exactly what Philippe was seeing. It was what he wanted. He smiled slightly to himself but did not respond. There was still some doubt in his mind about the man's voice.

"That is what they see, the directors. But truly, monsieur, these are not the plays being written for our times. Drawing-room comedies and bedroom farces— that is what they are casting. Oh, I do a smooth butler, even a credible philanderer. But no. They do not see that when they look at me. What they see, monsieur, is a burglar if I am lucky enough that one has been written into the script. Or perhaps some deus ex machina kitchen lackey letting the audience know that the cuckolded husband's coach has broken down and that he is on his way home to catch Madame with her lover. A fact, monsieur, a sad fact: There are not the rogue and villain roles there once were."

Philippe decided it was time to be blunt. "I'm looking for a vicious brute, a violent thief capable of rape and murder."

The actor sighed. "Physiognomy and circumstance have indeed made such parts my specialty, monsieur."

"Your voice?"

"Ah. I see." The features of the actor's face rearranged themselves before Philippe's eyes. Menace furrowed the brow, the eyes became predatory talons, the neck bulged with jungle muscle, a slavering snarl possessed the mouth—Robert Louis Stevenson's Mr. Hyde turned into Mary Shelley's monster. From the beast's maw sounded a voice—not loud—of the Paris sewers, a tone part beggar's whine, part Apache growl, a mutter to tear out throats by. Indeed, it was a voice designed to strike terror into the heart of the bravest victim. "Your jewelry, madame, and be quick about it! . . . Your virtue? Ha! Up with your skirts! . . . Later— later we will see about your life!"

Philippe nodded with satisfaction. The voice could not have been better, the perfect final touch. "The part," he told the actor, "is yours."

Leaving the actor at the Montparnasse bistro, Philippe proceeded to the House of Diamond offices on the Place de l'Opera across from La Bourse, the financial exchange, and not far from the Banque de France. There was a message there from his uncle, Lord Haran Diamond in London, the latest in a series of communications that had been shuttling back and forth between them for the last month. Like the others, it concerned Philippe's defiance of Lord Haran's decision to withdraw from the bidding for the Cullinan Diamond in Amsterdam.

Irritation and hubris showed through the businesslike wording of Lord Haran's message. He thought he had made his decision clear when he first transmitted it to his nephew, Philippe. What, then, was the difficulty? Why did Philippe persist in sending replies that continued to muddle a situation that had been settled? Why, by Jove?

Actually, there was no "By Jove!" in Lord Haran's missive. Philippe supplied it from memory. His uncle's frequent use of the exclamation in a business context was the British equivalent of "Subject closed!"

By Jove! Well, now, not quite. Philippe flicked the waxed ends of his blond mustache thoughtfully. Seating himself at his desk, he took out a sheet of parchment and dipped his quill pen:

> *Dear Uncle,*
> *We really must arrive at a final decision as to our top offering figure for the Cullinan. Our agent in Amsterdam reports himself much confused by our shilly-shallying. Also, he tends to agree with me that you seem inclined to go too high and cautions against our letting ourselves be stampeded by the Warburgs and the Rothschilds. In his opinion, the bid to exceed will be that of Sir Everard Hambro acting in concert with Lord Revelstoke of the House of Barings. I very much appreciate your many communications on this matter, and value your thoughts on it highly, but really, dear Uncle, it is time to establish a figure so that we may bring things to a conclusion.*

Philippe added fondest regards to his six London cousins, and to Lord Haran himself. He signed the letter "Your most obedient nephew, Philippe."

Rereading the letter, Philippe allowed himself a dry chuckle. It was gobbledygook, but Uncle Haran was as literal minded an Englishman as Britannia had adopted, and his first reaction would be to ingest it sentence by sentence and word by word, determined to answer his nephew rationally and put an end to the nebulous conflict between them. Finally, of course, his uncle would realize that the letter did not at all address his decision not to bid on the Cullinan. He was not a stupid man, and he would understand that all the verbiage about prices and bids was merely a way of mocking him. And then he would doubtless fire off another letter clearly declaring that the House of Diamond should not bid on the Cullinan. And, Philippe smiled to himself, he would reply with yet another innocent demand that Uncle Haran establish a reasonable ceiling for their bid lest they be pushed into buying too high.

The Cullinan was the world's largest uncut diamond, weighing in at 2,000 carats, and Philippe was determined to have it.

"By telegraph, Monsieur Diamant?" inquired his secretary when Philippe handed him the message.

"Oh, no. This is a very important message. By all means by pigeon." Philippe laughed. Such a precaution would doubtless make the letter all the more confusing to Uncle Haran.

The House of Diamond carrier pigeons were a hedge against the vulnerability of the telegraph. In the frenzy of toppling governments accompanying the winding down of the infamous Dreyfus Case, Paris was seething with espionage and counterespionage. Many Parisian telegraph operators were spies, double agents, even triple agents. Who could say where news entrusted to the telegraph might be delivered? The headquarters of the Anti-Semitic Party presently trying to oust Georges Clemenceau as premier of France was certainly one possibility. The German secret service was another, as was its Russian equivalent. The Rothschilds had no doubt securely positioned themselves to intercept House of

Diamond cables, just as Diamond agents had a pipeline into the communications system of the Rothschilds. News from either house, if leaked, might have a chaotic effect on the money markets of the world.

Since the message was being sent through House of Diamond private channels, the secretary secured it with sealing wax and personally handed it to the company courier. The courier immediately took horse for Calais. Here, on an isolated bluff overlooking the English Channel, an agent of the House of Diamond lived in a small cottage. On the flat, shingled roof of the cottage stood the House of Diamond carrier pigeon coops. After the laying of the telegraph cable across the channel, these pigeons had been used much less frequently than they once had been. But when they flew, the top-secret news they invariably carried affected the financial exchanges in all the major cities of the world. Not that the letter Philippe was sending to his uncle contained anything of importance.

After the courier passed the message to the pigeon handler, the handler inserted it in a capsule and attached the capsule to the leg of one of the expertly trained birds. Within hours the homing pigeon would be in Dover. From there another horseman would carry the message to the London offices of the House of Diamond.

It would be waiting for Lord Haran on his desk the following morning.

Early that same morning, on one of the more obscure bridle paths of the Bois de Boulogne, a chestnut gelding trotted at a sedate pace. A petite young woman in a fashionable split-skirt riding habit and mid-March furs perched sidesaddle on the gelding and inhaled the crisp morning air deeply. It brought color to her cheeks and a sparkle to her wide brown eyes. It made her look younger than her thirty-three years and quite vulnerable.

Philippe Diamant stood beside his own tethered mount and observed the woman from the camouflage of a copse of dwarf pines. It was not the first time he had secluded himself there. She had been riding by every morning for the past two weeks, and Philippe had watched her frequently.

Now he found himself holding his breath as she approached the small bluff with its rock overhang just at the point where the bridle path turned. As she did every morning, the young woman reined in the chestnut and slowed down to negotiate the turn. Her movements were automatic, smooth, and graceful, the motions of an accomplished horsewoman who had been riding all her life.

"Stand fast!"

The man had fallen like a stone from the peak of the craggy bluff and landed gorillalike in the gelding's path. He crouched there with a pistol in each hand, waving them threateningly as the startled horse bucked and she fought to bring it under control. His face of warped flesh was twisted by a snarl and his muscle-bound, hulking, simian body looked quite capable of wrestling the horse to the ground if she couldn't rein it in.

That wasn't necessary. White-faced and fearful, she brought her steed under control. "What do you want?" Her voice quavered, but her expression revealed little of her true panic.

"Get down." It was a command, backed up by one of the gesturing pistols.

When she complied, the ruffian shoved one of the pistols into the waistband of his pants and wrenched the riding crop from her hand. He slashed her mount across the rump with it three times in rapid succession.

The horse whinnied, reared up, and then bolted. It would find its own way back to the stables.

In his place of concealment, Philippe nodded, satisfied. His stage directions were being followed to the letter. Silently, he unwound his own horse's reins from the branch where he had tethered him. He had to be ready to make his entrance. He awaited his cue.

"Your jewels!" The furs over her bodice were prodded with the pistol.

She removed the twin pearl-inlaid tortoiseshell combs that had been holding her chestnut ringlets in place against the wind. She slipped three wrought-silver bracelets from the arms under her furs, handed him two rings, one with twin rubies, the other a silver band with emerald chips.

"That one, too!"

"But that's my wedding ring."

"Be quick about it!" The muzzle of the gun poked the rise of her bosom once again.

Reluctantly, she removed the circle of gold and handed it to him. The jewelry vanished into a bag with a drawstring tied through a belt loop of his pants. She waited, fear now written plainly on her face.

"The muff."

She handed over her sable muff. That, too, vanished into the drawstring bag. As he contemplated her other furs, she hoped that he would realize they were too cumbersome for him to steal.

"Take them off." She took off the furs and stood shivering before him in her riding habit. "Lay them on the ground." She complied. He looked at her and licked his lips. He moved the muzzle of the gun against the collar of the blouse she was wearing. He hooked the loop button with the sight and ripped it open. A string of pearls was revealed. "Holding out on me, lady? Not smart!"

"I forgot about them." It was true. With trembling fingers, she reached behind her neck, unhooked the pearls, and handed them to him. The gesture thrust her small, shapely breasts forward prominently.

Behind the copse of dwarf pines, Philippe quietly mounted his horse.

The string of pearls followed the other jewels into the drawstring bag. "What else did you forget?"

"Nothing. I swear it."

"Well, we'll just see." He hooked the blouse with the barrel of his pistol below her bodice and ripped it apart with one vicious motion. The bare top halves of her breasts rose and fell rapidly above the whalebones of her corset. "Let's just make sure." He licked his lips. "Move." He prodded her off the path.

"Please, no! Don't—!"

"Have to do a search, lady. Who can say what else you might be holding out on me." Hidden from the path by the bushes now, he moved closer to her, the pistol separating the folds of the split riding skirt. "More to life," he leered, "than business."

Her scream galvanized Philippe into action. Digging his spurs into his steed's flanks, he charged into the scene through the underbrush. "Unhand her!" Melodrama has its conventions, and Philippe had opted for traditional dialogue. His riding crop slashed viciously, but harmlessly, over the padded shoulders of the assailant.

The villain fled as Philippe was leaping down from his horse. He knelt beside the young woman who had been borne to the cold floor of the forest only seconds before his arrival. "Are you all right, madame?" He helped her to a sitting position as she smoothed down her skirts.

"My jewels! He stole my jewels!"

Philippe patted her hand quickly, reassuringly. Then

he sprang to his feet and leapt back into the saddle. He galloped off down the path in the direction in which the assailant had fled.

The actor was waiting around the next bend. "Well done," Philippe told him as he reclaimed the drawstring bag full of jewelry in exchange for a pouch of gold coins, which the actor pocketed.

"One of my better performances, Monsieur. But the house could have been larger."

"*Adieu.*"

"Adieu, monsieur." A final bow, and the actor was gone.

Philippe returned to the woman. "Your jewels, madame." He handed her the drawstring sack.

"But how—?"

"The knave was all too glad to surrender them and escape with his worthless life."

"I am greatly in your debt, monsieur."

"The sight of such early-morning loveliness cancels the debt, I assure you, madame. Philippe Diamant at your service."

"*Merci.* My name is Babette." She blushed prettily, then looked around helplessly. "My horse—?"

"Seems to have departed, madame. But if I may make so bold . . . It would be a privilege to share my steed with you." Philippe jumped lightly to the ground and indicated the saddle.

"It would seem I have no choice but to accept your kind offer." She allowed him to help her mount. His hands were strong. Spiderweb lashes concealing the curiosity of her glance, she looked down at Philippe.

With his narrow, buccaneer face, his swarthy complexion contrasting with his straight ash-blond hair and fashionably waxed golden mustache, he was the sort of well-turned-out man who compelled the attention of ladies of station. His fawn-colored riding jacket and dark brown velvet jodphurs set off his slender figure to advantage. When he mounted behind her and reached between her arms and the sides of her body to take the reins, she felt the hard muscles of his arms, and of his thighs where they brushed her hips as well.

"It really is not safe for a young and beautiful woman to ride alone in the Bois de Boulogne early in the morning," Philippe remarked, his voice soft, his breath warm in her ear as they started off at a gentle trot.

She was flustered by the compliment, but pleased as well. "I have no choice. There is no one to ride with me."

"No one?"

"I am visiting in Paris. The only people I really know here are my sister and her husband. François is occupied with business, and Simone does not ride."

"I ride every morning." Philippe's arms were just a little unnecessarily tight around the sides of her breasts as he manipulated the reins. "Perhaps you would allow me to accompany you."

"I am a married woman," Babette blurted out, and immediately felt embarrassed by her gauche response.

"But your husband is not here in Paris with you." Philippe accepted her marital state easily. The muscles of his forearms flexed slightly, steadily against her rib cage. The tendon of his thigh rippled against her hip as the horse bent with the banking of the path. "Isn't that right?"

"How did you know—?"

"You said that you were alone in Paris."

"Oh."

"Surely your husband would be gratified to know that you were protected on your daily rides against such outrages as you experienced this morning."

Babette felt foolish. He was not suggesting an assignation after all. And if he were? This dashing young dragoon—for so she saw him—who had rescued her from a nightmare of sexual assault. He'd only suggested that they ride together in the park. There would surely be no harm in that. "I suppose he would be gratified," she said doubtfully.

"Then it's settled. I will be your escort."

"My cavalier." She turned in the saddle and looked into his eyes. They struck her as green pools of pleasure—pools into which it was going to be difficult to resist plunging.

It had been a strenuous morning, and Philippe was glad to relax over lunch—an omelette as light as a feather and a Sahara-dry white wine—in a corner of the private dining room at his club. Unfortunately, he had forgotten that it was also the club of Georges Clemenceau, the Premier of France.

His peace was destroyed when the sixty-five-year-old premier descended upon him like a plump and angry bantam rooster. Rumbling through substantial mustaches that managed to droop and bristle at the same time, he launched his assault while still halfway across the dining room from Philippe. "Bank of France!" he harrumphed. "Bonds, Diamant . . . House of Diamond depended upon . . . Betrayal . . ."

"Join me, Monsieur le Premier." Philippe was unruffled as he held up his wineglass. "Rothschild has outdone himself with this vintage. I promise you, it is the most superb of Mouton Rothschilds."

"A sip. No more. No, I shall not sit. And do not think to deflect me, young man. I was manipulating angry politicians before your father even reached an age to beget you. Now, what of the bonds, sir?" he asked of the bonds that were to underwrite his government.

"London has temporarily held up the funds."

"London!" Mouton Rothschild sprayed out from under the walrus mustache. "This is France, sir! What has London to do with us?"

"Purse strings. For the moment, unfortunately, the London House of Diamond controls the Paris House of Diamond purse strings."

"But they are Jews, these London Diamonds, are they not?" The premier was blunt.

"And the money will be forthcoming." His uncle, Lord Haran, might drag his feet to embarrass him, Philippe knew, but he would not ultimately put the Jews of France at risk. "The House of Diamond will guarantee the bonds," he assured Premier Clemenceau. "Please be patient just a little longer, Monsieur le Premier."

"Not too long, Philippe." He finished the glass of Mouton Rothschild, savoring it. "If the government's bonds go begging, the Bank of France has not the stability to withstand such public lack of faith by the House of Diamond. The signal that sends to the world financial markets could cause the bank's collapse. And if the bank goes, so, too, will my government, Philippe. I do not have to tell you what that means. The anti-Dreyfusards will take over. It is what they are waiting for, hoping for, praying for. Right now, Philippe, the Bank of France and my regime are all that stand between France and the Anti-Semites." Clemenceau bowed curtly. "Call on me soon, young Diamant."

Philippe watched the premier leave, head low like a charging bull, small feet pushing the carpet out from under him as he propelled himself from the dining room. Despite Clemenceau's pompous manner, Philippe was not resentful. What the premier said was perfectly true. Clemenceau's administration *was* presently all that stood between France and the politically powerful Anti-Semites.

For twelve long years they had been waiting to

pounce, poised to seize the government. For twelve long years they had stoked the fires of hatred toward Jews throughout France. For twelve long years they had held France in turmoil and shame as they rode the infamous whirlwind that the entire world had come to know—and frequently to protest—as the Dreyfus Affair.

Captain Alfred Dreyfus, a Jewish officer in the French Army, had been arrested and charged with high treason on October 15, 1894. Accused of having betrayed secret plans regarding French troop deployments to the German high command, within a month, he was tried, convicted, and sentenced to a life term on Devil's Island. The French press applauded the sentence as justified because Dreyfus was part of "the Jewish plot" to overthrow the French government in the interests of a German conquest.

Three years later, it came to light that a key document used to convict Dreyfus had actually been written by Major Charles-Ferdinand Esterhazy. When friends of Dreyfus petitioned to have the case reopened, however, the Army refused. The leadership feared that other high officers might be implicated and that the General Staff might not survive the revelations. The Esterhazy "forgery" was ascribed to the anti-Christ Jewish plot.

World opinion, however, was on the side of Dreyfus. In the autumn of 1899, it forced a new trial. Again the military tribunal found Dreyfus guilty. However, this verdict so contradicted the evidence that public outrage could not be stilled. Consequently, the French nation, and particularly Paris, split into Dreyfusards and anti-Dreyfusards. With the honor of the Army at stake, the issue became patriotism, and the scapegoat the Jews. Paris was seized by an orgy of anti-Semitism.

It continued through 1904, when Dreyfus was finally granted a new trial. With the spotlight of world opinion focused on France, this time Dreyfus was redeemed. Both houses of the French legislature passed a bill reinstating him as a captain in the Army. Lately, plans were afoot to make amends by awarding him the Legion of Honor.

Justice may have ultimately found Alfred Dreyfus, but there was little in France left over for other Jews. Defeat only hardened the hatred of the anti-Dreyfusards for the Jews. The legacy of the Dreyfus case was an anti-Jewish sentiment unprecedented in French history. And the more prominent the Jew, the more likely he was to be a target of that legacy.

As head of the House of Diamond, Philippe Diamant was thus a frequent target. Politically, those who attacked him ran the gamut from anti-Semitic Socialists leveling attacks against the "bloodsucking Jewish bankers" to Royalists and Clericalists reviving the accusation of a Jewish plot to take over the government in order to "crucify the Church of Our Lord as once Jews crucified Our Lord Himself." The Diamant family had even been accused of bankrolling the anarchists who had assassinated French President Carnot around the time the Dreyfus scandal first broke.

Philippe Diamant's town house on the Rue Saint-Antoine and the offices of the House of Diamond on the Place de l'Opera were constantly smeared with anti-Semitic slogans and symbols. The police, of course, looked the other way. They continued to look the other way on those occasions when hoodlums flung rocks through his windows.

All this Philippe abided with no appreciable diminishing of his aplomb. If he looked the gentleman with his waxed mustache and stylish clothes, and played the dandy as well as the rake, it could not make him any less Jewish in the eyes of the anti-Semites. But it did confuse them. Since French society accepted him, then how undo the blurring of the lines between Jewish gentleman and gentile? Philippe simply did not look the part of the Jewish conspirator, and he refused to act it. A fop and a roué, perhaps, but there was no denying he had style.

Damned devious, these Jews! Clever, too! They would gladly have lit the faggots of Philippe Diamant's burning stake, but the most virulent among the French upper-class anti-Semites could not entirely suppress a certain grudging admiration for the gentleman Jew.

It was not returned. Appearances were deceiving. Philippe was neither a fool, nor a mere poseur. Much as he turned a blithe other cheek to the offal winds of anti-Semitism sweeping over France, he was far from oblivious of their message. France was not the humanistic haven Jews had once thought it to be. The Dreyfus Affair had revealed France to be a country hanging by a thread—the snapping of which might prove fatal to any Jew, even—or particularly—Philippe Diamant.

Philippe and Babette had taken to riding together each morning, and one week to the day after his confrontation with Premier Clemenceau following the "rescue" of Babette, Philippe consummated her seduction. The ease of the conquest did not stop Philippe from feeling guilty. He had soon found out that Babette was neither a simpleminded woman, nor one of easy virtue. She succumbed with a depth of feeling that was a far cry from the casual affairs in which Philippe customarily embroiled himself.

It had been obvious to Philippe from the first that Babette was not a woman for such casual affairs. Although she had every reason to be deeply unhappy with her husband, Philippe knew that she had always been true to him. She considered fidelity in marriage a duty. She would not discard it lightly, out of boredom, or even for pleasure. That was why he had resorted to the melodramatic rescue to secure their introduction and ensure her gratitude. What he had not known was that only love could break the bond. And now her grave, wide eyes shone with it in Philippe's arms.

He was touched. Her passion, unlike that of so many other women, was not born of the secret joy inherent in infidelity but was directed solely toward Philippe. Her innocence completely negated the fact of adultery. Philippe's roué cynicism was no match for the combination. What had started out as the most carefully calculated and deliberate of any of his seductions had ricocheted, leaving him with strong feelings of guilt about his motives.

Yet his motives were worthy. Philippe could not doubt that. He loved his father, and he was bound to do everything in his power to save him from the predicament of his abduction. He could not allow himself the luxury of empathy with Babette's innocence and passion at the expense of the course of action he had embarked upon to save the Baron Immanuel.

In the aftermath of their lovemaking, he evaded that innocence, that heartbreakingly open affection. Taking a light tone, he steered the conversation in the direction it must eventually follow if his purposes were to be achieved. "Why did you marry your husband in the first place?" he asked Babette with studied casualness.

"Why did I marry him? Because I was very French and he was very German—different—exotic to me, you see."

"I see." Philippe's head was turned toward Babette on the pillow they shared. He was paying close, and unfeigned, attention. "And why did you fall out of love with him?"

"The same reason I married him." Babette's dimples flashed with wry humor. "He was so *very* German."

"I was born in Austria, you know. Some people don't consider me French at all," Philippe told her.

"Really?" The dimples again. "Well, they haven't been made love to by you."

"Perhaps the reasons are the same," Philippe suggested, still directing the conversation according to his purposes. "Why you were attracted to him. Why you're attracted to me."

"Well, you do have a dueling scar, and so does he, only his is much more fierce. Still, I don't think so. We were married a long time ago. I was very young. Only nineteen and now I'm"—Babette thought about lying, but didn't. There should not be lies between them— "thirty-three."

Her eyes, large and soft brown, were worried. It was only two years, but would it bother him that she was older? Her husband, twelve years her senior, had led Babette to believe that all men preferred the woman to be younger.

Truly, Philippe had never given a thought to the matter "And all that time you were faithful to him," he reflected. "Fourteen years."

"Do you mind that I'm so inexperienced?" she worried. "Perhaps I don't please you, and you're too gentlemanly to tell me."

"Of course you please me." Philippe was accustomed to lying to women who required reassurance, but he wasn't lying now. In his cold-blooded seduction of Babette he had not anticipated the unabashed warmth and intimacy of her flesh. It was not just sensuality; their coupling had touched him in a way alien to his experience. He had always taken it for granted that his casual affairs should be physically satisfying. But he was jolted by the emotional gratification of their lovemaking. He had not been prepared for it. "One would think that a woman as attractive as you would have taken a lover long ago," he told Babette, again steering the conversation.

"Perhaps no one asked me." Babette was not a coquette, but she instinctively fished for the compliment.

Philippe propped his head on his elbow and drew back the covers. Truly, she was lovely. Her flesh was smooth, her body petite, compact, slender, but not thin. She was perfectly proportioned like some porcelain figurine crafted by a master. Her face, with its large cinnamon eyes set off by dark, filigree lashes, was framed by a cascade of chestnut ringlets. When he had first observed her riding in the forest, she had appeared very French and very girlish. But now Philippe saw her face differently; there was a seriousness in its rounds and hollows that was mature, womanly. He was struck by the contrast between Babette's frivolous, Gallic persona and her grave expression and serious commitment. "Oh, you were asked." He smiled at her blush of pleasure. "But perhaps I just came along at the right moment. Perhaps you were ready."

"That wasn't it." Babette was defensive. "It was you. Nothing else has changed. I haven't been in love with my husband for a very long time, but if I hadn't met you, Philippe, I would have remained faithful to him."

"For your children's sake?" She had told Philippe about them during one of their early-morning rides. There were two, a boy and a girl, twelve and ten years old, respectively.

"Yes. But also because it is my nature to be true to one man."

"And will you remain faithful to me?" Philippe's voice was teasing, but the question was serious. He had to ascertain whether she would ever betray him.

"Of course I will." The question hurt Babette and bewildered her. "How can you ask?"

"Then that makes two men to whom you will remain

faithful." Again his tone was casual, his purpose hidden. "Myself, and your husband."

"Why are you saying these things, Philippe?" Her remarkable eyes reflected her recognition that this was not casual teasing. "They hurt me. Why do you want to hurt me?"

Philippe sighed. His regret at the pain he was inflicting was genuine. But that did not mean he could offer her a real explanation. Instead, he said in a low voice, "I'm jealous."

"Jealous? Oh, darling, of what? Can't you see that I adore you? There is no one else."

"There is your husband," he persisted.

"But I love *you*, Philippe."

"While you're here in Paris. But how long will that be? Only another few weeks. Then you'll return to Germany. You'll go back to him."

"What else can I do?" It was true, all true. She had pushed the thought of her return to the back of her mind, but now Babette was forced to face it. "My children—"

"You can do nothing." Philippe was despondent. Then, slowly, he turned to her, as if suddenly struck by an idea. "But perhaps I can," he said slowly. "Perhaps I could come to Germany. Perhaps we could arrange for me to visit. Not as your lover, of course, but as a friend you made in Paris—the man who came to your rescue when you were assaulted by a brigand. What do you think?"

"Oh, yes, Philippe. Helmut could not object to that. You could stay with us, be a guest in our house." Babette was blushing now at her own eager duplicity and at the opportunism her next words expressed. "My husband's duties frequently take him away on trips to other parts of the country. We could be alone. I mean, once the children were in bed . . ." Her blushes deepened.

"Alone. Deliciously alone." Philippe's narrow, elegant hand moved intimately under the covers. "As lovers are meant to be." He caressed her pliant flesh. "And you will be faithful to me," he murmured.

"Oh, yes, my darling."

"Not to him. To me."

"I swear it."

"Then I can ask no more." Philippe took her in his arms then and kissed her so that her petite body curved urgently into him.

Some time later, dozing, they were aroused by a discreet knock at the door. Philippe rose, put on a robe, and went to answer it. His secretary was standing there, an opened telegram in his hand. "I'm sorry, sir," he apologized. "It's from Emperor Franz Josef. I thought you'd want to see it immediately."

Philippe scanned the message quickly. The Austrian emperor had received demands from the kidnappers. From the emperor's cryptic message Philippe knew that these demands were complex. He asked that Philippe come to Vienna immediately so that they might discuss them before consulting with the other members of the House of Diamond.

The secretary was waiting for a response. Philippe glanced at his watch. It was almost midnight. "Rouse the coachman," he instructed the secretary. "Send him to the Gare du Nord with a message to hold the one-thirty train to Vienna for me. Then have him return immediately to take me there. I will be ready when he gets back." Philippe glanced over his shoulder at Babette sitting up sleepily in the bed. "The lady will leave with me," he said. "We will drop her off on the way to the station."

Philippe was careful not to mention the lady's name to his secretary. The fewer people who knew his bed had been shared that evening by Frau Helmut von

Koerner, the better. It was not in Philippe's interest to have Paris gossiping about his liaison with the wife of a field marshal who served on the German General Staff—a man who had been a childhood friend and was presently an intimate advisor of Kaiser Wilhelm himself.

2. VIENNA

"REALLY, PHILIPPE!" THE Austrian Emperor's blue eyes flashed disapproval. "Are you trying to upset the European balance of power single-handedly? A dalliance with the wife of the kaiser's closest confidante!"

"Sire, how did you—?"

"In Paris you all worry about the Germans, the English, even the Russians. And so my Austrian secret police go about their business unnoticed."

"Of course. With father missing, you would place me under surveillance." His tone was calm, but Philippe's mouth twitched with resentment.

"Nonsense, Philippe. My spies were not watching you. They were watching the lady. Routine. She is, after all, the Frau von Koerner. Her husband is a potential threat to Austria." The emperor wagged a long, bony, arthritic finger. "But why have you involved yourself with this Marseilles siren?"

" 'Marseilles'?"

"According to my secret police, that is where Frau von Koerner and her sister are from originally. They are the daughters of a Royalist family. The older sister married a Parisian businessman with ties to the Clericalist Party. And the younger sister, your inamorata, married Field Marshal Helmut von Koerner, Willie's pet Prussian. The sisters remain close and visit each other frequently in Paris and Berlin. But is it just sisterly devotion, Philippe? Or do the sisters serve a more devious purpose in the interests of their husbands? Could it be a continuation of the Esterhazy connection that brought France to its knees with the Dreyfus Case?"

Philippe shrugged. "The Dreyfus Case is over."

"Wrong, Philippe." The emperor spoke slowly, impressing his words on his listener. "The Dreyfus Case will never be over for France. Ten years from now, thirty years from now, a hundred years from now, France will still be haunted by the specter of Alfred Dreyfus."

"Are you suggesting, Excellency, that Frau von Koerner and her sister serve as couriers in some plot involving the German General Staff and the anti-Dreyfusards?"

"You can't ignore the possibility, Philippe. Yours would not be the first bed used by a clever woman for purposes of international intrigue. But how could you not perceive this and resist temptation? What would your father say if he knew of your compromising liaison with Frau von Koerner?"

"It is for my father's sake that I became involved."

"Really?" Franz Josef was sarcastic. "You copulated out of filial devotion, did you, Philippe?"

"Hear me out, Excellency. I had to have an entrée into the kaiser's inner circle. The seduction of Frau von Koerner seemed the shortest route."

"I'm listening, Philippe."

"Father held notes for loans to a member of Kaiser Wilhelm's council of advisors. He was Father's ear trumpet as regards German expansionism. From them he learned that the kaiser's men regarded his leadership tilting the House of Diamond in favor of your em-

pire, making it antithetical to German interests. Their
information made it clear that the one with the most
to gain by depriving the Austro-Hungarian government
of my father's support and advice was Kaiser Wilhelm
of Germany."

"Are you saying that you think Deutsche Willie is
behind the Baron Immanuel's abduction?"

"Yes." Philippe nodded. "The kaiser gains most from
Father's absence."

"And does the baron's German informant confirm this
suspicion?"

"I can't say. I don't know who he is. Only Father
knew his identity. But this, Excellency, is why I have
involved myself with Frau von Koerner. I will go to
Berlin to continue our liaison. There I hope to pick up
the trail of my father's abduction, or at the very least
to determine who his informant was and speak with
him as to German involvement."

The emperor thought a moment. "Your suspicion has
a certain logic," he said finally. "But the ransom demands point to anarchists as the kidnappers."

"The kaiser is devious. They may well be his personal 'anarchists.' The same 'anarchists' the kaiser infiltrated into Russia to destabilize the country and keep
the tsar off balance while at the same time he urged a
secret military treaty on him. It is my belief that Father
may well be in the hands of German provocateurs, Excellency, rather than genuine revolutionaries."

"Imposters?" Franz Josef sat back wearily in the tall
throne where he had automatically seated himself.
"Well, nothing is impossible." He thought in silence for
a moment. "But suppose you are wrong, Philippe? Suppose these anarchists who are holding your father are
genuine? After all, their terms do reflect radical concerns. Why would the kaiser—?"

"A red herring." Philippe sighed. "But you're right,

Sire. We can't take the chance that my theory is wrong. Not with my father's life at stake. The terms must be met."

"Easier said than done, Philippe. There are several nations involved, all with conflicting interests." The emperor ticked them off. "The United States, where the demand is for the release of Alexander Berkman, the anarchist who has been in jail for fourteen years for the attempted murder of Henry Clay Frick. Spain, which is to free sixty-one anarchists, anti-Clericals, Catalan Republicans, and other opponents of the regime held since eighteen-ninety-five at Rio de Oro on the flimsiest of conspiracy charges. Italy, where the four Syndicalist leaders of last year's Venice dockworkers' strike are to be let out of prison. France, which is to provide transportation from Devil's Island to Argentina for six anarchists imprisoned for the unsuccessful bombing of a passenger train five years ago. And Switzerland—" Here a certain controlled fury mottled the emperor's aging countenance. "—which is to free the assassin Luigi Lucheni."

"Lucheni!" Philippe was appalled. "I'm sorry, Highness. I didn't know."

On September 10, 1898, the anarchist Luigi Lucheni, concealing a dagger fashioned out of an old file that he had sharpened and fitted to a handle carved from a piece of firewood, accosted the Empress Elizabeth of Austria, Franz Josef's wife of forty-five years, during a state visit to Geneva. As she and her lady-in-waiting walked toward the Quai Mont Blanc, Lucheni squinted beneath her parasol to make sure he had the right woman, and then stabbed the empress through the heart. Elizabeth died four hours later. When informed of his victim's death, Lucheni had declared himself delighted. It was, he said, part of the ongoing anarchist war on the rich and the great.

"Lucheni," Franz Josef repeated the name bitterly to Philippe now. "They demand that this murderous maniac be turned loose to seek out other innocent victims."

Philippe sighed. "I love my father," he said gently, a reminder of what was at stake.

"I loved my wife."

"I hope my father is still alive." Philippe paused and said softly, "The empress is dead."

"Nevertheless, I loved her. Did you know that, Philippe? Ours was a rare marriage for royalty. It had been arranged that I should marry Elizabeth's sister. But when I went to Bavaria to finalize the betrothal, Elizabeth and I set eyes on each other and fell in love. There was a fine uproar, I tell you. But we held fast, and against everybody's objections—all those plans upset!—we were married. I never stopped loving her, Philippe. And then this insane anarchist assassin took her from me. And this is the man they want released!"

"Well, I suppose it will be up to the Swiss to decide." Philippe's tone was placating. "They are the ones holding him in jail."

"The Swiss"—the emperor's voice was abruptly icy—"will do what I tell them to do."

Instinctively, Philippe knew that he must not press the issue. He could only hope that Franz Josef's genuine affection for his father would outweigh his need for vengeance. "There will be problems with the other demands," Philippe observed, in an attempt to deflect the emperor's brooding. "I'll have to lean heavily on Clemenceau to get the railroad bombers pardoned in defiance of the right-wingers who even now are calling for his removal as premier. The New York House of Diamond may not have the political influence to contrive an amnesty for Berkman. Spain will have to be approached through my uncle, Lord Haran, who one hopes carries weight with those British business interests who are propping up the present Spanish regime. Carlo Diamante will do everything he can, of course, to influence the Italian government, but in the end, I suspect, the help of the Conte di Falco, my cousin Tamar's husband, may be more effective." Philippe fell silent for a moment. "It is significant, is it not," he said finally, "that neither Germany itself, nor any of its client states is mentioned in the anarchist demands?"

"That is true." The emperor nodded slowly. "Nor its new secret ally, Russia."

"Why is the kaiser off the hook?" Philippe persisted in his line of reasoning. "Unless he is involved."

"I don't rule out Willie's involvement," the emperor assured Philippe. "He is a devious and complicated man—a twisted man."

" 'Twisted'?"

"From birth. In two ways. He was related to my wife, Elizabeth, you know. Willie used to visit us as a child. Even then, he was consumed with envy and resentment of his Uncle Bertie, then the Prince of Wales. Bertie, who was eighteen years older, seemed to represent to Willie everything that he himself was not. Bertie was a sportsman and an outdoorsman, physically strong, very attractive—particularly to the ladies. He might have been Willy's idol, but Bertie always ignored him, you see. Quite apart from that, Willie was prevented from measuring up to him by his withered arm. That accident of birth atrophied far more than his limb. . . ."

"I wonder—" Philippe had a thought. "Would that explain why he surrounds himself with Prussian duelists and swordsmen like Field Marshal von Koerner?"

"We have a fellow here in Vienna who is creating quite a stir dealing with questions of why people are the way they are. Freud is his name, Sigmund Freud.

You should perhaps bring such questions to him," the emperor replied drily.

"As a general rule, I steer clear of soothsayers," Philippe countered. "But about the kaiser's being twisted. If I understand you right, Excellency, you do mean both his arm and his mind."

"Willie is warped." The emperor was firm. "He doesn't just demand loyalty from his subjects. He demands the impossible."

" 'The impossible'?"

"Rather than address the people of Germany, he addresses 'My Army,' by which he means all his people. They are soldiers of the kaiser first, you see, and subjects of the German nation second. He expects of his people precisely what he expects of his army. No less. Indeed, when he speaks to his soldiers, he speaks to the nation as a whole. And he does, indeed, demand the impossible of them. Recently, while he was addressing a company of young recruits, he said, 'If your kaiser commands you to do so, you must fire on your father and mother.' That is the German kaiser's twisted and impossible demand to all his people. And he means it literally."

If your kaiser commands you to do so, you must fire on your father and mother! Philippe's heart sank. Could his own father have fallen into the hands of such a man?

3 . YORKSHIRE

"MURDERERS!" MINERVA DIAMOND stood on the heath of her father's country estate with her hands on her hips and the wind off the moors blowing her hair as wild as that of a Valkyrie and confronted her father and his guest. "You are all murderers!"

"By Jove!" Lord Haran peered nervously past her into the distance, down the path upon which the royal party would at any moment appear. "Minerva, it is impudent enough that you embarrass me and my guest, but the king will be along at any moment. I beg of you—"

"To shoot helpless birds for no reason but the sport of it? Sport, ha! Well, then, His Majesty is also a murderer!"

"Minerva!"

Observing the confrontation between father and daughter, Sir Everard Hambro was amused, rather than embarrassed. At the age of almost seventy, few things embarrassed him anymore. He stood to one side with his arms akimbo and looked down on the scene from his six-foot-five-inch height. The girl was not beautiful, but her anger lent her a certain fire that was not without appeal. Perhaps, Sir Everard thought to himself, young Viscount Templeton had passed up a good thing. Like many of the London gentry, Sir Everard assumed that Ronald Templeton had trrned up his nose at Minerva Diamond. It never occurred to any of them that she might have rebuffed him.

"Will you not at least have mercy on these defenseless creatures, Sir Everard?" Sensing his tolerance of her outburst, Minerva turned to appeal to him.

Her nearsighted gaze as she strained to look up into his face was meant to be disconcerting. Sir Everard, however, was not a man whose composure could be easily ruffled. "I fear you are directing your plea to the wrong court, Miss Minerva. The Yorkshire grouse season has commanded my participation for over twenty years."

"But why?" Minerva's throaty voice was hoarse with despair.

"To achieve my heart's desire and break Lord Walsingham's record," Sir Everard told her with a twinkle in his rheumy eye.

" 'Lord Walsingham's record'?"

Her father explained patiently. "In Yorkshire, not far from here, in eighteen eighty-eight, Lord Walsingham, hunting alone, single-handedly bagged one thousand seventy birds in a day's shooting."

"Bagged?" Minerva's dark eyes grew large. Her fingers, combing through her windblown brown hair distractedly, were leaving a lopsided skew of tendrils in their wake. "You mean *killed*?"

"Miss Minerva"—Sir Everard tried to calm her—"have I not seen you eating meat at dinner, including fowl?"

"Did this Lord Walsingham dine on a thousand seventy birds in that one night, then?"

"Enough, Minerva!" Lord Haran was firm. He knew that he allowed his eldest daughter too much liberty, but there was a limit to his tolerance. "His Majesty approaches. Since you can't—or won't—control your tongue, I must insist that you leave us."

Minerva, sensing that she could do no more, quit the field. "As you wish, Father. I will leave you. I will leave you to your slaughter!" Skirts crushed by a fist holding them above the mud, Minerva flounced off.

Sir Everard watched as she intercepted the approaching party of King Edward VII. Minerva's curtsy was formidable, rather than graceful. The king, ever the *beau galant*, bent to kiss her hand with a charming smile and what were undoubtedly some cavalier words of greeting. Minerva's reply, whatever it was, left him gazing after her retreating figure with a bemused look on his still-handsome, if somewhat dissipated, face.

"By Jove!" Lord Haran moaned in despair as he observed the royal encounter with his unruly eldest daughter.

The king, flanked by two gunbearers, reached them. "Diamond. Hambro." His cheerful greetings snapped them erect from their deferential bows. "It's a bonny day for shooting, what?"

"The moors do sparkle, Sire," Sir Everard agreed.

"*Bertie*, Ev. Call me Bertie as in the old days. No formality here." The king, while still Prince of Wales, had been a frequent guest at Sir Everard's villa in Biarritz. The two had played cards together regularly; and when Bertie had gambled at the casino and lost more than his allowance from his mother, Queen Victoria, would cover, Sir Everard had advanced him money to make good his losses. He had also acted as a beard for the philandering prince in his affair with Lillie Langtry.

The friendship had worked to Sir Everard Hambro's advantage. While Queen Victoria had deplored her son's Biarritz debaucheries, she had counted, nevertheless, on Hambro to keep them within limits. His reward was to be knighted and to be made a director of the Bank of England. It was through Sir Everard Hambro that Lord Haran had met the king, eventually to become along with Sir Everard one of his most trusted financial advisors, as well as a sporting companion.

"The beaters are ready, Highness," Lord Haran now informed the king. "We can start at your pleasure."

"To render the English grouse extinct by royal firepower." The king laughed.

"Sire?"

"Your daughter's words, Diamond. Spoken when I remarked to her that it was fine weather for the hunt."

Lord Haran's cheeks were puffed red with embarrassment. "My daughter is out of sorts today, Your Highness. Please allow me to apologize for her."

"Nonsense, my dear chap. She could not have put it

more accurately. We are, indeed, going to have so fine a day's shooting as to decimate the flocks to the point of extinction. At least I hope we are. After all"—the king laughed—"why else are we here?"

"And Lord Haran has more than paved the way for us, Bertie." Sir Everard was approving. "He took pains last year to burn off the old heather on the moor so that a more vigorous growth might be encouraged." The heather was the chief food supply of the grouse. "Now the birds flock in greater and greater numbers to gorge themselves. The stock has multiplied. We can expect a very large bag today."

"Then let the beaters proceed." The king, in high spirits, beckoned to one of the bearers to produce a flask of aged-in-the-wood whiskey, which was poured into three crystal glasses unwrapped from linen napkins and served to the trio of sportsmen.

Lord Haran gave the order. The beaters formed a ragged line and thrashed their way slowly through the moor. The hunting dogs preceded them, roisting any stray birds to rejoin their flock. The three hunters leisurely finished their drinks and positioned themselves at the shooting stands that the bearers had set up for them.

When all was ready, the beaters startled the first flock of grouse into flight. Each of the shooters got off three rounds before the swarm resettled out of range. As the beaters proceeded to thrash through another section of the moor, retrievers—both human and canine—moved behind them to round up the dead birds. The shells had been premarked with a dye so that each kill might be attributed to the shooter who had brought it down. There was a scorekeeper to keep track of the kills and record them.

It went on for some two hours, with over one hundred and fifty birds brought down. The king was in the lead with Lord Haran a close second, and Sir Everard grumbling that a faultily aligned sight on one of his guns was responsible for his poor third. But they had to call a halt now, while the beaters circled around behind the roosting flocks in order to drive the birds back toward them.

During the break in activity the king decided to have a nap. Lord Haran and Sir Everard sat a little way off from him and talked softly, waiting for the shoot to resume. "I admire your courage, Diamond," Sir Everard remarked with a certain irony in his tone.

"Courage?"

"Shooting with that monocle screwed up in your eye. I'd be afraid of the recoil."

"By Jove! Never gave it a thought."

"It could splinter the monocle, shatter the eye with glass."

"I suppose I'm used to it." There was more than one way, Lord Haran realized, to close the gap in a shooting match. "Of course, it never bothered me," he added drily, "until now."

"Well, you're a brave man." Sir Everard changed the subject. "And a truly patriotic one. Withdrawing House of Diamond funds from the Panama Canal puts England in your debt. His Majesty"—he nodded toward the sleeping king—"is also grateful."

"Not prematurely, I hope. His Majesty should understand that the blocking of the ditch is only a temporary stopgap, just as it was thirteen years ago." Lord Haran referred to his earlier and successful attempt to halt the progress of the Panama Canal when the French were attempting to dig it. By exposing the bribing of one hundred and fifty members of the French Chamber of Deputies in the handing out of contracts to build the Panama Canal, Lord Haran's behind-the-scenes maneuvering had effectively brought to a halt French efforts to build the waterway, so crucial for international shipping, which would link the Atlantic and Pacific oceans. Subsequently, though, the site of the canal had been sold to the United States. And now they were faced with the same problem—and a temporary solution.

"'Temporary'? Perhaps. But with the House of Diamond withdrawing its financing, how will the United States government replace the money needed to complete the building of the canal?" Sir Everard wondered.

"Ask our mutual friend J.P. Morgan. He will tell you that, like my own American cousins, there are financiers in the colonies who will perceive our withdrawal as an opportunity. It's not patriotism that will finance the canal; it is the possibility of profit. I am afraid some deal will be worked out to compensate the bankrollers that will satisfy their greed."

"Well, any delay works to the benefit of British commerce."

"That is why I cut off the funds for the canal," Lord Haran replied. "Refinancing will not be found quickly. It will give Britain time to maneuver so that when the canal is finally built it will not interfere with our naval and shipping supremacy. Trade, after all, is the Englishman's lifeblood."

"Good Lord, Diamond!" Sir Everard laughed. "You sound just like young Winston." It was common gossip in the House of Lords that the thirty-two-year-old Winston Churchill was actively campaigning for a secretariat in the Department of the Navy.

"By Jove!" Lord Haran grimaced around his monocle. "Not that."

"Next you'll be telling tales of the bore's war." Churchill was well known for his propensity to corner members of his club and regale them with accounts of his exploits during the Boer War, which he had covered as a newspaper correspondent.

But Sir Everard knew that Haran's ruddy face and the monocle could be deceptive. Lord Haran was not a simple man.

"Actually, there's something else entirely that I wanted to chat with you about."

"Oh?"

"Spain." Lord Haran came directly to the point. "You and J.P. have some investments there, do you not?"

"We dabble in Iberia," Sir Everard confirmed.

Lord Haran knew that Sir Everard's casual characterization of his Spanish interests was undoubtedly in inverse proportion to the size of his holdings. "I need a favor." He remained blunt. "From the Spanish government."

"Ahh, the Spanish government." Sir Everard's smile was wicked. He and J.P. Morgan had split the Spanish government between their respective hip pockets. "What sort of favor?"

"The release of sixty-one assorted leftists from the Rio de Oro prison."

"So many anarchists?" Sir Everard raised an eyebrow. "Will you have them brought here for a shoot, Diamond? To replace the grouse? My word, that would be popular with our fellow Tories."

"I'm serious. Absolutely serious."

Sir Everard looked more closely at him and saw that he was. "I see." He thought a moment. "I suppose you have your reasons?"

"Yes."

"But you're not going to tell me what they are?"

"No."

"I see." Sir Everard was disturbed, although he didn't allow it to show. There was obviously something going on with the House of Diamond. There was that abrupt pullback on the Panama Canal, and the House had withdrawn support of the Vienna-Budapest railroad trunk line. They had not entered a bid for the Giotto frescoes in Florence. Other investments had been canceled, and—most disturbing—large blocks of House of Diamond stock had been unloaded on half a dozen exchanges around the world. The price had plunged. There was rumor of the unthinkable—a Diamond bankruptcy. Something drastic, indeed, must have happened. But what?

Sir Everard's momentary silence had set Lord Haran to reflecting as well. Hambro was no fool. He would not have missed the market shifts involving the House of Diamond. He would recognize that there must be a connection between them and Lord Haran's bizarre request regarding freedom for the Spanish leftists. In any case, the news of Baron Immanuel von Diamant's abduction could not be contained much longer. Such news would have many consequences—both in terms of the financial shape of the house and, no doubt, in terms of the baron's safety. Still, first things first. "The release of the anarchists," he prodded Sir Everard. "Can it be done?"

"In Spain, all things can be done." Sir Everard stood and stretched, his aging six-foot-five-inch frame looming over Lord Haran. "For a price," he added.

Sir Everard's words were not unexpected. "Of course."

"What you are proposing must be done quietly and most unofficially. That is always expensive."

"Whatever the cost, it will be paid," Lord Hambro assured him.

"Don't you want me to find out what it might be first?" Sir Everard inquired.

"No. I trust you. Our bank in Madrid will supply what is needed." Whatever the cost might be to bribe the pertinent Spaniards, he knew that Sir Everard would also expect something in return for his help. It was understood; there was no need for the awkwardness of words of condition.

"All right, then. I will make inquiries and get back to you."

Lord Haran nodded. It would be done. The Spanish anarchists would be released.

"We were speaking of young Winston before." Unexpectedly, Sir Everard brought the conversation back to Churchill. "He means no harm, you know, with his jingoistic carryover from his colonial war days in Africa."

"I suppose not." Churchill again? What was Sir Everard getting at?

"Winston's patriotism knows no sense of proportion. Did you know that he is absolutely determined that we should bring the Cullinan Diamond back to England?"

So that was it! Everard's request had not been long in coming. " 'Back'?" Lord Haran wondered.

"Well, it was mined in South Africa," Sir Everard reminded Lord Haran. "We do rule there. Despite Winston's participation, England did win the Boer War."

"Did we?" Lord Haran, who knew the cost, was not so sure.

"We did." Sir Everard was emphatic. "And so, yes, 'back' to England. That is where Winston wants the Cullinan. And in this instance, I confess I couldn't agree with him more."

Patriotism, Lord Haran thought, but did not say aloud, is the last refuge of jewel collectors. Ah, well. "I have no argument with that, Hambro," he declared. "Indeed, if there is any way that I can be of service . . ."

"Perhaps a word with your nephew, Philippe. It seems he has evinced some interest in bidding for the Cullinan. If he's successful, the world's greatest jewel will go to France. If that happened, Winston would be most unhappy."

As if Winston's happiness were of the slightest concern to Sir Everard Hambro, or anyone else of power in England! "Well, we don't want young Churchill unhappy," Lord Haran declared aloud. His eyes were downcast, observing the monocle in his hand as he polished it.

"I, myself, would be saddened to see the Cullinan sparkle in France," Sir Everard added. "And I think I'm safe in saying that His Majesty would be desolate as well."

" 'Desolate.' " Lord Haran's ruddy cheeks filled with air, which he then expelled in a sort of sympathetic snort that in no way expressed a lack of concern with the happiness of the head of the Royal House of England. "Well, I certainly wouldn't want that."

"Then you'll speak to Philippe?"

"I promise."

"And do you think he will be reasonable?" Sir Everard wondered.

"I'm sure he will." There was a certain grimness in Lord Haran's tone. Philippe had been playing an infuriating game regarding Lord Haran's decision not to bid on the Cullinan. Philippe's counterresponsive communications had sent his blood pressure soaring. Well, now the game was over. With his father's life at stake, Philippe would have to bow out of the bidding for the jewel. The infuriating letters would cease.

Lord Haran was content. He had not contrived the situation; he would not have played games with the life of a brother he loved even as he competed with him. But, as it worked out, once again he had killed two birds with one stone. First, the U.S. Diamonds had had to pull out of the Panama Canal deal. And, now, the

Spanish anarchists would be released—and Philippe would not be able to bid on the Cullinan.

The sound of birds' wings in flight, a distant thunder, informed them now that the beaters were driving the flocks back toward them. The king, having awakened, was clearing his head with the help of hot and cold cloths supplied by his bearers. The shooting stands were repositioned to the hunters' advantage. Three more glasses of aged-in-the-wood whiskey were poured from the king's flask. The hunters raised their glasses as the king proposed a toast to the afternoon's shooting.

"Let us get on with the extinction of the grouse," His Majesty declared. He smiled, and expressed an afterthought of attribution: "As Miss Minerva so aptly put it."

4 . LONDON

THERE SHE WAS again, the Diamond girl, His Lordship's daughter, intent and slender, sitting on the bench in Hyde Park. Jacob Steiner frowned. This was his fourth—no, his fifth—encounter with her. What did she want of him?

Not long ago, Lord Diamond had come to the Savile Row shop, where Jacob Steiner was an apprentice, to be fitted for a formal business suit of cutaway coat, striped trousers, and pearl-gray vest. Mr. Lemburger, the master tailor and owner himself, had attended to His Lordship. Jacob had only been summoned later for sleeves and cuffs. The young woman had been sitting there looking bored, observing the proceedings by squinting over the tops of her spectacles, when Jacob entered. Then she had played closer attention, not hiding her interest in him.

She saw a narrowly built and gangly young man with joints that extruded—elbows, knees, hips—and an Adam's apple that jutted out from his thin, long neck like a parrot's wattle. He appeared clumsy in all things save his work, where his deft hand was never anything but steady and sure. His face had a mournful look to it, pale with a shadow of dark beard. No amount of time in the sun, and no amount of shaving, would alter the combination; that was plain to see. His cheekbones were as prominent as his elbows, and his ears were somewhat large and set at right angles to his elongated face. His eyes were dark, hooded, and doleful-looking. In no conventional sense could he have been considered handsome, and yet she plainly found his ungainliness compelling.

Jacob could not have known it, but Minerva Diamond was experiencing an emotion so intense as she scrutinized him that she questioned whether or not her stays would contain it. For the first time in her life, the swelling of her chest seemed about to burst the confines of her corset.

Was this love? Well, of course it was, she said to herself. Did the symptoms lack dignity? Yes, they did. When has it ever been otherwise? It's possible to scoff at the notion of love at first sight, but to the one smitten, the emotion cannot be denied.

Minerva took a second look. She could hardly be blamed. There had to be something more than bony, jutting elbows and a haunting, doleful countenance to justify the hammering of her heart and the dizziness she felt as she looked at this young tailor. She squinted. Jacob Steiner's looks had not changed. I am nearsighted, she reminded herself. And, besides, what I *feel* is more important than what anybody may see.

As she struggled to come to terms with her feelings, her head cleared, and she gradually regained her composure. Having dealt with the impact of her emotions, as she felt it was important to do, she felt relatively calm now. She was quite able to relax in the grip of the love that had so suddenly and unexpectedly seized her.

Minerva's outward demeanor revealed no hint of the turmoil of her inner emotions, of the sudden attack of love that she was experiencing. Jacob had seen in her a young woman whose hair, a few of its tendrils escaping its neat coiffure, was a subtle shade of brown, not at all shiny in the style of so many of the aristocratic young ladies he saw every day driving about London in their fashionable open carriages. Cosmetically glittered hair, so much the rage among chic women of the day, was to Jacob a falseness not in keeping with his ideals of womanhood—ideals that were very high. He approved the more modest sheen of Lord Diamond's daughter's tresses.

Lord Haran, however, had his mind on other things. "A men's tailoring shop is no place for a young girl," he said to his daughter, as if continuing an earlier argument.

"Really? Well now, Father, I understand about your club, but tell me, what wicked masculine pleasures does this innocent-seeming tailor shop conceal?"

"Don't be ridiculous, Minerva."

"Well, if you won't tell me, perhaps Master Lemburger will."

Mr. Lemburger held up his hands, laughing and pleading to be uninvolved.

"Then you, sir." The young woman had addressed Jacob Steiner directly. "What say you, Master—?" She turned to the owner for an identification of the tailor's apprentice. Minerva had to know who he was. She had already made up her mind to marry him.

"Steiner. Jacob Steiner," he told her. "Come now, Steiner, you must reply to Miss Diamond."

Jacob Steiner had been very red in the face, and his mournful mouth had been full of pins.

"I am so sorry." She saw that she had embarrassed him. "My father is right. I do apologize, Mr. Steiner."

"Not necessary, miss," Jacob Steiner had mumbled around his mouthful of pins. "Not necessary."

But her eyes had held him, myopic and intent. "I really am sorry." Her gaze had leapt the chasm between their stations. "I honestly had no wish to cause you discomfort."

Her low voice, its earnest tone, unexpectedly thrilled Jacob Steiner. He felt a stirring that had nothing to do with the job at hand. He had nodded—recognition? forgiveness?—lowered his hooded eyes, and bent to pin His Lordship's cuffs.

Three days later she had come to the shop alone. She had come at noon, when Mr. Lemburger habitually went home to lunch. So it was Jacob Steiner who answered her ring.

"Yes, miss?"

"I'm Minerva Diamond, Lord Diamond's daughter. Do you remember me?"

"Yes, miss. Of course."

"I've come about my father's trousers." She had leaned across the counter, her strong, longish face very close to his.

Her conduct might have seemed aggressive, but he recognized her nearsightedness and sensed that this thrusting of her face into his was meant as a friendly overture. "Yes, miss? There is something wrong about the pants?" Close up this way, Jacob was aware of how much the Polish accents of his boyhood still clung to his speech despite all his efforts to Anglicize it.

"I believe he ordered two pleats at the waist on each side?" Made tremulous by her own boldness at having come to the shop alone, Minerva's normally husky voice nevertheless came out sounding even deeper and huskier.

Jacob had to think back to remember. "Yes, miss," he said finally. "I'm pretty sure that is so."

"Well, he has changed his mind. He wants only one pleat on each side. He asked me to stop by and change the instructions."

"One pleat on each side?" Jacob was doubtful. That was definitely not the style of the day. "Are you sure, Miss Diamond?"

"Oh, yes." Her face was still very close to his. Her eyes, squinting a little, were nervous. They held a plea that he not embarrass her by questioning her excuse for coming. "I'm sure."

"Very well, then, Miss Diamond. I'll tell Mr. Lemburger."

"Thank you." She maintained the proximity an instant longer than was necessary. Then she straightened up from the counter and picked up her muff. "It was very nice to see you again, Mr. Steiner."

"You, too, Miss Diamond." Pleasure reddened his long face.

Somehow Jacob was not surprised when a few days later Minerva Diamond returned to the shop, again during Mr. Lemburger's lunch hour, to say she had been mistaken: Her father wanted the original design of four pleats to stand, rather than changing them to two. She had evidently misunderstood him. Really, she was very sorry for any inconvenience.

"The pleating hasn't started yet," he had assured her.

"Don't worry, Miss Diamond. There has been no inconvenience."

"Have you worked for Mr. Lemburger long, Mr. Steiner?" The casual question belied her tone.

"I was apprenticed to him six years ago. For the last year I have been his journeyman tailor."

"That would mean that you have advanced?"

"Yes, miss."

"And what will your next step be?"

"My next step?" Jacob had stalled. Only one next step was possible, and that one highly unlikely. It was to have a tailor shop of his own.

"Yes. You are obviously an ambitious young man. I only wondered—?"

"Mr. Lemburger treats me very well." Jacob cut her off in his nervousness. His employer might return from lunch at any moment. "I am happy in my work."

"I'm sure. It's just that you seem to be so good at it that I wondered . . ." Minerva floundered. Her eyes begged him to relieve the situation.

"There is much to learn on Savile Row, Miss Diamond. The tailors here are artisans, perhaps even artists. It will be many years before I master all that they have to teach me."

"That is very interesting. Fascinating. I would so like to know more about it." Her face was thrusting into his again, the gesture making the words a sort of cue. "Could you tell me more about it sometime?"

" 'Sometime.' " His dark, hooded eyes stared at her. Surely she couldn't expect him to suggest a meeting. She was a daughter of a Lord of the Realm, he a tailor. True, this was England, not Poland, but still!

Jacob was saved by Mr. Lemburger's return. "Miss Diamond, how nice to see you. Has Steiner here been taking care of you properly?"

"Oh, yes. It was nothing, Mr. Lemburger. Only about the pleats."

"The pleats. I see." Lemburger glanced sidewise at Jacob. He knew nothing about any pleats.

"I have to be going." Minerva smiled at Lemburger, and then at Jacob, on whom the smile lingered.

After she left, Lemburger turned to Jacob and inquired what this business was about the pleats. Jacob told him that she had been in a few days ago to request an alteration concerning the pleats of her father's trousers, but that today she had come by to cancel the request.

"Why did you not tell me when Miss Diamond came in the first time?" Lemburger wondered.

"I would have when we got to the pleating," Jacob replied. But it wasn't true. The real reason he didn't tell Lemburger was that he had been certain Minerva would be back to cancel the order.

A few Sundays later, Jacob attended a band concert sponsored by the Amalgamated Society of Tailors, a former craft guild that had evolved into one of England's first trade unions. The small, unnamed park where the concert was to be performed was widely known to be frequented by Jews in the London clothing trades. Jacob, accompanied by another journeyman tailor, a friend of his named Chaim Zlotow, had stretched out on a grassy knoll under the branches of an early budding elm tree and folded their jackets under their heads. While the band rendered a Beethoven's Third that was heavy on the brass and light on the strings, the two young men stared up at an ephemeral sky of drifting clouds filled for them with the nostalgia of Polish boyhood memories. An unexpected, very English, and very husky female voice roused them.

"Hello, Mr. Steiner."

They both looked up. Jacob blinked, and then scrambled to a sitting position. "Miss Diamond, hello." His brain could not take in the fact of her being there. This was not a place for the daughter of an English lord. "What are you doing here?" he blurted out.

"I came for the Beethoven. And you?"

"We hoped for Chopin." It was Chaim who answered her. "But as frequently happens, the German prevailed." He looked at Jacob, who was still blinking. "I am Steiner's friend, Chaim Zlotow." He introduced himself.

"I'm glad to know you, Mister Zlotow. I am Minerva Diamond."

"So, Jacob, here is a young lady ..." Chaim observed. "So, why have you never mentioned—?"

"Miss Diamond is Lord Haran Diamond's daughter," Jacob blurted out.

Chaim gulped and fell silent.

"May I sit down?" Minerva inquired, ignoring the frightened looks on the faces of both young men.

"Of course. Of course." With a noticeable lack of coordination, Jacob spread his jacket on the grass for her.

She sat, leaning on her parasol, her chin resting on the hand that was holding it perpendicular to the ground. Her face was leaning in toward Jacob. She smiled politely at Chaim every so often, but mostly she ignored him. "You are a music lover, Mr. Steiner?" she inquired of Jacob.

"Yes. I love music."

"I, too." Her smile was warm. When Jacob did not respond, she continued. "We have that in common."

"Yes." Nervously, he hugged his arms. His elbows seemed very much in the way.

"I wonder what else we might have in common."

There was a silence that stretched into eternity.

Amazingly, it was Chaim Zlotow who broke it. "Jacob likes to go to Hyde Park," he informed Minerva.

"Hyde Park?"

"To hear the speakers. The craziness, you know." Being in the presence of the famous Lord Haran's daughter had made Chaim Zlotow nervous, too, and there was a certain desperation, a babbling quality, to his speech.

"Chaim!" Jacob sat up straight suddenly. "Miss Diamond isn't interested—"

"But I am. What is it that attracts you there, Mr. Steiner?"

"Ideas. That anybody can get up and say, no matter how silly."

"Are they all silly, then?"

"No—no." Jacob felt himself on the defensive, all arms and legs and big ears. How to make her understand without sounding like one of the Hyde Park crazies himself? "In Poland, I was only a boy, but old enough to know that you do not say what you think. From others I hear most of Europe is like that. But here in England, in London, in Hyde Park at least, is everybody talking what they think. Not the ideas so much I go to hear, but just that they can do this."

"I see." Minerva nodded very slowly. She had taken what he said very seriously. She understood.

The moment passed. They chatted a while longer, but the awkwardness had returned. Chaim Zlotow, who was silent, was very much a part of it, the awkwardness. Finally, Minerva had gotten to her feet and left.

"You have made me curious," she said to Jacob as she departed. "Perhaps one day I will see you in Hyde Park."

"But not for the speeches," Chaim Zlotow remarked to his friend after she was gone.

"What do you mean?" Jacob muttered.

"For you, schnook. The lady goes to Hyde Park to find you, same as today she comes here."

"*Meshugener mamzer!*" Jacob overreacted. "What should Lord Diamond's daughter want from me?"

"Maybe she likes jugs with big handles." Chaim grabbed Jacob by his protruding ears, shook his head once, and then scrambled away before his friend could retaliate. "And so," he called out over the cymbals concluding the Beethoven, "Lord Diamond's daughter will go to the Hyde Park for such a jug."

So now here she was in Hyde Park, sitting on a bench diagonally across from Jacob Steiner and smiling a greeting. He nodded back, his long face as tragic-looking as always. He was embarrassed that at the moment their eyes had met his mouth had been full with too large a bite of the bologna sandwich that was his lunch. He chewed and swallowed it quickly, threw the remainder of the uneaten sandwich into a trash barrel, and brushed the crumbs from his chest.

Minerva watched Jacob patiently, waiting for him to finish composing himself. Her smile remained unchanged. Her heart was beating wildly. Her feelings for him had not abated. Love, Minerva was finding, is the most stubborn bacillus. Finally she raised a white-gloved hand and crooked a finger to him to come and join her. Just as he did, a speaker mounted the stump across from them and clapped his hands rapidly to attract an audience.

"Hello, Mr. Steiner. It's so nice to see you again."

"Hello, Miss Diamond."

"Actually," Minerva informed him as though he had asked why she was in Hyde Park, "I am here because of you. What you said about the Hyde Park speakers that afternoon at the band concert aroused my curiosity. So I thought that I would come and see for myself.

I was on the other side of the hedgerow before. There was a speaker there from the Wildlife Preservation Society. I'm a member." Minerva giggled, a rare sort of laughter for her. She was aware that she was babbling, but she couldn't seem to stop herself. He was sitting so close beside her on the bench . . . Well, not really . . . Not too close . . . Not close enough . . . "Of course, my father would have a fit if he knew that I was a member. I mean, he knows I'm against slaughtering animals. I have made that clear." Minerva stopped talking, made a determined effort, and composed herself. She was outwardly calm now—in contrast to Jacob, who was patently nervous—and she remained so.

"Not too many ladies come here unescorted." He blurted it out—the effect she seemed to have on him— and immediately regretted it.

"Ahh, well, surely in these modern times with universal suffrage just around the corner—"

"Suffrage!" Jacob's eyes became very big. "Are you a suffragist, Miss Diamond?"

"Not actively, I confess. However, my sympathies are with them."

"But you are Jewish." Jacob was confused.

"Oh, yes." Minerva was amused by Jacob's shock but did not allow herself to show it. "But we are a very modern family, religiously speaking. My European uncle is intermittently pious, and my grandmother always, but my father is less so. Are you very religious, Mr. Steiner?"

"No. But I believe that all things—people, that is— have their place. Men. Women. Old. Young. I believe that Jehovah has decreed this, and we are bound to live by it."

"I see." Minerva saw how serious he was. "But," she asked carefully, "do you believe that people— individuals—can change, Mr. Steiner?"

"Yes." He was cautious, sensing a trap.

"And you? Can you change?"

"I do change from time to time. I will again, I'm sure."

"Well, good." Minerva beamed. "Very good."

"What?" Jacob was confused.

"I'm glad that's settled." She rearranged her glasses on her nose and peered out over them. "Oh, look. He's going to speak."

A small crowd had gathered around, and now the man who had been clapping earlier began to speak "Citizens!" His voice was thunderous, sweeping the murmur of the crowd away before it. "Workers! My topic is the eight-hour day."

"A Socialist." Jacob shrugged.

"You are not in sympathy with the Socialists?" Minerva inquired.

"We have different goals. They want to do away with the bosses. I want to be a boss." Jacob caught himself. "Someday in the distant future," he was careful to add.

"I once went to a Fabian Society meeting," Minerva confessed. "I thought some of their ideas were very impressive."

"Your father let you go to such a meeting?" Jacob was shocked.

"He didn't know about it."

"A daughter should not deceive her father." Jacob spoke the words that were one of the absolutes in which he believed.

"Diamond!" The name roared forth from the speaker's soapbox, the high point to which his oratorical rhythms had been propelling him. "Lord Haran Diamond! That's who!"

"Oh, dear!" Minerva's attention was claimed. "He's saying something about Father."

Jacob started to get up from the bench, intending to escort her out of the area. "Perhaps we'd better—"

"No. Please, no. Sit down. I'm interested. I want to hear what he has to say."

"The House of Diamond controls seventy-five percent of the industrial output of Manchester and Leeds. Six-day weeks, ten-to-twelve-hour days, and factory workers worn out and discharged for slowing down when they reach forty years of age. To form a union is forbidden. All goods purchased from stores also owned and run by House of Diamond subsidiaries. Houses for the workers—hovels—owned by the Diamond landlords. Now contrast this, comrades, with the dividends declared to Diamond stockholders—a small, elite, wealthy group, as you know. They grow fat on the sweat of the factory workers. Is that right? I submit that it is not only not right, it is downright evil. Exploitation is the devil's work. Lord Haran Diamond is an exploiter. Lord Diamond is the Devil!"

"I insist that we should now leave!" Jacob's white face was even whiter than usual. "It is not right you should sit here, Miss Diamond, and listen to such lies about your father."

"But are they lies?" Minerva wondered. "It's certainly true that he wants no part of the eight-hour day, or of unions."

"He is your father," Jacob pronounced, as if that were sufficient to close the subject. "We should go now."

"And the workers are exploited. My father and his friends—they do believe that that is how it should be."

"Well, they are right," Jacob declared. "God has decreed that there should be bosses and there should be workers. When has it ever been any different? A worker can hope to be a boss, but until he is, while he is a worker, then he should be satisfied to work. He should put in his time and earn his pay." Without realizing it, Jacob was flapping his bony arms with the fervor of his belief.

"No," Minerva realized a trifle sadly. "You are certainly not a Socialist, Jacob Steiner."

"I am ambitious. Why should I be?"

"No matter what else, Father will be relieved about that."

"Relieved about what?" Jacob was bewildered. "Why should your father care what I believe?"

Because, Minerva thought, someday you are going to be his son-in-law, Jacob Steiner. Someday you are going to marry me. And then you are going to change some of your ideas. Someday . . .

But Minerva did not say any of that aloud.

5. FRANKFURT

LONDON WAS MUCH on the mind of the Baron Immanuel von Diamant as he settled into captivity. It was undoubtedly there, he thought, that his fate would be decided. His brother, Haran, would have assumed control of the House of Diamond, and his first, formidable task would be to deal with the abduction and all the problems that must inevitably have spun off from it.

Haran. The baron sighed. For as long as he could remember, theirs had been a sibling love-hate relationship. Always he had known that Haran measured himself against him, the older brother. Still, the baron decided, he must not let his predicament distort his picture of Haran. His brother loved him, and—although he might be tempted to cut some corners that the baron would never have cut—he was honorable. Yes, Haran might take advantage of the situation to implement some policies of which the baron would not approve, but there could be no doubt that he would do everything in his power to keep his older brother from harm. All else aside, the baron was certain that his brother would act in his best interest.

This attic that was his prison was itself a reminder of the time when he and Haran had been children. Until they were grown, they had shared an attic room very much like this one. But that house had been different, not run-down at all, indeed quite a lavish dwelling for the Judengasse.

Before the baron and his brother were born, in the days when the fortunes of Zelik Diamant had begun to prosper, he had asked for and received permission from the Jewish Council of Elders to make an arrangement with his landlord to upgrade the dwelling his family occupied. In effect, he had rebuilt it from the bottom up, although his landlord continued to own both the land on which the house stood and the house itself. It was only later, after the unification of Germany with its easing of restrictions on Jews, that Zelik's son, Gershon—the baron's father—was able to buy both the land and the house.

By that time, however, taking advantage of their new freedoms, Jews were leaving the ghetto in droves. In their wake, many of the older houses were torn down, and tenements—new, but otherwise not really an improvement—had been put up in their place. A working-class Christian population took over the area that had once been the Jewish ghetto. They paid no toll to come and go, and there were no chains locking them in at night; nevertheless, poverty imprisoned them in the area as surely as it had the Jews. And, irony of ironies, poverty and the rapid decay of the new "ghetto" made of the area a breeding ground for Frankfurt's new wave of anti-Semitism.

Despite this, at the insistence of Rebekah Diamant, the family had continued to live in the house that was today looked upon as a landmark of the long-gone Jewish ghetto. The house in which he was being held, Baron Immanuel was sure, was not regarded as a landmark. It was simply one of the few old ghetto houses that had not yet been razed. It was a crumbling slum dwelling. If he ever did gain his freedom, he thought to himself, it shouldn't be too difficult to identify this house again. The attic room, at least, was indelibly imprinted on his memory.

He was hardly ever alone in it. Jerzy, or Ammal, or Gabrielle constantly stood guard over him. One of them was always in the room with him. Only when he used the chamber pot did they post themselves outside the door.

With Jerzy and Ammal, the language barrier still prevented any communication. Sometimes, though, Gabrielle would deign to exchange a few words with him. She was becoming less taciturn, if no less confrontational, in her attitude toward the baron. Her tone during such conversations tended to be hostile, and their relationship was clearly defined by the shotgun she held at the ready. Her words floated out at the baron on a haze of blue smoke from one of the small, brown cigarettes she smoked, lighting one from the other.

"Why," she demanded one evening, "does the House of Diamond prop up the backward and tyrannical Austro-Hungarian monarchy, which can only exist on the backs of the people?"

"There are worse rulers than Emperor Franz Josef," the baron replied. "Worse royal houses than the Hapsburgs. In Russia, for instance, they have the Romanoffs."

"You are not a part of the Russian tyranny as far as I know. But you are a collaborator of the Austrian emperor. He is a self-proclaimed despot, and you are so greedy for profit that you embrace him."

"It's not that simple."

"Oh?" She was skeptical. "Well, I have time. Explain it to me, then."

"You said you were Jewish, Gabrielle. Then try to understand. It has to do with being Jewish."

"A handy excuse." She snorted.

"No, it's not. From the very beginning of his reign, Franz Josef stood up for Jewish rights. As long ago as eighteen forty-eight, shortly after he was crowned emperor, he announced his support for Jewish emancipation. The next year he granted recognition to the Viennese Jewish community. Two years later, he designated a million talers that had been derived from fines imposed upon the Jews of Hungary for a fund for Jewish education, including a rabbinical seminary in Budapest. He intervened on the side of Jewish defendants in a famous case accusing Jews of ritual murder. In eighteen sixty, he issued a decree allowing Jews to work at occupations formerly forbidden to them, and allowing them for the first time to own land. He raised Jews to the status of full citizens of the empire in eighteen sixty-seven. Two years later he went to Jerusalem and contributed generously toward the building of a synagogue there."

"Ancient history!" Gabrielle was contemptuous.

"No. I am only stating the background. Throughout his tenure, the emperor has made a point of visiting synagogues and other places where Jews congregate. He constantly assured Jews of his favor and protection. He praised their adherence to family values and their charitable practices. And, always, he denounced anti-Semitism."

" 'Charitable practices'!" A cloud of blue smoke enveloped the phrase. "The emperor exploits the poor for the rich. It's that simple. So of course he is a great admirer of charity, Jewish and otherwise. Except that his own charity is royally withheld."

"Franz Josef has consistently put himself at risk for the Jewish people," the baron insisted. "When, in eighteen ninety-two, the lower Austrian Diet passed a tax on Jewish physicians, he went to their meeting place and publicly accused them of promulgating 'a scandal and disgrace in the eyes of the world.' Twenty Jews, among them my father, and later myself, have been raised to the ranks of the Austrian aristocracy by him."

"And you brag about that? You think more aristocrats are a good thing because they are Jewish aristocrats?"

The baron would not be deterred. "Most recently, when the poison spread by *The Protocols of Zion* resulted in the notorious anti-Semite Karl Leuger's being three times elected mayor of Vienna, the emperor twice refused to confirm him in that post. On the third occasion, he combined the by then unavoidable confirmation with the bestowal of an Order of the Empire on Moritz Guedemann, Chief Rabbi of Vienna."

"Chief Rabbi! You think that's any different from kings and popes? All self-proclaimed leaders with their self-proclaimed divine right to lead, to rule, are exploiters of the people."

"Even the anti-Semites, both in Austria-Hungary and Germany, refer to Franz Josef as the *Judenkaiser*."

"King of the Jews." Gabrielle shrugged. "Just what we need. Another king."

"Not King of the Jews," Baron Immanuel corrected her, "so much as 'the Jews' king,' their dupe, their willing tool in the Jewish banker–anarchist conspiracy of the Elders of Zion as spelled out in the *Protocols*. That's what the anti-Semites mean."

"Do the *Protocols* really say there's a conspiracy between Jewish bankers and Jewish anarchists?" Gabrielle found that amusing.

"It's a convenient linkage for them. It simplifies things. It makes just being Jewish the crime. You don't have to be a banker swindling the people. You don't have to be a radical fomenting revolution. All you have to be is Jewish."

"But that's absurd." Gabrielle was indignant. "What have we to do with Jewish bankers?"

"It doesn't matter. You'll be punished for our sins, if not for your own. And we, for yours."

"We have no sins. We stand with the masses, the proletariat, the people. We stand with all those who are exploited by your Emperor Franz Josef, and by your House of Diamond, too."

Baron Immanuel regarded her with curiosity. How strange a Jewish woman she was with her chain-smoking and her guns. Compact and sturdy, this warrior woman was not unattractive, but she was so—so—implacable. To the baron, women had always been malleable by definition. The gender precluded ideologues, did it not? Revolutionaries were dangerous, of course, but a woman in revolt? That was very dangerous, indeed. "Never have I met a woman like you before," the baron told Gabrielle honestly.

"We don't travel in the same circles," she retorted drily. "At the emperor's court, the weapon of women is sex. I prefer my shotgun." She slapped the barrel, a gesture that conveyed strength but was at the same time strangely sensual.

The baron was genuinely confused. "I don't think of sex as a weapon," he replied.

"Of course sex is a weapon. It's how women lay siege

to power. That actress of the emperor's, for instance. How close would she get to any throne if she didn't share his bed?"

"Katharina Schratt? You do her an injustice." Baron Immanuel's tone was reproving. "I can assure you that her affection for the emperor is quite genuine."

"She is half his age." Gabrielle was skeptical.

"Age doesn't always matter. Women often seek and find qualities in the men they take as lovers that render youth unimportant."

Gabrielle raised a dark, heavy eyebrow. "And how old are you, Baron von Diamant?"

The question took him by surprise. "Fifty-four."

"And I suppose that you have *had* many women?"

The way she stressed the word *had* seemed odd. "I have had my share of agreeable companions."

"And since—umm—middle age? You have *had* many younger women, I suppose."

Again the accent on "had." What was she getting at? "I have known a few younger ladies." He shrugged.

"Known?" Her laugh was harsh. "In the Old Testament sense? Don't worry, you don't have to answer that," she added quickly. "The answer is self-evident. But tell me, Baron, do you never wish to have had a more mature woman?"

"I don't quite see what you're . . ."

"Don't you, Baron?" Gabrielle stood up. "My shift is over," she announced. "It is time for Ammal to take over guarding you."

"Oh." The baron's puzzlement was not relieved by her announcement.

Gabrielle laughed. "Will you miss me?"

"Will I—?"

"—miss me. My presence?" She placed a hand on her hip and stood provocatively. "Why, Baron, is that a blush I see?"

It was no such thing. But what was she up to? Why, suddenly, this uncharacteristic behavior?

"Well, I will miss you, my exploiting, capitalist baron." Amazingly, Gabrielle brushed his cheek with a quick kiss, and then she was gone.

The baron stared at the door that had closed behind her. Was he crazy? Or was this formidable woman who was guarding him, who frequently was all that stood between him and his freedom, making advances to him?

6 . AMSTERDAM

BABETTE WAS THE first woman Philippe Diamant had ever made love to who exploded with a love so pure and so consuming that he was compelled to respond in kind. Was he falling in love with her? Absurd! One had affairs with married women; frequently other men's wives became infatuated, even obsessive, toward one; but never the other way around! Besides, his affair with Babette—its physical side and its emotional side—had been deliberately contrived for reasons that had nothing to do with love. Philippe had initiated it only because she was the shortest route to her husband, because her husband was a member of the kaiser's inner circle, and because there was good reason to think that the kaiser might be behind the kidnapping of Philippe's father. In such a scheme, there was no room for falling in love with a married woman with two children.

A message from Babette had reached Philippe in Vienna. She would not be in Paris when he returned. Her husband had to go to Amsterdam on the kaiser's business. He had directed her to cut short her Paris visit and meet him there. But, Babette had added, his days would be occupied. Was there any chance that Philippe might make a side trip to Amsterdam on his way back to Paris from Vienna?

Actually, Philippe had two reasons besides Babette for coming to Amsterdam. One had to do with the bidding for the Cullinan Diamond. The other was a long-term political commitment that had little to do with the House of Diamond. And so he replied to Babette in the affirmative, and they had arranged a tryst.

She was lovelier, even, than the image his mind had retained during their brief parting. The petite, perfect body abrim with energy, that Gallic face with those large, melting brown eyes and delicately sculpted, vulnerable mouth, her unique combination of fragility and voluptuousness . . . indeed, the reality of Babette overwhelmed the memory. And her passionate reception of Philippe in his Amsterdam hotel room had imposed a new dimension on their affair.

First they had made love quickly, frenziedly, as lovers do after a parting. Then they had taken each other more slowly, more deeply. As they approached their climax together, Philippe had looked down into Babette's eyes and seen such unquestioning love that he felt an instant's panic that he might drown in such pureness of emotion. The instant vanished with their release, and they were left with a happily weary intimacy that fell into the plotting of lovers who because of circumstance must painstakingly arrange future meetings.

"When does your husband arrive in Amsterdam?" Philippe asked, cradling Babette's tousled head on his bare chest.

"At eight this evening. We're to have dinner at our hotel."

"Good. Suppose I were to run into you accidentally? You could introduce me as your rescuer."

"And then what?" Babette wondered.

"Then what?" Philippe did not confide his scheme to expedite his larger aims. "Why then, beloved, we shall see."

The dining room glittered with the gaslight of eighteen teardrop chandeliers. The hotel was the best in Amsterdam, and the cuisine and service reflected that. Dress was formal, and Babette had donned the latest-style evening gown, a souvenir of her Paris visit, a strapless boned bodice of velvet rising from a floor-length, narrow sheath. Her husband wore the full-dress uniform of the Prussian General Staff, and Philippe cut an elegant figure in black broadcloth tails, complete with white vest and the requisite white tie.

He strode past the Von Koerner table without taking notice, sure that Babette would hail him, as she did. "Monsieur Diamant." Philippe turned, green eyes questioning. He allowed the puzzled gaze to linger as if he recognized the lady who had called his name but was having trouble putting her into context. "The Bois de Boulogne," Babette softly reminded him. "You rescued my jewels—and me, as well."

"Of course." He bent over her hand and kissed it. "Forgive me, madame. Business. Things on my mind. I do apologize."

"This is my husband, Field Marshal von Koerner. Helmut, this is Philippe Diamant. Remember, I wrote to you how he saved me from—well, I don't know what."

"You exaggerate, madame. It was nothing." Philippe made a move as if to continue on his way.

"Are you dining here?" Babette's question stopped him.

"Yes, madame. The menu was highly recommended to me."

"With friends?"

"Alas, no. Alone."

"Helmut?" Babette turned to her husband.

"Of course, my dear." He addressed Philippe directly: "You must join us for dinner, my dear fellow. We are greatly in your debt. The least we can do is give you a decent dinner with—I hope—not too boring company." As friendly as his words were, his tone maintained its habitual imperiousness.

"I don't want to intrude—"

"No intrusion." Von Koerner snapped his fingers at a waiter. "A chair," he commanded.

"Well, then, thank you very much." Beware the Prussian stereotype, Philippe thought. Often he is exactly what he seems to be. "Actually, I was dreading dining alone."

From there on, Philippe put himself out to be charming to Von Koerner while neglecting Babette, a men's-talk attitude he suspected the field marshal would approve. "You have dueled?" He led off with an allusion to Von Koerner's scar.

"Yes." The field marshal, in turn, noticed the faint crescent on Philippe's cheek. "And you, too, I see. Where?"

"Heidelberg." It was true. Philippe had been a student there. More important, the mention of the prestigious German university forged an instant bond.

The conversation went on to cover business, and each man's reason for being in Amsterdam. Babette was virtually ignored. Philippe was vague, talking in the most general terms about ongoing interests in the jewelry trade. The field marshal, reading signs of expertise in Philippe's very vagueness, said forthrightly that he was in Amsterdam to purchase industrial diamonds for armaments manufacture. Two jagged lines appeared at the corners of his very Prussian mouth—a smile—and he added that he would appreciate any advice.

Philippe, who knew the Amsterdam diamond industry well, did not hesitate to give Von Koerner advice. It was good, solid advice, and would wear well. Chilly as he was by appearance and nature, the Prussian staff officer warmed noticeably toward this foppish-appearing but actually quite businesslike Parisian.

"I am very grateful," he announced. "If ever I can return the favor . . ."

"But you can," Philippe assured him. "I am going to Berlin on business next week, and you can return the favor by allowing me the pleasure of taking you and your lovely wife," here he looked toward Babette for the first time, "to dinner."

"You are going to Berlin? Well, then, you must certainly stay with us. Our home is quite large, and comfortable, too, I think. Yes, you must stay with us. Tell him that he must, my dear." Von Koerner's square face with the close-cropped pewter-colored hair turned to Babette as to a subaltern waiting at attention for orders. Behind her fan, she made a face at her husband to show her displeasure at his imposing a guest on her without prior consultation. He ignored it, as she knew he would.

"Thank you, madame." Philippe's green-eyed gaze was unfathomable, but Babette's heart beat as loudly as a pocket watch with its passionate message. "It will be quite delightful to be your guest."

The next afternoon, Philippe was the guest of a quite different sort of host and hostess. The rather unfashionable couple lived in a lower-middle-class Jewish section of Amsterdam, and their modest apartment had the

cluttered look of too much family. Philippe had been
introduced to them two years earlier by Theodor Herzl,
the founder and leader of the World Zionist movement.
Their names were Elijah and Belah Bronck, and they
were dedicated Zionists. They greeted Philippe's arrival
with remonstrances.

"If you wealthy and successful Jews will not support
us, who then?" Elijah Bronck was soon demanding.
"How can you of all people turn your backs on the
movement?" His blazing eyes implied that the fault was
Philippe's, although in fact Philippe supported the Zionist cause and was the least guilty of turning his back.
His sin to the Broncks was that he represented his class,
who for the most part were suspicious of the Zionists.

Philippe sighed. He had an answer, but it was not
one, he knew, that would satisfy the Broncks. The reaction he consistently met with whenever he broached
the subject to the very people that Elijah and Belah felt
had an obligation to help the cause was not merely
negative, but distrustful.

"Zionism?" Philippe's father, his uncle, and his cousins had all looked at him askance when he had announced his own commitment and suggested that the
House of Diamond support the establishment of a Jewish homeland. Like most wealthy Europeans, his family
thought Zionism a visionary scheme, socialist-tinged
twaddle that would likely boomerang and bring the
weight of public wrath down on the Jews of Europe.

Most well-off European Jews agreed. They deplored
the Zionist principle of cooperative land management,
which they considered unquestionably anticapitalist.
After all, Jews had long been denied the right to own
land, and now that they finally had it, here was a Jewish scheme to revive that notion. In their eyes, Zionism
was definitely a mask for socialism.

Many Jewish socialists, however, were themselves

anti-Zionist. As they saw it, by creating a homeland and separating Jewish and gentile workers, Zionism undermined the solidarity necessary to fight capitalist exploitation in Europe and America. Some Zionists might consider themselves socialist, but most Jewish Socialists regarded Zionism as a harebrained deviation.

Nor was there wide support among Jewish religious leaders. The orthodox regarded Zionism as a religious heresy. The conservative rabbis saw it as both a distraction from Torah—the righteous way—and as a threat to their own authority. Jewish religious leaders, both rabbinical and lay, of all sects, even the most liberal of the few new reformed synagogues, feared that the gentile rulers would view Zionism as a confirmation of the Jewish-conspiracy charges that were now being spread by *The Protocols of the Elders of Zion*. To them it was a provocation that could only result in increased anti-Semitic laws and violent reprisals.

And yet, among rank-and-file Jews, the dispossessed and the nonpolitical, the Zionist movement was slowly finding wider and wider acceptance in Europe. But nowhere—and Philippe Diamant had good reason to recognize this—were the Jews so ready to embrace Zionism as in France. The reason, of course, was the infamous Dreyfus Affair, which had stoked the fires of French anti-Semitism for twelve long years. Indeed, it was the Dreyfus Affair that had led Philippe to Zionism. Philippe loved France—its lighthearted mystique and free spirit reflected his own—but the dark side of the Dreyfus Affair was a denial of the rights of the French Republic to French Jews. As a response, Philippe had sought in vain for Jewish leadership to counter the stranglehold the anti-Semites were establishing on the French soul. Yet no such leadership seemed to exist in France, or in Europe, and then a pamphlet—*Der Judenstaat*—fell into his hands and he recognized that its author, Theodor Herzl, was a visionary with a plan that might be the salvation of the Jews of France and all Europe. Philippe decided to attend the Sixth Zionist Congress in Basel, Switzerland, in August of 1903. After hearing Herzl speak, Philippe had a private audience with him at his Geneva headquarters.

Herzl, as a correspondent for the Vienna-based *Neue Freie Presse*, one of Europe's most prestigious newspapers, had covered the opening chapters of the Dreyfus Affair in Paris. It was this experience that prompted him to formulate and particularize the idea of a separate Jewish state as a solution to anti-Semitism in Europe. He was thirty-six years old, he had a dream—*Yisrael*—and he spent the rest of his life campaigning for it at royal courts throughout Europe and the Middle East.

His efforts continued for eight years. He had many failures and some remarkable successes. On July 3, 1904, a month or so after a second meeting with Philippe Diamant, as Theodor Herzl was preparing to leave Switzerland for the latest in a series of private conferences aimed at persuading the Sultan of the Ottoman Empire in Constantinople to issue a charter allowing Jewish colonization of Palestine, he fell victim to a sudden heart attack. During the two years since his death, the movement had been gaining members, nevertheless declining due to lack of funds.

Now dedicated followers like the Broncks of Amsterdam were trying to resurrect Zionism from the grave of Theodor Herzl. To do this they needed money. Philippe was their contact with the powerful Jewish financiers. And when he was unable to gain support, they tended to blame him personally for the tycoons' lack of interest in the movement. It was a case of blaming the messenger, despite the fact that he was as committed to their cause as Philippe was.

Indeed, Philippe was totally committed. With anti-Semitism, sparked by the *Protocols*, spreading furiously across Europe, Philippe viewed the rebuilding of the Zionist movement as an urgent priority for Jews everywhere. His commitment had given new meaning to Philippe's life. And despite his absorption in plans to promote his father's release, the causes of Zionism were never far from his mind.

"More and more French Jews are embracing Zionism," Belah Bronck pointed out. She was softer and less demanding than her husband, but just as determined. "Proportionally, one and a half times as many of them have made application to emigrate to the Holy Land compared to Dutch Jews. We understand the politics of this, but what we don't understand is how the most powerful French Jews such as the House of Diamond can turn their backs. If not you, who else will provide the money for your countrymen to resettle in the Holy Land?" She came back to the question her husband had raised.

The bottom line. Philippe was being told to put his money where his mouth was. "I will make another contribution," he promised.

"And the others?"

"I will go back to them again and try. I will do my best."

"We can't function on promises. Do better than your best," Elijah Bronck told him. "Come see us the next time with money, not excuses."

Guilt! Nobody could make a Jew feel guilt like another Jew.

Despite his promises to the Broncks, Philippe knew that raising money for the Zionists would not be his priority when he returned to Paris. The plight of his father must come first. He would have to arrange for a private meeting with Clemenceau.

Philippe anticipated that it would not be a pleasant meeting. He would have to call in some favors that he well knew the premier was not in a very good position to redeem. The bottom line was that Clemenceau had been put into office with the help of House of Diamond money—a fact that, if it should become known, would provide the Anti-Semitic Party with the ammunition it needed to drive the fiery little leader from office.

Thus, to threaten exposure was a betrayal of Clemenceau to their common enemy. If his father's life were not at stake, Philippe would never have considered doing it. Indeed, he fervently hoped it wouldn't come to that. But if it did . . .

Clemenceau must be persuaded to release—either by public pardon, or secret arrangement—the six anarchist bombers being held on Devil's Island. The kidnappers' demand that they be transported to Argentina and released must be met. It would not be a popular thing to do, thus all the more reason to do it secretly. Even though their attempted bombing had not been successful, the very fact that they had targeted a passenger train—a reminder of past anarchist carnage that had resulted in the killing of fifty-odd people with one act— put public opinion squarely on the side of maximum punishment. Indeed, there had been a public outcry at the time of their trial that they be guillotined. A life sentence on Devil's Island was a punishment viewed by many as an overly lenient compromise.

Nevertheless, now they must be freed. Philippe would do what he had to do to bring about their release. Knowing this, however, didn't make him look forward to Paris.

In any case, before Philippe could leave Amsterdam, it was necessary that he visit the world-famous Diamond Exchange. His family had been among those who originally established the exchange. The man he went to see was well aware of that fact and greeted Philippe with rather more bowing and scraping than was necessary.

"I had not expected to see you in person, Meneer Diamant." He came close to knocking Philippe over with the chair he offered him. "Nor to hear your bid so soon."

Philippe did not tell him that he had come personally to place a response bid for the Cullinan Diamond before his uncle, Lord Haran, could catch up with him and interfere with his plans to buy the world's largest diamond. "I believe the last bid was from Sir Everard Hambro in London," he replied. "May I know what it was?"

The functionary told him. Philippe was taken aback. It was far lower than he had anticipated. Sir Everard must have known that he would go higher. With the bidding almost at an end, the other major bidders all eliminated, Philippe would have little problem going on record with an offer sure to secure the diamond for himself. Why had Sir Everard decided to let him have it?

Never look a gift horse in the mouth. Philippe shrugged. He jotted down a figure on a slip of paper, passed the paper to the functionary, and rose to leave.

"The usual twenty-four hours," the bid handler reminded him.

That was how long he had to change his mind—to raise, or to cancel. "I know." Philippe bowed and left.

Back at his hotel there was a messenger waiting for Philippe. He had come all the way from London to Amsterdam to hand-deliver a missive from his uncle. Philippe, fearing that it might be in regard to the diamond, considered refusing the delivery; but in the end he accepted the message and took it up to his suite to read.

The letter informed Philippe of the tacit agreement Lord Haran had reached with Sir Everard Hambro. The release of the Spanish anarchists from Rio de Oro would be arranged by Sir Everard out of concern for Baron Immanuel. Gratitude demanded that Philippe withdraw from the bidding for the Cullinan Diamond and leave Sir Everard a clear field. It was as he feared. In the end his uncle's will had prevailed. Philippe could not play cat-and-mouse with this demand as he had with those that had preceded it. Not with his father's life hanging in the balance. At least he knew that one more of the demands had been met.

Philippe picked up the telephone. He called the man he had just left at the Diamond Exchange and instructed him to cancel his bid on the Cullinan Diamond.

7. NEW YORK

"MY BOY, WE have backed the wrong horse." Marcus Diamond and his son, Noah, were sipping brandy from snifters in the library of the town house they shared on upper Fifth Avenue. "Somehow Lord Haran has pulled the rug out from under Philippe. The Cullinan has slipped through our cousin's fingers." Marcus did not have to add that any success for Lord Haran bore the seeds of defeat for them.

"Do you suppose Philippe's withdrawal has anything to do with his father's kidnapping?" Noah stretched his legs out toward the flames crackling in the marble-manteled fireplace.

"In the same sense that the rug's being pulled out from under our Panama Canal commitment has," Marcus snorted. "Our leadership—Philippe's and ours—no longer comes from benevolent Vienna, rather from me-first Uncle John Bull."

Noah smiled slightly at his father's phrasing. Marcus had a truly American suspicion of the British. "What will we do about the abductors' demands?" Noah wondered. "Will it be possible to engineer Alexander Berkman's release? Why is he in prison, anyway? What was his crime?"

"You don't remember the case?"

"It was fourteen years ago, Father," Noah reminded him. "I was only a boy. What was it all about?"

"*Cherchez la femme.*" Marcus smiled. "It began with a ménage à trois involving the anarchist Emma Goldman and Johann Most, who was editor of the socialist newspaper *Freiheit*, and Alexander Berkman, who like Red Emma was a firebrand Russian anarchist. It seems that Berkman became jealous of Most. It wasn't just sexual. Most was a prominent radical, while Berkman was a nobody. Anyway, he became convinced that Emma was slipping away from him, and that Most's prestige was the reason. It was not true, as later became obvious. Emma loved her 'Sacha'—that's what she called Berkman—best. But Berkman was blind to the reality."

Marcus Diamond warmed to the subject. "Now, at the very time that Berkman's jealousy and feelings of inferiority were at a peak, a strike broke out against the Carnegie Steel Company in Pennsylvania. Andrew Carnegie, refusing to be intimidated, went off to fish for salmon and left his blue-blood, socially connected plant manager Henry Clay Frick in charge. Frick, following instructions—and no doubt elaborating on them—brought in strikebreakers, and violence broke out. Ten men were killed. Many more were wounded, and eight thousand militia were called up to ensure that the Carnegie plant could continue to operate.

"Crazily enough, in these circumstances Berkman thought he saw a way to impress Emma and to overshadow her other lover, his rival, Johann Most. He went to the Carnegie Steel Company and—incredibly—bluffed his way into Frick's office, by pretending to be the representative of an outfit that could provide more strikebreakers. Once inside the office he pulled out a revolver and shot Frick, wounding him in the neck and in the right side. Guards rushed into the office and wrestled the gun away from Berkman." Marcus paused dramatically. "He then produced a dagger and stabbed Frick repeatedly in the side and the legs. He inflicted at least seven more stab wounds before he was finally pulled off him and subdued.

"Amazingly, Frick lived. Berkman was convicted and sent to prison, where he still languishes. But that isn't the end of the story. Shortly after the trial, Johann Most denounced Berkman's deed in his newspaper, *Freiheit*, claiming it was counterproductive and had hurt the cause of labor. He repeated this denunciation from the speaker's podium of a socialist meeting when suddenly, from the audience, up sprang Emma Goldman with a horsewhip. She publicly flayed her lover for criticizing the 'legitimate anarchist act' of her other—and now favored—lover, Alexander 'Sacha' Berkman."

"But what Emma Goldman did had nothing really to do with Berkman's crime," Noah protested.

"In the public mind it did. The papers had a field day. Public opinion was stirred up against all those 'crazy anarchists,' and of course against the strikers as well. The strike was broken. For the American public, Berkman and Red Emma and their ménage à trois came to

symbolize the immorality and violence of the anarchists."

"All that was a long time ago," Noah reminded his
father. "People forget. Perhaps if a pardon could be
arranged discreetly . . ."

"In America, all things are possible." Marcus took out
a cigar and snipped off the end of it with a bejeweled
cutter. "I shall arrange a quiet talk with Andrew."

"Carnegie? But isn't it out of his hands? Isn't Berkman under the jurisdiction of the prison system now?"

"The prison system? Do you mean the government,
Noah?" His father's smile was sweet and innocent and
not at all cynical, as it might well have been. "Carnegie
Steel's government? Andrew's government?"

"I see."

"Mercy, Andrew. Mercy for the worst among us.
Berkman's crime was the deed of a crazy man. An insane act. But as we all know, while criminality is cul-
pable, insanity passes. And when it does, should we not
show leniency, forgiveness? We are, after all, as my
good friend Andrew keeps reminding me, a Christian
country."

Inadvertently, Marcus had touched on a sore point
with his son. "That was not your attitude, Father," Noah
reminded him, "when we discussed my feelings toward
Olivia Hamilton."

"I said the country was Christian, Noah. I did not say
that we were." Marcus held up a hand that gleamed
white against the mahogany of the library's wood pan-
eling. "Let's not rehash that argument, my boy. You
know my feelings. You are an adult. You will most
likely do as you wish." He puffed deeply on his cigar
and slowly exhaled a controlled curl of smoke. "By the
way, where is the fair Olivia? I note with pleasure that
this is the third night running that I have had the plea-

sure of your company. Are you running up against some competition, my boy?"

"No. She's in Virginia with her family."

"Oh? I had the impression she came to New York to get away from her family."

"It's the start of the fox-hunting season," Noah informed his father stiffly.

"The fox-hunting season." Marcus was amused. "Well, there's no competing with that. No matter how hard those heretic Belmonts with their stables and race course try to pretend to horsemanship, we Jews are not born to the saddle. One has only to observe the Goog girls suffering the bridle paths of Central Park to confirm that equestrianism is not our heritage."

"I understand you've had some conflict with the One Hundred." Noah picked up on his father's allusion to the wealthy uptown German-Jewish families by the conceit they had assigned to themselves. The "One Hundred" was meant to imply a greater exclusivity than New York gentile society's "Four Hundred."

"The Old Guard is on one of its periodic reform rampages." Marcus was disapproving. "I swear it's one of our less desirable German-Jewish traits. No sooner do our young women graduate from their exclusive New York City finishing schools, whose screening processes we went to such pains to subvert in order to have them admitted, than they troop off to the Lower East Side to perform good works in the settlement houses and among the immigrant dregs of Italy, Poland, and Russia."

"Those Poles and Russians are mostly Jews," Noah reminded his father.

"Eastern Jewry." Marcus shrugged his disdain. "Not like us, my boy. Unlettered, or Hassid, or even socialist. Night and day from the German Jews. No culture. None. And they are flooding into New York in truly alarming numbers. Mark my word, they will never assimilate as we have done."

"Why are you so upset? What do the do-gooders want from you?"

"They're on a rampage about the Lower East Side sweatshops. Child labor. Unsafe working conditions. The more outrageous among them are even talking about a minimum wage and an eight-hour working day. I swear, Noah, they go down there to teach these people's children how to read and write English and they come back Bolsheviks. I think the radicals have a program aimed at subverting altruistic women."

"But we don't run sweatshops," Noah pointed out. "We're not involved in the garment industry."

"It seems that we own six buildings with sweatshops in them." Marcus held up his hands as if denying some charge. "I swear, I wasn't even aware of it myself, Noah. I knew we owned property downtown, but I had no idea who the tenants were. One of the do-gooders went down to City Hall and looked up the real estate records. Now they want us as the landlord to do something about conditions in the buildings. Bring them up to code, and so forth. A delegation of them called on me the other day. I play pinochle with some of their fathers. Of course, I said we'd look into it."

"But don't we employ people to manage these buildings for us?" Noah remembered.

"Yes. There is a management firm. And they assign a superintendent, of course. But the sweatshop operators buy him off first thing. And he, I suppose, takes care of the city inspectors. It's a corrupt system all the way up and down the line." Marcus sighed, grinding out his cigar. "I had to say that we would check to see if there were violations and correct them if there were."

"We being me, Papa?" Noah laughed.

"Would you, my boy? I'd be eternally grateful."

"Eternally?" Noah laughed. "Why then, of course I will, Papa."

A few days later, Noah went by hired coach to Division Street, disembarking in what was clearly a slum area. There was a miasma over the street—steam off the pressing irons coming from the sweatshops of the high, narrow buildings on every side—and the smell of human waste and garbage. The streets were teeming. Having never been down there before, Noah was appalled by the sights and smells.

Children were everywhere, their faces dirty, their clothes ragged. No matter the age, their eyes were feral, narrowed, as if on the lookout for opportunity. Noah watched as a fight broke out among one group of them over a discarded cigar butt. Even the little girls cocked their heads at him with a disturbing air of adult wisdom. Only slightly older were the obvious prostitutes. As they solicited, they bypassed small groups of men on their knees shooting dice. But they left the gamblers alone. They knew from experience that gambling men could not be distracted by offers of sex—not until they were way ahead in their winnings, anyway, and then the men would find them.

Many hacking coughs split the chill air. Noah had heard that tuberculosis was epidemic among the immigrant poor, even though many were turned back from Ellis Island because they showed symptoms of the disease. Still, the people in the street seemed to ignore the icy breeze knifing in off the East River.

Communication was carried on at top volume. Many tongues filled the air, although Sicilian Italian and Yiddish predominated. The screaming was particularly harsh around the outdoor stalls of the vendors selling every kind of goods.

Noah felt conspicuous. His customary business suit

with the light duster over it stuck out in a forest of raggedy garments. His silver-knobbed cane drew acquisitive glances. Some of the unshaven faces seemed to be regarding him as wolves eye a caribou slogging through high snow.

Finally he found the building for which he had been looking. The super was respectful and obliging, and considerably worried by his presence. He agreed uneasily to Noah's suggestion that they start their inspection at the top and work their way down.

They trudged up eight narrow, dark flights of stairs. When they reached the top, the exit door was stuck. Noah tugged at it with all his strength, but it wouldn't budge. He turned to the super questioningly.

"Kessler Ready-to-Wear," the super explained. "The Heinie, Kessler, he keeps the door locked so his cutters can't sneak out for a smoke."

"Isn't having the door locked against the fire laws?"

"I guess so." The super scratched his head.

"Is there another door to Kessler's?"

"Oh, sure. He's got the whole loft, the whole top floor. There's two other doors, plus there's a sort of steel ladder runs up to the roof."

"Well, what about those doors? Are they left opened?"

The super scratched his head again. "I doubt it. Kessler's a real Dutchman, know what I mean? I think he locks everything and only opens up when the workday is over."

"What about the roof?"

"He had me nail that one shut." The super smiled slightly. "Caught one of his cutters sparking a sleeve girl up there. They tried to say they were on their lunch break, but Kessler, he's got a rule they have to eat their lunch at their machines, so he fired them both and then he had me nail the door."

"And you nailed it for him? Just like that? Without checking with my father, or me?"

"Didn't want to bother anybody," the super mumbled. "Kessler's the tenant. My orders is to keep the tenants happy. So that's what I done."

"Let's go in." Noah indicated the locked door.

"Okay. Okay." The super began pounding on the door and yelling "Mister Kessler!" repeatedly and loudly until finally the door was opened.

"What is it?" The fat, red-faced man standing there glaring at them from small, pig eyes was clearly annoyed. "It's working time now. Why do you bother me?" His accent was guttural.

"This here is Mr. Diamond."

"So?" He stood barring the door.

"He's your landlord."

"*Ja?* Hello, landlord. I always pay my rent on time. It's not due until next week. Now, I've got a factory to run here." He started to close the door in their faces.

"This loft isn't zoned for a factory." Noah made it up on the spur of the moment. He didn't think Kessler would know one way or the other how the property was zoned. "That's why I'm here. To inspect the premises."

"I pay my rent. That's your only business with me. Why should I let you inspect my premises?"

"Because if you don't," Noah told him, "I'll evict you."

Kessler stared at him, malevolence gleaming in the porcine eyes. "All right," he relented. "Inspect."

Trailed by the super, Noah entered the sweatshop. Over twenty girls with tired eyes and beetled brows, poorly dressed and washed-out looking, sat over their sewing machines stitching together cheap children's summer dresses. Up the line from them, seated around a large table, were the cutters, scissoring sleeves and bodices and skirts according to preset patterns and sizes. Behind them were two pattern-makers who were working out the specifications for various sizes and materials. At the other end of the line, two boys, scarcely into their teens, packed boxes of the finished goods, labeled them, and stacked them for delivery.

Even as he walked beside Noah and the super, Kessler kept darting off to the side to make sure the line kept moving. An idle girl at one of the sewing machines was a sure sign that the girl just before her was dawdling. Even with Noah there, he was harsh and threatened the malingerers who held up his line. Time was money, and sewing-machine girls were a dime a dozen, and jobs—he reminded them—were hard to get. The "girls," ranging in age from prepuberty to over sixty, were all intimidated.

One, however, Noah noticed, seemed slightly less intimidated than the rest. She had been working quickly and effortlessly, her fingers nimble, her movements sure. Nevertheless, she was forced to pause to allow the girl on the line before her to catch up. When Kessler came rushing over to harangue the slowpoke, telling her to pump the pedal harder so that the needle would fly more swiftly over the material, the red-headed girl with the quick fingers remonstrated with him. "You want her to put the needle through her finger, Mr. Kessler?" Her English was pure New York with no trace of a foreign accent. "She's new. Give her a chance to pick up the rhythm."

"This is not a training school. And you butt out, girlie, or maybe two of you will be looking for jobs."

"You don't scare me, Mr. Kessler. I'm experienced and fast, and I can get a job anyplace and they'll be glad to have me. And you know that." She stared him down.

"All right. All right," he mumbled. "Get back to work, both of you. Time is money. My money."

She must be Irish, Noah decided. She had curly red hair and her rolled-up sleeves revealed arms covered with freckles. And the way she spoke up. Oh yes, she must be Irish.

When Noah had finished his tour of the premises, he turned to Kessler. They were only a few feet away from the redheaded girl bent over her sewing machine. He had to speak loudly to be heard over the cacophonous noise of dozens of sewing machines. "You have to make some changes," he told Kessler, his tone a reminder of the threat of eviction he'd made before. "All three doors have to be kept unbolted. That's a fire law. You have to open the trapdoor to the roof for ventilation. You have to put in another toilet."

"Another toilet!" Kessler exploded. "You're crazy."

"You have men and women here. You have to have a toilet for each. It's the law. And you have to keep them both in working order. The one you have is all stopped up."

"I'm not a plumber," Kessler protested.

"Then get a plumber," Noah told him. "And oh, yes, in the summer, you have to pry out the nails holding those windows shut and let some air into this place. With all this steam from the irons, I don't even know how your employees can stand it now."

"Are you crazy? My materials will blow every which way."

"Your employees are entitled to breathe, and to have some relief from the heat in the summer."

"You're so concerned about my employees, Mr. Diamond, let me tell you something." In his excitement, Kessler's words ran together more gutturally than ever. "I open those windows and the material flies, it's their fingers will get all tangled up with the needles in the machines."

The redheaded girl rattled off two quick sentences to

the girl next to her. Noah stared at her, amazed. She had spoken in fluent Yiddish. What she said was: "If he hires two boys to work the line and hold the material out of the breeze, that's enough so nobody's fingers get tangled. That's what the big uptown apparel places do."

"Hire two boys to keep the material from getting blown around," Noah told Kessler. "That's what the reputable manufacturers do."

The redhead spun quickly around from her machine and shot him a broad grin. Curving under her pug nose the way it did, it made her look more Irish than ever. Then, before Kessler could come down on her, she turned back, and the material was once again flying between her fingers.

"All right. All right." Kessler backed down quickly, agreeing to everything.

He just wanted him out of there. Noah saw that. "Someone will be back to check from time to time," he warned him. "If you don't take care of the things I mentioned, Mr. Kessler, make no mistake about it, I will evict you." Noah left then, and along with the super climbed down the flight of stairs to the floor below.

It was after nightfall when Noah finished with the building. He had planned to inspect all six properties on his father's list in one day, but there were many more violations than he had anticipated. Writing them down was time-consuming. Noah had filled a thick pad with notes for follow-up to ensure the sweatshops complied at least minimally with the law. His ears were ringing from the noise, and he was exhausted and hungry.

He exited to the thunder of footsteps descending the narrow staircase. The sound marked the end of the workday. They would be back at six the next morning. Noah recognized the red-haired girl from Kessler's with a group of other women. Then she was swallowed up by the crowded street.

Rubbing his eyes and squinting into the poorly lit streets, Noah realized that he had no idea of how to get home. It hadn't occurred to him before, but it was a most unlikely area to find a coach for hire. He started to walk uptown.

The crowd thinned out. Somehow he had gotten turned around on Division Street and couldn't seem to find his way back to East Broadway. He passed an alley, and peering down its tunnel-length, saw bright street-lights at the other end. It appeared to be a shopping district. He cut down the alley.

No sooner had he entered it than there was a rush of footsteps from behind him. He swung around with his cane raised to ward off the expected attack, but he wasn't quick enough. One of the men ducked under the walking stick and grabbed Noah by the throat. The other lunged for the cane, wrenched it from Noah's grasp, and struck him a glancing blow on the side of the head with it. Still struggling, Noah was borne to the garbage-littered ground.

Even as he grappled with the first thug, the second one was attempting to go through his pockets. Noah sank his teeth in the searcher's wrist and at the same time managed to jam a thumb into the eye of the man on top of him. The weight atop him eased and Noah tried to scramble out from under it. A fist of metallic knuckles glanced off his cheekbone, splitting the skin, and he went down again.

"Bastard bit me!"

"You get his dibs?"

"Not yet. He drew blood." The hoodlum raised Noah's cane. "Let's finish him. It'll be easier."

"Beats sitting on him. Go ahead."

Noah saw the silver knob of the cane describe a vicious arc toward his skull and barely managed to jerk his head out of the way. Even so, it grazed him, leaving more sharp pain and some dizziness in its wake. Struggling for his life now, Noah felt faint and weak and at their mercy.

Suddenly, from behind the two men, a slight figure appeared wielding a wooden plank with a rusty nail sticking out of one end of it. The plank bounced hard off the shoulder of one of Noah's assailants, and then the nail raked the cheek of the other one. With the weight off him, Noah summoned the last of his strength and came up swinging. The plank struck again. First one of the attackers, and then the other, turned heel and fled down the alley.

"Are you all right?" To Noah's amazement, it was a woman's voice.

"Yes." Even as he spoke, a sharp pain crossed Noah's scalp. He put his hand up to it and found his hair matted with blood. "I think so." His voice was doubtful.

"Let's get you out into the light and see." She took his arm and put it around her shoulder so that his weight was on her. "Slow and easy. That's it. Lean on me."

Out in the street, under the gaslight, Noah saw the woman's face. It was the redhead from Kessler's sweatshop. Her features came into focus, and then blurred. The lampposts tilted and his legs wobbled under him.

"You need to lie down and rest for a little while. And your head should be bandaged." She put an arm around his waist and guided him down one block and into another.

She turned into a building entrance. They traversed a narrow, dark hallway and went up a creaky flight of stairs. She let them into a small apartment, struck a match, lit the gaslight, and turned it up. She led Noah to a sofa, where he gratefully sat down. "Stretch out.

Lie back. I'll get some water to clean up those cuts."
She vanished back into the hallway again. There was
no bathroom and no water tap in the apartment.

Without moving—he still felt weak and dizzy—Noah
looked around him. Clearly there was only the one
room. The only other door besides the one they'd entered by was ajar and revealed an overflowing closet.
There was a bed across from the couch on which he
was lying, a stove against one wall, and a small icebox
and some food cabinets. There was one window, and
Noah could make out a fire escape outside it.

The redhead returned with a basin filled with water
and some clean cloths. She examined Noah's head.
"Mostly just scratches," she told him. "But there's one
real gash. I'll bandage it for you."

"This is very kind of you." Noah expressed appreci-
ation as she gently sponged his wounds.

"I'm glad to do it. I liked the way you talked to Kessler before. With us, he has all the power, but not with
you. You were pushing him to make the workplace
better for us, and he was giving in. It's the only good
feeling I ever had on the job at Kessler's. It's like I read
in one of those books at night school: 'The enemy of
my enemy is my friend.' So you're my friend, Mr. Diamond." Her broad grin lit up her face.

"How do you know my name?"

"I heard Mr. Kessler call you by it."

"I see. And might I know yours?"

"Levine. Naomi Levine."

"I thought you were Irish until"—Noah remembered—"I heard you speak Yiddish."

"Other people have made that mistake. Is it my pug
nose, do you think? Or my belligerent chin." Naomi
Levine laughed. "I know it couldn't be my freckles."
She had finished cleaning the gash on his head. "Actually, my people were Polish. And 'Levine' was what

was left of their name after Immigration got through shaving most of the letters off it." She started to wind the bandage around his forehead. "And you, Mr. Diamond? Are you Irish?" she teased.

"*Bist meshugeh?*" He answered her in Yiddish. "Are you crazy?"

Naomi Levine laughed and stood up. Like Noah, she was of medium height, a little shorter than he, her figure slender, but sturdy, competent-looking. She examined his head from the top. "I think we've covered the battleground. How do you feel?"

"All right. A little wobbly maybe."

"Then rest awhile. Get your walking legs back."

"Do you live here alone?" Noah wondered idly.

"With a roommate. She's on the night shift at Triangle Shirtwaist. We hardly ever see each other." Naomi Levine followed his eyes. "The bed is hers. I sleep on this couch. I have no family," she added matter-of-factly. "I'm an orphan."

"I'm sorry."

"No need to be. I've been an orphan since I was eight years old. I'm used to it."

"Lucky for me you came along when you did." Noah shifted topics.

"It wasn't an accident. I saw Kessler finger you."

"Kessler fingered me?" Noah blinked. "You mean he paid those hoodlums to beat me up?"

"Oh, no." Naomi laughed. "Kessler's too cheap for that. As much labor trouble as he's got, he never hires goons. No, all he did was point you out to them. Dressed all spiffy the way you are, they knew a target of opportunity when they saw one. Everybody in the neighborhood knows them for the jackrollers they are."

"I think they might have killed me."

"Well"—her blue eyes were twinkling—"you shouldn't have antagonized them."

"Antagonized them?"

"Oh, yes. There are two choices down here when you're being robbed, Mr. Diamond. Your money, or your life. The wise man surrenders his money without provoking the jackrollers. Better a simple business transaction than that blood should flow."

"A business transaction?"

"Oh, yes. Not so very different from the way you do business uptown, when you stop to think about it. Except you're more fastidious, so you don't have to personally get your victims' blood on your hands."

"You sound like a Socialist," Noah realized.

"I am a Socialist," Naomi said matter of factly. "What else should I be? I'm not rich enough to be a Republican. And I don't have the Tammany connections to succeed as a Democrat. Besides, it's the Democrats keep the Kesslers in business and look the other way at the sweatshops. Only the Socialists can offer a solution to poor people like me because, you see, they're not part of the problem."

"You're the first Socialist I've ever met," Noah confessed.

"And you expected horns and a tail?"

"Well, no. But I have heard that Socialists espouse some pretty outrageous ideas."

"Such as?"

"Well . . . free love, for instance." Noah blurted it out.

Naomi Levine threw back her head, copper curls swirling in the gaslight, and laughed without humor. "It's what I always tell my Socialist sisters. The capitalists are all men. Never mind about the eight-hour day and the minimum wage. It's free love will put their backs to the wall every time." Her blue eyes flashed cynically. "That's a double standard, Mr. Diamond. Men can rove at will, but a woman who does the same—

who believes in free love—is immoral. That's it, isn't it?"

Actually, that was exactly what Noah believed. "Women aren't the same as men," he said helplessly, feeling trapped. Wanting to end the discussion, he struggled to his feet, still a touch wobbly. "I am in your debt," he acknowledged. "I should like to show my gratitude." He reached inside his jacket for his wallet.

"Oh, money!" She clapped her hands. "You're going to give me some of your money."

"Well, I only thought—"

"Oh, it's perfectly all right." Naomi touched his arm in assurance. "It's fine. You have so much, and I, frankly, have none at all. At least until payday. How much will you give me?"

Red in the face, Noah examined his wallet. There was eighty dollars in tens and twenties in it, but he would have to keep some for a cab—if he could find a cab in this godforsaken corner of the city. He took out sixty dollars and handed it to Naomi.

She counted it. "Sixty dollars. Is that what your life is worth, Mr. Diamond?" There was no malice in her tone. She asked it as if it were the most innocent question in the world, as if she were simply requesting information.

"If you will write down your address, I will send you more."

"Oh, I was going to write down my address for you anyway. I was hoping you'd come back so we could talk about socialism some more. And," she added, looking up almost shyly, "free love."

" 'Free love,' " Noah echoed.

"Why, yes, Mr. Diamond." Her look was bolder now. "I have told you my views on free love, but you haven't told me yours."

"I don't understand." Noah was wary.

"It's very simple. You appeal to me. I am exercising my right to freely choose a partner with whom to make love. Now the only question is whether or not your choice coincides with mine." Despite the bold words, Naomi's face was faintly flushed.

Noah stared at her. The cloud of her red hair shimmered in the gaslight, and her slim figure stood taut with the tension of what she was proposing. Her small breasts rose and fell rapidly, but she did not lower her eyes.

"Yes," he decided impulsively, before he echoed her words. "My choice coincides with yours."

"Very well, then." She gravely held out her hand to him with the bills he had given her still in it.

Noah looked down at the money uncomprehendingly.

"I will take your money, or I will share my bed with you, but not both. Prostitution is a capitalist enterprise."

Noah took the money back without protest. He replaced it in his wallet and carefully put the wallet back in his inside jacket pocket.

Naomi grinned her wide grin again. "Although I'll probably hate myself tomorrow when I think of all the things I could have done with the money . . ." She stooped and gathered up the folds of her rather shabby dress. When she straightened up, the skirt came with her. She paused for a moment, then raised her arms and pulled it over her head. From deep in its folds, her voice addressed Noah. "Would you help me out of this, Mr. Diamond?"

Noah walked to her and helped her remove the dress. As he was fumbling with buttons and snaps, he felt her hands unbuckling his belt. Then, quickly, they were deep inside his trousers. "What's your first name, Mr. Diamond?" she whispered huskily.

"Noah."

This was, Noah thought as they slid to the floor, very different from his experience with Olivia Hamilton of the Virginia fox-hunting Hamiltons.

8 . VENICE

IN CONTE GUIDO di Falco's hand was a message of the utmost urgency from his wife's cousin, Carlo Diamante in Rome, but it was the heavy aroma of a woman's perfume rising from the envelope that interested him more. Was it Carlo's wife's perfume? Of course not. The scent of his mistress, then, Signora Noella Corri? Sì. Without a doubt.

Conte di Falco had good reason to be sure of that. He had been aware of Carlo Diamante's affair with the wife of the Italian Minister of Trade for some time. Indeed, on more than one occasion, unbeknownst to the lovers, the conte had contrived to lure the Minister of Trade away from Rome so that they might be together. It was not that the conte considered Carlo Diamante a friend and desired to assist him in his affairs of passion. No, the count's assistance was inspired by his patriotism. In the view of the Conte di Falco and many other wealthy Venetian patriots, the House of Diamond represented Austro-Hungarian, and not Italian, interests. In Venice, in particular, the House of Diamond monopolized shipping for the benefit of the Austro-Hungarian Emperor. The conte was a leader in the movement to get his nation out from under the thumb of the Austro-Hungarian Empire, where it had been ever since its unification by Napoleon.

When Minister of Trade Corri was away from Rome, the allure of his wife was a major distraction to Carlo Diamante. So much so that it undermined his stewardship of the Italian House of Diamond. To the conte and his allies, Signora Noella Corri's service in the arms of Carlo Diamante was a patriotic act—albeit an unwitting one.

Now Conte di Falco opened the letter from Carlo Diamante and read it. His high, noble brow furrowed as he took in its meaning. Then his chiseled, heraldic features settled into their customary repose—revealing nothing of his thoughts—as he considered its import.

A demand from the baron's kidnappers had been passed along to Carlo Diamante in Rome from the Emperor Franz Josef in Vienna. It was for the release of four Syndicalists who had led a dockworkers' strike in Venice a little more than a year ago. There were many ramifications to meeting this demand, and as Conte di Falco sat tracing the razor-sharp crease in his trousers with the letter, he considered some of them.

When Italy's Monarchist government jailed the leaders of the strike, there had been protest riots in the squares of Venice, and on the streets of Rome as well. Italian working people, it was true, did not consider themselves radicals, but at the same time, there had been wide support of the Venice dock strike. Privately, the conte himself had not been unsympathetic to the strikers. They were being exploited in the interests of a foreign power—Austria-Hungary. And the instrument of their exploitation was the House of Diamond under the inept hand of Carlo Diamante.

Nevertheless, the conte and his fellow aristocrats could not condone Syndicalist tactics. The prospect of an organized labor force was far more heinous to them than their resentment of Austro-Hungarian hegemony. They had tacitly acquiesced when the House of Diamond pressured the government to bring in troops to break the strike, and to imprison its Syndicalist leaders.

In one way, the kidnapping of the Baron Immanuel von Diamant represented an opportunity to the Conte di Falco's faction. It had always been the baron's iron hand behind the House of Diamond financing of Austro-Hungarian exploitation of Italian resources and sea-ports. Carlo Diamante only followed the baron's orders. Obviously, the anarchist allies of the Syndicalists had realized this when they abducted him.

Perhaps, however, it might be best if the kidnappers' demands were not met. The interests of Venice might be better served if the Syndicalist strike leaders remained in prison and the baron was not returned to leadership of the House of Diamond. By himself, Carlo Diamante did not have the influence to secure their release against what was bound to be strong opposition from the Italian noblemen, industrialists, and financiers who propped up the faltering monarchy. The conte was a leader of this group, and so, in the name of family, Carlo had turned to his cousin's husband.

The conte, however, felt no obligation to his wife's family. The conte did indeed love his wife, but that was another matter. Her family he held responsible for the exploitation of his country by Austria-Hungary. Why, then, should he use his influence to meet the demands of the abductors of the Baron von Diamant? Without the baron behind him, Carlo Diamante's ineptitude might well bring about the fall of the Italian House of Diamond. That alone made it desirable simply to wait and do nothing about the kidnappers' demands.

A knock at the door of the study where the conte had retired to read the letter from Rome interrupted his thoughts. "Come in," he responded.

The woman who entered was middle-aged and dowdily dressed. She curtsied and waited nervously for the conte's permission to speak.

"You have information for me?"

"Sì, Conte." She had a sparse, dark mustache on her upper lip and large, luminescent eyes that begged to be trusted. She was the contessa's personal maid, and Tamar did indeed trust her utterly. Her name was Gina, and from the day she had first entered Tamar's service, she had been in the employ of her mistress's husband as an informant. "There is a new one," she revealed triumphantly to him now.

"Really." The conte was surprised, but otherwise unruffled. He had known about both of his wife's previous lovers and did not regard them as a threat to him at all. With supreme self-confidence he knew that she would realize in time that they were quite second-rate in comparison with him, and of course she had. Even so, it now seemed there was a third one. Well, it had been a while since the second. Sure of himself, the conte felt no more threatened than by the first two. He was, however, curious. "What is he like?"

"Young."

The conte was himself ten years older than his wife. "How young?"

"In his middle to late twenties, I should think, Conte."

"Continue. His appearance, other than youth?"

"A gentleman, from his dress. Soft-spoken. Tall. Slender. Not unhandsome."

"What does that mean? 'Not unhandsome'?"

"Handsome, Il Conte," Gina amended. "Really quite handsome."

Well, after all, he would not expect Tamar to choose an aging grotesque as a lover. "Their trysting place?" he inquired.

"The gentleman's hotel room, Il Conte. The contessa goes to him there."

"Hotel room? Then he is not a Venetian?"

"No, Conte. He is here on business from Rome."

"Business? What business? And what is his name?"

"The gentleman is called Paolo Banducci. And his business is with the contessa."

"My wife is involved in business?" The conte was not really surprised. She was a Diamond, after all. Business was in her blood. "You were present at this tryst?" he asked Gina, trying to sort out the picture.

"In the gentleman's anteroom, Conte." The gleam in Gina's eye promised a faithful rendering of the fruits of her eavesdropping. "They were right next door, with only a drapery separating. Right next door, in the boudoir." Gina set the scene evocatively.

"How was it that you contrived to accompany my wife to this assignation?"

"It was yesterday afternoon, Conte. She was to meet you and some friends for dinner and then to go on to the ballet. The time was short. In order to be able to spend more of it with the gentleman, the contessa had me come along with her to carry her formal gown and various toilette articles, and to help her dress properly and do her hair for the evening. Then I was to bring her afternoon suit back to the villa, which I did."

"And so you were able to overhear them as they made love. And what did you overhear?"

"Many endearments, Conte." Gina was not without native literary skills and a sense of how to build suspense. "Also, sounds which were not words. Heavy breathing, sighs, and so forth."

" 'And so forth,' " the conte echoed. "Well, that will suffice for the carnal details, Gina. Now, about this business you mentioned between the contessa and— What did you say his name was?"

"Paolo Banducci, Conte."

"Paolo Banducci. Sì. Tell me about the business."

"It involves the cousin of the contessa in Rome."

"Carlo Diamante. Sì. Go on." The conte was growing impatient with Gina's insistence on dramatic impact.

"The cousin is having an affair with the wife of an important government official." Gina decided against another pregnant pause. What she had said was obviously no news to the conte. "The contessa learned of this."

"Of course." The conte had told Tamar himself. It was a tidbit of family gossip that he thought would amuse her.

"The contessa told Paolo Banducci about her cousin's affair."

"Yesterday?"

"No, Conte." Gina corrected the wrong impression she had given him. "Before yesterday. Some time ago, from their conversation. I'm not sure just how long."

"All right. Go on. What was said yesterday?"

"The gentleman—Signor Banducci—described to the contessa how he went to her cousin with what he had learned. He threatened to tell Signor Diamante's wife and the husband of his mistress about it unless Signor Diamante did certain business favors for him."

"Wait." The conte held up a long-fingered, graceful hand. "Let me understand this. My wife's lover, this Paolo Banducci, is blackmailing Carlo Diamante and Tamar is behind the scheme?"

"Sì."

"Did they discuss what the specific demands were?"

"Sì." Gina told him what she had heard regarding the bidding for the Giotto frescoes and arrangements for Banducci to buy into the House of Diamond Renaissance art collection.

The conte listened carefully. Slowly, a smile of understanding spread over his face. What a remarkable woman his wife really was! She had never resigned herself to being denied power in the House of Diamond merely because she was a woman. In particular, he knew it had always galled Tamar to watch an incompetent like Carlo Diamante wield power in Rome simply because he was fortunate enough to have been born a man. Now, obviously, she had evolved a plan to wrest that power from her cousin.

Denied entry by the front door, Tamar had found a way in via a boudoir window left indiscreetly open. This Paolo Banducci—the conte remembered now that he had heard the name in connection with certain small-scale, but highly profitable, stock manipulations that had taken place in Rome—had been chosen by her as a front man to further her interests in the strictly masculine world of the House of Diamond.

She had doubtless enticed Banducci by taking him as a lover. Still, the conte was sure that Tamar was being driven not by passion but by ambition. The Giotto frescoes and the Renaissance collection would be a substantial entrée into the House of Diamond. However, the conte knew they were not to bid on them, a fact that Tamar and Banducci evidently were not yet aware of. Tamar's plan was clear. Once in, Banducci, with her behind him providing guidance, would slowly but surely force Carlo Diamante out. With the baron gone and Rome in disarray anyway, that shouldn't be too difficult. Then Banducci, backed by Tamar and acting for her, would stage a takeover. The Roman branch of the House of Diamond would be his, and Paolo would be Tamar's.

Delicious! The conte allowed himself a quiet chuckle. Actually, the pressure that Tamar and her lover were bringing to bear on Carlo Diamante could not have suited the conte's own purposes better. Thus distracted, he would make even more of a botch of House of Diamond operations than he usually did. That could only work to Austria-Hungary's detriment and Italy's advantage.

And if Tamar and her lover should succeed? If they should gain control of the House and patch up the Austro-Hungarian alliance and reassert Emperor Franz Josef's dominance over Italy? Why, then the conte could go to Lord Haran in London and denounce his wife as unfaithful. It was Lord Haran, after all, who had arranged their marriage in the first place. He was an honorable old fussbudget, and he would quickly bring Tamar to heel. This would put an end to her affair with Banducci, and to her meddling in matters meant only to concern men. Whatever hold she might have established over Diamond affairs in Rome would quite naturally pass into the hands of an administrator who—while inevitably of the Diamond bloodline—would be agreeable to her husband.

No matter how things turned out, the Conte Guido di Falco couldn't lose.

9. ROME

"ASHES. MY LIFE is ashes."

"Nonsense." Signora Corri truly didn't know how to handle Carlo Diamante. In all the years they'd known each other, she had only known Carlo's hedonist side. Food, drink, dancing, fun, laughter—these had been the fuel for an energy level that was never anything less than overprimed. Now, for the first time, she was seeing the other side of the coin. It revealed that the normal, bubbling joie de vivre that had always been Carlo's hallmark was balanced by a willingness to plunge uncommonly deep into the throes of depression. "You're just having a little business trouble. That's all."

"Business trouble." He sighed. "My two youngest girls have measles. My oldest boy has been suspended from school for smuggling lewd pictures into his dormitory and abusing himself."

Noella suppressed a smile. "Sowing wild oats." She tried to be soothing. "And the measles will pass."

"Sì. They will probably pass to my other children." Carlo sighed tragically.

"And Leah?" Doggedly, Noella kept trying to distract him. "How are her sinuses? Did the honey-and-onion syrup help?"

"She was allergic to it. She swelled up like a balloon and broke out in hives."

"I'm so sorry."

Another hopeless sigh. "She blames me, of course."

"Well, then, just tell her it's my fault." Noella allowed herself an instant of pique. "Say your mistress did it on purpose."

"How can you make jokes?" Carlo rocked back and forth, in mourning for himself.

"I'm sorry, darling." Noella was remorseful. "I really do want to be more supportive. Tell me what I can do."

"Just listen, I suppose."

"I'm listening, darling."

"My daughters are covered with red spots. My son is a pervert. My wife is swelled up like a balloon. And my dog refuses to be housebroken. The carpet— you're laughing at me!"

"I'm sorry. I'm sorry. Really I am."

"You find me comic. Well, of course. I am laughable."

"Not you, my darling. Never you. It was the unhousebroken dog that I was laughing at." Noella stroked his brow.

"If it were your carpet, you would not be laughing."

"Come now, Carlo, that is all trivial, and you know it. I understand that with the baron gone you have a lot of business pressures. I know you're having a hard time with the negotiations for his release. But it's plain that something else is bothering you. Why don't you just tell me what it is? You'll feel better, darling, if you do."

Carlo regarded her unhappily for a long moment. "All right," he said finally. "I'll tell you." He revealed to Noella then for the first time how Paolo Banducci was threatening to tell her husband and his wife about their affair unless his demands were met regarding the Giotto frescoes and the Diamond collection of Renaissance art.

Noella was concerned. "My husband would banish me and destroy you if he found out about us."

"The worst of it is that I can't comply where the Giottos are concerned because, as you know, I've had orders from London to withdraw from the bidding."

"Did you tell this blackmailer that?"

"I tried to, but he wouldn't believe me. He said he'd carry out his threats and go to your husband immediately. I couldn't have that. So I told him I'd only been stalling and agreed to include him in for forty percent of the Giottos."

Noella thought for a long, silent moment. "Something in exchange." Finally she spoke aloud.

"What? What do you mean?"

"You can't cut him in on the Giotto bidding because there won't be any Giotto bidding. You have to give him something else instead."

"Sì. But what?" Carlo wondered.

"Licorice!" Noella said triumphantly.

"Licorice?" Carlo was bewildered.

"The House of Diamond must immediately buy up

the Southern European licorice crop. Listen to me, Carlo. I was going to pass this information on to you anyway, but now it is doubly important. My husband—"

"Yes, the Minister of Trade." Carlo was caught up in Noella's sudden enthusiasm.

"—is involved in negotiations with the United States government to lift the trade restrictions on licorice paste. It is to be removed from the list of quota items in exchange for Italy importing a specified amount of American surplus wheat."

"Licorice paste?"

Carlo had never been even an adequate businessman, Noella reminded herself. "Licorice paste," she explained, "comes from licorice roots. It is used in cigars, cigarettes, and chewing tobacco. No country consumes these items so heartily as the United States. I am told that the gold paving of the streets of her cities cannot be seen for the debris of butts and the rivers of licorice spittle. Hear me, Carlo. Tomorrow, futures for the licorice root crops of Sicily and Greece will be going for next to nothing. The day after, when the government breaks this news, the value of licorice futures will increase tenfold."

Buy low. Sell high. Wasn't that what Zelik Diamant, the founder of the House of Diamond, had advised? "I will have my brokers begin buying first thing in the morning," Carlo Diamante decided.

"Sì. And include this Banducci in on it. That should make him forget the Giottos and hold his tongue."

"Noella, my darling, you are a marvel!" Impulsively, Carlo Diamante seized his mistress in his arms and kissed her.

"The credit really should go to my husband," she murmured when the kiss was over. "If he were not the Minister of Trade . . ."

"I will be eternally grateful to him."

"Do you think you could manage to express that gratitude to me before he returns home?"

"Definitely," he said with his old, buoyant smile.

10. FRANKFURT

DURING THE TIMES when Gabrielle guarded the Baron, when they were alone, he drew her out and learned that she had been reared in a Latvian *shtetl* by a pious Jewish family that did not believe in educating its daughters. She could neither read, nor write. A pogrom had wiped out her family when she was a teenager, and this event had radicalized her. Anarchism—the making of the revolution—had taken up her entire adult life.

They were in all ways opposites. The baron was wealthy, Gabrielle poor, he a titled aristocrat, she a shtetl peasant, he well educated, she illiterate, he powerful, she one of the dispossessed, he true to his Jewish religion, she an apostate, he a stalwart of the status quo, she a revolutionary dedicated to its destruction. Still, the baron surmised that Gabrielle was infatuated with his worldliness. Behind her own glib spouting of radical catch phrases, he saw that she was naive, impressed by him, and curious.

Sometimes she fought the attraction, doubtless because it ran counter to her radical commitment. Gabrielle was one of the anarchist hard-liners that Josef Rothko had told the baron about, one of those who favored decapitating him. She frankly viewed carnage and assassination as the most direct route to a people's world. "Rothko is too soft," she had postured during one of their first talks. "You cannot make an omelette without breaking the eggs."

"And am I one of the eggs?" the baron wondered.

"You are a lynchpin of the capitalist structure." The words came out glibly, a piece of the dialectic she had committed to memory. "You are expendable." She had never been educated, but the anarchist experience had expanded her vocabulary. Despite the harshness of her words, however, Gabrielle's tone was teasing. Increasingly there was this element of flirtatiousness growing between them.

There was an erotic underside to the way in which she listened when he spoke. Gabrielle would draw him out, and then she would take in information from the baron as if collaborating in an act of love. The more serious the topic, the more it revealed itself in the intensity of Gabrielle's attention and the tautness of her body. Slowly their discussions deepened from provocative banter to exchanges of solemn import.

The baron lectured. Gabrielle listened. The sessions evolved into seduction by education.

"How did you become so outrageously wealthy?" she had inquired on one of the evenings when she stood guard over him. If the question was blunt, her curiosity was nevertheless genuine.

"I grew up." The baron smiled. "My father was rich, and so was my grandfather. All I had to do was become old enough to claim my share."

"Not brains, talent, and superior ability, then." Shtetl background or not, Gabrielle had learned how to be sarcastic. "Even so, how did your forebears do it?"

"Ahh, well, for that, we have to go back to the beginning."

"The beginning?"

"The days of early Christianity. The period before and after Mohammed established Islam."

"Islam?" Gabrielle wet her lips. He knew so much; even at this early stage, it was in her eyes.

"The Muslim religion. The religion of the Arabic civilization."

"Go on."

"Well, you see, in the Mideast, during the first thousand years after Christ, the Jews were persecuted by the Romans, and then the Christians. They were driven off their farms; they were no longer allowed to be landowners. They drifted to Arab lands where they enjoyed relative, but not absolute, freedom from oppression. The Arab culture was nomadic, rather than agrarian. It consisted of traders and merchants. And so the Jews also became traders and merchants. They—"

Gabrielle cut him off. "This lesson in ancient history you are giving me. It's all very well, but it doesn't explain how your family became so wealthy."

"You have to know the background." The baron looked at her shrewdly. Yes. He was right. Despite her protest, Gabrielle was reacting with a certain warmth to his pedantry. Her receptiveness was more than mere academic curiosity. "As traders and merchants"—he picked up where he had left off—"those old-time Jews gravitated to cities because they were the centers of commerce."

"Not my people," Gabrielle interrupted. "They moved from shtetl to shtetl."

"That was somewhat later. This was still the great period of the Moslem Empire, which extended from the Pyrenees to China, and with its concentration on conquest and territory, Islam neglected trade and commerce at home. More and more, this was left to the Jews of the empire. So it was for a few hundred years, until the Crusades."

"I've heard of the Crusades." A little pathetically, as the baron perceived it, Gabrielle tried to show him that she wasn't totally ignorant.

"The Crusades, while actually campaigns of pillage and conquest, were rationalized by European Christianity as wars against the infidels. Although by this they meant the followers of Mohammed, there was little distinction amongst the Crusaders between Moslems and Jews. They still believed the Jews killed Christ. Often the Crusaders slaughtered Jews even more fervently than they did Moslems."

"How do you know all this?" He could tell from Gabrielle's expression that the way history geysered out of him like lava from a volcano was titillating.

Between their times together, the baron thought about that reaction. The history lessons were melting whatever resistance she might have had to him. Their mutual Jewishness—even as she disavowed hers—was an emotional link. She had never been educated and she was hungry for knowledge. He felt his advantage was growing and pursued it when Gabrielle next came to guard him.

"We left off with the Crusades," he reminded her.

"Yes," Gabrielle said. "I remember. The way you tell it is like going to school. I never had a chance to go to school," she added wanly.

"I'm happy to be your teacher." The baron's tone was kindly. He intuited that Gabrielle would be vulnerable to kindliness. "So the slaughter of the Jews by the Crusaders had an unexpected effect. A large Jewish migration began, a countercurrent to the invading Crusaders, and so large numbers of Jews fled the Near East for the relative peace of the Western European countries—Spain, Portugal, France, England, Italy. The center of Jewish life shifted from east to west."

"But my people went from west to east," Gabrielle

remembered. "From France to Bavaria. From Bavaria to Prussia. From Prussia to Poland. And from Poland to Latvia." Contributing to the discussion increased her excitement. She hugged her shotgun tightly against her quick-breathing bosom. Her eyes shone, seeking his approval.

"*That* migration began with the Inquisition. At this earlier time, when the Jews migrated from the Near East to Western Europe, they brought with them a well-established tradition as traders. Because of their expertise in commerce, even as Crusaders were slaughtering their brethren in the Near East, Jews were being welcomed with open arms and invited to settle in Italy, France, and Germany. Indeed, the Jews were actually invited to various European countries to establish mercantile cities in places where trade routes crossed."

"You really could have been a teacher. A professor." Gabrielle was all eyes, her voice trembly.

"Eventually—and naturally—Jews were resented for their trading skills. You see, they had become the core group of the first European middle class. Peasants who work with their backs do not take kindly to merchants who don't perform hard labor. They feel exploited by them—and sometimes they are."

"Then you admit it!" Gabrielle's eyes flashed in triumph.

The baron, however, saw more in their depths than radical outrage. He perceived the desire of the victim for the oppressor. He was sure of it.

"I admit it." He spread his hands as if in a plea for understanding. "Jews are no less and no more scrupulous than any other people. In any case, deserved or not, this resentment found its outlet in the Inquisition. It started in Spain and spread over Western Europe like a plague. Jews were its main victims. Countless Jews perished. Everywhere they were subjected to anti-

Semitic laws and to persecution. Flare-ups were unpredictable, but in a general sense it pushed the Jews from west to east in Europe—from France and Spain and England to Prussia, Poland, and Russia. Like your people—and like mine."

"Yes." Gabrielle remembered the family horror stories she had heard. "They were beaten. All their goods were taken. They were driven from place to place." The way she said it reaffirmed her Jewish connectedness to the baron.

He nodded in agreement. "The same with my family."

"But they were rich."

"Not during the Inquisition and the period that followed they weren't. They were no better off than anybody else. They, too, lost everything and were driven from place to place."

"Then how—?"

But the answer had to wait. Ammal had come on duty. Reluctantly, the baron was sure of it, Gabrielle left the attic cell.

"You teach me history." Gabrielle plunged in abruptly when next she arrived for guard duty. "And I am grateful."

Surely the admission was a step forward leading into his arms. The baron smiled and waited for her to continue.

"But it doesn't explain how one Jewish family became rich while another ended up in a shtetl to perish in a pogrom."

"Chance," the baron told her gently. "One family was lucky. Another was not. There were no straight-line migrations during the Inquisition and the evil centuries that followed it. Circumstance forced all Jews to keep on the move. In the end, that worked to my family's advantage."

"But how?" Gabrielle's eyes were large with interest. Obviously it was a key question for her.

The baron explained carefully, observing her reaction. "Constantly on the move, the Jews were subject to edicts by local lords who were really little more than bandit chiefs. Most countries were split into principalities, each with its own prince, or graf, or duke, or whatever the head robber was called. More important—most important—each of these duchies had its own currency and coinage. The people of one principality often wouldn't accept the currency of another principality. Reigns were established and fell frequently. Governments were in flux; there was no stability. Currency honored today might be worthless tomorrow. This was a problem for forced-to-be wandering Jews like my family. But the solution of the problem became the foundation of the House of Diamond."

Gabrielle had picked up on a certain pride in the baron's voice now. She smiled. The baron thought the smile confirmed the allure of power. It was there on her face, plain to see. She would succumb to him. And then . . .

He went on with his account. "Because of these unstable currencies, the Jews, forced to be always on the move, took to hoarding gold, silver, and gems. Jewels and precious metals, you see, were universal tender, acceptable regardless of official currency or changes in the ruling houses. Even so, their value was a matter of time and place, and so the Jews also had to become expert in the conversation of currency."

Gabrielle's brow was knitted. This was an area foreign to her. Concentrating, her focus was completely on Baron Immanuel.

Not long now. The baron was sure. Possess a woman's mind, and her body will follow. "Am I going too quickly for you?" he inquired gently, considerately.

"No—no. Please go on." Gabrielle stood her shotgun on the floor and rested her angular chin on its muzzle. "Please."

"Very well. Because they had the knowledge and because they were forever on the run, Jews became the money changers for gentile traders who did not want the constant bother of exchanging currency. A Christian merchant might go through four or five duchies with differing currencies in a day, twenty in a week, eighty to ninety in a month. In most places, the Jews were forbidden to compete with them. By law, Jews couldn't sell goods. All they could do was traffic in currency. That was allowed, you see, because it was an important service to the gentiles. In many instances, Jewish money changers actually made gentile commerce possible. Soon, the first stop of a Christian trader when he arrived in a new place was the Jewish money changer. For this service the Jew took a small commission—one or two percent. But he dealt in volume, and it added up."

"And this is how the Von Diamant family became so rich." Gabrielle was obviously enthralled.

There was no chance to correct her. Their time together was once again at an end. But Gabrielle would think about it between then and the next time she stood guard. The baron was sure of that. Could it be that simple? she would wonder. Were great fortunes really born so easily? No, she would realize. The Von Diamants must have been very intelligent—more intelligent than her own family. She would hate that, the baron knew, and she would admire it. And that conflict of emotions should finally deliver Gabrielle to him.

The baron was not by nature cold-blooded. He did not usually go about affairs of the heart so callously.

He was not indifferent to Gabrielle's feelings. But his predicament superseded his character. He would use Gabrielle any way he could to obtain his freedom.

When she came to guard him the next evening, at first she chattered, recapitulating what he had told her the last time to make sure she understood it correctly. Then she sat and listened while the baron elaborated on it.

"The money changing for gentile traders was only the beginning," he explained. "From it, the practice of money lending naturally evolved. Travel was dangerous for traders. Highwaymen ran rampant and robbery was frequent. The Jewish money changers like my great-grandfather began removing the risk by exchanging currency for a letter of credit for a small fee. The letter of credit from the Jew in Frankfurt would be honored by the Jew in Hamburg and the trader would not have to carry money. The Jews evolved rough codes among themselves to authenticate such letters of credit. And if one were stolen, the original Jew who issued it would still honor it because he knew his customer. Soon, for a slightly higher fee, Jews were issuing letters of credit without actually having the money in hand. A rug trader would show the Jew his goods, tell him he had a buyer in Warsaw but that he needed financing for the journey to deliver the rugs. The Jew would advance the financing in the form of letters of credit to pay the trader's expenses at way stations, and the trader would repay the loan after he sold the rugs. Thus the Jew went from money exchanging to money lending to financing trade."

"It sounds so involved." Gabrielle was working hard to follow. There was a slight film of perspiration on her forehead. It was not merely from concentrating. Nor was it that warm in the attic room.

"Indeed it was, my dear." The term of endearment

was calculated. "But it was predicated on the interre-
lationships between the Jews in the various cities of
Europe. Because their trust in one another was so often
a matter of survival in a hostile world, it worked."

"And so the Von Diamants became bankers? And
then aristocrats?" Gabrielle's expression was that of a
child who has heard a romantically satisfying fairy
tale.

"Not quite. They survived and put by a little something for the bad times, but it wasn't until my grandfather Zelik that the House of Diamond was really born.
He was the numismatist."

Gabrielle pouted. "I hate it when you use words I
don't understand." The pout, however, was sensual.

"*Numismatist* means coin collector. You see, my
forebears before Zayde Zelik were frequently forced
out of places before they could redeem the local currency. Because of this, they accumulated old coins, currency of places that no longer existed in terms of their
former statehood. With time, these coins took on a
value apart from their denomination. They became an-
tiquities, something to collect."

"But who—?"

"When my grandfather Zelik was a young man, he
became aware that among the nobility—and including
the most powerful of them—it had become a chic fad
to collect old coins. Zelik began buying them up from
other Jews who had been stuck with them over the
years. They were grateful to get face value for them.
Then, slowly, he let it be known to the noble houses of
Europe that he was a seller of antique coins. His reputation spread. Soon, lords and dukes and princes were
coming to him to see if he had a specific coin needed
to round out a collection. If he didn't have it, he made
it his business to locate the coin for them. Once the

family had been stuck with them; now Zayde Zelik was selling them to aristocrats one at a time at a great profit. That was what it meant to be a numismatist."

"And just from old coins?" Gabrielle licked her lips. That fortune should be so easy! It was indecent. It was delicious.

"Not quite. It was entrée, you see. Entrée into the courts where the power was. Zelik kept his ears open. He learned which noblemen were short of money. He made loans to them. In exchange, they tipped him off to investment opportunities. Soon he was making loans to princes. Then to kings. Then to emperors. And finally, to the governments of powerful nations."

"Like Austria?" Gabrielle shifted her weight restlessly.

"My father was the first to establish contact with the Emperor Franz Josef of Austria." The baron moved closer to Gabrielle, standing on the other side from her gun. "He delivered some money to him for Zelik. The money was a loan from Zayde Zelik to the Prince of Hesse-Kassel, who owed it to the emperor. The emperor also collected coins. Zayde Zelik gave my father a coin to present to the emperor as a gift from—and he said this on the spur of the moment—the House of Diamond. The emperor was grateful. He took a shine to my father. Soon he was buying coins through him from Zelik. One day my father overheard a conversation about financing for a barge canal. He went to the emperor and told him the House of Diamond would be honored to provide the financing. It was no risk, you see. The Austrian Empire stood behind the canal. After that, the House of Diamond financed more and more projects for the Emperor Franz Josef."

"And so he made your father a baron." Gabrielle looked up into Baron Immanuel's face, not flinching, although he was standing directly over her, and very close.

"Probably as much to annoy the Austrian anti-Semites as for any other reason." Baron Immanuel laid the palm of his hand gently over the curve of her cheek. "I haven't forgotten that time you kissed my cheek," he said softly.

"Haven't you?" The breath Gabrielle took was deep and tremulous. "And then the emperor made you a baron, too," she added quickly.

"My rank is unimportant." He cupped her face with both hands.

"No, it's not," she murmured with absolute honesty. "It's not at all important."

The baron kissed her then. Still holding her shotgun, Gabrielle kissed him back passionately. She continued to clutch it as he led her to his cot.

Gabrielle succumbed to him willingly, easily. His words, the baron was sure, had opened the path for him. He had judged right. It was what she wanted. She rose to him with all the fullness of her sensuality. She enveloped him, and then she dropped her shotgun and clawed at him as they mounted together to the pinnacle of their lovemaking.

Afterward, tacitly, they prolonged the coupling embrace. The baron's mind was racing. Gabrielle was his. She would do as he wanted now. She would no more be able to help herself than she had been able to resist making love with him. Oh, yes, he had truly—as with men and women always—bent Gabrielle to his will. That's what the baron thought.

But then, he couldn't see Gabrielle's face.

11. BERLIN

PHILIPPE HAD BEEN in Berlin four days as a guest in the house of the Von Koerners. The field marshal, busy with affairs of state, left the house every day after an early breakfast and only returned for a late dinner. In his absence, Philippe had filled the quartet of long, lazy afternoons making love to the field marshal's wife, Babette.

Despite himself, his feelings for her were deepening. It was not just passion. Indeed, it was in the aftermath of their lovemaking that Philippe experienced his most intense feelings toward Babette. During those tired, happy moments when their desire was spent and—he would tell himself later—his guard was down, Philippe would be caught up in her outpouring of love and unable to restrain his own feelings of answered affection.

She had been in love with him from the start. Now he was falling in love with her. He could deny it to himself no longer. But his helplessness in the grip of this emotion inevitably fired his paranoia.

Suppose the Emperor Franz Josef had been right? Suppose Babette's trips to Paris constituted a connection between the German General Staff of which her husband was a member and the French anti-Semitic, anti-Clemenceau coalition, to which her brother-in-law belonged? Babette could be a pawn knowingly or unknowingly smuggling messages between Berlin and Paris, or she could be a player who deliberately became the mistress of the head of the Paris House of Diamond to obtain inside information about the extremely shaky French economy.

Surely Von Koerner would be aware of the dependency of the Bank of France on the House of Diamond. Germany's desire for expansionism—the kaiser's passion—was no secret. It was in Germany's interest to encourage the French anti-Semites because splitting off the great Jewish banking houses from the French Republic would bring about financial chaos and tip the balance of power strongly in favor of Germany. A weak France meant a strengthened and more aggressive Germany.

Would Von Koerner use his wife—encourage her affair—to further German national interests? Prussians had invented blind patriotism. Perhaps Von Koerner would do that. Perhaps.

If it were so, then Babette was using him just as Philippe had been using her. Philippe's goal, which he hoped to attain through her husband, was to find his father's informant among the kaiser's inner circle, to determine the kaiser's role in his father's abduction, to gather information to help secure the baron's release. But what was Babette's goal?

There was a glint of amusement in her eyes this particular evening. She would be dining along with her two children. Her husband, Helmut, was taking Philippe to a stag party. It was a very special "smoker," one of the kaiser's exclusive get-togethers to which only his most intimate male friends were invited. It was a tribute to how well Philippe had hit it off with Helmut that her husband had contrived to include the Frenchman in such an elite gathering. Even so, it was all such ridiculous male posturing—"Not," she had predicted to Philippe, "unlike boys at soccer slapping one another's bottoms even as each tries to prove himself the manliest among men."

There were some twenty male intimates, mostly middle-aged and the majority of them in full-dress uniform, present at the kaiser's smoker. The kaiser, and of course

Field Marshal von Koerner, were particularly resplendent. All the men greeted one another punctiliously, each accepting in turn and rather formally an introduction to Philippe. Then, however, the schnapps flowed freely, voices rose boisterously, even raucously, and a certain bawdy spirit took over.

In this atmosphere, with the kaiser making a point of being "a regular fellow, just one of the boys," it seemed quite possible to Philippe that one of the host's cronies might be his father's agent. The man was supposed to be a member of the "inner circle." If this wasn't the kaiser's inner circle, what was? But then something happened to make Philippe wonder.

"Restrain yourself, Klemperer." At one point the kaiser chided a crony whose face was particularly ruddy with drink. "You know"—he stood ramrod straight, but the eye behind his monocle twinkled meanly—"when we were boys at school, Klemperer here always won the contest of who could break wind the loudest. He is still winning the contest, only when he drinks he gets his ends mixed up and mistakes his words for gas."

Klemperer stood, blinking, in his watery eyes the look of an unruly child who does not know how to make things right with an angry schoolmaster. He obviously was not regarding Kaiser Wilhelm as one of the boys. He shifted from one foot to the other in front of the kaiser. He was a foot taller than his monarch, who was under medium height and slightly built. When Klemperer opened his mouth to speak, it was obvious he was still seeking his words. And then, unintentionally, he burped quite loudly.

"You see?" The kaiser turned to the others and spread his hands. "We pride ourselves on self-discipline, but Klemperer has none." Wilhelm's abundant, waxed mustache overwhelmed his thin face. "He is not a man among men. He is still a schoolboy. And so we must punish him like a schoolboy. Go and stand in the corner, Klemperer."

Klemperer blinked down at the kaiser.

"In the corner!" Kaiser Wilhelm roared, his withered arm snapping out to point as if it held a dueling pistol.

Face quivering, Klemperer went and stood in the corner.

The kaiser turned to Philippe and asked quite conversationally, as if nothing unusual had occurred, "So will your House underwrite Clemenceau's bonds?"

Philippe was taken by surprise, but he concealed the fact. "That is not my decision to make, Excellency," he replied.

"Has your father not confided in you?" There was a note of mockery in the kaiser's high-pitched voice.

"My father usually keeps his own counsel," Philippe answered carefully. Did the mockery he detected indicate that the kaiser knew of his father's abduction? Perhaps even had a hand in it? If the kaiser didn't know, Philippe would certainly not reveal it.

"Clemenceau is a Socialist."

"He calls himself a Republican, Excellency."

"A Radical Republican." The monocle of the forty-seven-year-old kaiser was like a magnifying glass focusing the rays of an angry sun on Philippe.

"Labels are not always what they seem in France, Highness. Clemenceau's last act as Minister of the Interior before he took office as Premier of France was to send troops to crush the coal miners' strike in Pas-de-Calais."

"A sop to you bankers." The kaiser's tone insisted on his opinion of Clemenceau. "I still say he is a Socialist. You Diamonds are financiers. Is it true that you and the Rothschilds financed his latest campaign?"

"Gossip, Excellency. It grows out of the fact that only

Clemenceau provided a viable alternative to the Anti-Semitic Party."

"Young Diamant here is a Jew." The kaiser addressed the group at large.

Field Marshal von Koerner looked uncomfortable. Philippe had, after all, come as his guest. Philippe himself merely smiled, his composure unruffled. There was a lull in the conversation as a servant passed among them refilling glasses.

Standing in the corner, Klemperer angled his head around and looked at the kaiser pleadingly. "Ja. Ja." The kaiser's withered arm indicated that the servant should fill Klemperer's glass as well.

"I am not anti-Semitic." Abruptly, having downed his whiskey at a gulp, the kaiser once again turned on Philippe. "Some of my best frie—" He caught himself. "Did you know, Herr Diamant, that I was one of Herzl's first supporters? You know who Herzl is, don't you?"

"Indeed I do, Highness." Philippe also knew that the kaiser had dropped Herzl like a frankfurter fresh from the fire when his foreign minister, Bernhard von Buelow, had pointed out to him that Jewish bankers, liberal Jews, and the Jewish press all opposed the Zionist movement. Whatever his feeling toward Jews, the kaiser needed their money.

"I granted Herzl an audience in Constantinople and another one in the Holy Land when I made my pilgrimage to the east. I accepted the sponsorship of his Jewish Land Company for Syria and Palestine. I even spoke to the Turkish Sultan in favor of Zionism."

That had been eight years ago. Philippe did not point out that since that time the kaiser had completely deserted the Zionist movement. Nor did he bring up the fact that the kaiser's underlings were constantly conspiring with the Anti-Semitic Party in France.

"Enough of you troublesome Jews." The kaiser said

it good-humoredly, although Philippe did not hear it that way. "We are here for fellowship, not Zionist protocol." The mean-spirited reference to the infamous document angered Philippe, but he did not betray his feelings. Wilhelm turned to the larger group. "In the interest of fellowship, your kaiser has a gift for each of you." Again he signaled the servant.

A fair-sized pearl-inlaid box was produced. When the kaiser opened it, the contents were revealed to be a dozen or more tie pins each adorned with a huge, solid-gold, Gothic W. No explanation was necessary. The W stood for Wilhelm.

Kaiser Wilhelm presented one of the tie pins to each of his guests. Finally he turned to Philippe. "Some might consider it a sort of graven image." His jocular tone hid the affront. "Are Jews permitted to accept such gifts?"

"I would be honored, Excellency." Actually, Philippe thought the tie pin quite vulgar. He dropped it in his pocket.

"Look! Look!" The kaiser waved toward Klemperer.

The tall man, his body gone to flab so that his uniform bunched out in all the wrong places, was again craning his head over his shoulder. All this time he had been standing in the corner as ordered and drinking. There was sweat on his forehead and his eyes were not quite focusing.

"He wants an imperial gift, too!" The kaiser was amused. "Ask me for it properly, then, Klemperer."

Klemperer turned around and took a step toward them. Suddenly his eyes rolled back in his head and he stumbled and started to fall. Several of the men moved to catch him before he hit the floor. Klemperer, however, barreled into Philippe. Bracing Klemperer's weight against himself, Philippe felt the others pressing in on him as they also tried to be helpful. For a moment, he and Klemperer, in a sort of forced embrace, were the centerpiece of a small, very close crowd.

The others backed off. Philippe half-carried Klemperer to a couch and laid him down on it. A servant was summoned. Cold cloths were applied to Klemperer's face. After a while he seemed to struggle back to consciousness. One of the other men said he'd see that he got home, and that signaled the breakup of the party. Philippe thanked the kaiser for his hospitality and left with Field Marshal von Koerner.

In the coach going back to the Von Koerner house, the field marshal was uncharacteristically loquacious. He sang the praises of the kaiser as a hail-fellow-well-met and left just enough pauses in between for Philippe to agree. Philippe managed it, but he was glad when the coach pulled up in front of the town house and he was able to get away from the field marshal.

Alone in his room, he sighed. He had hoped the evening would somehow put him in contact with his father's agent among the kaiser's intimates. The hope, it seemed, had been in vain.

Philippe took off his jacket and automatically reached in the pocket to remove the Gothic W tie pin. He came up with an unexpected piece of paper. On it were pasted-down letters of newspaper type spelling out the name and address of a brauhaus and a time: five P.M., Thursday.

The brauhaus was in a working-class quarter of Berlin. At five in the afternoon it was just beginning to fill up with men coming from their jobs. There was a nearby wholesale butcher market, and many of those who came in were meat cutters still wearing their bloodstained aprons. The air was thick with smoke, the smell of stale beer, and the sweat-and-blood body odors the men brought in with them.

Philippe moved among them seeking the man he had come to meet. He had no trouble spotting him. It was Klemperer.

"I'm sorry." With a wave of his hand, Klemperer apologized for the setting and waved Philippe to a chair. "I had to pick a place where we wouldn't be seen together."

Philippe nodded, waited.

"Your father—" Klemperer groped for words. "He holds notes of mine. Overdue loans— Do you intend to call them in?" Klemperer blurted it out.

Philippe shrugged noncommittally.

"I would be ruined!"

"You provided my father with information. If you provide me with information that is useful, then I, too, will see that your notes are not called. If not . . ." Again Philippe shrugged.

"What do you want to know?"

"I want to know everything you know about my father," Philippe told Klemperer.

"I know that he has been kidnapped by anarchists."

Philippe was surprised. "How do you know that?"

"From the kaiser." Klemperer was sweating profusely. He drained off a stein of beer and signaled the waiter for another.

Philippe did not touch the beer in front of him. "How does the kaiser know?"

"He's known from the first."

"Is he behind my father's abduction?"

"No, Herr Diamant. He is not." Klemperer drank off half of the second beer the waiter had brought him. It didn't stem the flow of perspiration. Finally he came out with it: "One of the anarchists is his agent. This agent was infiltrated into the anarchist movement some time ago. Then it had nothing to do with your father. It was just so that the kaiser would have an ear in their midst. You know, in case they decided to assassinate him like Umberto of Italy, or President McKinley of the United States."

"Go on." Philippe tapped his fawn-gray kid gloves on the table impatiently.

"This agent has been in on the abduction from the first. The kaiser says the agent has access to the baron. The agent—" Klemperer bit his lower lip. "The agent has orders from the kaiser."

"What are the orders?"

"If the anarchist demands are met, and they decide to set him free, the agent's orders from the kaiser are to immediately kill the Baron von Diamant."

"Who is this agent? What do you know about him?" Philippe was pale with concern.

"I don't know who the agent is. If the kaiser knows more about him, he hasn't told me."

Philippe stared at Klemperer for a long moment. "Why?" he asked finally. "Why does the kaiser want my father dead?"

"France," Klemperer said. "Austro-Hungary. These are the areas of His Excellency's ambitions. Your father is a stabilizing power to the east, and through you, to the west. It is to the kaiser's benefit that London should be in control."

"I see." Philippe thought. Yes. It made sense. "Do you know where they are holding my father?" he asked finally.

"Nein."

"Does the kaiser know?"

"He may. I'm not sure. I don't think he will tell me if he does."

"He doesn't have a very high opinion of you," Philippe remembered. It gave him doubts about Klemperer's value.

"Don't let last night deceive you, Herr Diamant. At

such parties the kaiser always singles one man out to humiliate. But it is never the same man twice. Next time it will be someone else. Field Marshal von Koerner perhaps. And in a few days, he will be confiding in me again."

Perhaps it was true. Certainly it was worth taking the chance on Klemperer, Philippe decided. Another thought struck him. "What do you know about Frau von Koerner?" he asked.

"Frau von Koerner?" Klemperer looked blank. "Nothing. Nothing at all."

"She makes frequent trips to Paris."

"I believe she has a sister there."

"And that's all? She isn't acting as a courier?"

"Not to my knowledge."

Philippe stood up. "So long as you keep me informed on anything you hear about my father and this agent of the kaiser's who is guarding him, your loans will not be called," he assured Klemperer.

"*Danke*, Herr Diamant! *Danke! Danke!*"

But Philippe was already halfway to the door.

Philippe walked from the working-class brauhaus where he had left Klemperer to a block of upper-class shops on Unter den Linden. It was after six in the evening, and so the chic boutiques and antique stores and expensive jewelry establishments were already closed. Nevertheless, Philippe rang the bell of one of the jewelry shops and stood so that his face would be visible when the shutters were pulled aside.

This shop was owned and run by a Berliner named Goldschmidt. Many years before, Zelik Diamant, Philippe's great-grandfather, had loaned the Goldschmidt family money to escape one of the periodic outbreaks of violence in Frankfurt and flee to the more tolerant metropolis of Berlin. The Goldschmidt jewelry store, initially financed by Zelik, had prospered over three generations. The loan had long since been paid back. But their indebtedness to the Diamant family was an article of faith that had been passed down to Uriah Goldschmidt, the present proprietor of the jewelry store.

The House of Diamond took only the slightest advantage of this indebtedness. They had no branch in Berlin, and so the exclusive Goldschmidt jewelry store was used as a contact point when one was needed there. Agents of the House of Diamond could pick up instructions there. Advance market information could be relayed. And when one of the principals of the House such as Philippe was in Berlin, he could pick up his messages there.

Now Uriah Goldschmidt unbolted the shop door and welcomed Philippe with genuine warmth. He had known him since boyhood when Philippe had first been brought to the shop by his father, Baron Immanuel von Diamant. Of all the principals of the House of Diamond, Uriah Goldschmidt felt most at ease with Philippe.

"Have you heard the news?" He was a small, cheerful man, overweight, with cheeks that jiggled when he was excited. "About the Cullinan?" As a jeweler, Uriah Goldschmidt, of course, followed the news of the Amsterdam Diamond Exchange closely.

"That Sir Everard Hambro bid it in. Yes," Philippe told him. "I have heard that."

"No—no. That was how it looked, but at the last minute he was outbid by a cartel."

Hambro outbid! Philippe's mind raced. His initial reaction was one of satisfaction. Even if he himself had been forced out of the bidding because of his father, at least Lord Haran's friend and colleague Sir Everard would not have it.

Immediately, though, the sense of satisfaction waned.

Philippe realized that if Sir Everard Hambro were denied the Cullinan, he might not cooperate in having the Spanish radicals being held in the Rio de Oro prison released as the abductors demanded. And this at a time when Philippe himself was still jockeying to persuade Clemenceau to release the six French dynamiters being held on Devil's Island. Philippe did not know Hambro well enough to predict just what his reaction would be to losing the diamond.

"Who comprises this cartel?" Philippe asked Uriah Goldschmidt.

"Nobody knows for sure. An agent handled the bidding, outfoxing Hambro neatly. But it is whispered that Seligman, Lehman, and Cohen are involved."

"Seligman, Lehman, and Cohen?" Philippe stared at him. The three Jewish families were prominent French political allies of his, and like him secret backers of Clemenceau. All three were forces in the world of international finance, although none was quite as prestigious as the House of Diamond. "But they don't usually involve themselves with gems."

"Now it would seem that they have." Uriah Goldschmidt nodded his head, loose flesh quivering on either side of his face.

It was a puzzle, Philippe decided, that would doubtless sort itself out at some future date. "Has anything come for me?" he asked Uriah Goldschmidt.

"This was delivered by hand from Paris." He gave Philippe a large envelope.

Philippe opened it. There was a Paris newspaper inside with a note attached. He unfolded the newspaper. The headline proclaimed the abduction of the Baron Immanuel von Diamant by anarchists.

The cat was out of the bag! Philippe knew that the revelation would cause tremors to reverberate throughout the financial markets of the world. It was impossible to forecast exactly what the repercussions would be, only that they would be considerable and widespread. In the short term, each branch of the House of Diamond would have to deal with them as best it could. As to the long-term consequences, unhappily Philippe realized that they would be determined by Lord Haran in London.

More important, Philippe thought as he scanned the newspaper story and saw that all the kidnappers' demands had been listed, it made his father's position much more dangerous. In each country there was sure to be some—possibly considerable—opposition to caving in to anarchists for the sake of one rich Jew. Yes, the peril to his father was much greater now than it had been while his abduction had been kept secret.

How had the newspaper learned of the kidnapping? Philippe looked at the enclosed memorandum. It was from his trusted secretary in Paris. One sentence leapt out at him:

"Our sources have determined that the paper obtained the story of the Baron von Diamant's abduction from Berlin."

BOOK THREE

1. NEW YORK

ETHNIC REMEDIES OUTLAST both assimilation and upward mobility; they prevail. Let the most minor illness strike—heartburn, athlete's foot, poison ivy—and folk medicine snatches back the soul from homogeneity every time. Always, the chicken soup rises to the top of the melting pot.

"*Shvitz bod.*" The Yiddish fell from the tongue of Marcus Diamond dissonantly. As a monied German Jew, his vocabulary, like his clothing, was Eastern Establishment, indistinguishable from that of the Tory aristocrats of the Hudson River Valley, as American as prep school apple pie. But Marcus was afflicted with one equal share of a father-and-son head cold, and so had turned to not only the treatment, but also the language of his forebears. "Shvitz bod," he groaned and, with Noah in tow, he had made tracks for the exclusive William Street Club and its rejuvenating steam bath.

The William Street Club, frequented by the most elite

among the moguls of Wall Street, was one of the few posh establishments of its kind that did not enforce a restrictive membership policy barring Jews from its premises. Because of this its membership was heavily German-Jewish, consisting mainly of such masculine "Our Crowd" luminaries as Loebs and Guggenheims, Lehmans and Diamonds. It was a place of rich leathers pocketing deep armchairs, of oiled mahogany walls and bookshelves and first editions, of hearty culinary offerings served on oversize silverplate to make the portions seem smaller than they really were, of best-year sherry, of brandy fresh from the keg and the worm. In short, it was a place for men of wealth and distinction, Jewish or not, and its steam baths were serviced with discreet, albeit lavish, concern.

Wrapped in oversize Turkish towels, barely able to see each other through the thick clouds of billowing steam, father and son languished in padded, contoured sling chairs that anticipated the Danes. Their pores were open; the perspiration was escaping at a rapid rate. Beside Marcus and Noah were small rattan tables with trays of canapes made of fish eggs and North Sea salmon and the limbs of small squabs. To wash down the hors d'eouvres, there were goblets half-filled with *slivovitz*, the Slavic plum brandy that had found its way via the trade routes to Frankfurt and become the schnapps of preference for those Diamants who drank only on special occasions and equated sweetness with celebration.

Nondrinkers, the only other occasion for schnapps was when the head cold struck. Slivovitz cleared the nasal passages and generated perspiration. This folk remedy, too, had survived the Americanization of the New York branch of the Diamond family.

"Of course," Marcus complained to his son, "this shvitz bod and slivovitz are what we are reduced to because you don't do your duty and go out and marry a nice Jewish girl."

"What are you talking about, Father?" Noah sniffled.

"If you would marry some nice Jewish girl, she would boil a chicken for soup and we would be rid of these damnable head colds in no time. There is only one cure, my boy, and that is it. This steam and schnapps is only a holding action."

"Why don't *you* go out and marry some nice Jewish girl since you're so determined to reclaim your heritage? An attitude, incidentally, that you haven't displayed before this. Is it a cold symptom, Father?" Noah was used to talking frankly with his father, but his cold brought out his sarcasm.

"I did marry a nice Jewish girl. How do you think you got here, my boy? And she did indeed make the most marvelous chicken soup I have ever tasted. Knock out a head cold overnight."

Naomi Levine was a Jewish girl, Noah thought to himself. Not by his father's standards "nice," though. Nice Jewish girls didn't make love to men outside of matrimony. Nice Jewish girls didn't enjoy it as wholeheartedly as Naomi evidently did. Noah continued to think about her as his father droned on—whined, really; Marcus did not suffer a stuffed nose with even mild stoicism.

Noah was seeing Naomi regularly now. After that first time, he had gone back to her small cold-water flat on the Lower East Side more and more often. Always she had welcomed him without coyness. And she had taken him into her bed—the couch on which she slept, really—the same way. Remembering, even now, with his stuffed head and his body melting in the steam, Noah felt a stirring in his loins.

Once hair the shade of raw carrots and freckled flesh had seemed to Noah a coarse version of the feminine ideal. His preference had been tresses of gold with 'twining curls, and smooth, satiny skin, delicate as porcelain. Soft, doe eyes that gave a man back his manliness were what captivated him, not a blue-eyed gaze that engaged his own boldly from defiant orbs that were never demure, never downcast. Before he met Naomi, the enchantment had been in the teasing. Back then he had longed for fulfillment, but never appreciated how satisfying it could be. Then, he had been in love with Olivia Hamilton.

But he was still in love with Olivia, wasn't he? Wasn't she what he wanted, what he had always wanted? Naomi was just a—convenience—yes, a willing plaything, uninhibited by morality—that's what Naomi was. There was nothing wrong with his taking advantage of that. She was willing—even eager. Any man would do as he was doing. But he mustn't let it confuse him. Olivia was the one he wanted to marry. Naomi Levine was just an interlude. And yet . . .

Why was he always so miserable when he was with Olivia, and so happy when with Naomi?

An attendant in spotless white entering the Diamonds' private steam room interrupted Noah's reverie. He shoveled the red hot bricks from the bottom of the grate to the top where a carefully adjusted fine spray of water would draw new clouds of steam from them. The thick heat momentarily cleared Noah's nostrils and his clogged ears. The steam brought a new clarity to his father's voice that claimed his attention.

". . . reached the turning point," Marcus was saying.

"I'm sorry, Father. I didn't catch that. What did you say?"

"I don't wonder. It's these damn sinuses. I can't understand my words myself. Why should you?" Marcus took a deep sip of slivovitz, laid a long finger against one nostril to close it off, and tried unsuccessfully to breathe in the steam through the other one. "I was saying the manipulation has reached its turning point," he repeated unhappily, his nose as stuffed as before.

"Manipulation?"

"House of Diamond stock. I hate to say it, but Haran was right. Selling off early was a smart move. Now that the cat is out of the bag regarding the baron's abduction, the panic is on. Our stock is at the bottom and going begging. Thanks to our English cousin's foresight, we've been cushioned against the run on House of Diamond securities. But yes, now is definitely the turning point. Our stock is at an unheard-of low. It's time to buy back what we sold as per Haran's plan."

"Why, Father, you sound positively admiring of Lord Haran."

"I never said he didn't know his financial onions, my boy. I only said he's Rule Britannia through and through, and America be damned."

"Even so, he's under a lot of pressure," Noah reminded his father. "It's his brother who's been kidnapped and whose life is at stake."

"Well, Baron Immanuel may not be my brother, but he is family. I'm concerned, too." Marcus Diamond signaled the Irish attendant that they needed more steam. As it billowed up, obscuring him from his son, he finished his slivovitz and poured some more plum brandy from the decanter into his glass. When the mist cleared a little, he continued. "I've spoken to Andrew Carnegie," he told Noah. "He'd like to see that would-be assassin Berkman on the gallows, but he has European interests that he'd much rather pursue in a climate of the balance of power the baron maintained than under the tipped balance Haran might institute. He's putting the wheels in motion for Alexander Berkman's release as per the demands."

"That's good news, Father." Noah's fingers snarled in

his hair; the steam had curled it closely to his scalp. His cold didn't feel any better. He felt hot, wet through, and uncomfortable. Actually, he didn't share his father's liking for the shvitz bod.

"Haran is smart, but we can't let him be too smart," Marcus was saying. "He forced us to withdraw our backing from the Panama Canal stock, but now that we're buying back House of Diamond securities, we should reinvest in the canal as well."

"Isn't that against Lord Haran's explicit instructions?" Noah remembered.

"Is it?" The slivovitz rendered Marcus droll. "I don't remember that."

Noah smiled and blew his nose. Maybe his father was right about the steam. His head did feel clearer.

"Actually," Marcus continued, "it should work out well, just as with our own stock. When we withdrew our backing from the canal, the value of the government bonds we'd guaranteed plummeted. We should be able to pick them up for a song now. Then we can issue a statement saying we're guaranteeing the bond issue again, and we'll do better than Harriman and Tweed on the railroads."

"There will be an uproar. They'll accuse us of dumping the canal unethically just so we could profiteer on the buyback."

"And in a sense they'll be right, my boy. But then, do we want to be respected, or do we want to be rich? John D. Rockefeller answered that one for us a long time ago."

"All right, Father." Noah sniffled. "I'll take care of it first thing in the morning."

Still sniffling, Noah was at the stock exchange when it opened the next day. He went to the private quarters that the House of Diamond maintained there, summoned their head floor-man to him, and instructed him to buy Panama Canal bonds as quickly and as heavily as possible just as soon as the bell rang to signal the beginning of trading. Then Noah used the private telegraph line to call the the House of Diamond man in Washington and instructed him to go to the Engineering Division of the Department of the Army to negotiate new backing for the canal by the House of Diamond.

"Army will be delighted," the Washington man wired back. "Engineering desolate when we withdrew."

"Say unfortunate decision," was the message Noah had the House of Diamond operator transmit. "Apologies. Assure them announcement no later than tomorrow House of Diamond will guarantee necessary financing to finish Canal."

"Most happily, sir," was the message the Washington man could not restrain himself from sending.

The message he sent an hour later was not happy at all. By that time, though, Noah was prepared for it. By then the House of Diamond floor man had reported to him that there were no Panama Canal bonds for sale. Someone had bought them all up. Likewise, Washington informed him now, the Department of the Army was not offering any further investment opportunities in the Panama Canal.

Someone had beat them to the canal! But who? It wasn't hard to find out. The floor man made a few discreet inquiries. The answer was no secret.

Immediately after the House of Diamond bowed out—with obvious foreknowledge of the move—the financing of the Panama Canal and its latest bond issue had been taken over by the Virginia-based brokerage firm of Hamilton & Sons, which was owned and run by Olivia Hamilton's father and two uncles!

2 . LONDON

"IT IS NOT ethical." Jacob Steiner was guilt ridden and morose. "What we are doing is a betrayal."

"But we are not 'doing' anything," Minerva Diamond replied with some exasperation. "Who are we betraying?"

"You are betraying your father, who has every right to a suitor for his daughter from her own—what do they call it?—station in life. I am betraying Mr. Lemburger, who employs me, by putting at risk the patronage of his prize customer."

They were seated in a closed carriage belonging to the household of Lord Haran. The Diamond crest was emblazoned on the side of the coach. Jacob, noticing it when he climbed inside to join Minerva, huddled in a corner lest he be seen. That it was night, and drizzling, and that the street where the coach stood was deserted at this hour did not reassure him. Nor was he convinced by Minerva's assurances that the coachman and footman would be discreet. They might be mere servants to her, barely noticed by habit, but Jacob was sure they must be wondering what their mistress was doing in this unlikely part of London with this fellow whose status was closer to theirs than hers.

The carriage was parked on Savile Row, a street of custom-made tailoring establishments catering mostly to gentlemen. At this hour, naturally, all the shops were closed and shuttered. The light rain washed down their darkened windows. With business hours long past, there was no sound of footfall on the cobblestoned street. No other coach passed their stationary carriage, the horses resting, the coachman and the footman nodding side by side under cover of their drawn-up collars and tipped stovepipe hats and rain cloaks.

Almost a month had passed since that afternoon in Hyde Park. During that time, Minerva and Jacob had met frequently. Without quite realizing that it was happening—or how—Jacob acknowledged that they had fallen in love with each other. Indeed, he loved Minerva deeply and truly, but he was not finding it a pleasant experience.

Despite all the obstacles they faced, Minerva did not understand this. "Love should make you happy," she insisted to Jacob now in the back of the carriage.

"Indigestion is less painful. Toothache, too."

"But why? I'm happy. I'm in love and I'm happy."

"You're *meshugineh*. We both are. This is not some fairy tale where the toad gets the princess. This is real life."

"Toad." Minerva chuckled. "Listen to me, my Savile Row Frog Prince. People make fairy tales, not the other way around. And people make real life. Anything can happen if you make it happen."

"If you're the daughter of an English lord, perhaps. If you're an immigrant Polish tailor, what happens happens and if you're lucky, you survive."

"You have dreams. I know you do. You've told me. Well, they can come true. We'll make them come true together." Minerva put her arms around his neck and peered into his eyes with earnestness and love. "Together," she repeated. "Now, kiss me."

Jacob kissed her. Even as their lips touched, his dolor was dispensed, his awkwardness vanished. He lost himself in the response of this gentle yet strong woman, of her surprising and enveloping love for him.

"Yes. I have dreams," he murmured when the kiss was over. He rubbed the film from the coach window so that they could look at the tailoring shops across from them. "Not to be answerable to a boss. To have my own establishment. To be recognized as a master craftsman of my trade like Gittelman the shirtmaker"—Jacob pointed out his shop—"and Gluck in outerwear"—again he gestured—"and most of all, Mordecai Schnitzler."

"Who is Mordecai Schnitzler?" Minerva asked softly, struck by the intensity of ambition mirrored in Jacob's shining face.

"Was. He's dead now. He was the master tailor who went by appointment to Buckingham Palace some years back to design and fit the clothes for Prince Albert." Jacob smiled. "The prince was Hanoverian, you know, and he had the *deutsche* appetite. He developed a little pot belly, which, according to Savile Row legend, greatly disturbed him. And so Schnitzler was set the problem of concealing this bulge while at the same time not compromising Prince Albert's position as a leader of fashion."

"How did he do that?" Minerva asked, regarding Jacob as a proud mother might regard a child home from school with tales of his day's adventures.

"He designed the most famous frock coat of the Victorian Era." Jacob laughed with delight at the cleverness of the solution. "Mordecai Schnitzler tailored a long, double-breasted garment that both concealed the bulge and presented a straight, sleek line. And he called it the Prince Albert."

"A major stride forward for mankind." Minerva was indulgent, but humorous.

Jacob missed the humor. "It was an inspiration for every tailor who followed. If I could fashion just one garment—" He broke off. "But of course I am only a journeyman. I cut cloth as I am told to cut. I am Lemburger's scissors—accurate, but never original."

"You should leave Lemburger. You should open your

own shop." Minerva knew that was his dream, and she intended to go on encouraging it at every opportunity.

"That takes money. I don't have any."

"We will get some. You will do it. It will happen. You will see."

"A dream." Jacob shrugged.

"Dreams can come true. I told you."

"And I believe you." Jacob smiled, happier now in spite of himself. "It's just the means I'm still hazy about."

"The means will present themselves." Minerva took his hand in hers. "And am I part of your dreams?" she asked in her fond, throaty voice.

"You know you are."

"Then you must go to my father, Jacob. You must tell him straight out that you want to marry me."

"I might as well ask for a share of the House of Diamond." Jacob shuddered. "How can a journeyman tailor with nothing approach a great lord to ask for his daughter's hand in marriage?"

Minerva tried to brush aside his fears. "I will prepare him. I will tell him it is my wish as well."

"And that will solve everything." Jacob was sarcastic. "Don't you understand, Minerva? I see it all too clearly from *his* point of view. If I were a great lord and some nobody wanted to marry my daughter, I would have the servants throw him out of my house. I would pack off my daughter to Switzerland, or wherever. I would take every precaution to make sure she never saw the scoundrel again."

Minerva sighed. There was more than a slight possibility that his scenario was right on the mark. Even though her father had always indulged her. In this case Jacob might be right. Her father would turn him out. And he probably would send her abroad to get her away from what he would perceive to be a lower-class fortune hunter.

But how absurd! A fortune hunter! What had Viscount Ronald Templeton been if not just that? What had all the other young aristocrats—younger sons of old, impoverished, landed families—been but fortune hunters? Why did a poor Jewish tailor deserve the epithet any more than they did?

"Your father would never agree to our marrying," Jacob added. "It is hopeless."

"It is not!" Minerva, as much as she loved him, was irritated with Jacob. Why couldn't he be a bit more forceful? "You must confront him. You must stand up to him. You must not let yourself be overawed by him."

"But I *am* overawed by him." Jacob spread his hands, his Polish accent thicker now as he despaired. "He is mighty Lord Haran of the House of Diamond. I'm a journeyman tailor, one short step away from my apprenticeship. I would be tongue-tied before him."

"You are not a coward!" Minerva objected firmly.

"But I am. That is the truth of it, Minerva. The idea of facing your father fills me with fear. I am a coward."

"You only think you are a coward." Minerva was unconvinced. "But you aren't really. I could not love a coward. Someday you will see for yourself how brave you can be. No matter what you think, our love is not hopeless."

"Not hopeless?" Jacob sighed. "But what can we do?"

"We can be brave together," Minerva told him. "We can disregard my father. We can secure our future for ourselves. We can take action."

"Action?" Jacob squinted at her in the dim illumination from the desolate, gaslit street as the drizzle patterned the window of the coach. "What kind of action?"

Then Minerva began to tell him what she had been thinking—planning—all along.

3. VENICE

PAOLO BANDUCCI REGARDED Tamar with a look of restrained, nevertheless total, infatuation. He had poured her a liquore against the chill night of early springtime and now he sat watching her sip it as she stared into the blaze he had kindled in the fireplace of his hotel suite. "I'd like to think your mind is dwelling on love, but I suspect it's business."

He was quite right, of course. Tamar did not spend time thinking about love. Lovemaking, after all, required little planning. You did it; that was all. Whereas to succeed in business, sequential plotting was a necessity. Business was a complex web of cause and effect and side effect and response prompting counterresponse that demanded never-ending and constantly revised planning. So, even as she warmed to the liquore, and the fire, and the passion smoldering in her lover's peat-coal eyes, Tamar was going over recent events in her mind. A lover, she thought, did not really require attention—only passion.

"Ahh, *caro*, don't be silly. It is you and being here with you that fills my mind." Gazing on him, her violet eyes grew luminous with what he thought was desire.

They drew him to her, and as her bee-stung lips pursed invitingly, Paolo bent and kissed her.

"I adore you." Paolo's hands were cupping her face. "You are beautiful."

Ahh, well, Tamar thought not for the first time, men did romanticize. They seemed to find it necessary to the enjoyment of their passion. Women were really the practical ones. Women knew instinctively that orgasm was its own reward. Only the need to please men—

those little boys who still believed in Santa Claus and
Cupid—caused them to bat their eyes and flutter their
fans and sigh deep sighs for a love that was pure and
only incidentally carnal. Convention, Tamar specu-
lated, might dictate that men lust and woman submit,
but then convention, like morality, was male ordained,
and so, not surprisingly, had it backwards.

"And you are so handsome, caro." It was true. Paolo
Banducci was the beau ideal of that period in Italy. Half
a head taller than Tamar, who was quite majestically
tall for a woman, he had hair like black silk, wavy, and
worn just a little long so that it curled to draw women's
fingers to the nape of his neck. His eyes were black
pools, heavy lidded and lazy with sensual invitation.
There was even a dimple in his chin to buff the most
proper *donna*'s heels to roundness. Whatever clothes
he chose to wear were enhanced by his elegant figure,
and when he removed them, his athletic build enhanced the most exquisite gymnastics of love.

Tamar enjoyed Paolo immensely. Sometimes,
though, she wondered why she did not enjoy him more.
These were the same times when she told herself she
really should enjoy her husband less. For the truth was
that the conte possessed her, and Tamar did not suffer
gladly being possessed by anybody.

"Let me undress you," Paolo murmured now, following a second kiss.

Women dress painstakingly to be undressed by their
lovers. The thought flashed through Tamar's mind as
Paolo fumbled with the first of the velvet buttons descending the back of her gown. Immediately, she realized where she had heard it. Guido, her husband, had
tossed it off to female titters and masculine winks during a recent dinner party they had attended. Damn him
with his falcon face, all bone and a touch of cruelty, his
cynical, knowing eyes, and yes, his often infuriating

maturity, too. The conte was the only man Tamar had ever known who could make her lose control.

Even so, Tamar grimaced, she had indeed dressed to be undressed by her lover. Her amethyst evening gown had been selected to match her caressing violet eyes, its silk taffeta enhancing the upward thrust of her bosom even as its deep V drew attention to the pronounced cleavage. The long, heavily boned corset looked formidable, but its clasps were designed for easy removal. Her petticoat was magenta, silk and pleated, and ruffled at the bottom. Closely fitted, it was the latest style, an "Anna Held," fastened at the back with glove snaps. Her white heavily embroidered "drawers," reaching halfway to her knees, hung loosely from the waist. Their design was matched by the white lace of her stockings, which were skin-tight to the sleek curves of Tamar's long legs.

These garments would be removed slowly, and for maximum effect. Á la her husband's *mot*, they had been donned with that in mind. She had even arranged her hairpins so that the removal of only one or two would cause the shining mass of her blue-black hair to cascade sensually over the creamy flesh of her shoulders.

Paolo drew her to her feet now in order to reach the lower buttons at the back of her gown. "Lovely!" he exclaimed, although in truth in the voluptuous flame dance from the fireplace he was looking at very little of the bare flesh of Tamar's back and mostly at her undergarments, the silk magenta petticoat, the stiff corset. "Your flesh is aphrodisiac," he murmured in Tamar's ear, his breath tickling with the words.

"Ahh." Her hand slid inside his shirt, her fingertips caressing the hardness of his chest. But the response was automatic. Tamar had picked up her thought from before. Licorice futures . . .

She and Paolo would do well with them. Very well.

Already that was obvious. It had been a better than even exchange for losing out on participation in the bidding on the Giotto frescoes. In any case, the House of Diamond was not making an offer on the frescoes. Her cousin Carlo had told Paolo the truth about that, a fact that Tamar had confirmed by idly questioning her husband. The conte had freely revealed that Lord Haran had instructed Carlo Diamante not to bid on the frescoes. So she and Paolo had accepted Carlo's offer, and a few days later the Ministry of Trade had announced the lifting of restrictions by the United States on imports of licorice paste and the price of licorice had soared. But not before her husband had somehow—

A sigh, so heartfelt, came out of Paolo with a whoosh and reclaimed Tamar's attention. He had removed her gown and was now standing back to look at her. The creamy top-halves of her breasts rose deliciously from the push-up support of her formidable corset. Paolo, embracing her in the firelight, covered the quick-breathing mounds with intense, hot kisses. When his tongue tried to push under the boned stays to reach her nipple, or at the very least the areola around it, Tamar laughed and moved away from him.

"It's warm in here," she remarked teasingly.

"Sì."

Her violet eyes dropped momentarily, noting the distension of his trousers, and then rose to regard him innocently. "Why don't you take off your shirt?" she suggested.

His naked chest was tan with only a sparse amount of curly black hair like twin umbrellas guarding his rippling pectorals. Tamar went to him again and moved her lips over his chest in a series of small kisses. She could feel him hard and throbbing through their clothes against her belly. Her lips and then her tongue teased his nipples. His hands moved quickly to remove her petticoat.

Tamar was aroused. Paolo's lean body pushed insistently against her more pliable flesh; it seemed to burn through her. However, she knew from experience that consummation would be a while in coming, and though her body continued to respond, her mind drifted. . . .

Licorice . . . Her husband had somehow found out about the trade restrictions being lifted and bought up licorice futures, too. What was the source of his information? At first Tamar had suspected her cousin Carlo Diamante, but only a few days ago Carlo had come to Venice to offer to include Guido in on the venture if he would only stop procrastinating and use his influence to have the leaders of the Venice dock strike released. But the conte had virtually—if politely—laughed in Carlo's face. He had already bought up licorice futures, he had told Carlo. He, too, had his sources of information.

What sources? Tamar wondered now as Paolo held her against him, her petticoat removed, his hands greedy over the loose material of her drawers below the corset. Could it be, Tamar worried, that she talked in her sleep? Or could her lover, perhaps, be reporting back to her husband? That might be just the sort of arrangement on which the devious conte would thrive.

But Paolo would not, Tamar realized. His passion for her was too genuine. His desire for her was greater than his ambition. No, she thought as Paolo opened the last snap of her corset and removed it, whatever Paolo might be, he was not the conte's agent.

Carlo Diamante's current visit to Venice made it necessary to reevaluate him. Tamar had always regarded him as a hopeless incompetent who would have been easy to replace if she had only been a man. But recent events made her appreciate that while he was inept a good deal of the time, Carlo also had his moments of competence.

Tamar would have expected him to be devastated by the conte's refusal to help in securing the release of the Syndicalists, and thereby the eventual release of his mentor, Baron von Diamant. He had been upset, but not despondent. Carlo's next move had surprised her even more. He had gone to the pertinent Venitian officials himself, bribing them with the licorice futures originally intended for the conte. In effect, he had successfully gone around the conte to secure his ends. Yes, she must not let her contempt for Carlo allow her to go on underestimating him.

"Now what are you thinking about?" Paolo was distressed. He had taken off his trousers. But he had caught her out, the wheels of her mind clicking even as she gazed on his blatant lust.

"I'm sorry," Tamar apologized. "It's just, my darling, that we really must firm up our plans so that this licorice deal can be used to force Carlo out in order for you to take over the House of Diamond."

"You mean so that you can take over the House of Diamond. And my plans—damn it—are firmed up." Blatantly, he showed her the proof.

"I do apologize, my angel. You're right. There will be time for that later. And please don't think I am any less ready, any less eager than you." Her tongue delicately circled her lips. Without letting her gaze fall from his naked body, she placed both hands on the waistband of her drawers at the hips and slowly pushed them down, wriggling slightly as she removed them. By the look on Paolo's face Tamar knew that he had forgotten his pique. She stepped naked out of the drawers and into his arms.

Their kiss this time was long and deep. Their hands moved greedily over each other's flesh. They sank to their knees on the sheepskin rug in front of the crackling fireplace, their limbs, like their tongues, entwined. Impatiently, Tamar urged Paolo onto his back, the cloud of her black hair swirling over them.

All thoughts of business were blotted from her mind now. Pure sensation possessed them both for a long, long time.

There followed the pressure of his release and the dizzying sensation of her own, and Tamar was a long time coming down from the crest of the experience. When she did, the first thing she noticed was the smug expression of Paolo's mouth above his dimple. Unwanted, there flashed through her mind the falcon face of her husband, its harshness and dominance, which she resented, in such moments as this. Damn him! The thought, too, was unwanted. What logic made the conte, her husband, the more satisfying lover?

A long time later—Paolo never made love less than twice during any one tryst—Tamar had to leave his hotel to go home for dinner and the ballet with her husband. Paolo took her downstairs to a waiting gondola and, standing on the dock, he kissed her passionately by way of temporary farewell.

They did not see the gondola that glided past them, coming quite close to the dock, just as the moon emerged from behind the clouds to illuminate their intimate embrace. The passenger in the gondola, however, did see them. He recognized them, too: his cousin the Contessa Tamar di Falco, and Paolo Banducci, the man who was blackmailing him.

Carlo Diamante stared at the couple, his mind racing, until his gondola turned the corner of the canale.

4. NEW YORK

NOAH DIAMOND WAS muddled as to how he would handle Olivia Hamilton when they were alone. Indeed, considering the hubbub preceding the Hudson River Valley fox hunt to which Olivia had contrived to have him invited, he wondered if he would be able to isolate her at all. His concern, however, was still blurred by images of Naomi—her flame-colored curls and milk-white arms, her slender, sturdy body that enveloped his own as blue eyes laughed up at him with the joy of coupling.

"I'm glad you're over your cold." Unashamedly naked, the spattering of freckles over the top rise of her bosom made deeper in color and more pronounced by their lovemaking, Naomi had been as frank about this as she was about all things. "You were such a *nudje* with those sniffles." She'd wrinkled her pert nose.

"You should have said something," Noah had replied. "If the sniffling bothered you, we didn't have to—"

"Which is why I didn't say something." Naomi cut him off with a kiss and mussed his tight-curled hair. "Better to have my lover with the sniffles than not to have him."

"Is that a socialist principle?"

"Absolutely." Her laugh had been hearty. "Now will you give all your money to the party and join it?"

"Very tempting." Noah had joined in her laughter.

That's how it was with Naomi. It wasn't just the lovemaking. He always felt so . . . so comfortable with her. He could be himself. No facade was necessary. He didn't have to put on an act. He didn't have to pretend to be something he wasn't.

This, now, was pretense, Noah reflected as he strode back and forth in the hunt-club locker room, trying to walk the pinching tightness out of his new riding boots. He felt a bit nervous about riding in the hunt. Not, Noah thought to himself, that he was such a complete *klotz* on horseback. Curious how much Yiddish had crept into his vocabulary since he'd been seeing Naomi.

When Noah had first been smitten by Olivia and learned that fox hunting was her passion, he had made it his business to take riding lessons and to learn everything about the sport that he could. He would not fall off the horse, or disgrace himself in any way. Only he would know how uncomfortable he was on his mount.

His being there at all—at a Hudson River Valley hunt club on the cusp of Duchess County—was an indication of shifting sands in his relationship with Olivia Hamilton. She might not have been ready to invite him to the ancestral family mansion in Virginia to ride to the hounds, but all she had had to do was bat her gray-green eyes at one or two of her more deeply smitten New York State suitors and the rules were bent, his Jewishness overlooked. The embossed invitation to join the hunt had been on the silver tray with which the Diamond butler greeted him every morning when he came downstairs to breakfast with his father at their Fifth Avenue town house. Accompanying it was a terse note from the young Harriman cousin responsible for the invitation. It said simply: "At the request of Miss Olivia Hamilton."

Oh, yes, shifting sands. At some point recently, Olivia must have cast a quick, coy look over her shoulder, anticipating Noah following in her footsteps as loyally as a spaniel, and he hadn't been there. She must have realized he hadn't been there on more than one occasion of late. This, in any case, was Noah's reading of the invitation.

More surprising to him was the realization, when he received it, that he hadn't really missed seeing Olivia. He had reason to be angry with her, but still, in the past—before he'd met Naomi—he would have been desolate. Now, though, he found himself approaching their meeting with rather less enthusiasm than heretofore.

He came out of the clubhouse to encounter a vista of just-budding trees—oak and elm and maple—that stretched over a rather rocky countryside toward the ridge concealing the Hudson River. The breeze off the river gave the air a crisp feel, more like autumn than springtime. The breeze carried an aroma of manure and horses. The prehunt confusion had not abated.

Viewing the groups milling around and waiting for the hunt to begin, Noah did not feel quite so conspicuous in his scarlet coat, top hat, and formal mid-gray riding breeches. Only his matching, mid-gray stock failed to blend. One of the fine points of fashion, it seemed, had eluded him. The other male hunters were all part of the conspiracy to standardize white cravats, not gray, as the huntsman's neckwear of the season.

The women were likewise dressed uniformly. They wore black velvet caps in the shape of pheasants banked in flight and green and yellow riding jackets, as well as scarlet. All their skirts were black, long, and split so that they might ride a-straddle. Like the men, their black patent-leather riding boots were scuffed and caked with mud, or at the very least smeared with dirt.

Noah, realizing immediately that his own boots were too new and shiny-looking, took pains to kick heel-and-toe through a mudslick. This maneuver brought him within sight of Olivia Hamilton, holding court in the center of a large group of young men. There were two other groups, one to either side of them. One consisted of young women Olivia's age. None among them could compete with her lissome blond beauty, and so they had clustered out of its radiance. The second group was of slightly older people, men and women possessed of a solid look that struck a compromise between the anachronism of chaperoning the young and the need for it in these too-liberal modern times.

Noah walked toward the circle of men around Olivia. They were passing around a stirrup cup—not as clandestinely as they might have—and Olivia's cheeks were already flushed from having sampled its contents. Approaching, Noah contemplated the young men and wondered which among them had wangled him his invitation. It didn't matter. They all looked alike. The only nod to nonconformity was a spattering of small, thin mustaches, waxed at the ends.

"Noah, darling." Olivia spied him and called out. "Where have you been hiding?"

"I haven't." He joined them.

"We were just discussing the Master of Foxhounds' plan," Olivia told him. "What do you think of it?"

It was the old tease. Noah recognized it immediately. Presenting him with an "in" topic when she knew very well he wasn't "in," was Olivia's way of keeping him off balance. But one effect of his satisfying relationship with Naomi was that Noah didn't feel off balance anymore. "The plan has its merits." He replied to Olivia noncommittally. "But perhaps more study . . ."

"Precisely!" One of the unmustached young men greeted Noah's response as agreement with his own opinion. "More study. It won't do just to jump in and set up a Master of Foxhounds Association and allot territories and register hunt colors. We have to be sure we protect the exclusivity of the sport. We can't have just anybody hunting foxes. Nouveau riche merchants, Jews—"

"Do come and tell me everything you've been up to lately." Olivia hastily linked arms with Noah and led him away from what was now her disconsolate group of admirers.

Behind them, Noah heard a harsh whisper. "Bromley, you ass, that fellow is Noah Diamond."

"The Jew? But they aren't allowed . . ." The voice of the would-be protector of the social integrity of the burgeoning Master of Foxhounds Association faded out of Noah's hearing.

"I am sorry." Olivia's gray-green eyes did look truly contrite. "It's just that they take it for granted that we're all Christians."

"Naturally. Since the club is restricted." Noah's tone was flat.

Nevertheless, Olivia did not miss the bitterness. She chose, however, to ignore it. "They're going to start." She gestured toward where the grooms were leading out the horses for the hunt. "I want to be sure you ride alongside me. Perhaps we'll find a chance to rest and talk."

"Ladies and gentlemen, please to mount your horses." Olivia was right. The Master of the Hunt spoke the traditional words signaling that the hunt was about to begin.

The grooms sprang into position with bent backs and clasped hands to give the ladies a foot up. Only after they were mounted did the men take to their saddles. Then the Master of the Hunt turned to the Huntsman and said, "Please to proceed, Mr. MacPherson."

Nodding to the whippers-in to position themselves to herd the hounds, the Huntsman raised his horn. It was a copper tube, slightly curved, about eight inches long. The sunlight glanced off it as the Huntsman blew two notes. These were not loud, but they had a peculiar carrying and penetrating quility to which the hounds responded. It was the signal that the hunt had officially begun.

Guided by the Huntsman's cheers, the voice sounds by which he commanded them, the hounds moved to search the covert, which was a mixture of woodland and field. Led by the Master of the Hunt, the other hunters followed behind at a slow trot. Only when the fox had been flushed would they speed up their pace to a canter and take the hurdles that made fox hunting the exciting sport it was.

It was almost an hour before the Huntsman's horn sounded again, signaling that the hounds had picked up the spoor of the prey. The Master of the Hunt reined in his horse, stood up in the stirrups, and proclaimed, "Tally ho!" Then he dug his heels into his steed's flank and was off at a swift canter in the wake of the yipping pack of dogs. The rest of the group followed.

The chase was spirited. Noah was careful to stay close beside Olivia as she had asked him to do. It was half an hour or more before they caught up with the stragglers among the hounds, and another fifteen minutes before they reached the Huntsman. When they did, the Master of the Hunt conferred with him and then gave courteous directions to the members of the hunt as to how they should position themselves in order that the group might best run down the fox when next the hounds flushed him. Patiently, the Master of the Hunt passed on to them the Huntsman's best estimate of which way the prey would bolt and added his own words of advice on the complicated terrain over which they might next expect to ride.

Some ten minutes later, the Huntsman's horn sounded again and they were off like thunder. The pace was no faster than before, but the country through which they were riding now was much more difficult. It took all of Noah's concentration to both maintain his position on Olivia's flank and manage the fieldstone-wall and pasture-fence jumps at the same time. It was not Noah, however, but Olivia who failed to navigate one of these barriers.

At least Noah thought she had failed to navigate it. Had he been watching, he might have seen Olivia deliberately rein in her horse in mid-jump and then pick her spot to land as she was thrown. It was a soft and grassy patch shielded from casual view by a clump of tall bushes.

Concerned, Noah rode back to her and dismounted. Olivia sat up with her head tilted artfully and regarded him from hurt, doe's eyes. She had lost her soft felt hat in the fall, and the sun glinted becomingly on her slightly mussed golden hair.

"Are you all right?" Noah knelt beside her.

"Shaken up."

"Do you feel as if you've broken anything?"

"No. I just feel so awfully faint." Olivia's voice was weak, trembly, vulnerable.

"The wind's been knocked out of you. Just lie here and rest. Get your breath back."

"We'll never catch up to the others."

"I think they can manage to do in the fox without us," Noah assured her.

"I still feel faint. Maybe I'd better take off my jacket." Olivia took off her scarlet riding jacket and handed it to Noah. "Would you?"

Noah folded it and propped it under her head, as she wished him to. She closed her eyes and lay prone on the ground. Her face was slightly flushed, not pale, and her golden hair rumpled in a becoming disarray.

Once again Noah was struck by her beauty, but he was less affected than he had been on previous occasions. He did not speak.

"We're all alone now," she noted after a moment's silence.

"So we are."

"And even if we weren't, nobody could see us behind these bushes."

"I suppose not."

"Noah Diamond!" Olivia pouted. "I don't have the strength to strike you over the head. Are you going to kiss me, or not?"

"Not."

"What?" Olivia sat bolt upright, forgetting she was supposed to be feeling faint. "What do you mean? Why not?"

"Because I'm not feeling affectionate toward you. That's why not."

Olivia stared at him. This was very uncharacteristic behavior. Particularly since they hadn't been alone together for a while. "What is the matter?" she demanded.

"The Panama Canal," he told her. "That's what's the matter."

"Oh." She put her head back down on the pillow of her jacket. "Oh. I see."

"What I told you regarding our plans to withdraw backing from the canal was in confidence."

"I know." Olivia's tone was unhappy.

"Never did I think that you would pass it along for your relatives to capitalize on."

"I am so sorry."

"Nor could I have anticipated that the noble Virginia Hamiltons would leap in to corner the canal in such a way as to make it impossible for my father—myself, our firm—to regain entrée to the financing."

"I never meant—"

"Didn't you?" Noah's voice was cold.

"Listen to me, Noah. You have to. I really didn't mean

for anything like that to happen. I was stupid. I was showing off when I told Father about the canal financing. He'd found out I was seeing you. Someone up from Virginia saw us together at the theater in New York and went back and told him. He was carrying on about you, and your family, and the Jews generally. I was trying to defend you. I said how he was only jealous because Jews were better businessmen than Christians. He said they were just more grasping, that all that counted was squeezing out another dollar. He said Jews had no loyalty and no discipline. I said that wasn't true, and to prove it, I told him about how you were getting out of the canal because your family had to stick together and do what your cousin in London wanted because your other cousin had been kidnapped. That's how it happened. I was defending you. I swear it. I never thought Father would violate my confidence and take advantage of what I told him that way."

Despite himself, Noah relented. The soft eyes, the pleading look, had not lost their power over him. Whatever else Olivia was, she wasn't a financial expert. She probably had chattered away to her father about the canal without realizing until after the fact that he would capitalize on the information to the detriment of the House of Diamond. It was pointless to blame her for a treachery committed mainly—if not altogether—in innocence.

"Please, Noah. You must forgive me."

"I forgive you." He spoke the words and he meant them, but the expression on his face did not soften.

"Then show it." She held up her face, eyes closed, lips parted, to be kissed.

After the kiss, the sound of a distant *holloa*, the Huntsman's high-pitched cry, reached their ears. "They've sighted the fox," Olivia realized.

"Then perhaps we'd better—"

"They're very far away." She held up her arms to claim another kiss. When his lips touched hers this time he felt a stirring as she responded and clung to him with a passion, an urgency he had not expected. Yet part of him was holding back. "I've missed you," she murmured.

"I've missed you, too," Noah responded obediently. He hadn't, he knew he hadn't, and he tried to end the embrace, but Olivia's arms encircled his back as her lips moved greedily over his. She was pulling him down until he was almost lying on top of her, until his own weight was crushing the soft curves of her body into his. Her hands moved down to his buttocks and, straining against her, he responded. "I've missed this," she murmured in that liquid southern voice that had once so captivated him.

The distant sounds of horses and hounds rang in his ears and the afternoon sun beat down on his back. Olivia shifted her weight as her hands guided his body onto hers, yet even as his lust asserted itself over his feelings, he realized that Olivia only wanted the reassurance of knowing his desire to possess her hadn't waned. She wasn't really ready to consummate their lovemaking, no matter how her body was teasing his now. With one quick movement, he pulled apart from her and scrambled to his feet. He looked out over the distant copse in an effort to evade her eyes.

Olivia sat up dazedly. Something—she didn't know what, but something important—had changed between them.

When he finally looked down, the expression on her face was enough to force him to relent. He sat down a few inches from her.

Clinging to him, she whispered endearments in his ear. They mingled with the excited cries of the hunters and the yelping of the hounds as they drew closer. Noah responded only tepidly and for the first time it occurred to Olivia that she might be losing him.

"Noah, I've been thinking a lot about us." Her voice was quavery. With the hunt drawing closer, she drew back from him and smoothed down her clothing. "About your proposal of marriage."

Noah pulled back with a start. It was true. He had asked Olivia to marry him—not once, but three or four times. Each time her response had been devastating. "It would be delicious." She had laughed. "The look on my family's face when I introduced you as my fiancé." She had never outright told him no. But she had never said yes, either.

Now Noah looked at her questioningly. He stood up again and brushed himself off. The hunt was closing in on them.

"If you should ask me again—" Olivia paused and then continued "—I would say yes. And never mind about your Jewishness." She thought she was being very courageous. "I'll just brazen it out with my family and make them accept you. Perhaps you could convert. You don't have to decide that now," she said hastily, cutting off his protest. "Father never could say no to me if it was something I really wanted badly enough. We'll just face them down together—my family, my father."

Noah stared at her. He'd been taken by surprise. He had wanted Olivia for so long, and now she was saying she would be his. But unbidden, the memory of Naomi sprang to mind.

Yet he did feel a quickening of his pulse at Olivia's offer. It was what he had sought for so long. "You shouldn't be hasty, Olivia," he said finally. "You don't want to alienate yourself from your people. I couldn't let you do that. What you're saying is a very big step—

an irretrievable one. You should think about it some more. We both should."

Now it was Olivia who was taken aback. This was not the response she had expected. Not at all.

There was a sudden savage snarling on the other side of the bushes behind which they were concealed. An instant later a thunder of hoofbeats caught up with it, and then there was abrupt silence. It was the finale of the hunt.

The hunters, Olivia knew, would be watching as the hounds ripped the live fox to pieces. When it was dead, the Huntmaster, aided by the whippers-in, would rescue what was left of the prey from the pack. These hirelings would butcher it on the spot and toss the carcass back to the dogs. Then the Master of the Hunt would award the brush (tail), mask (head), and pads (feet) of the slain fox as trophies to those among the hunters who in his judgment had best acquitted themselves during the hunt.

Olivia realized with bitter regret that she was not to have a trophy of the hunt. Not this time.

5. LONDON

"NEXT TIME," KING Edward VII of England had confided to his two guests just before he curled up on the red velvet couch in the anteroom to the Royal Box at Albert Hall, "we will leave the Wagner to Cousin Willie and send to Cousin Nicky for something tried and true by that Tchaikovsky fellow, something one can hum."

Now the king lay snoring softly, cut off from the Wagnerian thunder by the heavy velvet draperies that had been drawn between the antechamber and the concert hall. Later there was to be a reception and a dinner at the French Embassy that His Highness was duty-bound to attend. Still later, there would be cards and perhaps some scintillating female company. The king, therefore, was taking this opportunity to rest.

Across from him, seated at a small table over brandy and cigars, Lord Haran Diamond and his nephew, Philippe Diamant, spoke in hushed tones so as not to disturb the monarch. Both were relieved to have escaped the music. Lord Haran's ear, he said, was too sensitive for such cacophony, and the crashing cymbals only served to remind Philippe of the kaiser—King Edward's "Cousin Willie."

Dislike of Wagner's music was one of the few things on which the two men agreed. Otherwise, they were oil and water. Lord Haran viewed his blond nephew with his pointed, waxed mustache and flippant wit as a Frenchified dandy, a womanizer, a popinjay. Philippe, for his part, saw Lord Haran as a blustering Anglophile, humorless, pompous, and overbearing.

Only because of the present delicate situation, the kidnapping of Baron Immanuel von Diamant, had His Lordship arranged for Philippe to attend the concert with him and the king. Philippe had attended in hopes of finding a chance to privately discuss matters with His Highness that would come up more officially later in the evening at the French Embassy reception. For the moment, with the king napping through a surfeit of Wagnerian trumpets, that hope had been dashed.

In low voices, the friction between them just below the surface, uncle and nephew were discussing the abduction. "You're sure, are you, that the story was leaked to the newspapers from Berlin?" Lord Haran scrutinized Philippe from behind his monocle.

"*Oui.*" Philippe deliberately used the French affirmative to annoy his compulsively British uncle. "Our sources are unquestionable."

"And you think the kaiser is behind it? But why?"

"Franz Josef relies on Father. The kaiser is obsessed with expansion: west into the rich French coal-mining regions; east to assimilate German Austrians. He's even coined a term for this eastern expansion. He calls it *Anschluss*—the annexation of Austria by Germany. Anschluss requires discontent among Germanic Austrians. The large investments by the House of Diamond in Austrian development hold such discontent at bay. Franz Josef will never be popular in Austria, but so long as his government can maintain a certain level of prosperity, it will never be overthrown. The kaiser understands that Father and the House of Diamond investments are the lynchpin of the Austrian power he dreams of upsetting. Wanting Father out of the way, the kaiser saw to it that the press got the story of the abduction in order to increase the risk to him."

The woodwinds were blowing up a tornado on the other side of the Albert Hall curtains. Lord Haran raised his voice to be heard over them. "But surely if the kaiser antagonizes Franz Josef, he risks an Austrian alliance with Russia."

"Shortly before he was kidnapped," Philippe replied, "Father learned that a secret military treaty had been signed between Germany and Russia."

Lord Haran's bushy white eyebrows shot up. "England will not stand idly by while Russia and Germany wreck the balance of power."

"The kaiser evidently thinks otherwise." Philippe stared his uncle down. "Perhaps he has reason."

Lord Haran removed his monocle. He took a starched white handkerchief from his pocket and polished the lens. Then he replaced the monocle in his eye socket. The stare now directed at Philippe was even colder than before. "By Jove, I don't know what you think you know, Philippe," he told him, "but what you should know is that my brother's safety will always come first with me." Suspicion, Lord Haran knew, eats most at the one who suspects. Let Philippe mistrust his motives if he wanted to. He would reassure him no further.

"Before England?" Philippe's gaze drifted toward the softly snoring British sovereign. But he did not give voice to his doubts. "There is something else you should know," he informed his uncle instead. He told him about the agent whom the kaiser had planted among the anarchists, who was now one of the baron's captors, and that he had instructions to kill Baron Immanuel if it appeared that the anarchists were about to set him free.

Lord Haran took out a pinch of snuff from the silver monogrammed box he always carried with him. He consciously put aside his dislike of his nephew. "This is going to have to be handled very carefully." He inhaled the pinch and patted his nostrils lightly. "Perhaps we should stall on making the arrangements to meet the abductors' conditions." His sneeze was controlled.

"That might be even more dangerous," Philippe pointed out. "They've given us a deadline, an ultimatum. If we don't meet it, the anarchists will kill Father."

"And if we do, by Jove, the kaiser's agent may kill him."

The two men regarded each other, joined for a rare moment in their genuine concern for the Baron Immanuel. "Just where do we stand on meeting their demands?" Philippe asked after a moment.

"Considerable progress is being made. I had word from New York this morning that Marcus has secured the cooperation of Andrew Carnegie in obtaining the parole of Alexander Berkman." Lord Haran sighed. "I could wish I had shown the faith in Marcus that Carnegie demonstrates."

"The Panama Canal?"

"Yes." It was a grudging admission. "I had Marcus withdraw the House of Diamond from the project because I feared the effect of the canal on English shipping. I never dreamed the American government would find refinancing so quickly. But they did, and now construction will go forward. An investment group has been formed headed by a Virginia firm, Hamilton and Sons, and they have virtually taken over the canal investment opportunities. Marcus tried to put us back in, but it was too late. The very thing I wanted to avoid has come to pass. Without our involvement, American control of the canal will leave English shipping completely at the mercy of the United States."

"Well, at least the Berkman release has worked out." Philippe was secretly pleased that Lord Haran—and England—had suffered the setback. "But what of Italy? How is that coming?"

"To my surprise, Carlo Diamante has somehow secured the promise of the Italian authorities to pardon the four Syndicalist leaders of the Venice dockworkers' strike."

"Well, good for Cousin Carlo." Like his father, Philippe was fond of the good-natured, if bumbling, Venetian.

"It's the only thing he's done right," Lord Haran added disapprovingly. "I instructed him to conserve capital, and instead he has expended it buying up licorice futures in southern Italy and Greece."

"Licorice futures?" Philippe laughed.

"Yes. And as a result, he has no funds to buy back the Roman House of Diamond stock that was sold. All Carlo's lire are tied up in licorice. I had to wire him two million English pounds to make sure we didn't miss out altogether." Lord Haran obviously resented Philippe's amused reaction to this turn of events. Abruptly, he went back to the pressing matter of meeting the terms of the abductors. "There is," he told Philippe, "some question in my mind about the assassin Lucheni. I was hoping you might have some word from Franz Josef regarding his release."

Philippe had been to Vienna again since Franz Josef had passed along the anarchists' demands to him. Now he was cautiously optimistic. "Luigi Lucheni assassinated the emperor's wife. You can imagine Franz Josef's feelings. Nevertheless, he has real affection for Father. He has promised to appeal to the Swiss authorities to release his wife's killer."

"Thereby keeping his government afloat," Lord Haran murmured sarcastically.

Philippe frowned. "Father always said that the English have energy and enthusiasm, which leads to empire, but they have no flair for cynicism. That is a subtlety best left to the French."

His Majesty stirred on the couch as if registering some subconscious protest and muttered in his sleep.

Philippe ignored him. He was still brooding. He was particularly sensitive to criticism of his negotiations with the Austro-Hungarian emperor. It was a sore spot nurtured in France.

The powerful Anti-Semites pushed to the surface of French politics by the Dreyfus Case were also blind nationalists. The Dreyfus legacy insisted on a German-Jewish conspiracy to sell France down the river. This was gospel. To them a Jewish Diamond would only meet with the Austrian emperor at the behest of the German kaiser.

They would never have believed that Philippe, possessing proof from the kaiser's inner circle of Wilhelm's expansionist aims, had gone to see Franz Josef to discuss the possibility of an alliance between France, Austria-Hungary, and England against Germany. Of course, the possibility of including England, the ancient enemy of France, in such an alliance would particularly have infuriated them. In regard to Philippe's putting out feelers to the English concerning possible financial and military agreements, the Dreyfusards would simply have damned him as a nationless Jewish profiteer. Nevertheless, Philippe's motives were those of a patriotic Frenchman, and that patriotism had led him straight to London from Vienna. When the English king awoke from his catnap, Philippe hoped to discuss these matters with him. Regardless of the secret pact with Russia, if France, Austria-Hungary, and England could be aligned against him, the kaiser would have to restrain his ambitions.

"What about Clemenceau?" Lord Haran asked now, bringing them back to the subject of meeting the abductors' demands. "Will he cooperate?"

"Clemenceau is vulnerable," Philippe replied. "If it came out that he was releasing the anarchist dynamiters, the Anti-Semite Party would undoubtedly claim that Father, the victim, was in league with his kidnappers and that Clemenceau was a part of the left-wing anarchist–Jewish banker plot. Also, the French public generally would be outraged by releasing the six dynamiters to some Argentine sanctuary in exchange for the freedom of a German-born Jewish banker. We are asking Clemenceau to go very far out on a limb."

"And he refuses?"

"No. He is prepared to act clandestinely. But he insists that if he takes this risk, then the House of Diamond must no longer keep him dangling as regards the financing of the French government bonds. He is adamant. Either we take the financial steps necessary to prevent the toppling of the premier's government, or he will not help us save Father's life."

Lord Haran glowered. He truly loved his brother, but—"French government bonds are a terrible investment," he told Philippe flatly. "Clemenceau's government is bound to fall, no matter what. If we underwrite the bonds, our money will go with it."

"With all due respect, Uncle, sitting here in London you are in no position to make that judgment. I don't see it that way at all. If we do not underwrite the bonds, Clemenceau will fail and the Anti-Semites will prevail."

His Lordship repolished his monocle. "Would the Jews of France really be imperiled if Clemenceau were to fall?" he asked finally.

"Oui!" Philippe's reply was insultingly French and no more friendly than a pistol shot. "Such an event would deliver France to the pogrom. And," he added, "by delaying now, you are delivering my father—your brother—to the anarchist executioner."

"All right, then." Lord Haran replaced the monocle. The eye behind it was once again icy. "You may tell the premier the House of Diamond will underwrite his government's bonds. But, by Jove, there must be no delay as regards the release of the six dynamiters."

"Once his course is set, Clemenceau will not shilly-shally," Philippe assured his uncle.

There was a roll of drums and a blare of trumpets from the Albert Hall symphony orchestra. The king sat bolt upright, eyes opened. "The music of Wagner is a declaration of war!" he announced. He lay back down and closed his eyes. A moment later he was once again snoring gently.

"That leaves only the sixty-one leftists held by the Spanish." Philippe spoke softly so as not to disturb the king further.

"I've had considerable trouble with that," Lord Hambro told Philippe, not without some malice, "because of the Cullinan Diamond."

"But I withdrew from the bidding."

"I assured Sir Everard Hambro that you had. Nevertheless, his suspicions were aroused because the three-man cartel who bought the gem were all Jews. He evidently suspects they were acting for you. Understand me, Philippe." Lord Haran wagged a finger. "Sir Everard is an English gentleman, and an English gentleman would never set conditions for doing a favor for another English gentleman. Nevertheless, he suddenly found that the Spanish government was not being as cooperative as he had anticipated. There was a bureaucratic foul-up, a change in personnel, papers lost in transit. Sir Everard was most perplexed, most apologetic."

The son of a bitch! Philippe was furious. This "English gentleman" was playing games with his father's life.

"I don't mean to provoke you, Philippe," Lord Haran said, not quite meaning it, "but you are partly to blame. That Zionist business—"

"What has that to do with it?" Philippe was genuinely puzzled.

"Sir Everard believes that Seligman, Lehman, and Cohen are in it with you, that they're Zionists, too. He believes they bought the Cullinan for you because of the Zionist connection. Somewhere he picked up the story of the French Rothschild and his Palestine investment company, and he sees that as proof implicating all Jewish bankers in Zionism."

"But Baron Rothschild is not a Zionist."

"He financed Jewish settlements in the Holy Land."

"What Baron Rothschild did"—Philippe corrected his uncle—"was to underwrite emigration as an *investment*. That is not Zionism!"

What it was, without a doubt, was a classic case of how the road to hell is paved. Some years ago, before Zionism and prompted by Rabbi Samuel Mohilever's accounts of Russian pogroms, the French Baron Edmond Rothschild had financed an agricultural settlement of one hundred and one Russian Jews not far from Jaffa. The enterprise had thrived, and subsequently Rothschild brought pressure to bear on the Ottoman Empire, which still ruled Palestine, to open up more land for Jewish agricultural settlement. Eventually there were seven such Jewish farming communities in Palestine. Rothschild financing had made it possible for settlers to emigrate, to clear the swamps, put up homes and outbuildings, irrigate, plant their crops, and reap their harvests. When there were problems—drought, typhoid and cholera epidemics, crop failures—Rothschild money saw the farmers through. Three of the seven Jewish settlements were saved from bankruptcy by the baron. The original hundred and one Jewish settlers grew to hundreds and then thousands more.

Along with his money, however, the baron imposed strict conditions. When he underwrote their emigration, he indemnified the settlers he financed. He obligated them to him, virtually turning them into indentured servants.

The settlements had to be laid out to his exact specifications. Emigration into the existing colonies was to be determined solely by him. He dictated terms for the buying of farm implements and for the selling of crops. The moneys earned by the crops had to be divided up according to rules he laid down. He considered that he had made a charitable investment, and so expected, and took, a modest profit. Thus, his paternalism evolved into tyranny.

Russian Jews who had fled tsarist persecution now

found themselves expected to submit to a more benevolent, but nevertheless restrictive, rule. Finally, a dep-
utation of them called on the baron with a list of
reforms for the governing of the settlements. Their reception was apoplectic. "These are my colonies and I
shall do with them as I like!" was the baron's response.

Power corrupts, Philippe reflected, paraphrasing Lord
Acton's recent and much quoted epigram to himself.
He hoped that the Zionist ideal would prevent that. But
there was no way he was ever going to make his uncle
Haran see it that way.

Finally, Lord Haran spoke, breaking the silence between them, which in any case was being overwhelmed by an ear-piercing string section straining for
the high notes soon to be shattered by the bombastic
Wagnerian climax. "I don't understand your Zionism,
Philippe," he said. "Common ownership of land. Why,
that's nothing but socialism."

"I'm not a Socialist, Uncle," Philippe protested. "I do
think the European royal houses are on their way out,
though. I do believe that French democracy, imperfect
and chaotic as it is, will lead the way for all Europe in
the future."

"French democracy, which gave us the Dreyfus Case?
And what of your *Judenkaiser*, Franz Josef? What happens to the royal House of Hapsburg, which has been
such a friend of the Jews, when your democracy takes
over Europe? No, Philippe. I am committed to main-
taining a balance of power by economic means among
the various royal houses of Europe. I truly believe in
the system of monarchy."

"But you are a businessman and a pragmatist, Uncle.
Open your eyes to the future," Philippe urged. "If we
merchant bankers are to survive, we must make alliances with more democratic interests. You will yet see

that France is our wisest investment. The days of kings are numbered."

"Numbered kings." His Majesty sat up, yawning, stretching, and idly echoing the words that had roused him. He cocked his head. There was silence, and then, suddenly, a thunderclap of drums and cymbals. "Not over yet—the days of kings." He lay back down on the couch and closed his eyes again. He appeared to be dozing as he had been before, but actually King Edward was simply lying there with his eyes closed.

"What is to be done about Sir Everard Hambro?" Philippe returned to the point in a low voice. "All of the other abductors' demands are being met except Spain. If he is the key, a way must be found to make him cooperate."

"I've already found a way." Lord Haran reassured him. "To make up for the loss of the Cullinan, I have let Sir Everard in on a munitions deal with Germany."

"And this will ensure his cooperation?"

"By Jove, it is not tit for tat, Philippe. That is not the way we do things here in England. But to answer your question, yes, he will cooperate."

"This munitions deal with Germany?" he inquired instead. "Does it involve arms meant for aggression against France?"

Lord Haran shrugged. "The House of Diamond will be glad also to sell arms to France. Arms deter wars. They don't cause them."

"Ahh, yes, Uncle. I remember how well they deterred the Franco-Prussian war. All that dead cannon fodder was deterred remarkably. You can wager they'll never fight another war."

"Simplistic, by Jove. Munitions are often the only means for peace-loving nations to protect themselves against aggression."

Philippe, leaning back, cocked an eyebrow. "Peace-loving nations like Germany?"

The music was reaching a crescendo now, which even the king with his eyes closed could no longer ignore. "I have been listening," he informed them over it. "As you know, Lord Haran, I don't usually interfere in the world of commerce, but I must say that I agree with your nephew. Arming Germany can't be a wise course. Cousin Willie is a demented child filled with hostility. You don't give a loaded gun to such a child. Providing arms to Germany cannot be in England's best interests."

"The sale was cleared with the Ministry of Trade, Sire." Lord Haran was conciliatory. "The munitions are manufactured in Manchester. Our plants there enjoy some twenty-five thousand workers. If they don't produce, they shut down. If we don't sell arms to the Germans, the Hungarians will."

Philippe knew that was true. Even the Emperor Franz Josef would not be able to prevent the sale of arms manufactured in Hungary to Germany. As in England, there were investment capital and profit and jobs involved.

"Even so"—the king yawned—"give Germany the means, and she will swallow up all Europe."

Philippe, seeing his opportunity, took it. "Your Majesty is quite correct," he said quickly, before his uncle might devise still more rationalizations. He went on to reveal to the king that Germany had signed a secret nonaggression and mutual defense treaty with Russia.

"That is very serious." The king spoke loudly so as to be heard over the finale of the Wagner. "Does Henry know about this?" he asked Lord Haran, referring to the Liberal Prime Minister of Great Britain, Henry Campbell-Bannerman.

"I had hoped to have a chance to inform him of it

tonight, Your Majesty," Philippe interjected quickly. "I have certain—ahh—suggestions I would like to put before you, Sire, and the prime minister."

"I would like to point out, Sire," Lord Haran said, "that the prime minister and his party are a large part of the reason that Manchester armaments are being sold to Germany. The Liberal policy of disarmament is systematically depriving us of the British market. Winston believes it is endangering the national security."

"If Winston had his way, he would provide cannon to those Boy Guide Troops that Baden-Powell is trying to recruit." The king had reservations about the idea of organizing boys. He had been a boy once himself. "It is my policy, Lord Haran, to refuse rides on young Winston's bandwagons on principle." The king scowled at the still-mounting volume of the never-ending Wagner. "Even so, I am only the king, while Campbell-Bannerman is the elected representative of the people and therefore empowered to decide policy for the nation."

Philippe shot his uncle a look. Did he appreciate the import of the king's admission? Did he understand that this, too, signaled the end of monarchy in all respects save its trappings? And in solid England, too, not one of the more shaky courts of decadent Europe. Still, Philippe recognized that monarchy was not completely without its influence. To have the king on his side when he spoke with the prime minister would be a decided asset. "I have just come from Vienna, Excellency," he told King Edward.

"The old emperor is well, I trust?"

"He is, Sire."

"And still shocking the burghers with the fair Katharina?"

"Yes, Majesty."

"By God, I have to hand it to the old goat. I can only hope I'm half the man he is when I reach his age."

"I'm sure you will be, Sire." Philippe knew that the king was only eleven years younger than the emperor, but he liked to pretend the difference was greater—particularly where his exploits with the ladies were concerned. Still, it was true that the emperor was in much better health. "I discussed the secret German-Russian pact with the emperor," Philippe continued quickly, not wanting the king to detour further on the topic of Franz Josef's sexual prowess. "Like yourself, Majesty, he was gravely concerned. So concerned, in fact, that I am authorized to broach the subject with you, Sire, and with the prime minister, of a protective alliance."

"An alliance with the Austrians?" King Edward nodded his approval. "By God, the idea has merit."

"The P.M. may not think so, Sire," Lord Haran reminded him. "His party is opposed to all alliances on principle, fearing they may embroil England in armed conflict."

"Cousin Willie may do that anyway. Better to have an ally than to stand alone." The king smiled at Philippe. "Young man, you bring this up to Henry, and I will be there beside you to urge him to control his negativity."

"Thank you, Sire." Philippe took a deep breath. "Actually, His Excellency the Emperor has committed himself, if England will agree, to a three-way alliance to counter the Germans and Russians."

The king and Lord Haran responded simultaneously. "The third party?"

"Oh, no!" Lord Haran guessed the answer even as the question was being raised.

"France," Philippe replied. "The emperor envisions a triple alliance against Germany and Russia consisting of England, France, and Austria-Hungary." He did not add that the idea had been solely his and that the emperor had only agreed on condition that both the other participants join.

"England and France allies, eh? Bury the ancient battle-ax?" The king was both cautious and bemused by the idea. "Has Clemenceau agreed to this?"

"He has not yet been approached, Sire," Philippe admitted. "The emperor thought, and I agree, that it might be best to have a concrete proposition to which both England and Austria-Hungary agreed before inviting Clemenceau to join."

"Quite so." The king laughed. "What choice will he have if we agree, eh? He can't very well ally France with the Bosche."

"Opposition to Clemenceau is strong," Lord Haran reminded them. "I have grave doubts that he could get such a treaty through the Senate, not to mention the Chamber of Deputies."

"They will have no more choice than he has," Philippe pointed out. "No one wishes to ally France with Germany."

"Well, I've no love for the Frenchies—begging your pardon, young man—but I fear Cousin Willie's *soldaten* a lot more," the king said. "Let us get on to this reception, Monsieur Diamant, and you and I together shall see what we can do with my Liberal P.M." He was practically shouting now to be heard over the music's ear-splitting finale.

In the eerie silence that followed it, there was a knock at the door separating the anteroom from the corridor of Albert Hall. Lord Haran answered it. He recognized a liveried footman from his home in the charge of one of the fusiliers guarding the Royal Box. The servant had a message for him.

"With your permission, Sire?"

"Of course, Lord Haran, go on and read it."

Lord Haran tore open the envelope and perused the

note inside. A dazed look spread over his face. Fearing for his father, Philippe inquired if it was bad news.

"By Jove!" Lord Haran replied, his voice disbelieving. "My daughter Minerva . . ."

"What has happened, Uncle?"

"She has eloped. She has run away with a tailor." Anger mixed now with Lord Haran's disbelief. "Minerva has run off and married a journeyman tailor. By Jove!"

6. FRANKFURT

"RUN AWAY?" GABRIELLE'S voice was doubtful. "Escape?"

"Together," Baron Immanuel was careful to specify. "We could be together always."

They were stretched out facing each other on the Baron's narrow cot in the small attic room that was his prison. They had just finished making love, as they had made love every night since that first time. The baron was naked under the sheet. But Gabrielle was not. There was always the chance that her relief might show up early, or that Josef Rothko might arrive unexpectedly, or that there might be some other unanticipated interruption. The baron under covers on his cot might explain away his nudity if necessary, but logic would mitigate against any such explanation from her. And so Gabrielle made love with her clothes on—half off, really—her skirt raised, her buttons opened, her underwear in the pocket of the workingman's jacket she wore over her homespun dress.

"I don't know." The baron could see that the idea

made her uneasy. "It would be a betrayal of my comrades."

"We love each other," the baron said, stroking her brown hair. "I love you. I want to be with you. If we don't escape together, I may be killed. Even if I'm released, how could we ever find each other again? But if you were to help me escape . . ."

"I've never been disloyal to the anarchist cause. I've never gone against what we all agreed was policy."

"Policy?" The baron looked at her with dismay. "I thought you loved me as I love you."

"I do. But—"

"If we could get out of here," the baron rhapsodized, changing tactics, "we could lie in each other's arms all night, every night, without fear. I would make you so happy." His touch was intimate.

"Ahh." She responded. "When you do that, I would do anything you wanted."

The baron moved his hand. "Then help me escape."

"I have to think," Gabrielle moaned. "I can't think clearly when you do that. . . ."

The next night the baron deliberately held back when he made love to Gabrielle. Calculatedly, he remained inside her. "Have you thought about it?" He moved cunningly. "Will you arrange things so we can run away together?" His mouth swooped down to tease the tip of her breast. "Will you?"

"I'm so confused." Gabrielle stared down at the steel-gray hair. Her body arched, rising to him.

"Will you?" The baron raised his head and looked adoringly into her eyes. He thrust deeply, fully.

"I don't know." Gabrielle felt the fierce onrush of her second orgasm. "Yes. No. I don't know."

* * *

"Not tonight," the baron said the next time. "I can't. This prison has me in its grip like hands around my throat. I want only to be with you, but I will die here, and you won't help me. It's all I can think about. You. Our love. That you won't help me. And so tonight I can't."

"But you can." Gabrielle held the sheet high and pointed. "You see? You can. You are ready."

"No." The baron's thin face was tragic. His slender, athletic body pulled away from her. "I can no longer make love to you when you do not love me enough in return to help me. I am only facing the truth. Your anarchists are dearer to you than I am."

"But that isn't so," Gabrielle protested. "I do love you. I do."

"If only I could believe that."

"I want you." She grasped him. "I want you so much." She guided his hand. "So much."

"But not enough to help me escape."

"Oh, I do. I will." Gabrielle surrendered to him. "I will help you escape."

"You will help me escape." The baron began to move deeply, rhythmically.

"I will help you escape." Her arms, her legs, her gaze, all clutched him. "I will help you escape."

"How?" was the baron's next question as they lay together in the aftermath of lovemaking. "How shall we manage our escape together, my dearest one?"

"We'll plan it very carefully," Gabrielle assured him. "Oh, you are a devil," she said as he kissed the nape of her neck. "What woman could resist you? Not many, I'm sure."

"You are the only woman for me, my angel," the baron responded automatically. Unexpectedly, he found himself ready to make love again. His hands moved to cup her breasts as he pushed his erection against her belly.

"And you are a marvelous lover." She turned to gaze into his eyes. "But then, you've *had* so many women." Unexpectedly, Gabrielle shifted her weight and straddled him. "Are you glad you *had* them all? Will you be glad you *had* me?"

The baron was disconcerted. What was all this about the women he had had? But the position was such that he could not direct his attention to analyzing her words. She was moving over him now, and the question eluded him as he moved with her.

"Such a great lover," she singsonged as she rose and descended, and described small, tight circles. "To have 'had' so many women. Gentile women. Jewish women. Me. To have had me. Will you be glad," she asked once again, "to have had me?"

"Yes," he gasped. "When we get away from here—"

"To have had me now. Right now." Gabrielle raked his shoulders with her fingernails. "Right now!"

"Now!" the baron echoed and joined in Gabrielle's release.

"And so now I have once again, like all the others, been *had*," Gabrielle declared when they were once again lying side by side, their passion spent. "Or have I?"

"What do you mean, my dearest?"

"Are you so sure you had me? Are you sure it wasn't I who had you?"

"I don't understand."

"Then I will explain," Gabrielle told him. "I will explain to you as you have explained so many things to me. All those women you had. You used them. Just as you've been trying to use me to help you escape. But you made a fatal error, my darling. You see, all this time, I've been using you. You thought you were in control—the wealthy man, the man of substance—but you were wrong. *I* was in control. From the very start,

I was in control." Gabrielle smiled in triumph. "I just wanted to see how far you would go for something you wanted."

"My freedom," the baron realized. He pulled away and regarded her. "I see."

"Exactly. A poor girl sells her body for food and what do you call her? A whore, that's what. Well, Baron, I've been a whore. I've been used by men. Yes, even by wealthy men, by men like you. They used my body just as I've been using your body for my satisfaction. I sold them my flesh just as you've been selling me your flesh in exchange for a chance at freedom. You're the whore, Baron. How do you like it?"

"The escape? You were just leading me on."

"Yes. I wanted to see if you were any different from the rest of us, any different from folk like me, the people on the bottom. It turns out you're not. You, too, will do what you have to do to survive. You will be a prostitute. You will sell yourself. You will abase yourself."

"Then our lovemaking was just your way of making a political statement?" The baron carefully kept his reaction under control.

"You mean I wasn't feeling real love as you were? My God, Baron, is there no limit to how much your kind underestimates my kind? If I made love in the interests of anarchism, although there is always the possibility that all I was doing was scratching an itch just as you rich men so often do with your courtesans, is that any worse than you making love in order to contrive your escape so you could scamper back to your millions and set your foot on the backs of the masses once again?"

The baron drew the sheet close around him. "That a Jewish woman should behave so . . ." He shook his head in wonder as the words trailed off.

"A Jewish woman?" There was an unpleasant braying quality to Gabrielle's voice. "Who better understands the exploitation by Jewish men like you? You're not satisfied with grinding us down with your wealth. You use religion to do it also. I need no rich capitalist to teach me that. I learned it at my father's knee. Where else? Your wealth is only one tool of the paternalistic exploitation of Jewish women by Jewish men. That exploitation starts with Talmudic law and Hassidic custom. It starts with the ritual baths, with the shaved heads, with having to sit behind a screen in the synagogue so as not to tempt the men at prayer to the heresy of erection. I dealt with that a long time ago."

"And so now you are no longer Jewish?" The baron was sarcastic.

"I stopped being Jewish when I started being a woman." Gabrielle's words were scathing. "There was a choice to be made. I chose womanhood."

"And all the Jewish women who chose otherwise? Are they inferior to you because they remain true to the religion into which they were born?"

"Will the good Jewish men permit them to be anything but inferior?" Gabrielle rose and quickly smoothed down her clothing. The gesture said the conversation was at an end.

The baron stared at her. He did not allow it to show, but he was devastated. He really had thought that his seduction of Gabrielle was leading to her cooperation in securing his freedom. And all the time she had been using him, laughing at him. Yes, she had *had* him right enough.

He had never met her like before. Indeed, he had not dreamed that a woman who could harbor such feelings existed. A woman who could feel the hatred she felt, do what she had done . . . Such a woman could kill him.

7. PARIS

PHILIPPE'S CURRENT QUEST was for the man who wanted
to kill him. It led him to the Maison Gardien, an exclusive Parisian men's club frequented by Clericalists and
members of the Royalist Party who were jointly committed to returning to the Church the lands and tax
powers seized by the Third Republic, and to the resto-
ration of the French monarchy. Combined, the two
groups constituted only a political minority. Their importance lay in the balance of power they held between the ruling coalition of Republicans and Socialists
on the one hand and the Anti-Semitic opposition party
on the other. So far, they had sided publicly with Clemenceau's coalition. Privately, however, the members
of the elite Maison Gardien leaned toward the philosophy of the Anti-Semites. No Jews were allowed as either members or guests of the club.

This did not stop Philippe from striding purposefully
across the circular "square" of the Place des Victoires,
past the bronze statue of Louis XIV by Bosio, and into
the entrance to Number Four, one of the dozen buildings designed in the same monumental style by archi-
tect Jules Hardouin-Mansart. The edifice conformed to
its surroundings just as the members of Maison Gardien, which it housed, conformed to one another. The
setting, like those who took their relaxation there, was
conservative, traditional, and hidebound.

The doorman of the Maison Gardien was as dodder-
ing and creaky as the political philosophy of its members, many of whom where somewhat younger than
the ideas they espoused. He did not know what to make
of the fashionably dressed, blond young man with the

impeccably waxed mustache who came through the portals emanating such confidence. The gentleman wasn't a member—the doorman knew all the members—he was not an expected guest, and yet . . . "May I be of service, Monsieur?" The young man's air of importance made the doorman proceed cautiously.

"The *salle à manger*?" Peremptorily, Philippe inquired about the location of the dining room as he handed the doorman his hat, walking stick, and gloves.

The gesture further unnerved the doorman. It was not his job to relieve gentlemen of their outerwear. There was a cloakroom attendant for that. He was trying to find the tactful words to explain this when Philippe spoke more brusquely.

"Come come, my man!" Marvelous how a few days in England could sharpen one's manner toward menials, Philippe reflected even as he spoke. "I don't want to keep Monsieur Devereaux waiting."

The name tipped the balance for the doorman. Monsieur Armand Devereaux was the Minister of the Department of Taxation and Levies and a very important member of the Maison Gardien. He served on the Board of Trustees, responsible for overseeing the club's hiring and firing policies. Obviously this gentleman must be expected. Either Monsieur Devereaux had forgotten to leave his name, or he, the doorman, his memory blunted by his years of faithful service, had himself lost track.

Now, reacting to Philippe's impatiently tapping foot, the doorman directed him up the broad staircase to the salle à manger. Watching the slender, erect, stylish figure ascend the stairs, it never occurred to the doorman that the dapper young gentleman might be one of those barred by club policy from the premises. It never occurred to him that Philippe might be a Jew.

Philippe entered the gloomy dining room and

scanned the tables. The draperies had been drawn against the glare of day, and the modulated gaslighting gave off a diffuse light that seemed to enhance an aura of somber weight. Tables were spaced widely apart for privacy, and in the murmured conversations concerning business and politics the spaces between the words were often as weighted as the words themselves. The atmosphere contributed to the awareness that important men dined here, and between the sips of their mellowed brandy and the small bites of their *canard à l'orange*, the fate of France was redefined daily.

The man Philippe sought, the man who wanted to kill him, Armand Devereaux, was seated at a corner table with three other men. His square figure, its stockiness typical of the landed bourgeoisie gentry from which he sprang, was positioned with its back to the dining room, facing the wall against which two of his three companions sat. They were deep in a conversation that was punctuated more by sips of their brandy than attention to the food they had ordered.

Philippe strode purposefully across the salle à manger, his course calculated to take him past Devereaux's table. He did not pause as he came abreast of it, but he did deliberately hook his foot out under Devereaux's chair in order to kick the seated man's ankle as painfully as possible. Then, without breaking stride, Philippe tossed an apology of sorts over his shoulder. "Pardon, Monsieur, but you should not stick such large feet out where people must walk."

Automatically, Devereaux had started to apologize himself, or at least to return the apology he had expected to receive. But at that moment Philippe half turned to look at him from over his shoulder. Devereaux saw who the man was who had kicked him so painfully and immediately all thought of dismissing a trivial accident, a stumble, was banished. Instead, Devereaux rose to his feet in what seemed to be a decided overreaction, and loudly accused Philippe of being deliberately clumsy, rude, and bad mannered.

Philippe responded haughtily. "You should pull in your peasant feet, Monsieur," he informed Devereaux. "You should not present them as unsightly objects to trip up innocent passersby." His voice, too, resonated.

The hum of conversation in the softly lit dining room died down. Heads turned. Eyes refocused. Monocles were repositioned. A prominent member of the Anti-Semite Party who was dining at the Maison Gardien as a guest recognized Philippe and wondered aloud, "What is that Jew doing here?"

"You dare to deliberately provoke me, Monsieur?" Devereaux was livid.

"Your outsize appendages were the provocation, sir." Philippe replied calmly. "Tripped up by them as I was, I might have done myself harm."

"You confront me! You!" Devereaux sputtered. "You dare to show yourself here? You! Here, where I dine? Here, at my club? You— You—"

"Please be so good as to control yourself, Monsieur. You are embarrassing me before this company." Philippe spread his hands and turned to the room at large as if requesting their understanding of a situation in which he had been placed through no fault of his own.

"I?" Devereaux's voice rose several octaves. "I am embarrassing you?"

"Do not shout at me, Monsieur. It is insulting. I caution you that it is not wise to insult me."

"The Jew is a crack shot," the Anti-Semite whispered to his companion.

"Not wise? Not wise?" Devereaux answered Philippe. "When it is you who have insulted me, who have besmirched my honor, compromised my good name, dragged me through the mud?" He was quivering with rage.

"By tripping over your outstretched feet, Monsieur?" Once again Philippe spoke to the room at large, soliciting their sympathy for the ridiculous accusation, rather than appealing directly to his adversary.

"What is it all about?" one mystified diner inquired of another.

"More than Devereaux's big feet," the other replied. He bent to whisper in his friend's ear.

"Really?" The first man giggled at what he was hearing. "How delicious!"

"Satisfaction!" Devereaux was snarling now. "I demand satisfaction."

"Because of this paltry matter?" Philippe shrugged wearily. "Go back to your luncheon, Monsieur. And I will continue to my appointment."

"Not this paltry matter!" Devereaux pronounced each word slowly and distinctly. "You know that very well," he added in a tone so low as to constitute a hiss. "I demand satisfaction!" he repeated.

"I have no idea what you are talking about," Philippe dissembled.

"No? Then I will tell you."

"I advise against that, Monsieur," Philippe cautioned him in a voice so low that only the two of them could hear the comment. "You will only embarrass your own house."

Despite his rage, Devereaux managed to curb his tongue. Not, however, his desire for revenge. "Satisfaction!" he repeated stubbornly. He took a step backward and then, with a long stroke, slapped Philippe full in the face. "The time and the place are yours to name, Monsieur." He spoke the ritual words challenging Philippe to a duel.

"Devereaux is an accomplished marksman," one of

the challenger's fellow Royalists confided to a Clericalist.

"But the Jew, Diamant, has fought many duels and
never lost one," the Clericalist responded.

"That is true." A pause. "What is a Jew doing here,
anyway?"

His palm against his reddened cheek, Philippe responded to Devereaux: "It would be ridiculous to fight
a duel because I tripped over your foot. I decline."

A sigh spread over the dining room. Every man there
saw the common sense in Philippe's response. Every
man there also suspected cowardice behind it.

"My seconds will call on you." Devereaux ignored
Philippe's response. He refused to let the matter drop.

Philippe looked away from Devereaux's face. "I will
not be at home to them," he muttered.

The common sigh turned into a hum of disapproval.
It was no longer a question of being reasonable. The
blond dandy's manhood had been openly questioned,
and he had failed the challenge. There was no further
room for doubt. The man was a poltroon.

"Am I to understand that you deny me satisfaction,
sir?" Devereaux was perspiring heavily, torn between
his blood lust and the satisfaction of exposing the cow-
ardliness of the man he wanted to kill.

"It is too unimportant a matter to fight a duel over."
Staring at his boot tops, Philippe gave his answer.

"You know better, sir. You know that I have long
since announced my intention to reclaim my honor
from you on the dueling ground."

"I will not fight you, Monsieur."

"Then you are a coward!" Devereaux pronounced
the words loudly.

Philippe shrugged.

"You are a yellow kike!"

The room buzzed with the spreading scandal that

somehow a Jew had penetrated the premises of the exclusive Maison Gardien.

Philippe turned away from Devereaux then and started toward the exit.

"Cowardly kike!" The repetition of the insult by Devereaux followed Philippe out of the salle à manger.

Behind him, his identification spread like wildfire. This was the Jew Diamant, a renowned duelist, a crack pistol shot, who had intruded himself here only to be challenged and to respond by showing the white feather. A coward was the judgment of the room. And, confirming the club's bias, it was duly noted that Philippe Diamant was a Jewish coward.

Soon, as the story quickly spread, all of fashionable Paris shared that opinion.

8. NEW YORK

NAOMI LEVINE'S DRAWN-OUT trill of satisfied laughter still echoed in Noah's ears. Never had he known anybody who could become so intoxicated just from intellectual stimulus. Usually, Noah would have shared her exuberance gladly, easily, but tonight . . .

"I walk my wits and I am drunk!" Naomi spun around on the crumbly sidewalk along Avenue B, and her bubbling joy rebounded from the tenement walls on every side. Her freckles were beacons of happiness, her red curls a blaze proclaiming her excitement to the gaslight. "Who else but Jacob Adler could turn Shakespeare on his head and turn Shylock into the righteous one, an upright Jewish capitalist. Like you." Again her laughter exploded. "Ahh, if you were only a capitalist like Adler's Shylock, how I could love you."

"Could?" Noah responded immediately, his face falling. "I thought you did love me."

"Oh, I do. But if you were like that, then I could love you without feeling guilty." She grabbed Noah and spun him around and made him dance with her over the unevenly cobblestoned gutter. In a tenement doorway, a derelict set down his wine bottle and clapped his hands to provide a rhythm for them.

Noah danced with Naomi. Her body was warm and pliant in his arms. Her love was generous, tangible, physical, and so much more than physical as well. And she never held back. Never.

They danced. Her joy was contagious. For a moment it filled him. Never had Noah been so happy. Never had he been so miserable.

They were on their way back to Naomi's from a Yiddish Theater revival of *The Merchant of Venice* starring the actor who was then the toast of the Lower East Side, Jacob Adler. Although it was an English-language production, Adler had delivered all of Shylock's lines in Yiddish. His interpretation was very controversial and had created a stir that reached well beyond the Yiddish Theater. To justify Shylock by the way one played him, to give this most despised of dramatic Jews dignity and standing and ethical motivation, and all without changing a line—his translation from Yiddish to English was scrupulously exact. . . . This was what Adler had done for his people. The Broadway critics may have been divided on how successful he had been, but with the Yiddish-speaking audiences below Fourteenth Street, there was no doubt. Jacob Adler's Shylock was the only Shylock for them. It was so powerful that even Naomi, who might have been the first to denounce Shylock as a capitalist exploiter, had been co-opted by it.

At the beginning of the evening when she had met Noah for dinner at Orlovsky's Rumanian Dairy Restaurant, Naomi was very tired. She had put in her usual dawn-to-dusk day at one of Kessler's sewing machines and, walking to meet Noah, her slim, young body had felt the ache of muscles and the weariness of bone. But the play had changed that. It had revived her. She felt completely alive, and as they walked the dimly gaslit streets to her apartment, she was—uninhibited as always—sharing her exuberant feelings with the world.

It was good that she had her energy back. When they got to her apartment, they would make love. It would be the perfect climax to an emotionally and intellectually stimulating evening, an evening that had brought them very close together in a way that was not just sexual. Lately there had been many evenings like that. Their affair was becoming quite serious, and they both knew it.

At first Noah had been mostly caught up in the sex part. Naomi amazed him. She was always completely frank and never lied about their lovemaking. "Was I too fast?" he had asked her following the climax of one of their first times together. "Yes," she had told him. "Next time hold back. Calculate your investments in pork-belly futures or something. And for now—" She had shown him without embarrassment what she wanted him to do.

His timing had improved. Each tryst had been better for both of them. At least part of the reason was Naomi's openness. Everything they did was open for discussion. Noah never had to guess what she wanted. He never had to restrain himself from revealing his own desires. And so they made love uninhibitedly and it got better and better and better. Indeed, he became a wonderful lover. And much of the credit was Naomi's.

She had taken the trouble to come to know his body intimately. Trial and error had taught her quickly just where to touch him and when. She never made love in silence. She always asked, teased, told. Always the pitch of their mutual excitement grew to the accompaniment of the dialogues she sparked. The comfortable silences were reserved for the aftermath of their lovemaking.

But making love had not been enough for them. Life had so much to offer, and they discovered that all of it was twice as enjoyable in each other's company as it might have been alone. They went on ferry rides, took the bus to the Brooklyn seashore, strolled hand in hand in the shadows of the bridges on the East River waterfront. They went to inexpensive restaurants, mostly kosher, on the Lower East Side. And once or twice, like tonight, they went to the Yiddish Theater.

During the long walk back now, the sounds of tenement life, of the Lower East Side ghetto, intruded on their closeness unrelentingly. A shouted dispute in Sicilian-spiced Italian, the clatter of the feet of children playing tag up and down the fire-escape ladders of the buildings they passed, the distant singsong of food peddlers on Delancey Street hawking their wares in Yiddish, the squall of tomcats, the yelp of a mutt losing a fight, the clatter of carriages filled with young men from uptown on their way to the brothels below Division Street, were but some of the sights and sounds that intruded on their privacy. The shrill staccato of the policeman's whistle, the running footsteps, the sound of a gun being fired, a mother's shriek at a child scampering nimbly out from under the hooves of a fast-moving coach horse, the foghorns and ships' bells off the East River, the brassy rhythms of an organ grinder, the snarls of family disputes from ground-floor apartments, the flushing of the community toilet in the hall of one of the tenements they passed, a tortured violin in the hands of an unwilling child, a drunk hit-missing his way down a flight of steps, the repeated rattle of dice being rolled in an alley crap game—all these sounds and more filled the night. The ghetto never slept; its population was bursting at the seams, and the more the noisier.

Naomi hardly noticed the sounds. Noah registered every one. It was her milieu, familiar, relegated to an unimportant background as she hugged her lover's pale, strong arm to her breast while they walked. But to him it was a constant reminder that no matter the feelings between them, down here in the ghetto with Naomi he was a fish out of water.

His family, the Diamonds, had pulled themselves up out of the ghetto. Why should anyone in his right mind willingly return? And yet he had been returning as often as he could manage. Being with Naomi smothered his doubts with intimacy. Nevertheless, there were questions that could not easily be set aside.

Olivia Hamilton? What should he do about her? Once she had seemed the epitome of everything Noah wanted. Their torrid embraces, always aborted, had left him lying awake nights lusting to possess her. At the same time, her cool, blond beauty, her southern background, her poise and self-assurance had formed the contours of his impossible dream—the dream of marriage. To possess Olivia totally, and to spend the rest of his life with her as man and wife: It was a twin goal he had thought beyond his grasp.

And now it was within it.

She would wed him. She would stand up to her family. She would accept his Jewishness, defend him if necessary, make love to him with no drawing back in the legitimacy of their marriage bed. Olivia now wanted Noah as much as he had once wanted her. But . . .

But now he didn't want her anymore; he wanted only Naomi Levine!

Truly, the tables were turned. Naomi would be no more acceptable to his father, his family, his intimates of the "Our Crowd" set than he would be acceptable to the world of Virginia fox hunting. A Polish Jewess from the ghetto was no more suitable a bride for Noah Diamond than a New York Hebrew was a fitting groom for Olivia Hamilton.

To marry Olivia might be frowned upon by the older traditionalists of the House of Diamond because she wasn't Jewish; nevertheless, it would be a coup; to marry Naomi would be a more subtle, but greater, and more resented betrayal of all that had always been expected of him. But to marry Olivia would be to resign himself to a life of posturing and pretense. Only with Naomi did he feel comfortable, and passionate, and able to be himself. His pondering was a trap; his feelings were overwhelming. Noah decided to follow his feelings.

"Naomi." He stopped short in the middle of the sidewalk. "What do you think about our getting married?"

She backed away a step, suddenly defensive, arms folded over her breasts, freckles shimmering in the moonlight that had squeezed between the tenements to lend Essex Street a bit of unaccustomed romance. "I don't," she said slowly. "I don't think about it at all. I didn't think it would ever come up."

"That's not the response I expected." Noah was learning from her. He said what he thought.

"And that wasn't a proposal your average blushing maiden dreams of hearing." Her hands were on her on hips now, and her freckles were suddenly prominent.

Under her shawl, her small, sharp breasts inflated with indignation.

"I didn't think the niceties were important between us."

"Oh, yes. That's right." Naomi's sudden smile was insincere. "I'm sorry. I forgot myself for a minute, standing on ceremony that way. Let's start over. Now, what was the question?"

"Getting married. You and me. That's the question."

"Why?" Naomi moved her shoulders in small circles to relieve the tension that sitting all day at the sewing machine had left. "Why should we?"

"Why?" Noah was bewildered. "Because we love each other, I guess."

"Is that what you guess?" Suddenly, from the hip, Naomi's small fist shot out and punched Noah's belly hard. "You great lummox!" A passing drayman, on his way home late from work, saw and brayed a laugh he'd learned from his cart horse.

"What are you so—?"

"You guess! Don't you know? Don't you know I love you? And don't you know I know that you love me? You guess!" She jabbed him hard in the same place with her other fist.

"Oof!" The breath went out of Noah. Nevertheless, he was filled with joy. "Well, then, since you love me and I love you, then why don't we get married? If I survive these blows, that is."

"You're serious!" Naomi turned abruptly from him. Then she took his arm, her face still averted, and made him start walking downtown again.

"Well, of course I am."

"Why? Because we make love? Is our illicit relationship giving you a guilt complex, Noah? Is that it?"

"Night school really is doing wonders for your vocabulary." Stung, Noah responded hotly.

"Ver derharget!" Naomi told him to drop dead. "I didn't learn that in night school, you *mamzer!*"

"Why are we fighting?" Noah stopped again and took her by the shoulders. "I don't get it."

Naomi sat down on an empty stoop. "Let me think a minute." She turned halfway away from him. Finally she turned back. "We're fighting because you're making complications in this beautiful affair we've been having."

"Getting married is a complication?"

"You bet your uptown shoeshine it is."

"Why?" Noah demanded. "Why is it?"

"For starters, ladies and gents, we've got Bertha the Sewing Machine Girl"—Naomi was alluding to a currently popular Yiddish Theater drama—"and the evil banker twisting his mustache, foreclosure notices bulging from every pocket, plotting how to relieve her of her virtue."

"I don't have a mustache. And I'm not trying to relieve you of your virtue; I'm trying to marry you and make an honest woman of you."

"You don't have to marry me to make me an honest woman," Naomi said softly. "I'm not fooling now, Noah. Try to hear this. I am an honest woman. Who I sleep with has no bearing on my being an honest woman. Neither does a certificate of marriage." Naomi really meant what she was saying. It was more than a conviction with her; it was a commitment. It was an article of her own deeply held socialist faith that relationships could only be personal, never institutionalized.

The problem was that Noah didn't really understand how deeply Naomi believed this. He thought it was abstract polemics. He didn't perceive that such convictions went to Naomi's very core. And so he responded lightly, not realizing that this would only make Naomi dig in her heels even more against his proposal. "A marriage certificate can't hurt," he wheedled. "Listen, like it or not, we live in a society where women who have sex outside of marriage are not looked on tolerantly."

"That's society's problem. Not mine." She found it infuriating the way he waved her beliefs aside. And yet Naomi knew that Noah didn't mean to be insensitive. It was just that his background dictated it. Yes, his background caused the gulf between them.

"Society will make you pay. Why make an issue out of it? You admit we love each other. Why not just do it the easy way?" Noah pleaded.

"I don't believe in marriage. I really don't. I don't believe the state can legitimatize my relationship with a man. The state is the oppressor. Why should I let it tell me who to embrace?" She was repeating herself, she knew—and with the dialectic, no less. Yet she wanted so much for Noah to understand, even as she knew such understanding was beyond him.

"Forget the state. We'll get a rabbi to marry us. A religious ceremony."

"Since when are you religious?" Naomi was taken aback.

"I'm not, but—"

"It's religion that keeps the Jewish immigrants slaving in the sweatshops," she declared, cutting him off. "It tells them to be complacent about their suffering. The rabbis tell them they'll get their reward in heaven, and so they let the bosses walk all over them here on earth."

"You mean like Karl Marx?" Noah sneered. " 'Religion is the opiate of the people.' Is that what you mean?"

"Well, isn't it?"

"If you say so."

"I'd never let some hypocrite *daven* over me just to satisfy the world I was married."

"What about children?" Noah tried a different tack. "Aren't they entitled to legitimacy? Religious. Legal. Whatever. Are you ready to bring children into the world as bastards?"

"I don't want children. Not until the world can be changed so it's fit for them to live in."

As the truth sunk in, Noah's breath tightened in his stomach just as if she had punched him again. "You really are a hopeless Socialist."

"That's news to you? What else should I be? And I'll tell you something else," Naomi added defensively. "I still believe in free love, free choice for women just the same as for men—and I don't believe in restricting that with marriage." She knew that would hurt him. But it had been unfair of him to drag in religion when he was as much removed from it as she was herself.

"You want other men?" Noah cried out in disbelief.

Naomi persisted in the course she had set upon. "I might. Someday. And someday you may want another woman. Things change. Relationships change. People change. It's the way people are."

"I'm sorry I brought up marriage." Noah was bitter.

"I'm not. We've cleared the air." Naomi made an effort to dispel the bad feelings between them. She loved him. Let the question of marriage be settled and forgotten, and they would go on from there. She truly had not thought of marriage before, and she didn't want to think of it now. Their differences were too great. "Now that's out of the way," she declared, "we can be loving with each other again." She leaned across the stoop and took his face in her hands and kissed him tenderly.

"Then you really won't marry me?"

"It's a temptation. A Socialist wife, a Polish immigrant from the ghetto—that would really rock the House of Diamond to its foundations. But no, my Noah, my darling, my love. I won't marry you." Naomi stood and pulled him to his feet. "Your people are bankers." She linked her arm in his and started walking toward her tenement, explaining her position to him in its simplest terms. "You're an exploiter." They crossed Grand Street and turned east. "I abhor everything that you and your family stand for." They turned into her block. "I'm a Socialist." They reached her stoop. "I will remain true to my class and my socialist principles." She led him up the outside steps and into the hallway. "And so I won't marry you, my beloved Noah." They went up the interior staircase. "But I will go on sleeping with you for just as long as you want me." She laughed and led the way into her apartment. "Starting now, my dearest Noah."

Marriage, Naomi thought as she undressed. What we have together is truly wonderful, but it would never survive marriage.

9. PARIS

ONLY AFTER THEY had made love and were satisfying their appetite for food did Babette broach the subject of the duel Philippe had refused to fight. She had heard about it the very day she arrived in Paris from Berlin. Her brother-in-law, whose business entwined him with the Clericalist Party, had brimmed over with the story. He knew that Babette and Field Marshal von Koerner had entertained Philippe in Berlin, and now took some satisfaction in unmasking the Jew they had befriended for the coward he was.

By not mentioning it when she first arrived at Philippe's town house on the Rue Saint-Antoine, Babette was not merely being tactful. She was being both self-ish and sensitive to the man she had come to love. Selfish because she desired him with an intensity that made her blush to contemplate. Sensitive because no matter what stories were circulating through fashionable Paris concerning him, Babette knew that Philippe was a proud man in every respect and could never be a coward.

Now they sat in their robes over a small table that had been laid in the sitting room adjoining Philippe's bedroom. One of his menservants had brought a cold supper—sliced chicken and endive salad, a plate of lobster meat fresh from the shell, and small, cold Swedish meatballs, each speared on its own individual gold toothpick—the latest Parisian rage from Stockholm—along with two bottles of champagne in a large, silver bucket of slivered ice and an insulated carafe of hot coffee to go with the *macarons*, *glaces*, and *petits fours* arranged on the serving cart. Philippe had given the servant permission to retire for the night, and then he and Babette had fallen on the viands with the gluttony of happy children. Only when they were laughing and pushing the sweets away and dawdling over their coffee did Babette mention the matter of the duel he had refused to fight.

"You could never be anything but brave. I know that." Babette's luminous eyes shone with her faith in Philippe. "Why did you turn away from Armand Devereaux's challenge?"

"Tripping over a bumpkin's big feet is not a good enough reason to risk one's life in a duel."

"That may be an answer for others, but not for me." Babette's petite body quivered with emotion in her robe. "Such flippancy demeans our love. Devereaux insulted you. He insulted your faith. That it makes good sense not to duel over words is not the point. You did not turn away because it was inconsequential any more than you turned away out of cowardice. No, Philippe, you can't shrug me off with a glib excuse as you might some casual acquaintance."

With another woman Philippe might have been annoyed at her presumption, perhaps feel a trifle threatened by her possessiveness, her right to know the truth and her ability to see it. His reaction would have been to put distance between them. Possessiveness in a married woman with whom one was having an affair was normally considered a danger signal. It might even signify that it was time to withdraw. His affair with Babette had reaped the desired consequences. He had made contact with Klemperer, and truly no longer needed to continue the affair.

All of this world-weary roué wisdom, however, was meaningless. Because Philippe felt as strongly and as possessively toward Babette as she did toward him. He could not deny her love for him. He could not deny it because he had fallen hopelessly in love with her.

"You're right." Philippe reached across the table and took her small hand in his. "I'm sorry. But the truth is complicated and difficult to explain."

"Start at the beginning." She squeezed his hand, the gesture expressing her trust in him. "Why did you go to the Maison Gardien that day? You knew that Jews were not permitted."

Philippe sighed. "I went because I knew that Armand Devereaux was lunching there."

"But why? My brother-in-law says that Devereaux had been threatening all over Paris to kill you if he ever had the chance. You must have known that. Why seek him out? And why was Devereaux making such threats?"

"I told you it was complicated."

"The challenge wasn't just over the tripping incident in the salle à manger of the Maison Gardien."

"No," Philippe admitted. "Of course not."

"What, then?"

"Some years ago, I had an affair with Devereaux's wife, Danielle." Philippe kept his eyes steadily on hers. "Recently, Danielle left Devereaux. She ran off to South America with another man. She left behind a diary in which she had written down an intimate account of our really quite short-lived relationship. Armand Devereaux found it. Unable to lay hands on her present lover, or on Danielle, his wrath focused on me. You were right in what you said before. He let it be known all over Paris that he would kill me given the most trivial opportunity."

"A casual affair?" Loverlike, Babette narrowed her sights on his definition.

"Very casual. Nothing like us."

"We are not casual, Philippe, are we?" Babette did not think their affair in any way casual. She truly believed Philippe was as deeply in love with her as she was with him. And yet, she could not have stood it if she was deceiving herself.

"No. With us it has never been casual." The words were as true as their reality had been unexpected. "This thing with Danielle Devereaux was over a long time ago. Truly, it has nothing to do with us, Babette."

"Irresistible Philippe." Babette's words were rueful. "Irresistible to so many women." Her delicate, heart-shaped face was resigned. "And now to me as well."

"You are different. We are different." He was sincere. "You must know that."

"Oui." Babette sighed and returned to the topic of the duel that Philippe had declined to fight. "I still don't understand why you didn't accept the challenge once the matter had been brought to a head. You've fought many duels for similar reasons. You're an expert shot. Surely you would have won."

"Don't be so sure. Devereaux also has a reputation as a crack shot."

"I know that you weren't afraid of him," Babette insisted. "If you were, you wouldn't have sought him out at the Maison Gardien."

"That's true," Philippe admitted. "There was another reason." He went on to explain.

The week before the incident at the Maison Gardien, Philippe told Babette, when he had returned from London, he had received a short note from Henri Seligman, of Seligman & Co., asking him to call at his offices. An appointment was made. When Philippe arrived to keep it, he found Jean Lehman of the Paris branch of Lehman Brothers and Lazarre Cohen of Banque du Cohen waiting to receive him with Henri Seligman. This was the triumvirate that had outbid Sir Everard Hambro for the Cullinan Diamond.

Seligman had inquired about arrangements for Philippe's father's ransom, the details of which he had read in the Paris newspapers. Philippe told them that things were working out. In America, Italy, Spain, and Switzerland the demands were being met.

"And here in France? Clemenceau?" It was Lazarre Cohen, a rotund man with a complexion like ripe olives, who raised the question.

"In confidence, gentlemen. This concerns my father's safety, and perhaps the safety of other French Jews as well."

Their assurances were punctuated by billows of cigar smoke. Philippe accepted them; these were shrewd businessmen, but they were honorable men as well. And the bond of their each being Jewish in a France where anti-Semitism in the wake of the Dreyfus Case was a constant threat ensured that the common safety of their people would be held above any thought of personal gain.

"Clemenceau is quietly arranging for the release of the dynamiters from Devil's Island," Philippe revealed.

"Then all the anarchist demands have been met and Baron von Diamant will soon be out of their hands. Praise be to God the Almighty." Jean Lehman held to the old orthodoxy. He was a genuinely pious man with eyes that were dark and deep set and that could blaze with Old Testament fervor. His sentiment was genuine. He not only liked the baron but recognized that any one of them could be a victim, seized for ransom, or murdered by anarchists or rabid anti-Semites.

Henri Seligman sounded a more practical note. "If the release of the dynamiters should become public knowledge, the Anti-Semite Party will have a field day with Clemenceau."

"Which is why it must not come out," Philippe quickly responded.

"Then there are arrangements to—ahh—buttress the premier's position?" Henri Seligman's eyes were sharp behind his pince-nez.

"Oui." With these men, no further explanation was necessary. They all understood that the House of Diamond must be underwriting the bonds for the Bank of France. This was an injection of adrenaline to the depressed French economy that would energize the public faith in Clemenceau. The markets would react most positively, not just in Paris but around the world.

Patting his belly as if it were a pet poodle, Lazarre Cohen now led the conversation around to the reason behind the meeting. "About the Cullinan . . ." The name of the world-famous diamond hung in the air as if the jewel itself were being swung from a chain to attract attention, to hold it, perhaps to hypnotize. After a moment he looked up at Philippe from soft, dark, innocent eyes.

Philippe shrugged.

The gesture gained their respect. They were just beginning to realize that this too-handsome young fellow always in the vanguard of foppish fashion was not the lightweight he so often seemed to be. To know what to say and when to say it was one thing; to know when to remain silent and wait was everything.

"Our motives in acquiring the Cullinan were mixed." Lazarre Cohen continued speaking. "Naturally we saw the profit if the stone is properly cut and marketed. We have the connections in Amsterdam for the cutting, and in other jewelry markets around the world to sell the gems. Just as you do," he added. "But we also wanted the Cullinan for patriotic reasons."

"Patriotic reasons?" Philippe raised a skeptical eyebrow.

"We hold France dear just as you do, Philippe. If you had stayed in the bidding, we would not have entered. We had no wish to drive the price up against a *landsman*. But there was a certain transparent arrogance to the lowness of the British bid, as if perhaps Sir Everard Hambro had advance knowledge that you would drop out. Perhaps from your uncle, Lord Haran?" It was a shot in the dark. Lord Haran's Anglophilia was well known in the financial community.

Philippe's swarthy face with its romantically faded dueling scar remained impassive. He was here to listen, not to provide answers. He dropped a small smile into the silence now, but that was all.

"We've recently heard that the Cullinan will provide sixty perfect stones," Jean Lehman intoned. "Praise be to the Almighty."

"A handsome profit," Philippe remarked, inhaling the aroma of his brandy, "for outwitting the English."

"Who thought they won it in the Boer War!" Lazarre Cohen rumbled, his hands clasped over his round stomach now as if restraining it.

"Ahh, well." Philippe smiled. Actually he sympathized with Cohen's resentment. But he didn't show it.

"Nevertheless, we feel some contrition," Henri Seligman declared. "The House of Diamond should have had the stone. Having deprived the British of it, we would now like to offer you a share of the Cullinan equal to each of ours at cost."

"That's very nice of you." Philippe elegantly puffed his cigar. "Very brotherly." Philippe puffed. "I do wish I could think of something nice to do for you gentlemen in return." He puffed.

"There may be." Henri Seligman looked at Lazarre Cohen and Jean Lehman. He cleared his throat. "If I may bring up a rather delicate matter?"

"Of course." Ahead by twenty percent on the profit of sixty diamonds for a reason he sensed he was about to learn, Philippe was expansive. "Be frank, I beg you."

"It concerns one Armand Devereaux."

"Devereaux?" Philippe did not think to hide his surprise. "What has Devereaux to do with the Cullinan?"

"He threatens to kill you," Lazarre Cohen answered Philippe.

"I know that."

"A matter of honor, he says." Jean Lehman's pale face was slightly pink with embarrassment.

"Concerning a certain lady." Henri Seligman saw no need to mention that the lady was Armand Devereaux's wife.

"I know all that, too."

"Armand Devereaux's behavior would seem to indicate that sooner or later he will find an opportunity to challenge you."

"Oui." Philippe shrugged. "So?"

"If it is at all possible, we would like to avoid such a duel being fought."

Philippe looked from one to the other of the three financiers. "I am truly touched," he said slowly, the sarcasm coming through, "by your concern for my safety."

"If the duel were to be fought, we are sure that you would be the winner." Henri Seligman conceded that Philippe's safety was not uppermost in their minds. "It is the death of Armand Devereaux that we wish to avoid."

"Why?"

Henri Seligman looked at his two companions. Each of them nodded slightly. "Armand Devereaux is the government Minister of Taxation and Levies. He is our man," he told Philippe bluntly. "He is our cushion against the excesses of the Anti-Semite Party. Devereaux sees to it that taxes are not applied unequally to us. For a stipend, he provides insurance that our Jewish enterprises will be levied at the same rate as gentile businesses."

"But if Devereaux forces a duel on me—" Philippe protested.

"If Devereaux falls on the dueling field, his replacement will not be a Clericalist or a Monarchist. Most certainly it will not be a Socialist or a Republican. It will be an Anti-Semite, Monsieur Diamant. You may be sure of that." Henri Seligman regarded him earnestly. "That will be a disaster for us, and quite possibly for other Jewish businessmen in France as well."

"Nevertheless, he will challenge me. He has said so publicly more than once."

"You must not kill him. We want you to promise us that if you duel him, you will inflict no more than a flesh wound on him."

"How can I do that?" Philippe wondered. "Devereaux has the reputation of being a crack shot. If I fire only to wound and he shoots to kill, why then, gentlemen, the three of you will be meeting with seven other Jewish men to make up a *minyan* to say kaddish for me."

"Is there no way you could avoid this duel?" Jean Lehman formed his fingers into a church-and-steeple, and then frowned, unhappy with the result.

Philippe thought for a long moment. Here was a chance. Finally he spoke. "I don't want an equal share of the Cullinan investment," he told them. "I want you to relinquish all the profits."

"Monsieur Diamant!"

"I want the profits from the Cullinan to go to the Zionist cause," Philippe explained.

"But we are not Zionists!" Lazarre Cohen protested, thumping the round drum of his stomach once for emphasis.

"And I am not a wild duck to be shot at without shooting back," Philippe responded in a reasonable tone. "Think what you are asking of me, gentlemen. My life, or at the very least my honor. And all I ask of you is the profit from one investment for a good cause, a Jewish cause."

"But is it a good cause?" Jean Lehman worried. "We Jews are a religion, not a nation. God's Law does not tell us to settle the Holy Land, but rather to suffer His Will. Jehovah is a jealous God. He has given no sign that His People should create a secular state."

"And these Zionists with their talk of communes and such," Henri Seligman protested. "They will form their state. France will say, 'So let the Jews go there and stop disturbing us.' And when we get there, it will be share the wealth—our wealth!"

"If we try to take back the ancient land of Yisrael,

how long before all of the philistine nations unite to wipe us out?" Lazarre Cohen wondered. "Dispersed, we Jews are a difficult target. All together in one country ... I see us surrounded by enemies bent on our destruction."

"It will be a haven," Philippe replied, speaking with fervor, "from the *Protocols*, from the pogroms, from the Cossacks in Russia and the Anti-Semite Party in France and the ghettos springing up again in Germany and Holland and Austria-Hungary. It will be our own place, a Jewish place. Our land. For the first time we will have land and no one to tell us we can't own it."

"Jointly own it," Henri Seligman noted glumly. "And what about the people who live on this land now? Will they give it up so easily?"

"Historically, it is our land."

"Historically, America belonged to the Indians. But the United States government is not about to turn Florida back to the Seminoles."

"In Jerusalem it's not like that," insisted Philippe, who had never been there. "The people are Arabs, Bedouins, nomads. They drift with the sands. Zionism won't be taking the land from them, because they have never put down roots there."

"I wonder," Henri Seligman said. "Would those Arab-Bedouin-nomads agree with what you say? And if they did now, would they later?"

"It is the Land of David. The Land of Solomon. The Land of Saul," Philippe urged.

"Kings and sinners," Jean Lehmann told Philippe. "Read the Testament. Yisrael was lost to the Jews because of their sins. But where is it writ that Our Lord says the time is at hand to take it back?"

"The time is when it presents itself," Philippe insisted. "If not Palestine, where? If not now, when?"

They argued more. In truth, Philippe could not dispel their doubts. But he did wear them down to the point that they agreed the profits from the Cullinan should go to the Broncks in Amsterdam for the Zionist cause. And only then did Philippe promise not to slay the Minister of Taxation and Levies Armand Devereaux on the dueling field.

"But why didn't you just avoid him?" Babette wondered when Philippe had concluded. "Why did you seek Devereaux out?"

"Sooner or later, we would have met. He would have found some excuse to challenge me. Why wait? Better that I should pick the time and the place. Better that the matter should be out of the way."

"Poor Philippe. Now all Paris labels you a coward."

"They don't matter. You matter. And you don't think I'm a coward."

"No." Babette had been holding his hand throughout; now she pressed it to her cheek. "Are you so committed to the Zionist cause as to sacrifice the reputation of your honor to it?" she wondered.

"It is my true commitment."

"And are you not committed to me?" Babette asked lightly, the tone not concealing the depth of her feeling for him.

Philippe faced the question. So much had happened between them so quickly. First he had seen Babette as a dupe. Then, alerted by the emperor's suspicions, he had wondered if she was not playing a game counter to his own. He could only smile wryly at that memory: Babette as an agent of the kaiser; how truly absurd that suspicion had been. Now she was his true love. He did not doubt her; he did not doubt his own deep feelings. If that was not commitment, what was it?

"Yes." He acknowledged it to her. "I am committed

to you." He took a deep breath and then said what he had wanted to say for some time but had not dared because he feared that by doing so he might lose her. "I want you to leave your husband," he told Babette. "I want us to be together all the time."

"Oh, Philippe." It was a small, sad moan. "My children . . . How can I?"

"You would bring your children with you, of course. I will love them because they are yours. I will rear them as my own. They will lack for nothing."

"My marriage—"

"You would get a divorce. Then we will marry."

"But my husband . . ."

He was silent. Babette didn't love the field marshal. Philippe knew that. But her sense of obligation was strong. He knew that, too. It was for her to decide, only her.

"Where would we go? We couldn't live in Paris. You are too well known and I have family here. The disgrace—"

"Palestine." Philippe had thought about it carefully. "We would emigrate to Palestine. It is a new land. We could start with a clean slate there. I believe in the future of Palestine, and I believe we can have a role to play in it."

"But I'm not Jewish," Babette exclaimed.

"That won't matter." Philippe was sure that the marital traditions of the House of Diamond would be superfluous in this new land they would pioneer.

"I don't know, Philippe." She withdrew her hand from his. "I just don't know."

He said nothing. The decision would be hers.

"I want to be with you with all my heart. You know that. But the children. Breaking up my marriage. My husband. I have to think about it, Philippe. I cannot decide hastily. I love you so much, but . . . I must consider carefully."

"Of course."

"Oh, I do love you, Philippe. I'm not saying no. You do understand that. I'm not saying no."

"I understand."

The situation was left unresolved between them when Babette departed for her sister's home a while later. Shortly after her departure, a man on horseback reined up in front of Philippe's town house on the Rue Saint-Antoine. His horse was well lathered, and his face was lined with exhaustion. He had ridden at top speed from Bar-le-Duc with a letter for Philippe relayed from Berlin.

The letter was from Klemperer, the baron's, now Philippe's, informant among the kaiser's intimates. Philippe was wakened and he read it immediately. The kaiser had learned from his agent in the anarchist camp that all the kidnappers' demands had been met. It would take some ten days before the five countries involved had all complied. The anarchists had decided in the interests of future negotiations to keep their part of the bargain, and so at that time the Baron Immanuel von Diamant was to be set free. The kaiser's reply to his agent confirmed the orders already given: Before Baron Immanuel could be released, he was to be killed.

Philippe turned pale. The order had gone out. The kaiser's agent, posing as an anarchist, had been directed to kill the Baron Immanuel von Diamant without delay.

BOOK FOUR

1. ROME

CONTESSA TAMAR DI Falco had been in Rome on many occasions, but this was her first time in Trastevere. She had heard of it, of course. It was a theatrical and artistic neighborhood populated by artists, writers, and sculptors, its narrow, crooked byways enhanced by mimes and fire-eaters and street musicians. Boisterous carousing mixed with spicy foods and strong drinks amid naughty entertainments and carnal encounters made Trastevere Rome's turn-of-the-century Montmartre, a place where poetry met prurience in the shadows of twelfth-century Romanesque mosaics.

The coach had been too wide to navigate Trastevere's narrow streets, and so Tamar had disembarked in early-evening darkness at the bottom of its steep incline and proceeded on foot to her appointment. The narrow cobblestone walkways offered a maze of perilous choices. Should she follow a byway twisting into blackness, or a gaslit alley leading to a group of lounging rascals with insolent eyes? Soon she was hopelessly lost.

She walked tall, shoulders back, seemingly ignorant of the lustful looks she drew as she mounted the slopes of Trastevere. Apparently they did not penetrate her haughty mien. Her high-piled pompadour of lustrous blue-black curls under a sugar-scoop hat with its up-turned brim and dotted veil, her long beige cloak with its matching pillow muff in which her hands were buried, her glacé kid high shoes with their velvet tops and French heels—all these attested to a status not often encountered among females in Trastevere. Groups of Roman gentlemen sowing their wild oats were a common enough sight at the tables of the outdoor cafés and in the back-street brothels, but ladies of the aristocracy were not. This was a neighborhood where poor women catered to rich men. The artists and poets of Trastevere might peddle their sketches and couplets for a glass of wine or an ounce of tobacco, but the women, no matter their other talents, were expected to provide but one commodity, and that the world's oldest. And so, as Tamar wandered, the men's eyes lusted for that which was out of reach, exotic, and expensive; but the women's gazes were cold and unfriendly. They resented being reminded that there were privileged women who did not have to sell themselves.

They would not have believed that this fashionable lady, too, had struck her devil's bargain. Wending her way through a gauntlet of rouged cheeks and chill eyes, Tamar could not deny her connectedness with these creatures. In this man's world, she reflected, it wasn't a question of whether or not a woman sold her body, it was only a question of how.

Finally, with the help of a priest, Tamar found the out-door café that was her destination. The owner of Po-

pollo's tripped all over himself ushering the fashionable lady to a sidewalk table. He scampered to fetch her a glass of wine. The man she was to meet had not yet arrived. This annoyed Tamar, but she did not show it. She sat proud and alone.

"Tamar?" The male voice was husky with surprise.

She looked up to find Paolo Banducci beside her table. She had not come all the way from Venice to Rome to meet Paolo, and was as surprised to see him as he was to encounter her.

"What are you doing here?" Paolo demanded. "I didn't even know that you were in Rome. I thought you were in Venice." There was a suspicious note in his voice, the slight whine of the lover who is not quite sure of his loved one's fidelity.

"I was summoned to Rome unexpectedly. On business," Tamar explained.

"And you didn't contact me? You didn't inform me that you were here? You didn't let me know so that we might make arrangements to be together?" Paolo's tone was tragic. "Didn't you want to see me, Tamar?"

"Of course I did. I intended to contact you just as soon as my business was out of the way."

"What business?"

Tamar avoided the question. There was a more pressing consideration: Paolo turning up this way was most compromising. They must not be seen together. "You have to leave," she told him. "I'm here to meet my cousin, Carlo."

"Carlo Diamante?" He stared at her. "But that's why I'm here. I, too, have an appointment with him."

"I don't understand." She stared at Paolo. Her appointment with Carlo, his cryptic letter asking her to come to Rome, its urgency, was the reason she had hastened here from Venice. But why would Carlo ask Paolo Banducci, the man who was blackmailing him, to meet with them at the same place at the same time? Unless . . .

As the only possible answer was dawning on Tamar, Carlo Diamante appeared. He doffed his *boulevardier*'s silk hat to them and made a sweeping bow in his too sharply styled frock coat. His brown eyes were soft and friendly and dancing with mischief. "Buona sera, cousin." He brushed Tamar's gloved knuckles with his full, sensual lips. "Buona sera, Signor Banducci." His rich baritone voice boomed out jovially. "Isn't it a glorious springtime night?"

Sitting down, he called to the owner to bring them a bottle of fine wine. "And some of your new ripe olives to nibble on," he added.

Carlo Diamante turned to Tamar and Paolo. "Isn't this pleasant? A soft breeze, the perfume of budding lilacs in the air, good wine, ripe olives, a beautiful woman, and my most valued business partner. Come, now." He poured wine into their glasses. "Let us drink to the night and the music and above all to us."

"You have not introduced me to this lady, Signor Diamante," Paolo tried desperately.

Carlo Diamante threw back his head and laughed.

"It's no good," Tamar explained to Paolo. "He knows. If he didn't, we wouldn't be here. The question is, what now, Carlo? What do you want?"

"To drink my wine. To eat my olives. I wish to feast on your cousinly beauty, dearest Tamar."

"Don't play cat-and-mouse, cousin. Why did you summon me from Venice to this godforsaken café in the middle of this Roman slum?"

"Don't you like Trastevere, cousin? I myself find it picturesque, filled with quaint characters, spilling over with the arts, and with exquisite pre-Renaissance architecture. And this café— What better spot for a rendezvous with you and Signor Banducci? Nobody that you know, cousin, would be likely to see you here," Carlo added with pointed good humor.

"How did you find out?" Paolo was shaken.

"I saw the two of you embracing on the dock of your hotel in Venice. Imagine my surprise to find that my new business partner was my cousin's lover. I realized you must have learned of my affair with Signora Corri from her."

"What do you want, Carlo?" Tamar was forthright.

Carlo was specific. "An end to my partnership with Signor Banducci. An end to your ambition at my expense, Tamar. All our investments to revert to me at their original cost."

"But the licorice futures are worth three times as much now as when they were purchased!" Paolo Banducci's protest edged on being a howl. "Why should we—?"

"Because," Tamar explained wearily, "if we do not do as Carlo says, he will inform my husband of our relationship."

"Then I'll tell the Minister of Trade about Signor Diamante's affair with his wife," Paolo countered.

"It's a standoff, Paolo." Good Lord, he was slow. "You can't blackmail Carlo anymore, because now he's blackmailing us."

"More wine?" Carlo Diamante was solicitous. He poured for everyone.

"I don't care." Paolo's face was particularly handsome when he pouted. "Let your husband know. Then you can leave him and we can be together always."

Carlo Diamante, who was not a very good businessman, was, however, attuned to the nuances of amorous affairs. One eyebrow rose slightly as he looked at his cousin. Paolo's all-for-love message was not reflected in Tamar's lovely face.

"No, Paolo." Falling back on convention, she was less

than honest. She could not tell him that she didn't love him; that she had taken him as a lover in order to get the things she wanted most—power and control. "There is my honor and the good name of my son to consider. I cannot disgrace myself, or the house of Di Falco. Our secret must be kept." She nodded slightly at Carlo. "Nobody tells tales on anybody," she said. "Will that satisfy you?"

"Sì. That and the return at cost of my licorice futures."

"Then it's not a condition that we end our . . . friendship," Paolo realized.

"I would not sleep nights if I were such a spoilsport." Carlo was magnanimous. "We are all free to pursue our amorous interests as before. Only now we will no longer confuse them with matters of business."

Paolo was relieved. "At least," he told Tamar, "we will have our love."

Carlo met Tamar's eyes. Her sigh was very slight, but he did not miss it. He read its meaning correctly. Paolo Banducci was of no further use to Tamar. Lovers came cheap and were easy to find. "If you'll excuse me." Carlo diplomatically went to the *gabinetto per signori.*

"Listen to me, Paolo," Tamar said as soon as Carlo was gone. "We must end our affair. Being found out like this makes me realize what an awful thing we're doing to my unsuspecting husband. I feel too guilty to go on."

"There's someone else!" Paolo leapt to the usual jealous lover's conclusion.

"That's not true!" Tamar willed her eyes to fill with tears. "How can you even think that? No other man but you could ever make me be unfaithful to my marriage vows."

"Then how can you deny us our love?" Paolo demanded.

"We have to be strong enough to give it up," she told him. "You have to be strong, my darling. You have to get up now and walk away from me. And you must promise me not to look back."

"But, Tamar—"

"No. No. Do not destroy me." Her voice rose a little hysterically. "Go now. Go quickly." Her face dissolved in tears.

Head bowed, feet dragging, Paolo Banducci left.

A moment later, as she was drying her tears, Tamar's cousin, Carlo Diamante, returned to the table. "Are you all right?" he inquired.

"Sì. I have ended an ill-starred affair. That is all." She did not say aloud what she was thinking, that in truth she would not miss Paolo Banducci very much.

2 . NEW YORK

NAOMI LEVINE SAT on the fire escape of her apartment with her legs dangling over the side and regarded Noah Diamond with disapproving blue eyes. "This is the biggest watermelon I've ever seen. It's obscene."

"If it offends you, I'll return it."

"It's a rich people's watermelon. Only rich people could afford it."

"I bought it on Delancey Street," Noah told her drily. His response was automatic. His mind wasn't really on their banter.

"No matter where you bought it, I tell you it's a watermelon for bankers' bellies. Poor people like me will get tummy aches from it."

"That settles it. I will take it back." Noah wrested it from her and made a move as though to go down the fire escape ladder with it.

"Over my dead body!" Naomi snatched it from him and ran into the one-room apartment. When she returned a few moments later, it was with two slabs carved from the watermelon. "One for the plutocrat." She handed it to him. "And one for his lady."

They sat munching watermelon, she contentedly, Noah with concealed unhappiness. The breeze off the East River was warm and pungent. Soon spring would be slipping into summer. Soon these apartments would be sweatboxes and people would be leaning off the fire escapes with their tongues hanging out for just the taste of a breath of fresh air. But right now the Lower East Side was at its most livable—no baking in the oven apartments, no freezing in the heatless hovels while the landlords grew fat on the shortage of housing for poor people. Yes, it was a rare in-between night on the Lower East Side, a night without rain or snow, a perfect night for lovers. Indeed, Naomi's was not the only fire escape where couples huddled, the gaslight in the rooms behind them turned down as much to provide privacy as to save money.

"Any napkins?" Noah asked, watermelon juice running down his chin.

"That's what sleeves are for." She demonstrated with her bare arm.

Noah looked at the sleeve of his custom-made suit and made a face. He climbed through the window into the apartment and then went out to the bathroom in the hallway. Here he washed his face and wiped it dry with toilet paper. Then he returned to Naomi on the fire escape.

"All spanking clean?" Her grin was mischievous.

"I just don't like being sticky." He was defensive.

"Don't you?" Suddenly she had him by the shoulders and was pushing him backwards, in toward the window. Her mouth covered his, sweet with the watermelon juices. "And did I leave you sticky," she asked when the kiss was over. "Should I lick it spanky clean?"

Noah felt amused, aroused, and guilty all at the same time. Her small, sharp tongue darted at his lips. Her hand moved intimately over his thighs. "Shouldn't we go inside?" He felt still guiltier asking it.

"What kind of girl do you think I am?" Naomi teased him. The moonlight lit up her freckles and washed over the red of her hair. "Just because I allow you to take certain liberties out here on the fire escape doesn't mean I hold my virtue cheap." She leaned in and kissed him again. "A good girl may pet on the fire escape," she told him breathlessly when the kiss was over, "but that doesn't mean she's easy."

Drawing back from him, Naomi sighed. "I saw in the paper today that the House of Diamond is backing the Panama Canal again." She frowned disapprovingly. "Didn't you tell me that your people were out of the Panama venture?"

"They were. Now they're back in."

"It's just greed." The Panama Canal offended Naomi's socialist conscience for many reasons. "Nothing but greed."

"Trade. Development. Business." Noah ticked off the points defensively. "In the end, the canal will be a boon to both Central and South America."

"With the investors clearing so much per ton passing through from now to eternity." Naomi had been taking a course in economics uptown at Cooper Union.

"The bonds will pay a dividend," Noah granted. "Why

not? Aren't the backers entitled to a return on their money in such a risky venture?"

"Money has no right to earn money." It was a first principle of socialism. "And every cent of profit will be drenched in the blood of those who sickened and died building the canal."

"Yellow Fever is not a Wall Street product," Noah objected.

"And the revolution that separated the Panamanian isthmus from Colombia and established a government whose first act was to sign an agreement allowing the United States to take over the French excavations and complete the building of the canal? Was that revolution a Wall Street product?" Cooper Union also offered a course in current events.

"The House of Diamond had no part in that."

"Of course," she jeered. "What's done is done, and today your responsibility is to the stockholders."

"I don't want to argue about this anymore." Noah was placating. "It's true that the House of Diamond is once again financing the canal. That's what you wanted to know, and now you do. Can't we just drop it?" he asked wearily.

"But I don't know why. You withdrew. That's what you told me. Your hands were clean. Now they're dirty again. Why?"

"You don't really want an explanation; you want a *mea culpa.*"

"I suppose you're right." Naomi sighed. How could she have fallen in love with a man so involved in everything she was against? Their principles would never be the same. Yet she was in love with him, and the proposal of marriage she had so blithely declined just a few weeks previously had affected her deeply. If only she could make Noah understand . . .

Noah was relieved to have the subject shelved. If

Naomi had persisted, he would have been forced to open a can of worms involving the topic he had been skirting all evening. It would still have to be faced, but Noah didn't want the remoteness of their Panama Canal dispute to blur a matter so painful and personal. Their love—its resolution—was one thing; the Panama Canal, a thing apart.

Nevertheless, the two were related. It had begun not with Naomi, but with Noah's early obsession with Olivia Hamilton. He had struggled to maintain some semblance of dignity as Olivia wound him around her little finger. To Olivia he had been both exotic and off limits. Still, he had pursued her and he had convinced himself that his feelings for her would win out in the end. But when they had, things had changed and he was no longer sure the prize he'd sought was one he wished to claim.

Noah had grown in the relationship with Naomi. He had seen past the immediate sexual gratification, although its intensity had shaken him profoundly, to the genuine depth of his feelings for her. Regardless of the consequences, of his duty to his family, he wanted to spend his life with her. The night Naomi had rejected his offer of marriage, Noah had gone home and lain awake until dawn. He felt bitter and angry. He knew that Naomi's decision was firm. She was against everything he and his family stood for. She cared more for her principles than for him. Was love never equal?

At least Olivia Hamilton was willing to make changes for him, to stand against her family. Or so he reasoned. And thus, his attitude was softened toward Olivia when next they met.

She was not, on that occasion, the self-assured young woman he had come to know. There was an air of desperation in the depths of her gray-green eyes. In truth, their last encounter, in which Noah had been so uncharacteristically blasé regarding the future of their relationship, had left Olivia deeply shaken. Always she had been sure of him, and of his desire for her; now she couldn't tell. Perversely, she now felt he was more irresistible than ever.

"I have no shame," she'd told him bluntly. "I want us to marry. If you turn away from me now, I don't know what I'll do."

At that moment the image of Naomi's laughing face as she rejected him sprang to his mind. He empathized with Olivia's desperation. He reached out to her. A spark passed between them with the touch. Then Olivia was in his arms and she was crying.

Perhaps it was the tears—the contrast between Olivia's woeful countenance and Naomi's smiling rejection. Perhaps it was that once he had wanted Olivia so desperately, despaired of having her, and now she wanted him. The unattainable was attainable, and Noah heard himself saying yes—yes, of course they would marry.

Thus it was decided. Olivia told her father. Noah told his. The patriarchs, true to form, disapproved equally.

Olivia set about convincing her father that she was serious about marrying Noah. Since childhood, his beautiful blond daughter had evidenced a will of iron, and now she was determined to merge the blue blood of the Hamiltons with the House of Diamond. Finally the senior Hamilton capitulated, never dreaming that Noah's family might view the match even more negatively than he did.

"We Diamond men do not marry out of our faith," Marcus Diamond had reminded his son. "Our daughters may marry suitable Christians to strengthen the family, but our sons may not marry gentile women no matter how prestigious their families. That way the House of Diamond remains always in Jewish hands. The sons of Jewish mothers are Jewish always. The sons of gentile

mothers may not be. If you insist on marrying Olivia
Hamilton, all the elders of the House of Diamond will
stand opposed. They may even drive you out of the
firm."

"All, Father?" Noah had pinned him down. "Including you?"

Marcus had sighed. "I will stand up for you, my boy.
You are, after all, my only son. But I can't promise it
will do any good. You are flying in the face of family
tradition. And why? Do you really love Olivia so
much?" Marcus had looked at his son piercingly. He
knew him well. He didn't think so.

Nevertheless, at Noah's urging, Marcus Diamond
agreed to a meeting with Olivia's father. Of course, the
two men detested each other on sight. But it didn't matter. Their children were determined to marry.

Marcus perceived immediately that only Hamilton's
love for his daughter was stronger than his anti-
Semitism. And the minx had persuaded her father that
what he had always believed might really be true: The
Jews really did know the secret of making money.

With that as a foundation, they had put aside their
mutual dislike. Their discussion had been far-ranging,
beginning with the Panama Canal. In the end, an accommodation had been reached between the House of
Diamond and Hamilton & Sons. The House of Diamond would now be an equal partner in underwriting
the canal.

In exchange, Marcus Diamond had brought Hamilton
& Sons in on a refinancing deal involving a young
Dearborn, Michigan, horseless-carriage manufacturer
named Henry Ford who had devised an assembly-line
system of making automobiles. Ford had insisted on
retaining majority stock control of his company, but
the joint Diamond-Hamilton venture controlled a substantial minority block of shares. Marcus had himself

gone to Michigan, toured the Ford factory, as well as the older, more traditional plant founded by Olds, and seen for himself what impact Ford's mechanical genius would have on a market hungry for affordable transportation.

"It's the ground floor," Marcus had told the eldest Hamilton, "of an enterprise that will put a vehicle in the barn of every farmer from Maine to California. The key is mass production, low price, and volume. It will take Ford a year or more to go into production with the Model T, but when he does, the American automobile will have been turned from a luxury and a plaything into a necessity. In the end, there will be more profit from the Model T than from the canal itself."

Hamilton's two brothers, who were also his partners, had been dubious. To them, the Ford proposition had all the earmarks of "a smart-ass Yankee deal." Why should they surrender a virtual monopoly over the Panama Canal financing in exchange for this pipe dream?

Olivia's marriage, of course, was the answer. As she had prevailed over her father, he now prevailed over his two younger brothers. He didn't ask them, he told them.

The final compromise centered on the wedding ceremony itself. They concluded on a large wedding at the Hamilton family plantation mansion in Virginia and a small religious ceremony in the rabbi's study of Beth Israel Synagogue in New York.

All the details were worked out, except for Noah's telling Naomi Levine.

Above all else, Noah didn't want Naomi to be angry with him. It was crazy. He was about to tell her he was going to end their affair and marry another woman, yet Noah didn't want Naomi to be angry with him. He valued her good opinion of him more even than anything else.

Good-bye forever. Just like that. But don't be mad. He couldn't stand it if she was mad. He didn't even like it that she was miffed with him about the Panama Canal.

"Do you know Alexander Berkman?" Noah asked now, cradling Naomi in his arms. Maybe this would placate her.

"Not personally." He had her full attention. She already knew about the kidnapping and the anarchists' demands.

"But you're aware of the situation?"

Naomi nodded.

"Well, my father, together with Andrew Carnegie, has persuaded the government to parole him."

"In exchange for your relative's release?"

"Part of the exchange. Yes."

"Well, good."

"So perhaps we Diamonds aren't all bad," Noah cajoled.

"You're not bad, Noah. I adore you, and you know it. As for Berkman—well, he's an anarchist. I'm a Socialist. He believes in violence and I believe in changing things as peacefully as possible. Action when necessary, yes, but restrained action. Shooting Frick accomplished nothing, and if we adopt the tactics of the persecutors, then we become the persecutors. Eugene Debs understands that. Not all Socialists do, but many do, and I am one who does."

"Then you don't care if Berkman is paroled?"

"He's a political prisoner." She shrugged. "He shouldn't be held in jail. Carnegie authorized the slaughter of the strikers, and he walks free. His crime is far worse than Berkman's. Frick still lives. So why not free Berkman?" Naomi had a sudden thought. "If something goes wrong with the release of your relative, will Berkman still be paroled?"

"Probably not," Noah granted. "At least not immediately."

"My God, we are at your mercy!" Naomi's voice was filled with despair. "Every one of you is Kessler"—she named her boss—"with a shave and haircut and a manicure to boot. You're sleek and polished, but you are all Kessler under the skin."

Noah was dismayed. He did not want to part on such a note, but he would have to tell her. The evening was growing late. "Kessler," he said carefully. "How is it going there, Naomi?"

"He's a pig." She answered bluntly. "But soon now, I'll leave Kessler's."

"Where will you go?"

"My roommate has a friend who is a foreman at the Triangle Shirtwaist. She thinks he can get me a job there as a sleeve cutter. It's a step up. Mostly the cutters are all men. Also"—Naomi grinned—"I'll be organizing for the union there. That's more important than the job. Organizing the union at Triangle, that would be some step forward for the labor movement in the garment industry. Triangle is major, *kappish*?"

" '*Kappish*'? That's not Yiddish."

"Italian." Naomi's grin broadened. "I'm branching out." She studied him for a long, silent moment. "So all right, Noah," she said finally. "What is it? All night there's been something bothering you. It's like you are walking on eggs. So tell me."

"I don't know how." He blurted out his misery.

"That bad?" Naomi leaned back against the fire escape, hugging herself. "Well, you'd better tell me. And then I have something to tell you."

"What?" Any distraction was welcome to Noah.

"Later. First you tell me what's bothering you."

And so, finally, he told her. "If you had agreed to

marry me—" he began, trying to excuse himself. "But you wouldn't, and so—"

"No strings." Naomi nodded. She had turned very white. Her freckles were barely discernible under the pallor. "You're right, Noah. I wouldn't let you entangle me, and I have no right to demand anything of you. So you'll marry." She nodded again. "Well, I truly wish you happiness."

"Naomi," he groaned. "Naomi, I—"

"*Sha. Sha.* It's all right. You will do what is right for you. Marriage. A woman of your own class. A home. Truly, I wish you well. I wish you happiness."

"I'll miss you so much." Noah held her.

"Miss me?" She pushed him away and held him at arm's length a moment. "We are not to see each other anymore, then?"

"I'm getting married, Naomi. I can't continue our affair as if that weren't happening."

"Why not?" She held up her hand quickly. "No. No. I withdraw the question. I'm sorry, Noah, those are my principles—not yours. Of course I can't expect you to go on seeing me, go on sleeping with me, go on making love to me. You're going to sign a marriage contract, a legal document, doubtless backed up by clergy—a rabbi, Noah? Never mind, it's not important—and to you that is a binding pledge." Her words tripped off her tongue as her face grew whiter and whiter. Now she laughed without humor. "And so it's over with us. But no hard feelings, Noah, really. Really, I mean that. I wish you happiness. I wish you much happiness."

Naomi stopped talking then. The silence was dreadful. Noah felt as if the dark evening sky were closing in on him. The brightness of Naomi's smile was like a whiplash on his cheek. Finally, he steeled himself and turned his eyes to hers for this, their last good-bye.

"There was something you said you had to tell me," he remembered, postponing that final moment.

"It was nothing." Her smile was unchanging, her blue eyes clear, terribly clear.

"Are you sure?"

"I've forgotten what it was myself." She cupped his face in her hands. "Good-bye, Noah." She kissed him. "Good-bye, my love." She pushed him gently through the window and toward the door. An instant later he'd crossed the room and the door was closed behind him, and the tears began to fall down her cheeks. Naomi was alone, and she had not told him that she was pregnant.

3. FRANKFURT

THE DOOR TO the Baron von Diamant's attic prison opened to admit the Polish peasant guard Jerzy. The baron felt a flash of disappointment. Despite himself, he had been hoping it might be Gabrielle. He missed her, even though he was afraid of her. But his ordeal was empty without her.

There had never been any communication with Jerzy. The baron had always assumed that he spoke only Polish. Now, however, the stocky guard surprised him by addressing him in broken German.

At first the baron didn't understand what he was telling him. The Polish man was grinning through uneven snaggle teeth, one missing in front, and repeating the same distorted German words over and over. Finally the baron separated out the mangled syllables and comprehended. Jerzy was saying that the anarchists' demands were being met and soon he would be released.

The baron found himself grinning back, his lips curved in a smile so broad that it bisected his narrow face from ear to ear. It was so broad, indeed, that the dimple on his cheek found daylight from under the tangle of his unshaven side-whiskers. He was to be set free!

He questioned Jerzy carefully, listening patiently to his answers, making him repeat them until he gleaned meaning from the thick Polish accent overlaying the German words. Agreement had been reached. The arrangements had been made. As soon as the physical exchange had been effectuated by the other side, the anarchists would keep their part of the bargain and turn the baron loose.

There had been, Jerzy informed him, some sentiment for reneging by hard-liners. They were for delivering his dead body to those who had ransomed him as a statement of justice for all capitalist oppressors. But in the end, establishing the precedent of releasing the hostage when ransom demands were met had prevailed. There would be future abductions, future situations like this one, and credibility had to be maintained. The moderates had imposed their will; consequently, the baron was to be returned alive and unharmed. It would only be a matter of days now. Josef Rothko was in touch with those coordinating the arrangements in the different countries, and when all the exchange prisoners were in the hands of the anarchists, he would come here for the baron to escort him to a prearranged spot where he would be set free.

The baron wondered how Gabrielle would feel about his being giving his freedom. He remembered their last time together, and he shuddered. He had thought to make love to her and to use her, and she had turned the tables on him. She had used him, and then she had peeled back the pretense and shown him the true depths of her loathing.

It had been humiliating. Strange. He still felt humiliated by his thoughts of Gabrielle, the knowledge that this woman considered him *drek*. Fanatic that she was, she saw the baron as the embodiment of all that she detested—this he knew. But she had not dealt with him as a symbol. She had dealt with him as a man, granting him intimacy and using that intimacy to humiliate him. Even now the baron found that difficult to accept. If it had been up to her, the baron reflected, she would have pulled the trigger to execute him herself.

Days later, when Rothko did come, he woke the baron from a fitful sleep. It was night, and since his captors had long since deprived him of the gold pocket watch presented to him by the Emperor Franz Josef of Austria, he did not know the time. Because there was no guard in the room with him, the baron had deduced that it must be Gabrielle's shift. Since their confrontation, she had remained on the other side of his prison door when it was her turn to stand guard over him.

At first he looked up at Rothko sleepily, but then he came wide awake as the air of freedom filled his nostrils. "You've come!" the baron exclaimed, rubbing his eyes. "At last, you've come!"

"I'm sorry to have kept you waiting, baron." The youthful face was as earnest and amiable as ever under the sandy hair. "Even we anarchists, it seems, must negotiate bureaucratic pitfalls."

"But what Jerzy told me? It's true, isn't it? I am to be freed?"

"That was the consensus." Rothko's boyish smile was reassuring. "And I can see that you're eager to leave our custody."

The baron shrugged off the irony. "What happens now?" he asked.

"We will take a carriage ride, you and I. Not unlike the one that brought you here. I'm sorry, but I'm afraid you'll have to be blindfolded again." Rothko stepped over to the door. "Gabrielle," he called.

Gabrielle entered. She looked right through the baron and did not return his greeting. Her Slavic face was expressionless, although the baron fathomed a certain dark dislike lingering in her eyes. Stepping behind the baron, she tied a blindfold over his eyes. Her hands were competent and unnecessarily rough, and the cords she tied to bind his hands behind his back cut into his wrists.

Her grip was rough on his arm as she pushed him toward the top of the stairs. By contrast, Rothko's touch was friendly as he held Baron Immanuel's other arm. Maneuvering the baron between them, Rothko and Gabrielle guided him down the steps and out the back door. They ushered him into the waiting coach and seated him.

A moment later they were moving over the cobblestones, and the baron guessed they were reversing the journey that had brought him to his Frankfurt prison. The rough jostling of the wheels and the strong odor of slum offal receded after a while. The baron's nostrils picked up the aroma of springtime thistle blooming in open country and the smell of fertilizer spread over newly planted fields. There was a dirt road under the coach wheels now, and there were occasional sounds of a cow lowing, or of bleating sheep.

Finally the carriage drew to a halt. The baron couldn't be sure, but judging from the time traveled and from other signs, it seemed likely to him that he had been taken back to the farmhouse in which he had first been held prisoner following his abduction. Joseph

Rothko alit first. Then Gabrielle guided him out of the coach, her movements rough again, so that he stumbled.

"Gently, Gabrielle," Josef Rothko's educated voice chided her.

"Gently!" She snorted. "He'll be back in the lap of luxury soon enough."

Well, that, the baron told himself, was reassuring.

"I'll take charge of him from here," Josef Rothko told Gabrielle. "You can wait, and we'll ride back together." Although his tone was pleasant enough, it was clearly an order.

There was no reply from Gabrielle, no farewell for the baron. Was she sorry to see him go? Miffed to see him released alive? The baron would never know. Josef Rothko took Baron Immanuel's arm and led him down some sort of path.

Obviously they were not going into the farmhouse, if that, indeed, was the spot to which they had returned. As far as the baron could tell from the branches that brushed him as they walked, they were entering a copse of woods adjacent to the area where they had disembarked from the coach. Blindfolded, hands bound behind him, he had a sudden sickening feeling that he was being led to his execution.

"Stop here, Herr Baron." His hands gentle, Josef Rothko brought him to a halt against the trunk of a tree.

"Can't you untie me now?" His tone was almost plaintive. "And take off the blindfold."

"All in good time, Herr Baron."

"Am I not to be set free? Isn't that why you have brought me here?"

"Oh, yes, Herr Baron. The ultimate release."

An odd choice of words. The baron was bewildered,

his mind trying to hold on to a sense of assurance that his stomach was rejecting. What was happening?

As if by way of an answer, he felt something cold and hard pressed against his temple. The muzzle of a pistol! There could be no doubt! "What?"

"Rothko!"

At the sound of Gabrielle's voice, the cold, hard pressure was instantly removed. The baron heard the sound of Josef Rothko wheeling around toward the speaker. Even as the sound of his heel crunching the earth underfoot hung in the air, the roar of his pistol firing filled it. It was immediately followed by a second blast.

There was a high-pitched scream of pain. Even as it reached his ears, the baron, his blindfold still in place, was moving to escape the scene. He plunged into the woods, stumbling, bumping into trees, scratching himself with brambles. Behind him the scream was followed by the sound of a body falling to the ground.

And then a hand fell on the baron's shoulder. It was no longer gentle. Nor was Josef Rothko's voice amiable and boyish as it had always seemed in the past. It was a harsh and slightly guttural snarl now. "Oh, no, Herr Baron! You are going nowhere." He half pulled, half dragged him back to the small clearing and positioned him against the tree once again.

This time the fingers of one of Josef Rothko's hands squeezed together over Baron Immanuel's thin nostrils. To breathe, he had to open his mouth. When he did, the barrel of Rothko's pistol was shoved into it. There was the click of the hammer being drawn back.

Then there was a second click. The trigger had been pulled, but the gun did not fire. Josef Rothko cursed. He had forgotten to reload after having fired both barrels before.

The gun was removed from the baron's mouth. Still blindfolded, his hands still tied behind his back, the baron made another vain attempt at escape as Rothko reloaded. Again the baron was retrieved and positioned against the trunk of the tree. And again the barrel of the gun was forced into his mouth.

"Rothko!" It was a banshee wail, not of this world.

The gun was yanked free of the baron's mouth even as Rothko was whirling toward the sound. Too late! The clap of gunfire this time was not from Rothko's pistol. A heavy weight fell against the baron's chest, and a warm, sticky liquid gushed over him.

Baron Immanuel scrambled sideways, and the body of Josef Rothko crumpled to the ground. Everything was very quiet then. Even the birds had been stilled, had taken flight with the roar of gunfire, silent flight, respectful flight, a tribute to man's terrible weapons. "Gabrielle?" The blindfolded baron, his shirt soaked with Rothko's blood, spoke into the void.

A moan, faint, barely a whisper on the breath of the breeze, was his only answer.

Frantically, the baron turned to the tree against which he'd been standing and scraped the bark of the trunk with his forehead until he had worked the blindfold loose. Then he turned around. Joseph Rothko lay faceless and dead at his feet. A few yards away was the crumpled figure of Gabrielle. The baron hurried to her.

Hands still tied behind his back, he fell to his knees beside her. One side of her blouse was bloodsoaked. Her eyes were open, staring, and she was still breathing, a harsh rasp.

"Gabrielle." On his knees, the baron bent his neck, brought his face close to hers.

The staring eyes refocused, looked at him. He could detect no softness in her gaze, no affection. Her contempt of him was unchanged.

"You saved my life." The baron was moved by the

enormity of what she had done and still shaken by his brush with death.

"Not worth saving." Her grimace became a snarl. "You're a capitalist exploiter and a pig."

"Please, Gabrielle—"

"Go back to your trough."

The baron regarded her uncomprehendingly. "But then why—?"

Gabrielle's words came out in a hoarse whisper. "The consensus of the comrades was to let you live and set you free. Rothko was an agent provocateur, a spy for the kaiser. Did you know the kaiser wants you dead, Herr Baron? It would seem I'm not alone in hating you. Strange bedfellows, no? Me and the kaiser." Pain contorted Gabrielle's angular features and cut off the outpouring of words.

"I don't understand. If you knew that Rothko was a German agent—?"

"Better to know the spy in our midst than to have to guess who it might be." Even her anguish did not blur the contempt in Gabrielle's voice for the baron's naivete. "My job was to watch him and, finally, to save the life of the man I most despise."

"It doesn't matter why, Gabrielle. I will be in your debt always."

"Did you think I acted out of concern for you, love for you?" She barked a harsh laugh. Some blood bubbled from between her lips. "You arrogant plutocrat!"

"*Sha*, Gabrielle. *Sha. Sha.*" The baron pressed his cheek to hers. "We've got to get you to a doctor. I've got to get my hands untied so I can carry you."

"Too late, you fool. Look at me. No, not my face. Can't you see I'm bleeding to death? I won't last out the hour."

"Gabrielle." The baron was distraught. "Our intimacy

. . . it wasn't all just to get you to help me escape. I felt something. I— There was something between—"

"Don't flatter yourself, Baron." Her eyes were cruel. "You may be a successful banker, but you were a failure as a lover."

"You don't mean that, Gabrielle. What we had—"

"Would I lie on my deathbed?" Her irony, her hatred, was her final pleasure. Suddenly she half sat up. Her hand, one finger extended, shaking, pointed at the baron. "You are a dreadful lover." Gabrielle's laugh was terrible, harsh, final, and then she fell back and was still.

The baron struggled to his feet. He backed up against the nearest tree. Frantically, he sawed at his bonds, not caring that the blood from his wrists was soon flowing freely behind his back. After what seemed an eternity, they parted and his hands were free.

He hurried back to Gabrielle and cradled her in his arms. He put his ear to her mouth, and then to her bloody chest. It was no use. She was dead.

Some time later, the baron stood and walked back through the woods to the road where the carriage had deposited them. There was a farmhouse there, possibly the one in which he had been held captive when he had first been abducted. He didn't try to enter it. Instead, he started walking down the dirt road in the direction of Frankfurt.

Dawn was breaking as he reached the city. He made directly for what had once been the Judengasse. There were no guards, no chains there now. Head bowed, he walked wearily down Jew Street. Finally he reached the tall, narrow house in which his mother still lived.

The Baron Immanuel von Diamant had come home.

4. LONDON

MRS. JACOB STEINER, née Minerva Diamond, had thought about this meeting long and hard, and now, finally, it was taking place. On neutral ground, of course, which meant Claridge's, high tea and crumpets, little cucumber sandwiches on squares of feathery white bread with the crusts carefully removed. Not that the setting seemed so neutral on the face of it: The aura of white gloves and parasols, bejeweled bodices, and immaculately piled pompadours surely appeared closer to her father Lord Haran's milieu than to that of her new husband.

Jacob would not appreciate that the pastel decor and female murmurings of Claridge's at teatime were no more to the taste of Lord Haran than they were in keeping with his own idea of tea, which was of a beverage to be ingested through a cube of sugar steaming hot from a tall glass, not sipped lukewarm and bland with cream from fragile, hand-painted Spode cups balanced above wafer-thin saucers with extended manicured pinkies. Her husband would not know that this was the time of day when His Lordship customarily sought the sanctuary of his club, where whiskey-soda was served by an ancient, pensioned-off batman, and the low, comforting rumble of masculine voices prevailed. Jacob would see only the trappings of wealth in the teatime dining room of Claridge's, and he would not appreciate that he and Lord Haran were equally uncomfortable and actually united in their unwillingness to be there.

Which was precisely why Minerva had chosen high tea at Claridge's for the first face-to-face meeting following their marriage. Neither her father nor her husband had welcomed the meeting. Both had resisted it. All right, then, Minerva had reasoned, let them be equally uncomfortable with the setting.

"Cream or lemon, Jacob?" Naturally Minerva had poured.

"No." Jacob Steiner had not understood that he was being offered a choice, and Minerva did not embarrass him by pressing the point.

She poured his cup of tea. "Sugar?"

"Yes, please."

"One lump, or two?"

In such a thimble of a cup? "No sugar." Jacob changed his mind.

"Father?"

"Spare me the tea, Minerva."

"Would you prefer something else, Father? Cocoa, perhaps?"

"Cocoa!" Lord Haran grimaced. "By Jove!"

"Well, then." Minerva took a watercress sandwich and nibbled at it.

"No whiskey." The words were a lament, not a question.

"Father," Minerva reproached him. He knew better than to expect whiskey in Claridge's at teatime.

"All right. All right," Lord Haran grumbled. "If you can catch that hostess between flittings, order me a glass of sherry, then." He scowled in anticipation of the unwonted sweetness. "Order a glass for your husband, too, by Jove."

"Jacob doesn't drink intoxicating beverages, Father."

"Really?" Lord Haran regarded his new son-in-law through his monocle as the deceased French scientist Pasteur might once have regarded an *Anthrax baccillus* under the lens of his microscope. "Well, order it anyway. I'll have it if he won't."

Jacob Steiner drained his cup of tea at one gulp and continued looking down into it so as not to have to raise his eyes and meet the gaze of Lord Haran. Under the table, Minerva found his hand and squeezed it. Courage, the gesture told him. Have courage.

"It's so nice that the three of us are here together," Minerva said in a deep voice that contrasted noticeably with the fashionable chirpings around them. She appeared to be completely ignorant of the men's discomfort. "The two men I love most." She beamed at them, peering nearsightedly over the tops of her spectacles. "You know, I never realized it before, but being with the two of you together like this, I see that you are very alike."

Lord Haran and Jacob Steiner regarded each other in mutual astonishment. Jacob looked away quickly, his eyes still confused. Lord Haran continued staring at him. Alike? This creature of disjointed movements and graceless gestures, of mumbling, Polish shtetl speech patterns, this creature who was without poise and who possessed an unfortunate tendency to grovel—alike! Infatuation and marriage must have unbalanced his daughter's mind!

But Minerva had truly meant what she said. Love had pointed up every invisible similarity between her husband and her father and blurred the all-too-obvious differences. She regarded them both from the pinnacle of her new self-confident wifeliness and had reached the conclusion that they were two small boys, each self-important, unsure of himself, each ambitious in his own way and jealous of the other as regarded her affections, both fearful of losing her, one coping by bravado and the other by hiding inside himself. Her men. Minerva sighed. Little boys. She smiled. She would, like the American President Theodore Roosevelt, have to speak softly to them but carry a big stick for the times when firmness was required, as it most surely would be from time to time. Yes, she would have to be tender, but she would have to be strong.

"You will have a scone, Jacob." She was politely telling him, not asking. Jacob would need fortitude to get through this first meeting with her father. Minerva recognized how formidable Lord Haran must seem to him, what an ordeal this was. Poor, brave Jacob. Braver than he knew. She broke a tea-cake in half and applied a thin coating of Devonshire cream to the warm, crumbly, biscuitlike surface. She added a dollop of fresh strawberry preserves and handed it to her husband.

He took it hesitantly and regarded it skeptically. Finally, under Minerva's gaze, the tips of his ears red with embarrassment, he bit into the scone. Immediately his expression changed. The pleasure of a child tasting chocolate for the very first time suffused his mournful face. "This is very good!" His voice was warm and Polish with surprise.

"Sticky crumbs!" Lord Haran snorted. "Can't abide the things myself." He watched Jacob gobble down his cake with open disapproval. Never had he dreamed that one of his daughters would marry anyone so un-English.

Lord Haran looked sidewise at Minerva. She was glowing, by Jove! The silly girl was actually ga-ga over this shtetl refugee. And married to him, too, Lord Haran reminded himself. Not just the infatuation of courtship, not anymore. She was his wife now, and still she was all cow-eyes over the immigrant blighter. A journeyman tailor! Lord Haran splashed the sherry down his throat quickly so as not to have to taste it. Well, that was Minerva for you.

And it was a fait accompli. Behind all his British above-the-salt posturing, Lord Haran was a hardheaded businessman, a realist. He truly loved his daughter, and he knew when to cut his losses. Yes, a fait accompli. One way or another, he would have to be accommodating. He looked at Jacob Steiner. His elbows and knees were like bramble hazards on the smooth paths between the white linen tables of Claridge's. His lack of poise bore the stamp of the ghetto. Lord Haran shuddered. No matter. He was Minerva's husband, and Lord Haran would be accommodating.

"I don't mind telling you, Minerva, and you, too, young man, that your elopement put my nose out of joint." Characteristically, having decided that compromise and accommodation were in order, Lord Haran began by frankly stating his disapproval of the course they had chosen. "As a father, at the very least I feel deprived not to have been present at my eldest daughter's wedding."

Jacob mumbled his agreement with what Lord Haran was saying. He had warned Minerva that this was a terrible thing to do to her father. But she had not listened. So strong willed. Jacob sighed. Her character was intimidating and yet he found he loved Minerva for it.

"And I say to your face, Steiner, that you are not the husband that I would have chosen for Minerva."

Actually Lord Haran said it to the tight and spilling curls on top of Jacob Steiner's head, which was bowed so that he would not have to look at Lord Haran as he vented his all-too-justifiable fatherly spleen. Jacob felt horribly guilty. He was not worthy. Lord Haran's daughter! How could he have married her?

"All right," Lord Haran continued. "That's water under the bridge now. You're married, and there, we have it."

"We are married, and we are very happy to be married, Father." Minerva knew that her father had to let out his anger, and she was willing to suffer through his catharsis, but at the same time she wanted to be sure that certain things were clear to him, and to Jacob as well. "If you had known of our intention to wed, you would have put all sorts of obstacles in our way. Since we would have married in any case, but only probably after having been forced to defy you, it is better this way."

"Your logic has merit, Minerva," Lord Haran granted. "But only if we grant that you were better qualified to select a suitable husband than I."

Oy! That was so right. He was in perfect accord with Lord Haran. The father should decide on the husband. That was Jewish tradition. The child, particularly the daughter, should bend to his will. What had Minerva done? What had they done? The father knew what was best. He should decide, and who could say Lord Haran was wrong to not want a journeyman tailor from Savile Row as a husband for his eldest daughter? Jacob's head sank lower toward the embroidered white tablecloth. The match was the father's and only the father's to make.

Minerva again took Jacob's hand under the table and squeezed it reassuringly. She had come to know her husband. She understood that her father's words were rekindling his guilt. Believing that Jehovah always punished wrongdoing, Jacob equated guilt with having sinned and so was fearful of the punishment that would surely come. This was such a constant state with him that he appeared to be a fearful man. Indeed, he thought himself cowardly. But he wasn't cowardly. Minerva knew that. Indeed, he was much braver than he knew himself to be.

"You were saying, Father—" She smiled at Lord Haran. It was calculated; Minerva realized as a very little girl that she was not beautiful; at the same time, she comprehended that her smile was capable of lighting up her small, plain face in a way that delighted her father and that was capable of changing him temporarily from being critical to doting. "You were saying, Father, that our marriage is a fait accompli and that your objections are water under the bridge, and I do believe that you were about to address the realities of our situation."

Despite the glittering eye behind his monocle, Lord Haran was charmed. Ahh, Minerva! Her sisters were more attractive, but she was the one who had always been best able to wrap him 'round her little finger. "Your husband is your husband." He nodded. "You are my daughter. And I am a Lord of the Realm. And we must make arrangements in accord with family obligations and station."

As far as Jacob was concerned, all this fell on bewildered ears.

Lord Haran took his watch from its fob, opened the case, looked at the face, closed it, and replaced it. "I have an appointment to meet Sir Everard," he announced. "We are going on to the palace."

Jacob Steiner's eyes became very large.

"Give my regards to Sir Everard," Minerva responded. "And to His Majesty, too."

Jacob shut his eyes. It was too much.

"All right, then." Lord Haran was brusque now. "Down to business, by Jove." He tossed back his second sherry. "You are a tailor, Steiner. Isn't that so?"

Jacob's mumbled acknowledgment that this was so came out more garbled than if his mouth had still been full of pins.

"All right, then. As it happens, the House of Diamond controls three large clothing factories in Leeds. Since your position as Minerva's husband—my son-in-law—calls for a position more prestigious than that of a salaried journeyman on Savile Row, I propose that you take over the running of one of these factories with an eye toward eventually assuming control of all three. Now how does that strike you, Steiner?"

"That's very generous, Father." Minerva's smile was a benediction.

"A factory," Jacob whispered. "I don't know anything about running a factory."

"You'll learn, my boy. Rest assured, there will be people there to guide you every step of the way."

"But Jacob will be in charge." Minerva wanted to be sure. "After he learns—and I assure you, Father, that Jacob is a very quick learner—he will have full authority. That is so, isn't it?"

By Jove! Minerva was right to be skeptical. He had been mentally hedging that issue. Well, it was her happiness, and she wouldn't want a figurehead for a husband, because she understood that such a man could never be happy with himself. His daughter, by Jove! She understood intuitively how the world worked. "You have my word," Lord Haran capitulated. "A reasonable training period, and then full authority."

"Isn't that wonderful, Jacob?" Minerva turned to him.

"But a factory," he repeated miserably. "A factory to make clothing." His tone of voice identified such a place as *traif*, unkosher, forbidden.

"I don't understand." Lord Haran focused on Jacob. "Is there something wrong with a clothing factory?"

"Yes." Jacob was terrified by this powerful man whom circumstance had made his father-in-law. Nevertheless, he would not hold the word back from his lips. "It is machines. Ready-to-wear clothes, all the same—to be sold off the rack."

"I could be insulted by that, but I'm not," Lord Haran responded. "What you say is absolutely true. The House of Diamond factories in Leeds make cheap clothes to be sold at cheap prices, and we are not very much concerned with style. Is there something wrong with that?"

"No. No." Jacob tripped all over himself denying that he had meant any offense. But, he thought, it is not for me. It could never be for me.

"Your husband does not exactly seem overwhelmed by my offer." Lord Haran, frowning, addressed Minerva.

She smiled and did not answer. You dropped the child in the river and he either sank or swam. It didn't matter how much you loved him, or that he was your husband and not your child. He either sank or swam.

"Well, young man?" Lord Haran turned back to Jacob. "What do you say?"

Jacob opened his mouth, but no words came out. Minerva saw how overawed he was by her father. But to come to his aid now would be to destroy him. It was sink or swim.

"By Jove! Is your husband going to accept my offer, or not?" Lord Haran was miffed to find his generosity responded to in this way.

"He can speak for himself," Minerva calmly told her father.

"Seemingly not."

"Thank you, Your Lordship." Jacob found his voice and his courage. "But I must decline your kind offer."

Minerva expelled her breath, a whoosh of relief.

"Are you sure?" Lord Haran's eye squinted fiercely behind his monocle.

"Yes, sir. I don't want to run a factory."

Minerva beamed. Jacob was not a coward. He was standing up to her father.

There was silence among the three of them for a moment. Around them the soft hum and feminine rustle of Claridge's at teatime prevailed. Lord Haran nodded. He didn't like the position in which he found himself, but he accepted it. "Very well, then," he said to Jacob, "just what do you want to do by way of a career? After all, my daughter must be supported—and not, I insist, at some poverty level."

"Jacob aspires to run a tailor shop in Savile Row," Minerva told her father. "Isn't that so, darling?"

"Yes," Jacob whispered, having once again lost his voice.

"If you'd set us up in a Savile Row tailor shop, Father, that would be the nicest wedding present you could give us." Minerva peered over the tops of her glasses from her father to her husband and then back at her father again.

"And do you really think that he is that accomplished a tailor?" Lord Haran was dubious.

"Just look at the way that suit hangs on you, Father." Minerva leapt to her husband's defense. "That is Jacob's work. My husband is a wonderful tailor, Father. Have you ever been better fitted? And just think, you will be his foremost customer. Why, Father, one day you will be a trendsetter at Court, the one who introduces the latest new Steiner designs in gentlemen's clothing, which all the aristocracy will be vying to wear."

"Minerva!" Jacob was suddenly very firm with his wife. "Don't exaggerate."

"Could you really handle your own shop?" Lord Haran asked his son-in-law.

"With Minerva to do the books, yes. I do believe I could, Your Lordship."

"My daughter, the wife of a shopkeeper, herself a bookkeeper." Lord Haran was appalled.

"Isn't that how our family started out?" Minerva reminded him.

"We were never tailors."

"That's right. We were money changers, and then

money lenders. Come now, Father. Be fair. Give us your blessing. It would be such a lovely wedding present, Father."

"A tailor shop! By Jove!"

"Before long," Minerva assured Lord Haran as she looked at her brave husband with loving eyes, "it will be the most prestigious custom-made gentlemen's clothing store in all London." She turned to her father, and once again the smile transforming Minerva's plain face melted him.

"Very well." Lord Haran sensed the years creeping up on him. He did not want them to be devoid of the smile of his eldest daughter. "That will be my wedding present to you, then. You may select a suitable shop in Savile Row, and I will purchase it for you."

"And you will send Sir Everard and all your other friends to Jacob for their clothes, won't you, Father?" Minerva pushed.

"Yes. Yes."

"And His Highness, too?"

Jacob Steiner's jaw dropped open.

"I will suggest it to His Highness, too," Lord Haran agreed, looking at his watch again. "I really must be going." He might lose his daughter, but he knew when it was precipitate to leave.

Minerva kissed him good-bye. Jacob shook his hand so fervently that he barely avoided knocking Claridge's Spode teacups to the floor. Smiling despite himself, he made his way to the exit, and Lord Haran left his daughter and her new husband. If he had stayed any longer, who knows what further concessions he might have been forced to make.

In the coach on his way to Sir Everard Hambro's, Lord Haran felt a twinge of regret. It would be incongruous to the Yorkshire set with which he traveled that the head of the House of Diamond should have a

Savile Row tailor for a son-in-law. But then he was struck by another thought and he realized that such an incongruity was less embarrassing than it might have been: He was no longer the head of the House of Diamond.

His brother was free now, back in Vienna, and so it was not Lord Haran's iron hand, but Baron Immanuel von Diamant's, that would once again control the House of Diamond.

5. VIENNA

SCHOOLED NOT TO show emotion, Baron von Diamant was nevertheless deeply moved by his reunion with his son, Philippe. They had not always been as close as they might have been, but the baron loved his flamboyant son very much. If he had sometimes wondered in the privacy of his heart if Philippe returned this love, now he need wonder no more. It was plain to see as Philippe, straight from the Paris night train, his normal sartorial splendor rumpled from the journey, embraced his father with a fervor that all but brought tears to the stern baron's eyes.

"Thank God you're safe, Father." Philippe spoke from the heart.

For the first time in a long while, the baron saw his son as something more than the bon vivant who overindulged in vintage wines and clandestine affairs but who nevertheless had a shrewd head for business. He saw—he felt—a serious concern that had little to do with that surface image. It was good to be alive and to feel the love of such a son.

The setting for their reunion was neither private, nor particularly fitting. Philippe had located his father at an indoor riding rink on the grounds of the Hofburg Palace. Baron Immanuel was sitting in the Royal Box in the center of the bleachers circling the show ring. He was chatting with the Emperor Franz Josef as they waited for the monarch's inamorata, Katharina Schratt, to make her appearance. The emperor had given Katharina a Lippizaner riding horse for her birthday some months back, and she had been spending her spare time training it. Now she was ready to show the results of her efforts.

Servants in livery hovered around the Royal Box poised to provide various snacks, including the sinfully rich Vienna pastries that neither man's stomach could tolerate but that Katharina with her full figure adored. The men did sip some champagne from bottles nestling in buckets of slivered ice, and the baron indulged in a specially blended Turkish cigar, a treat forbidden the aging emperor by his physicians. The luxury was in sharp contrast to the sawdust on the floor of the rink and the strong, mingled odor of horseflesh and manure.

The emperor was explaining to the baron the difficult process of training Lippizaners, a breed that acquired its name from the Austrian imperial stud farm at Lippiza, near Trieste. The Lippizaner dated back to the sixteenth century, and from 1700 on it had been bred with an eye toward improving its intelligence and performing ability. In addition to being in demand from circuses because of their ability to master complicated maneuvers, the snow-white steeds, with their powerful torsos and legs bred for balance, were also favored by the Royal House for ceremonial purposes. Thus, Katharina, mounted suitably, would do the emperor honor when she rode by his side in the various pageants that claimed his presence.

"Katharina has been at it for three months now, and this, one hopes, will be her big moment," the emperor confided to the Baron Immanuel.

Now, waiting for Katharina to enter, the emperor invited Philippe to join him and the baron. Glad of the chance to be with his father, Philippe thanked Franz Josef and accepted a glass of champagne. He nibbled a biscuit with caviar; he had skipped breakfast: Philippe could not abide eating on trains.

"I was frantic that you might be killed." Philippe leaned over and half whispered to his father. "I had learned through Klemperer that the kaiser had an agent among the anarchists with instructions to murder you if they decided to set you free."

"Yes. Josef Rothko." The baron nodded. "He was a double agent. He did try to kill me. Indeed, he almost succeeded. I was saved by another anarchist—a woman." The baron said no more than that about Gabrielle. It would be too difficult to explain his relationship with the dead woman. Besides, he wasn't sure he understood it himself.

"It was a tremendous relief to hear that you'd escaped."

"I was myself amazed when your father turned up in Vienna," the emperor interjected. "Negotiations for his release had been completed, an agreement and date arrived at, but the actual exchange hadn't been effectuated yet. They were too precipitate in their actions." Franz Josef nodded to himself. "Fortunately," he added.

"The agreement will not be honored," the baron confirmed. "None of the prisoners will be released. I'm not convinced, however, that we shouldn't have lived up to all the commitments we made."

"It was blackmail!" The emperor objected angrily.

"By Bolsheviks and murderers! No bargain with them deserves to be honored!"

"They feel the same about us—we who rule, we who are rich," the baron pointed out. "But they were prepared to live up to the agreement. They would have let me go once their people were in their hands. It wasn't their fault that a German agent tried to kill me. The anarchists could have decided to renege, but they didn't."

"Honorable rascals!" the emperor snorted. "How can you romanticize them so, my dear baron?"

Philippe, too, wondered at his father's conciliatory tone.

"Perhaps I'm only being practical," the baron dissembled. He could never explain how his experience, Gabrielle's effect on him, had altered the outlook of a lifetime. Indeed, he didn't understand it himself. "If we don't deal honestly with them," he suggested instead, "then the next time, they won't deal honestly with us. They'll abduct some member of the ruling elite, we'll meet their demands, and the head of the kidnap victim will be returned in a hatbox."

"They'll probably do that anyway." The emperor snorted. "What do you think, Philippe?"

Philippe was saved from having to answer by the entrance into the show ring at that moment of Katharina Schratt on her snow-white steed. Her seat atop the Lippizaner was classic, her weight balanced deep in the middle of the saddle, her legs hanging naturally and in light contact with the body of the horse, her forearms straight and on a level with the bit, her head erect with just the trace of a smile on her red bow of a mouth. *"Grand dressage,"* she announced to her small audience, and then made the conventional circle of the ring slowly, just as if the bleachers were filled with spectators who must be greeted before the demonstration began.

It was a slow and time-consuming ceremony. Initially, the emperor's gaze followed Katharina dotingly, but she had not moved very far up the oval before she became a blur in front of his aging eyes. He turned his attention back to his guests. "Gentlemen," he suggested, "let us have some more champagne." As it was being poured, the emperor recalled his last meeting with Philippe, how hopeful their plans for an alliance against the Germans had been, and how now those hopes were dashed. For a moment he looked very much like the frail old man he was. "Let us drink to the crumbling of the old order in Austria." He sighed. "To the end of what is most pleasant and civilized as the Hun looms over the empire."

"I am sorry, Excellency." Philippe was sincere. "I really had thought—"

"They are too strong for me, my boy. And I am getting too old to stand up to them as I once did." A coalition of Austrian Anti-Semites and Germanic Austrians had learned of the proposed anti-German alliance with England and France and had aborted it. Only two days ago, the *Kaiserstadt*, the Austrian Congress, had voted overwhelmingly against even holding such discussions. "The Germanic Austrians," he told the baron and his son, "now threaten to depose me unless I negotiate a military pact with Germany instead. An ultimatum: Agree or abdicate." Franz Josef sighed. "I will agree. I have been emperor too long to take up some new profession at my age."

Katharina Schratt had arrived back at a point in front of the Royal Box. She was ready to put the Lippizaner through a series of increasingly complicated paces. To begin, she established how the steed's gait had been shortened and raised so that when she shifted her

weight smoothly in the saddle, the result was a graceful, almost girlish sort of prancing. This proceeded from
a walk to a trot to a canter in which both horse and
rider banked sideways as they circled in front of the
emperor and his guests.

"Matters may not be as bad as they seem, Excellency," Baron Immanuel tried to reassure the emperor
as they politely applauded Katharina.

"No?" Franz Josef was skeptical. "How long before
these Germanic Austrians force my poor country into
an alliance with Russia as well? And then what? Anschluss for Germanic Austrians. And annexation for
Hungarian Austrians. With such allies, the empire will
have no need for enemies."

Encouraged by the applause, Katharina now eased
the Lippizaner into a more complex series of *haute
école* movements.

"You don't have to worry about Russia, Excellency,"
the baron told him, smiling and clapping as Katharina
executed a trot in place. "I can assure you that the
balance of power is being restored."

"That phrase ... that sounds very much like your
brother Lord Haran in London. That is his phrase, is it
not? Balance of power? England's diplomacy to guarantee its supremacy over European commerce."

"I have had word from Lord Haran. Yes." The baron
exchanged amused glances with his son. The emperor
might be old, but he was a long way from senile. "I
think there is a very good chance that the not-so-secret
treaty between the kaiser and the tsar is about to un-
ravel."

Horse and rider now executed a pirouette. The Lippizaner made a complete circle in place on its
haunches, four or five controlled strides executed at an
impressive canter. Katharina's imposing figure sat mo-

tionless and regal in the saddle as the swift, gliding
movement was completed.

Philippe nodded approval of her grace to the emperor. His mind, however, was still on what his father
had revealed. He, too, had had confirmation from Lord
Haran that the secret Russo-German military treaty was
coming apart. Indeed, Philippe had been instrumental
in bringing this about. From Klemperer, the House of
Diamond informant in the kaiser's inner circle, Philippe
had been able to obtain documentation of the kaiser's
fomenting of unrest among Russia's armed forces. In
part, Germany's aim had been to weaken the tsar's control over his armies so that he would welcome a military alliance that would provide Prussian troops to put
down a rebellion like the one that had just occurred in
Russia. For some time, Philippe's father, the baron, had
been aware of the kaiser's scheme, but he had never
had proof of it. Now Klemperer had provided the proof
to Philippe, and Philippe had passed it on to Lord Haran, who had turned it over to England's King Edward.
The king had paid a visit to his "Cousin Nicky" in St.
Petersburg and shown him the evidence. The result was
that Russia was prepared to scrap its treaty with Germany and join in an anti-German alliance with England
and France. The balance of power was indeed restored—at least for the time being.

"The *lévade*," Katharina's voice broke into their
thoughts. "To be followed by the *capriole*." Philippe,
like his father and the emperor, leaned forward to observe these most difficult feats more closely.

With a flick of the rein, Katharina signaled the Lippizaner. The white stallion whinnied a reply. He was
ready. Katharina arched her torso smoothly back in the
saddle. As she did so, the beast reared up slowly on its
hind legs. At the same time, with exquisite grace, it
raised its forelegs and drew them in toward its power-

ful chest. There was not the slightest flicker of daylight between the seat of Katharina's seamless jodphurs and the buffed leather of the saddle as the Lippizaner slowly turned a circle in this difficult vertical maneuver.

"Bravo!" The emperor's enthusiasm reflected how impressed he was with Katharina. Would this generously fleshed, doll-faced young woman never cease to amaze him with her unexpected accomplishments? That she was intelligent he had long ago accepted. But Katharina was still capable of surprising him with her talents. "Bravo! Bravo!" Beside him the baron and his son echoed the emperor.

Katharina walked the Lippizaner now to ease its tension before guiding it into the most difficult maneuver of all, the capriole. The emperor took advantage of this interim to focus once again on what the baron had just told him. "If the tsar should cut himself loose from Willie," he asked bluntly, "will that mean that a Russian entente with France and England is in the offing?"

"It is certainly a possibility, Excellency."

"And the House of Diamond approves this even though the Russian tsar is surely the worst enemy that the Jews have today? It was he, was it not, Baron, who contrived *The Protocols of Zion*?"

"It was, Excellency." The baron was far from indifferent to the implications. "I have sent my brother a letter reminding him of that."

"Will it influence the English?" For enlightenment, the emperor turned to Philippe, who had recently been in London.

"I doubt it, Excellency. The English fear the Bosche far more than they despise the Muscovite."

"As do the French, I'm sure." The emperor frowned.

"In France the situation is complicated," Philippe told him. "The Anti-Semite Party, of course, will leap at the chance for an alliance with the Jew-hating tsar. They gnaw at the Dreyfus Case as a dog worries a bone, and what passes for statesmanship with them is really the specter of German aggression, which, of course, extends to Austria-Hungary. They have always vilified the House of Diamond for its friendship with you, Excellency, always seen it as a Jewish treachery designed in Berlin, and always ignored the reality of friction between Germany and Austria-Hungary. And of course to the Anti-Semites, the tsar is a hero for spawning the *Protocols*."

"Why should they damn the House of Diamond," the emperor wondered, "when it is the House that is underwriting the French government bonds?"

"They perceive that—with some justification—as a ploy to stabilize Clemenceau's government and the Third Republic." Philippe spread his hands. "Actually, Clemenceau is relieved that the alliance will probably involve Russia rather than Austria-Hungary. It takes the Anti-Semite pressure off him."

The emperor snorted and turned his attention back to the rink. Katharina and her Lippizaner were ready for their grand finale. Her soft, round face was quite serious and intent as she poised to execute the capriole.

It went off flawlessly. Responding to the gentle pressure of her thighs, the Lippizaner leapt straight up in the air, forelegs drawn in, hind legs kicking back horizontally, and without bending. Horse and rider twisted in midair—Katharina's posture perfect, its proscribed straight lines unaltered—and then the Lippizaner landed smoothly on its hind legs in exactly the same spot from which it had leapt.

Atop her steed, Katharina spread her arms wide in a very theatrical sort of bow. She trotted off with the Lippizaner showing off its final accomplishment, a sort of waltz-time dance in which it pranced and side-stepped and then backed and reared rhythmically. More heartfelt *bravos* from the emperor and his two guests followed her.

As they waited for Katharina to change and see to her toilette, the emperor returned one last time to the topic that had been bothering him. "So that is what democracy means—an accommodation with anti-Semites."

"Oui." Philippe would have liked to be able to deny it, but he could not. "It's imperfect, and yes, bigoted, but in France it is the future."

"It is anarchy!" The thunderous response transformed the emperor's lined face.

"Not really. The anarchists are only the most extreme manifestation against the last of the feudal system."

"Do you agree with your son?" The emperor turned to the baron. "Is the empire doomed?"

Once the baron would have denied the possibility with every fiber of his being. He had spent his life supporting the empire. He had believed it necessary to the maintenance of order, and he had believed that without order Europe would descend into bloody chaos. But his ordeal—and particularly Gabrielle's effect on him—had left their mark. He was beginning to face the fact that autocratic systems of government, monarchies ruling by divine right, were indeed doomed. "Yes," he said sadly. "I do believe Philippe is right. The old order will pass."

"Then so be it." The emperor observed Katharina emerging and smiled wanly. "But I will tell you one thing, Baron Immanuel. God help the Jews after I am gone and they are left to the mercy of the unrestrained citizenry of Austria. There will be no emperor to protect them then. Government without an emperor, I promise you, will seal the fate of the Austrian Jews."

Yes, thought the baron, rising to kiss the hand of the emperor's mistress, that might well be so.

6. PARIS

PHILIPPE DID NOT tarry in Vienna. He returned to Paris to await word from Babette. It was not long in coming.

She wrote from Berlin that she had made up her mind to tell her husband that she was leaving him. She would ask him for a divorce and come to Paris with her children as soon as the arrangements could be made. The three of them and Philippe could then leave for Palestine to begin their new life together. How Philippe hugged this letter to his heart! He was euphoric.

But his happiness didn't last long. The aim of love affairs may be happiness, but happiness has little to do with the nature of love itself. The course of love is unpredictable, and for Philippe and Babette this had been particularly true. Philippe's mind was not perfectly at ease. His conscience was not clear, and he saw the ravages of a guilty conscience plainly in his shaving mirror the morning he prepared to meet Babette. The features were the same, and yet the face was that of a man unalterably changed by love. The swarthiness seemed sallow now, the eyes suffered, the once-gay mouth pulled down the ends of the mustache. Where was the boulevardier, the bon vivant who had heretofore winked back at Philippe while he shaved? Love had spawned conscience, and conscience, guilt, and this unhappily introspective visage was the result.

While in Paris, Babette had written in her letter, she did not wish to embarrass her sister and brother-in-law by being seen publicly with Philippe. So it was that she was in the city for three days before they were able to arrange a meeting. The tryst, they decided, would combine discretion with nostalgia and would take place on one of the more obscure early-morning horseback-riding trails of the Bois de Boulogne.

This reminder of their first encounter was one reason for Philippe's wild mood swing from the euphoria of winning Babette to his unhappiness as he shaved on the morning the meeting was to take place. The other reason was a historic occasion that Philippe had been present for the day before—the military ceremony awarding the French Legion of Honor to Captain Alfred Dreyfus. What had this to do with Philippe and Babette? Love has a logic all its own.

The presentation of France's highest honor to France's most famous Jew was an exoneration ending ten years of disgrace, vilification, and imprisonment for Captain Dreyfus. And if it did not scratch the surface of French anti-Semitism, it was nevertheless a symbolic victory for all French Jews, including Philippe. It gave them back their honor, and suddenly Philippe found himself driven by love to reexamine that honor in the most personal terms. He had fought duels for his honor, but he had never really scrutinized it before. The honor of brave men had been the most potent weapon in the fight for justice for Alfred Dreyfus. But there was another kind of honor, one that existed in the privacy of one's mind. This intensely personal honor did not just have to do with men; it had to do with women as well.

Before Babette, Philippe had never taken women seriously. They had been partners, sometimes opponents in a game with elastic rules. He took it for granted that the woman's attitude was as lighthearted and frivolous toward whatever affair they shared as his own. His relationships with these creatures were earthy, nevertheless ephemeral, and he assumed that the women he took to bed lied to him as casually as he did to them.

But with Babette, almost from the start, it had been different. They had fallen deeply in love, and the first casualty of that love had been Philippe's cavalier attitude. Being serious about a woman was an awakening for him. Now his new awareness demanded that the standards of honor that had prevailed in the Dreyfus Affair be applied to this most important relationship in Philippe's life.

He had lied to Babette at the very beginning. He had let the lie stand throughout their love affair, and he knew that it stood between them still. No matter the consequences, he must have the honor—the courage—to set it right before accepting her commitment to go to Palestine with him. He must, even at the risk of losing her. As he rode at a canter down a bridle path of the Bois de Boulogne to meet Babette, he was steeling himself to take this necessary measure to ensure that they would not start their new life together with a lie between them.

Babette had dismounted and was waiting under the leafy bough of a weathered elm tree. Philippe rode up to her and leapt smoothly to the ground. He took her in his arms, not noticing that her heart-shaped face was as filled with some deep emotion as his own.

"How I missed you!" He held her tenderly. She was so petite, so fragile. And the soft womanliness of her response to him weakened his determination.

"There is something I must say—" Babette spoke the same words at the same time that Philippe did.

"Let me speak first." Philippe tethered his horse beside hers. It was a warm morning, and he removed his riding jacket. He spread it on the grass so that he and Babette might sit on it. When they were seated, he put his arm around her again. He did not notice how distraught she was. He was not even aware that the long, loving kiss they exchanged now shut off the words she was summoning the courage to speak to him. "Now listen to me," he whispered in her delicate ear when the kiss was over. "I have lied to you."

"What?" Babette was confused. Indeed, her mind was only half on what Philippe was saying.

"I have been living out a lie to you," Philippe amended. "Listen, Babette. Pretend that you haven't yet made up your mind to leave your husband to go to Palestine with me. Pretend that decision is still to be made."

"Why?"

"Don't speak." He put a finger over her lips. "Remember when we first met, here in the Bois de Boulogne, how we first met?"

Babette nodded.

"You had been accosted, robbed. Possibly you were about to be assaulted. I came to your rescue. Remember?"

She smiled wanly.

"That wasn't what happened," Philippe told her bluntly.

"What do you mean?" Even now, Philippe did not have her full attention.

"The man who accosted you was not a robber. He was an actor. I hired him to do it. I wanted an excuse to save you, to make your acquaintance in a way that would leave you beholden to me."

"So that you could seduce me?" Through her misery, the thought bemused Babette momentarily.

"Oui."

Babette, not yet understanding all, was flattered by Philippe's deception.

"It wasn't because I was attracted to you."

Her eyes grew large, and the slight smile on her face faded.

"I seduced you in order to meet your husband."

Babette's long lashes fluttered over large cinnamon eyes that questioned him. What was he trying to say? That he didn't love her?

"He was a member of the kaiser's inner circle. My father had been kidnapped." Philippe went on to explain in detail his suspicions regarding German involvement in his father's abduction. "In the beginning, I even suspected that you might be acting for German Intelligence," he told Babette.

"I? German Intelligence?" She was dazed.

"I know now how ridiculous that was. I stopped suspecting you of any involvement like that a long time ago. But I did contrive to meet you, to seduce you, and to use you. I lied in the beginning, and I have let the lie stand right up until now."

"But the things you said—?"

"I meant them," Philippe assured her.

"About loving me, wanting me to leave my husband, wanting to be with me always . . . ?"

"I meant it all. I still do. But if we're going to start a new life together, it can't be with a lie between us. I had to tell you, Babette. And now that you know, it's for you to say if you still want to divorce your husband and come to Palestine with me as my wife."

"I can't," Babette said miserably.

Philippe caught his breath sharply. It wasn't the response he had expected. Somehow, loverlike, he had expected that all the guilt he suffered in advance of telling Babette would have satisfied the need for further punishment. He had, of course, envisioned rejection, but he had not really expected it. He had believed instead in understanding, love, instant forgiveness. He looked down at the grass, his neck bent, his face not visible. He said nothing.

"Not because of what you've told me," Babette whispered. "Please, Philippe, look at me." When he raised his face, her gaze locked his. "You must believe that. What you've told me is unimportant. It doesn't alter what I feel about you at all."

"Then why are you changing your mind?"

"It was changed before I met you today." Babette plucked a wildflower. She looked at it. She smiled. She threw it away. A tear rolled silently down her cheek. "I can't leave my husband. I can't go with you to Palestine."

"But you wrote me—"

"That I would ask Helmut for a divorce. I did. He agreed to give me one. Only—" Babette's voice quavered. She brought it under control. "He would not give up custody of his children—our children. He forbids me to take them to Palestine. He won't allow them to leave Germany. He wouldn't even let me bring them to Paris with me." Babette bit her lip to keep from sobbing aloud. The tears splashed over her unhappy face.

"My darling." Philippe tried to comfort her.

"No!" She pushed away from him. "Don't take me in your arms. I can't stand it if you take me in your arms."

"Babette!"

"It's no good, Philippe. I can't leave my children. I can't marry you."

And there it was. Honor was not restricted to the larger issues in life like the Dreyfus Case. Nor was it solely a masculine obligation. Women, too, have their honor. In an instant Philippe recognized that the honor of women—of mothers—was the stuff of moment piled on moment, day added to day, and year to year until a lifetime passes. Such honor fights no duels. Whatever ego motivates, Philippe understood that it was quiet and hidden. And it could entail much pain, which is why, most often, it's called sacrifice. In the end Babette's honor left Philippe no choice: He had to let her go.

7. VENICE

CONTE GUIDO DI Falco bestowed a smile on his wife at the other end of the polished rosewood table where they were finishing a rare dinner for two in the dining room of their palazzo. Tamar, regarding her husband from the length of the table, was reflecting that the planes of his aristocratic face in the fickle candlelight would have been a challenge to any Renaissance sculptor.

Signaling to one of the footmen to remove their dinner plates, Tamar's eyes met the conte's. All night his had been resting appreciatively on her bare shoulders and the rise of her provocative bosom from the deep, wine-colored velvet of her dinner gown. They had eaten their dinner in uncomfortable silence, Tamar watching her husband warily as if trying to fathom his next move.

Finally, he spoke. "Business keeps me away from home so often, we rarely see each other. Is it business that keeps you from home and hearth as well?"

"Business?" she echoed mockingly and then nodded to the second footman to serve their coffee and *strega*. Concealing her bitterness, she said softly, "I have no business. I am a woman."

"Wasn't it business that took you to Rome?"

"No. I went to see my couturier. I needed some new clothes. That was all."

"Clothes? But that *is* a woman's business." Her husband's eyes were teasing over the ruffled shirt and formal dinner jacket.

"I suppose it is," she replied noncommittally. What was he driving at?

"But Rome, Tamar?" His raised eyebrow was curved, cynical. "I could understand Paris, even Milan, but an emergency journey to replenish your wardrobe in Rome . . . You must really have been desperate."

"I was." The *bastardo*! What did he know? Nothing. The trip to Rome had left her on edge, that was all. Guido could know nothing about Paolo Banducci, about her failed efforts to take over the Roman house of Diamond. "I had to have new nightgowns." Tamar smiled her most seductive smile, one she bestowed on her husband only rarely. "For the sake of my marriage," she added, fluttering her eyes for all the world as if she had been born to Italian coquetry.

"Ahh!" The conte waved away the footman before he could pour him a second cup of coffee and pushed back from the table. He walked around behind her tall, brocaded chair and held it for Tamar until she stood. "I thought we might retire early." He folded her arm in his. The knuckles of his long, graceful fingers grazed the purplish-red velvet of her bodice. His eyes were admiring, smoldering, possessive. They asked for nothing, but they claimed all.

"I would like to stroll in the garden first." To tease and then frustrate the conte, even temporarily, was a small victory for Tamar.

"But not too long a stroll." He led her toward the French doors leading out onto the terrace. His voice was pleasant, but firm. "Twenty minutes, and then to bed."

Tamar could not abide his tone. "Or else what?"

"Or else"—the conte threw back his head and laughed—"we shall *not* stroll for twenty minutes and we shall *not* retire."

The conte had never made an issue of husbandly prerogatives or connubial rights. He had made plain what he wanted, and somehow he had always claimed it without insisting. Invariably, this air of easy command had infuriated Tamar; invariably, by some alchemy she could not fathom, he had transformed her resentment into passion.

In any marriage, there are many things to forgive. Most of them, Tamar did forgive the conte. But that he aroused her in spite of herself—that was hard to forgive.

The sculpted gardens of the Di Falco palazzo were laid out to the rear of the dwelling, away from the canals. Statues of Carrera marble by some of the greatest of the Florentine masters, Renaissance pieces of inestimable value, marked the turnings of the paths through the shrubbery and flower beds all the way to the Di Falco olive groves and the small, trellised vineyard. It was spring, and the gardens spilled over with the blooming of lilac and violets, daffodils and hyancinth. There were bushes rife with forsythia and tangled vines of red and yellow roses gleaming moistly in the moonlight. Tulips marched in segregated formation—gold, ivory, scarlet. And finally there was the greenhouse reflecting back the starlight, a haven for delicate, exotic, specially bred and hand-tended orchids. They were russet, the orchids, russet and lavender and topaz. The perfume of the flowers filled the warm night.

Tamar seated herself on the polished stone bench just outside the greenhouse. The conte paused a moment, shrugged, smiled, and then sat down beside her.

He was a patient man. It was the patience born of self-assurance. His patience irritated her.

Early in life, Tamar had learned to conceal her displeasures, whatever they were, and whomever they were directed against. She did so now. She spoke of something else entirely. "And so the crisis is resolved," she observed. "The baron is redeemed, safe and unharmed."

"So it would seem."

"And nothing is changed." Now a small bitterness did indeed creep into Tamar's voice.

"Everything is changed." The conte corrected her mildly. "Such an upheaval as has taken place in the House of Diamond cannot but have an effect."

"Oh? And just what do you perceive that effect to be?"

"Well"—he smiled slightly—"your cousin Carlo in Rome will surely be happy to have his mentor back."

"You call that an effect? I regard it as business as usual." Tamar's violet eyes studied her husband shrewdly from under the spiderwebbing of her long lashes. "I shouldn't think you would be content to have the baron back in the catbird's seat, Guido. Isn't he the one that guides the hand of Rome as regards the House of Diamond's Austrian investments in Italy? Doesn't Carlo do what the baron tells him to do?"

"Not altogether." The conte's face swooped down, taking Tamar by surprise. He kissed her swiftly, and full on the lips. "Not anymore."

"What do you mean?" Tamar ignored the quickening of her pulses. "What has changed?" More than anything, Tamar disliked being kept in the dark.

"For one thing, Austria-Hungary has competition from a new quarter in Italy. Particularly in Venice." He put his arm around Tamar's bare shoulders. "You should have brought a wrap," he chided her. "The night air can turn chill."

Tamar fidgeted in the casual embrace. "The Japanese?" It wasn't hard to guess. She had long been aware of the conte's negotiations with Japanese investors. "But surely they don't pose a serious threat to Austrian control. The Venice docks—"

"An accommodation will be reached." He drew her to her feet. "One that Baron von Diamant cannot have anticipated." Linking her arm in his once again, he led her back toward the palazzo. When Tamar seemed to drag her feet, he stopped talking, only resuming when her pace once again matched his. "Carlo now recognizes the advantage of working with the Japanese." They had reached the terrace. The conte guided Tamar firmly up the broad steps to the verandah of the palazzo. They entered and mounted the staircase leading to their second-floor boudoir. The conte paused at the top of the stairs and kissed his wife again. "In future Carlo will assert his right to make decisions as head of the Rome House of Diamond without running to Vienna for guidance."

"But why?" Tamar was breathless, reluctant, and divided not only in her desire to know more but to enter their sleeping chambers.

"Your cousin Carlo has realized that he is an Italian as well as a member of the Jewish House of Diamond. He now understands that in some things he must act for the benefit of Italy rather than Austria-Hungary." The conte led Tamar into their bedroom and closed the door behind them. With his hands on her bare shoulders, he turned Tamar around and began undoing the snaps at the back of her wine-colored velvet gown.

Tamar's mind was racing. The conte had been doling out information to her in bits and pieces, a deliberate and tantalizing counterpoint to his gentle prodding toward the act of love. His fingers on her flesh as he undressed her now were meant to distract.

Even as they succeeded, Tamar did not completely succumb. Her naked breasts rose as her husband's firm, long-fingered hands slid around her to cup them. But she pursued the discussion of Carlo Diamante and the House of Diamond as the conte stepped away from her to take off his jacket and shirt. His gaze remained on her bare bosom gleaming white and firm in the gaslight as he replied. "There has been a mending of fences," he told her vaguely.

Tamar crossed her arms and covered her breasts. She waited for him to go on. The haughty expression on her proud face said she was prepared to wait for just as long as it might take.

Although the conte was amused and annoyed, his patience did not desert him. "One infidelity at a time has never been enough for your cousin Carlo," the conte reminded Tamar. He took his wife's wrists in his hands and moved her arms so that they were no longer blocking her breasts. "Most recently"—and now the conte veered cannily off on a tangent—"could Carlo have had something to celebrate?" he wondered.

"I can't imagine what you mean." Tamar turned away and walked to her dressing table. Sitting down before the mirror, she removed the pins from her coiffure. She shook her head, and the glory of her blue-black hair cascaded down over the creamy roundness of her shoulders and the breathtaking fullness of her breasts. "What would Carlo have to celebrate?"

"I wonder." The conte came to the dressing table and stood behind her. He put his hands on Tamar's shoulders and looked at her in the mirror. Tamar regarded her husband's reflection thoughtfully. His dark eyes glittered. His chest was bare. It was not the broad, yeoman's chest of Paolo Banducci, youthful and rippling with muscles. Rather it was sleek, long, of a piece with his slenderly aristocratic torso, sensual and serpentine. He bent and brushed Tamar's loose-flowing hair aside and put his lips close to the delicate shell of her ear. "I wonder." His lips brushed the pulse at the base of her neck.

Tamar shivered. A fever was spreading through her body, but she would resist. "You were telling me why Carlo is no longer under the thumb of the baron," she reminded the conte.

"So I was." Once again the conte led his wife back to their bed. He sat down in front of her, his hands on her hips signaling that he wished Tamar to remain standing. "Carlo did seem to have some cause for celebration," he told her. His hands were busy under her petticoat, peeling a lace-embroidered white stocking down from the trembling thigh of one leg. "This feeling, it seems, coincided with the Minister of Trade's catching his foot on a loose curbstone and breaking his ankle. This accident necessitated the minister's taking to his bed for a prolonged period of days—and nights— a convalescence that temporarily suspended his wife's affair with Carlo." The conte removed the first stocking and then began to slide the second one down Tamar's other leg. "Carlo's wife, Leah, lay victim to one of her recurrent attacks of sinusitis." The conte removed the second stocking and then the petticoat itself. "So here was poor Carlo filled with the need to celebrate for whatever reason, and deprived by cruel fate of both of the women in his life." He removed Tamar's petticoat and sat back and admired the shapely sweep of her long, graceful legs. The conte caught his breath. The sight of Tamar's body never failed to renew his belief that their marriage, regardless of her feelings in the matter when she had been a young bride, had been a coup for him. "And so, like many another

man, Carlo sought other company." The conte buried
his face between Tamar's extraordinary naked breasts.

"Ahh!" Her fingers tangled in his sleek, straight hair.
"But what other company"—Tamar could not help
gasping—"did Carlo seek?"

"The lady is an actress. Lucrezia Romano." The answer came muffled from lips buried in perfumed flesh.

"I've seen her." Tamar felt this sensation in her perfectly aligned white teeth. It was an itch almost, a com-
pulsion to bite, to bite deeply, to sink her teeth into
flesh, male flesh, her husband's flesh. "She was quite
good."

"Sì." His hands were behind her, kneading the roundness of Tamar's derriere through her underwear. "A
good actress. A bad choice for a partner in what was
meant to be a quick—and one-time-only—romantic interlude."

"Why a bad choice?" Tamar squirmed under his caress. Her body was on fire. She resented him for having
struck the match.

"Signorina Romano has a loose tongue. She bragged
about their brief romance—really a quick assignation,
nothing more. But she built it up in her mind. She let
it be known that it was but the beginning of what would
be a long-lived and passionate affair. Word spread."
The conte began rolling the waistband of Tamar's
bloomers down over her hips. "It spread so widely that
it even reached my ears."

"And what did you do?"

"As it happens, I am a major shareholder in the theatrical troupe of which Signora Romano is a star
player." The conte rolled the bloomers down slowly.
"When I became aware of poor Cousin Carlo's discom-
fiture over the fair Lucrezia's loose tongue, I made this
known to him." The conte paused to bestow a deep
kiss on his wife's twinkling navel.

"Oh! Don't! Don't!" Tamar's nails raked his shoulders. Twisting away, she fell to the bed beside him, half in and half out of her last undergarment. "What happened then?" she panted. "After you told Carlo?"

"We came to an agreement." The conte stood up and quickly stripped off the rest of his clothing. "I arranged to have the theatrical troupe sent on an extended tour of Sicily where Signora Romano's indiscreet tongue could not do Carlo any further harm. This meant that Carlo could conceal his indiscretion from his wife, and his mistress, who is probably much more jealous than his wife, and his patron, the baron, who regards Carlo's escapades as indicative of his frivolous attitude toward the business of the House of Diamond."

The conte regarded his wife's naked body. *Graza di Dio!* She was lovely! His desire was mixed with admiration and with true love for her.

Tamar writhed under his gaze. She resented his passion. Most of all, she resented it for arousing her own. "If you went to such trouble for Carlo," she realized, her voice unsteady, "then of course you got something in return." Unwittingly she circled her lips with her tongue as the conte stretched out beside her and took her in his arms. "What was it?"

"An accommodation," the conte admitted. He kissed her ear, her neck, the quivering tip of one of her breasts. "Carlo was very grateful and, as a result, I now have influence over the policy-making of the Roman House of Diamond." His hands were more forceful on Tamar's body now, searching, intimate.

"Don't touch me there. I don't like it."

"You adore it."

It was true. It was an indignity. She hated him for it. But it was true. When her husband probed her this way, Tamar melted. She was robbed of her resentments. Her independence was lost to her, and worst of all, she didn't care. "What will you do with this influence?" Her words came out as a breathless snarl. She reached for him, found what she sought, captured its tumescent heat in both her clutching hands.

"Use it to help free Italy from Austro-Hungarian domination." It was true. In this one area, the conte's motives were more patriotic than self-serving. He pulled himself up on the bed, his back against the headboard, and faced Tamar in a sitting position. "There is a re-alignment of power going on in Europe." He pulled Tamar over him, positioned her so that she straddled him. "Whichever way Austria-Hungary goes—with Germany and against England and France, or with England and France and against Germany—whichever way, Italy will go the opposite. One day it may come to war, and whatever else, you may be sure that Italy will fight against Austria."

"But the Roman House of Diamond?" Tamar rose up high and impaled herself upon her husband. "If Carlo is in your debt, then you really have him." He moved deeply, circling, tantalizing, arousing. She bent and kissed the conte deeply, her tongue probing. "You will dominate the Roman House of Diamond." She squashed her breasts, the nipples burning, against the bony hardness of his chest. She rocked, flinging her head back, her black hair swirling wildly. "What will you do with the House of Diamond?" she wondered, laughing, spinning, tilting with the building of the thrilling pressure deep inside her.

"Give it to you, Tamar! It will be my gift to you!" The conte pushed her over backwards, moving with her. She struggled against him. She was very strong. There was no winner. Thrashing wildly, they mounted together to their climax. "Because I love you."

"I love you, too." Tamar thought that she was just saying it in the heat of their lovemaking. She didn't know how much she meant it. Passion—unwelcome, overwhelming—obscured her love even from her.

Afterwards, Tamar thought to herself that control over the Roman House of Diamond would serve the conte's own interests, too. Even so, might not their interests merge? Tamar had long wanted to neutralize Carlo Diamante and take over the House of Diamond. She had long ago accepted that it would only be possible through some man, a proxy. Once that would have meant Paolo Banducci. Now, however, Banducci was out of the picture. So why not her husband? Wasn't it a better gift coming from him than from some milksop of a lover?

After all, her husband did love her. And when Tamar considered it, she just might love him, too. Wonder filled Tamar as she snuggled in the conte's arms and recognized that. She had never let herself face the possibility before that she might fall in love with her husband. It left Tamar unable, at that moment, to consider what she would do with her power in the Roman House of Diamond now that she had it.

Later, though, Tamar promised herself, she would think about it a great deal.

8. ROME

SIGNORA NOELLA CORRI was a practical woman, and abstract considerations such as pride never weighed as heavily on her mind as tangible satisfactions. Carlo Diamante undeniably provided such satisfactions. Even so, Signora Corri had occasional moments of doubt.

What would it be like, she often wondered, to be the mistress of a great man, rather than an average one? Best not to dwell on that, she decided. Surely the joys of the night outweigh shortcomings sharpened by daylight. By late afternoon, certainly, the glare of discrepancy should fade altogether. If that wasn't quite what was happening, surely it was only that her vision was jarred by the presence of her lover clothed, rather than pawing the ground of her boudoir in his magnificent buff.

It had been a very long time, Noella realized, since she had seen Carlo with his clothes on for any longer than it took to remove them, or later to go out the door still fumbling with hasty buttonings. Their daytime trysts had always been behind drawn draperies. Sunlight was not a usual part of their relationship. Flesh, not fashion, was what sustained their attraction to each other.

That was fortunate, Noella realized now as she sat across from Carlo at a small checker-clothed table in the dimness of the little café on the Piazza di Spagna. Carlo displayed little sartorial sense. His clothes were as loose and disorderly as his personality. Indeed, the clash of colors among his flowing cravat, afternoon shirt, and frock coat seemed as overstated as his bubbling bonhomie.

Well, one can't have everything. Her husband dressed impeccably, spoke sparsely, was never boisterous, and had a smile as dry as his personality. Noella and Carlo were meeting in this café at the foot of the Spanish Steps under the shadow of the house in which the poet John Keats had died some seventy-five years earlier because her decorous husband, the Minister of Trade, was still convalescing from his broken ankle. Since he was firmly ensconced in the bed where Noella and Carlo usually trysted, and since Noella's wifely

356 of TED GOTTFRIED

nursing duties ruled out an absence long enough to justify the taking of a hotel room for lovemaking, the lovers had settled for late-afternoon liqueurs. And so they
faced each other in shadowy daylight.

"How are your wife's sinuses?" Noella inquired, sipping her peach brandy.

"Adapting to the Maytime pollen. And your husband's ankle?"

"Healing slowly. Too slowly."

"Much too slowly," Carlo agreed.

"Your daughters are over the measles?"

"Sì. But they have hives."

"And your oldest boy's—umm—scholastic troubles?"

"We have sent him to the priests. They will shield
his eyes and tie his hands."

"And the dog?" Noella's eyes danced. "Is he housebroken yet?"

"The dog, alas, is still minimally continent." Carlo
reached across the table and took her hand in his. "All
of my problems are under control," he told her. "Right
now, my only problem is that we cannot find time and
place to be alone together."

"Poor frustrated Carlo." There was a slight mocking
note in Noella's voice that he didn't notice. "And is that
really your only problem? What about business? What
about that fellow who was blackmailing you?"

Carlo told her then how he had found out about Paolo
Banducci and his cousin Tamar and how he had confronted them and put an end to their harassment of
him. "I even forced them to give up Banducci's share
in the licorice futures at cost," he bragged.

"Your cousin Tamar has always wanted to usurp
you," Noella recalled. "She would like control of the
Rome House of Diamond for herself."

"No woman could ever do that. Besides, I have put
her back in her place."

"I see." Noella kept her reservations to herself. "Her husband, the Conte di Falco—he plunged heavily in licorice futures, too, didn't he?"

"Sì."

"I wonder how he knew about them?" Noella asked with exaggerated innocence.

Carlo shrugged. At first he had wondered himself. Now he was merely grateful that the conte *had* known about the licorice futures. It had made him appreciate Carlo's astuteness in business. It had made him want to have a commercial relationship with Carlo. Because of that, the conte had done him a favor involving that little scrape with the actress, Lucrezia Romano. It had worked out well. Carlo had gladly shown his gratitude by granting the conte a role in the affairs of the House of Diamond. The conte had important connections in high government places and among the Italian nobility. Carlo was sure that he himself would profit by such an arrangement.

Carlo was eager to tell Noella about his new relationship with the Conte di Falco. "His participation will be a great asset to the House of Diamond," he concluded.

"The conte will be an asset, but his wife would not." Noella spoke without inflection.

The statement confused Carlo. He did not know how to respond. He signaled the waiter for another brandy and gazed out the window, up the Scala di Spagna to the two-hundred-year-old Church of the Trinity at the top.

"Do you really think that if the conte has influence over your business his wife Tamar will sit by idly without making use of it for her own ends?" Noella inquired.

The thought had not occurred to Carlo. He regarded Noella now with large, worried eyes. He had been so content, felt so secure. Everything had seemed to be going so well. Why was Noella raising doubts? Why did she have to say that?

Noella did not tell Carlo that she knew about the actress Lucrezia Romano. Indeed, if he had not been so naive, he would have realized that the wagging tongues of Roman society would seek out her ear first. What moralistic gossip, after all, can resist informing an adultress that her lover is cheating on her? And with a young actress, no less? Noella had known about Carlo's affair with Lucrezia Romano before the sheets were cold. She had also heard how the Conte di Falco had stepped in to help her errant lover cover his tracks.

But Noella was wise, her youth was fleeting, and her affair with Carlo was an ongoing satisfaction to her. Even now she would not accuse him. Why spoil their time together? Besides, it is wise for a woman to always keep some ammunition in reserve.

And so now in the little café at the foot of the Spanish Steps, she smiled. She squeezed Carlo's hand. She said no more about the inevitability of Tamar's infiltrating the Rome House of Diamond through her husband.

Noella had opened the door to Carlo's anxiety. That was enough. She did not have to involve herself further in the retribution that Tamar would surely visit on Carlo. It would be Noella's revenge for his cheating on her, and Noella would never even have to confront him personally with his duplicity.

9. PARIS

LOVING BABETTE HAD changed Philippe. Now, in the void she left, he willed himself to change back. The remedy for an unhappy love affair, insisted the popinjays of turn-of-the-century Paris, is another love affair. The cure for losing a woman is another woman.

Knowing better, Philippe forced himself to plunge into this cynicism. He didn't merely revert to being the superficial roué he had been before Babette, he deliberately wallowed in the inconsequential conquest of flesh. Discrimination played little part in the succession of one-night affairs on which he embarked. Quantity, not quality, was what he wanted, to drown in meaningless passion, to forget.

Of course, his debauchery solved nothing. It did not blot out Babette's face. It did not satisfy his desire for her and only her. And in the end he was left with nothing but self-revulsion and the need to fight one more duel.

The lady's husband had returned from a business trip a day early to find Philippe and his wife drunk and together in his marriage bed. There was the inevitable challenge, and then the early-morning duel on a plain in the woods near Versailles. Even as the distance was paced off, Philippe was filled with self-disgust. When they turned to fire, Philippe deliberately squared his shoulders and waited without pulling the trigger. He did not consciously will his own death; but, on the other hand, without Babette, what was there to live for?

One of his opponent's two shots winged Philippe in the shoulder. The other missed him altogether. Philippe was so infuriated by the man's atrocious aim that on the spur of the moment he shot him in the foot. He was immediately sorry.

Later Philippe thought about it. Putting a bullet in the poor fellow's foot that way—it wasn't just unnecessary, it was an irrational thing to do. Pushing away from the brandy bottle, his too-constant companion since that day in the Bois de Boulogne when Babette had left him, Philippe considered the pattern of his recent actions. None of his escapades had been pleasurable—not the drinking, not the sex, not the companionship of the women involved. Nor had there been much in the way of satisfaction on those evenings he'd spent carousing with male friends.

Once he had floated like a contented feather on the breeze of this kind of life. Now Philippe was appalled by its lack of meaning. He thought about the plans he'd made with Babette, the plans to go to Palestine and begin a new life there together, a life dedicated to the Zionist ideal.

When Babette had gone back to her husband, he had put aside the plan to emigrate to Palestine. Now he forced himself to consider it again. There would be emptiness without Babette. But there would be a new land and commitment to an ideal. There would be a purpose to his existence.

It was the morning after he came to this decision that Philippe received the communication from Herr Klemperer. He was mildly surprised to see that it was postmarked Geneva, Switzerland, rather than Berlin. He began to read it with casual interest, but the letter soon claimed his total, heartfelt attention.

> *Dear Monsieur Diamant,*
> *I have been found out and forced to flee Germany.*
> *The tsar is furious with the kaiser for having secretly*

fomented unrest in the Russian Army, and the kaiser
would have me executed if he could for having pro-
vided you with the proof to show the tsar, and thereby
destroy the German-Russian alliance. You should know,
since you were a guest at his home when you were in
Berlin and since it was he who brought you to the kai-
ser's little gathering where first we met, that it was Field
Marshal Helmut von Koerner who discovered my dis-
closure to you of the Russian card and denounced me
to the kaiser. However, I have had my revenge.

When I took flight, I left behind documents implicat-
ing Field Marshal von Koerner as my confederate. These
papers have been accepted as proof that von Koerner's
involvement in my "treachery," the kaiser's word, was
why the field marshal infiltrated you—a French Jew—
into Kaiser Wilhelm's most intimate circle. As a result,
von Koerner, like myself, has been forced to flee Ger-
many in great haste, leaving his wife and children be-
hind.

The last word I had of him, von Koerner was in Tur-
key under an assumed name and desperately trying to
get documents for a passport to Uruguay in South
America where he would presumably be safely beyond
the kaiser's reach. As for my own predicament, only
money can alleviate it, which is why I am writing to
you, Monsieur Diamant, and asking if you can find it
in your heart . . .

Even as Philippe was finishing the letter, his telephone rang. "I'm in Paris!" It was Babette. "My children
are with me. Helmut—"

"I know." Philippe interrupted her exuberantly. "I've
just had word from—"

"He's gone. My husband. I don't know where. I'm
free."

They talked for a long, happy, semi-incoherent time.

Later, Philippe sat down and wrote a letter to his
father telling him that he wanted to give up his position
as head of the Paris House of Diamond as soon as pos-

sible. He knew that his father disapproved of Zionism, but Philippe tried very hard to make him understand how he felt about it. "Palestine is the future," he wrote. "Zionism will one day unite Jews all over Europe. It will make a homeland, a haven for Jews everywhere. I am going to make a new life there with the woman I love."

After he had finished writing it, Philippe reread the letter to his father. It was visionary, as well as lovestruck, self-serving to be sure, and perhaps naive. He did not attempt to answer all the arguments that could be made against the establishment of a Jewish state. He was not able to come to grips with what he knew to be his father's objections to Zionism. The letter could not be expected to satisfy his father any more than it would satisfy a Palestinian Arab questioning a claim four thousand years old to a scrap of desert that his people wandered over today. But it was enough for Philippe. It satisfied him.

Eight weeks later Philippe, Babette, and her two children sailed for Palestine.

10. FRANKFURT

PHILIPPE'S LETTER REACHED the Baron Immanuel von Diamant in Frankfurt. It was brought up to the suite he maintained at the Frankfurterhof by a bellhop as soon as it arrived. As a silent partner in the Steinburger chain that owned the hotel, the baron's mail was never pigeonholed like that of ordinary guests. It was always delivered immediately.

The baron read the letter over twice. Between the

lines he discerned the happiness of a man in love. But there was also determination and purpose. Philippe was going his own way, and if the baron felt saddened that his son was breaking with the House of Diamond—the family, as well as the financial empire it had struggled to build over the years—he also understood Philippe's newborn idealism, his yearnings, in a way that he would not have before his abduction—before Gabrielle.

How strange that Gabrielle, who had so despised her religion and the traditions of her people, should have been the one to provoke the baron into a reexamination of his Jewishness. This was not a religious, or a cultural, introspection, rather a pragmatic soul-searching. What did it mean to live as a Jew in the world today if one stripped away the wealth and power and titles of being the Baron von Diamant?

With all their wealth, it was only a moment in time since his family had been driven from place to place, despised, persecuted. Only the flip of a rare coin had elevated the House of Diamond from abject poverty to vast wealth. No amount of money and power exempted them from the growing force of anti-Semitism. Indeed, the baron felt its flick every time the Frankfurterhof doorman tugged his forelock and whistled him up a coach-for-hire. And the sly anti-Semitic grovelings of the doorman were only a symptom of the pogroms raging over Eastern Europe and spreading westward.

"Jews adapt." One of the few childhood memories that the baron retained was of his grandfather, Zelik Diamant, the founder of the House, pronouncing those words to settle a dispute between two of his sons. Jews adapt. That was survival. There was nothing else to be said.

Except that there was.

Beyond adapting, perhaps even above survival, there was pride. Ethnic pride was not always in the Jews' immediate best interests, but without it there was the question of whether it really could be called survival if a Jew did not survive as a Jew. During the Inquisition, Jews had been offered three choices: convert to Christianity, hold fast to their faith and burn at the stake, or flee for their lives.

The baron's ancestors had fled. Most Jews had. Others had converted, lived on, even prospered—but not as Jews. The martyrs had died, their eyes live coals burning hotter with the fierce fire of their Jewish zealotry than the flames licking at the soles of their feet and rising up to consume them.

Many Jews today revered the martyrs. The baron was not among them. Life was always better than death. One should die for concrete things—defending oneself, sacrificing for one's family, one's children, even one's friends. But not for an abstraction, be it king and country, God or Marx. Not for an ideal. Never die for an ideal!

The thought brought a sad smile to the baron's lips. Gabrielle would surely have called him a coward. She had not died to save his life. She had made that plain. She had sacrificed herself for the anarchist cause. She had died a martyr. She, who would have had nothing but sneers for those religious fanatics who chose the stake in preference to recantation, had died a true believer in anarchism.

The baron posed a question to himself: If one did not believe in dying for a belief, was one entitled to have the belief at all? As soon as the question was formed the answer came to him: Yes, because you can only do the best you can and hope to survive. If you're not alive to have it, what good is an ideal? And if you don't have any ideals, what good is being alive? It was a paradox, a Jewish paradox.

The baron put Philippe's letter back in its envelope,

placed the envelope in a drawer of his desk, put on his hat and coat, took his gloves in one hand and his walking stick in the other. It was time to go to his mother's house for the Shabbas meal.

"Ha!" Rebekah greeted him, small and ancient, her nostrils quivering in supervision of the *k'naidlech* simmering in the pot of chicken broth in the kitchen on the floor below. "The kaiser doubles his army. So where does he get his cannon?" As usual, she began with what was on her mind.

"Blame Haran." The baron did not disappoint her. "The Prussians are loading English bullets."

"Blame Haran!" Rebekah snorted. "Just like when you were boys. Immanuel did it. Haran did it. Always you blame each other."

"But it was Haran's doing, Mother. It really was."

"And he says it was your fault for letting yourself get kidnapped. He says he had to agree to the sale to persuade some English *shvindler* to do something or other with the Spaniards so the kidnappers would turn you loose."

It was the first the baron had heard of that. Probably it was true. Haran would not have mentioned it to him. Probably Haran had only told his mother to defend himself from her ire for selling guns to the kaiser. A cold English kipper, his brother Lord Haran, but a caring brother nevertheless. "Haran has a point, Mama," the baron placated her. "The blame is mine."

Rebekah nodded. A little laying of guilt reestablished motherhood. Too much, however, was not good. She changed the subject. "How is Philippe?" Speaking the name, her voice softened. Guilt—strictness—that was for her children. For her grandchildren, Rebekah had only love.

"I had a letter from him today." The baron took a deep breath. "He's going to Palestine."

The sharp, sparrow eyes regarded him narrowly. "To Palestine? Philippe has become such a beach lover?"

"It's a desert, Mama."

"It's the world's longest beach." Rebekah's eyes drilled into the baron's. "What else?" her intuition demanded.

"He plans to be married there." Diplomatically, the baron didn't mention that Philippe's bride-to-be had been married before, or that she had children—or, particularly, that she was a gentile.

"He has to go to Palestine for a bride?" Rebekah was indignant. "There are no marriageable girls in Paris? In Europe?"

Sensibly, the baron did not explain. He knew that each answer in this area would only open the door to another question. And the answers to these other questions would only make his mother unhappy, and then more unhappy. He was relieved when Rebekah did not pursue the topic of Philippe's marriage.

"Why Palestine?" she wondered instead. "What is there in Palestine for my grandson?"

"Philippe is a Zionist. He believes in the establishment of a Jewish homeland, in the creation of a new nation of Yisrael."

"My grandson?" Rebekah had been taken by surprise. "And what about the Paris branch?"

"I'll find someone to replace Philippe."

Rebekah thought a moment. "You approve of this, Immanuel? Of your son going off to Palestine like this?"

"Approve? No. Not really. But I understand."

"My son, the Talmudic scholar. A straight answer, please, Immanuel."

"I'm not a Zionist. I don't think a Jewish nation, a religious nation, is necessarily a good idea. I'm not sure about this claim to land based on the Torah. I don't think the Arabs there will welcome Jewish settlement with open arms. But on the other hand—"

" 'On the other hand'!" his mother jeered at him. "This is a banker? No. This is a Hassid splitting hairs!"

"On the other hand," the baron persisted, "looking at it through Philippe's eyes, if the Jews don't take steps to look out for the Jews, who will? If the Jews don't create a sanctuary, a haven, who will? There's an ebb and a flow to it, but on the whole anti-Semitism is a plague that persists. And there are other forces. . . ."

"My son the seesaw!"

"When Zayde created the House of Diamond, it was as a bulwark against persecution. There was safety in making ourselves indispensable to those who ruled—to the emperors and kings, to the princes and the dukes, to the nobility and the aristocracy. They had the power; making them need us, our monetary expertise, and later our financial acumen and our wealth—that was survival. But things are changing now, Mama. There are new forces sweeping over Europe. The peasants, the dispossessed, the landless, the poor are rising up. anarchism, socialism, bolshevism, unionism—call it what you will, there's a mass movement for reform. The people aren't begging; they're demanding a share of the wealth they produce. Along with the rulers and the landowners, bankers are their target. Whether gentile or Jew doesn't matter, except that it's inevitable that the anti-Semites will make Jews the scapegoat. First rich Jews like us, and then poor Jews as well."

"How did you arrive at these conclusions, Immanuel?" his mother wondered.

"When I was being held prisoner, there was a woman—"

"A woman." Rebekah missed nothing, and she knew her son. "And so now the head of the House of Diamond understands the anarchists and sympathizes with them. A woman!"

"I don't exactly sympathize with them. But I do believe it's imperative that I—we—understand them. We ignore them at our peril, Mama. If an accommodation is not reached, this turbulence will surely boil over and engulf us."

"Revolution?"

"It's certainly possible."

"And the House of Diamond will sell them the guns." It was a flat statement. Rebekah was eighty-two years old. She knew how things worked.

Baron Immanuel didn't answer.

"Don't worry about it." Still sarcastic, Rebekah continued. "Before they can make their revolution, the kaiser will make his war."

"I think we—the House of Diamond, the Rothschilds, the other great banking houses of Europe, Jewish and gentile—still have the power to prevent his doing that, Mama."

"So you told me before. Sometimes, my son, I don't understand you. A Bolshevik woman whispers in your ear and you quake and look under your bed every night to see if the revolution is beginning. But your House of Diamond invests in Manchester munitions, in Krupps and in Skoda, with one hand, and with the other you think to stop war by snapping your fingers and saying 'tut-tut' to the kaiser and the tsar."

"I really don't think there will be a war, Mother. The balance of power—"

"—is a juggling act, my son." There was a tinkling from downstairs. Bertha was ringing the dinner bell. Rebekah's narrow nostrils flared. The soup and the *k'naidlech* were ready. She got up and took the baron's arm. "We'll eat now," she told him. "Later you'll tell me about how to prevent wars and which way to run from revolutions." They started down the stairs. After a few steps, Rebekah paused. "But one thing, Immanuel. Whether I'm right or wrong—war or revolution—one thing."

"What's that, Mama?"

"Buy diamonds, my son. Put a few aside some place only you know. Buy diamonds and hold them. You never can tell."

The baron smiled. "Shall I buy them low, Mama?" he asked, chuckling. "Shall I sell them high?"

"Of course."

"But Zayde never really said that, Mama," the Baron Immanuel von Diamant reminded her. "Somebody made it up. Some anti-Semite, probably."

"Diamonds." Rebekah ignored the disclaimer. "Buy low. Sell high," she insisted. "But not too high."